Review

Legitimate Power is a spellbinding story that combines history and technology with international intrigue to create an intelligent thriller sure to satisfy every hardcore enthusiast of this genre. What makes *Legitimate Power* such a compelling book is that the author seamlessly combines the old and the new; the old being two old burial chests that contain bones and an unusual crystal. The new is the concept of solar energy and its various potential innovations, in the center of which lies the unique crystal. Add murder to this political intrigue and you've got one terrific story. The best part is that the prose is engaging and crisp without being overly technical, making *Legitimate Power* an easy read.

Readers' Favorite

Books by Stefan Vučak

General Fiction:
Cry of Eagles
All the Evils
Towers of Darkness
Strike for Honor
Proportional Response
Legitimate Power
Autumn Leaves
All My Sunsets
F/X-26
28th Amendment
Night Sirens
Broken Rose

Shadow Gods Saga:
In the Shadow of Death
Against the Gods of Shadow
A Whisper from Shadow
Shadow Masters
Immortal in Shadow
With Shadow and Thunder
Through the Valley of Shadow
Guardians of Shadow

Science Fiction:
Fulfillment
Lifeliners

Non-Fiction:
Writing Tips for Authors

Contact at:
www.stefanvucak.com

LEGITIMATE POWER

By

Stefan Vučak

Note:

This is a work of fiction. All names, characters, places, and events are the work of the author's imagination. Any resemblance to real persons, places, or events is coincidental.

Stefan Vučak ©2016
ISBN-10: 0-9942923-5-X
ISBN-13: 978-0-9942923-5-3

Dedication

To Vanessa...and the promise that life brings

Acknowledgments

To Charlotte Raby and her work proofreading the manuscript.
https://charlotteraby.wordpress.com/

Cover art by Laura Shinn.
http://laurashinn.yolasite.com

Chapter One

The pickaxe sang as it glanced off the rock and the handle vibrated in Cheber's hands, which made his palms tingle. He arched his back and grunted as aching muscles protested this unaccustomed abuse. After a loud exhale, he squinted at the pale blue sky unbroken by any cloud and adjusted his shades. The four olive trees that bordered the back stone fence offered meager protection from the relentless sun and he longed to rest his weary body under one, preferably with a cold beer in hand. Bees flirted around red amaryllis and hollyhock blooms. If only it were not so hot, clearing rocks from Alisa's growing garden plot wouldn't be such a burden.

"I've been waiting *weeks* for that ground to be cleared, Cheber Shaken!" she raged at him over breakfast, taking the fun out of getting up this morning. He winced, coffee cup poised before his lips, wishing she'd stop nagging for once, resigned to suffer another miserable day.

"I don't ask much from you, and as the Lord is my witness, you don't give me much. How I came to marry a sniveling worm like you, I'll never know."

"I'll get around to it," he grumbled sourly, not wanting to meet her eyes.

He *had* been putting off the unpleasant chore. Besides, the plot she already had was sufficiently large and kept her occupied enough. What did she want, a farm? The scraps of vegetables she managed to eke out of that parched soil weren't worth the labor, but eating natural was the current gossip in their social circle and Alisa did not want to be left behind. Besides, August was not a good time to be planting anything.

"You'll get to it this minute! I don't want to see you wasting the few days left of your vacation staring at the TV or loafing with your friends. Hear me?"

"I hear you," he said wearily, knowing he'd have no peace until he got the depressing job done.

Perhaps if he dug a deep enough hole in that dried-up plot, he could fit her in it. The problem he had, he still loved her. Still worse, she knew it and took advantage of it, making his life a drudgery. There didn't seem to be any way to satisfy her demands. What did the woman *want?*

"Look at you! Still only an accounting clerk—"

"Management accountant."

"—and Eran is already a supervisor, and both of you joined the company together. Neta will start high school this fall. She'll need things. On your worthless salary, I don't know how we'll make ends meet. You're a spineless weakling with no consideration for me or your daughter," she hissed and tightened the sash of her green nightgown.

Her breasts shook as she gestured at him, and he was momentarily distracted by more pleasant thoughts. That's all they were…thoughts. He could not recall the last time they shared any intimacy, and the way things were going, that was not likely to change. Doesn't the Torah say a woman is a man's field and he should till his field? Unfortunately, that field was mostly barren of any love and warmth these days, overgrown with weeds.

He lowered his cup and glared at her. "If you took a job—you're a qualified graphics designer—it would help, you know."

She planted her hands on shapely hips and snorted. "If I had married a *man*, I wouldn't need to work!"

After that, breakfast did not sparkle with conversation.

Cheber leaned against the pickaxe and frowned. He worked hard at his job, but he didn't play the office politics game. It simply wasn't in him. Eran told him he was due for promotion by end of year as a section manager administering the company's internal audits. It would mean at least eighteen hundred shekels a month more, but he knew it would not be enough to shut Alisa's prune face. He should never have moved to Arnona and built this fancy two-story stone mansion for her, saddling himself with a lifetime mortgage. Nothing he ever did pleased her; not even his unfailing love. Hers had dried up somewhere along the way and he wondered what he did to trigger it.

Did she love him, or was their existence reduced to a cohabitation contract until Neta was married off, leaving them free to find what they never had together? There *was* love somewhere long ago and he tried to figure out where they mislaid it—where *she* mislaid it. He had given her his all. He remembered clearly the chance meeting in the sprawling Tel Aviv University library one sunny afternoon between classes. She wore a knee-length beige skirt and black blouse, black hair tied in a bun, her large almond eyes drew him inexorably within striking range of her delicate perfume, his captivity completed by a radiant smile. Like every young man with raging hormones, he'd had fleeting relationships, but he knew immediately that this woman was different.

Going out, talking about themselves and their life plans, she displayed determination, a toughness to succeed in a commercial world dominated by men. All warning signs, but he ignored them, willing to die for her. He wanted to study mechanical engineering, but was too lazy to put in the required effort. Higher mathematics and physics demanded a lot of work, and he settled for an accountancy course, majoring in management. Both in their final year, studies took up most of their time, but mutual magnetism overcame such a minor obstacle. Those were mad days, exhilarating days, and each knew where it would lead. The road since had turned into endless days of weariness. Even the joy of having Neta only emphasized his growing loneliness.

On reflection, he should have stuck with mechanical engineering.

From the open garage doorway, the Sephardi number he'd

absently been listening to ended and the DJ let loose with a Ye-hudah Poliker light rock piece. As he stared at the broken ground at his feet, dry and unforgiving like Alisa, he sighed and shrugged. He would get her damned garden plot extended, which should take her off his back, if only for a little while. It was his own fault really. He always sought to please her and accede to her every whim, which only succeeded in generating scorn and contempt from her. He had been too accommodating, that was the prob-lem. Perhaps it was time to start pleasing himself for a change, no matter what the consequences. A man can take only so much.

In the valley below the rolling hillside, the crowding suburbia of Sur Bahar pushed back available land. Far in the east, the Ju-dean Desert shimmered in the rippling heat. He picked up the pickaxe and clenched his teeth. A beer would go down nicely right now, he reflected, but he would have to fetch it for himself. It would never occur to Alisa to bring him one—although long ago, she used to—or condescend to help him rake away cleared stones. He shook his head, figuring the beer wasn't worth facing her caustic invective.

The pickaxe clanged against the same rock and he swore. He drove the pointy end under the thing and heaved, but it refused to budge. Muscles straining, he gave a hard jerk on the handle and sprawled back as the rock gave way. He stood, patted the dust off his clothes, and glowered at what turned out to be a small boulder. As he bent down to roll it out of the way, he faced a black opening in the ground. He bit his lower lip, groped for a pebble, and dropped it into the hole. A hollow clang told him he'd struck a cavity, which made his shoulders sag in disgust. In-stead of an extended garden, Alisa now had a cellar! Perhaps if he shoveled in all the loose rock he'd dug up, he might fill it be-fore she noticed anything and gave him more hard time.

The back of his land sloped down slightly. A stone fence sep-arated it from the stepped terraces hugging the hillside all the way into the valley below. Water running down the hill long before

Arnona became settled, probably found an entry somewhere and dug out the hole—leaving him with a major complication. First things first, though. He needed to find out the size of his problem. It wouldn't do having the ground cave in under him. As he gazed at the opening, a grin creased his smeared face. It might be just large enough for Alisa. Nobody would ever find her.

Contemplating the pleasant thought, he reached for the spade and gingerly cut away soil around the gaping opening. It seemed like the hole extended toward the fence, which made sense. What he needed was some light. He straightened and strode quickly toward the doorway that led into the garage. Inside, he cast a glance at the neat shelves of tools and paraphernalia accumulated over time, and reached for a boxy orange 6V torch. He grasped the handle and walked out clicking the switch to make sure it worked. The radio DJ pontificated on a song he was about to unleash on his listeners, but Cheber paid no attention as he strode out.

He lay on the ground and thrust the torch into the cavity. The yellow beam revealed a rough chamber some one-and-a-half meters deep, not more than three meters long, nearly rectangular, the end sealed by a large white slab. He froze when the torch exposed two small stone chests. He had stumbled onto an ancient burial site! What a damn nuisance. Whoever lay entombed here was not very important as the chamber lacked any stone lining.

"Cheber!" a shrill voice shattered the silence, making him wince. "What on earth are you doing down there?"

He lifted his head and studied her for a moment. She had put on a white cotton blouse and cream pants that hugged her supple figure. As she stood behind the steel-railed balcony, black hair cascading over her shoulders, light lipstick outlining full lips, she looked pretty in bright sunshine. Her face though, creased with scorn, was devoid of warmth. Did she plan to go out again? Perhaps she was seeing another man? A stab of fiery jealousy made his teeth grind. No, she wouldn't do that, content to make his life a misery. He should sell the house; the proceeds would be enough to keep her and Neta comfortable, and he would move back to Tel Aviv. Lots of high paying jobs there, and he'd be shut of her.

Unfortunately, he'd been saying that to himself for some time, but never acted on the thought. He simply could not bring himself to cut the bond of love he had for her, even if it was not shared. Staring at her, his thoughts tumbled as he contemplated life without her.

"Come down and see," he shouted back indifferently as he got up and walked into the garage.

He took the small metal ladder off its wall hooks and carried it to the hole. When he lowered it, he heard Alisa gasp.

"What in the world…"

Not listening to her, he picked up the torch and climbed down, relishing the sudden coolness. He had to bend to prevent his head striking the jagged ceiling as he made his way to the stone chests. When he knelt down, he recognized them immediately—ossuaries. People found them all the time, tucked into shallow holes dug into hillsides. As a Jew, Torah law bound him not to desecrate the resting place of the dead, but Cheber wasn't orthodox, to the lament of his parents. He lifted the torch and played it over the large seal stone. Clearly, over time, water and erosion had piled up rubble and soil in front of the burial chamber, hiding all evidence of its existence.

Given the rough state of the chamber, the ossuaries did not hold anyone with wealth or status. Perhaps not, but they still may have some value. If he sold them to one of the dealers who peddled so-called genuine antiquities to tourists swarming Jerusalem's Old City, they might bring in badly needed shekels. It could also stop Alisa's whining, for a time anyway. Besides, he would need the money for material to fill the chamber.

"Come out of there at once!" Alisa demanded and he peered up at her, seeing her disgusted expression framed against the opening. "I cannot trust you to do a simple job without you complicating it. Lord preserve me."

Something snapped inside Cheber and he didn't care anymore to be her foot mat.

"If you don't shut up, this hole is large enough to hold you and your waspish tongue," he told her calmly, amazed to hear his words and feel the flood of relief they produced, a catharsis that burned away the layers of suffering surrounding his soul, leaving him clean and invigorated.

She gaped, her mouth hanging open in astonishment. "How dare you talk to me like that!"

"I should have done it long ago," he declared and crouched beside the nearest ossuary, feeling her oppressive weight roll off his shoulders. He *should* have told her off long ago. Unrequited love wasn't worth giving up his dignity. There were limits and she just crossed the dividing line.

Strange markings decorated the lid and sides. He gently pushed the ossuary, but it didn't budge. He placed both palms against the edge and applied more force. The chest leaned back slightly. With a nod, he worked his fingers under it and gently lifted. It wasn't overly heavy, perhaps eight to ten kilos. He shuffled toward the ladder and grunted as he lifted the stone chest through the hole onto solid ground. He heaved the second ossuary through the opening, picked up the torch and climbed out. When he stood beside Alisa, he tilted his head at the chests.

"What do you think of that?"

"Two burial caskets. Big deal. What are you going to do about the hole in my garden? I can't walk around with that thing here."

He clenched his fists, holding back his temper. "Don't you understand? This could be the break we've been looking for. They'll fetch twelve thousand at least."

"Who'll want to buy two ossuaries?" she scoffed. "The markets are filled with them."

Stefan Vučak

"Maybe you're right, but let's take a look at what's inside before we throw them back, okay?"

"Bones, that's what's in there." A frown creased her brow. "Shouldn't we report this or something? The Antiquities Authority could give us a bad time if they found out."

"We dug them up in our backyard, for crying out loud. This isn't a declared archaeological site."

"Talk to Eran. He collects such trash."

"I don't have to talk to anybody. I know what I'm doing."

"Just like you knew when you dug up that hole."

"Peace, woman!"

Cheber picked up one of the ossuaries and carried it into the garage, bent under its weight. He placed it on the workbench, switched off the radio and reached for a long screwdriver mounted in a rack. The narrow blade slid easily into the groove between the lid and carved stone side. He levered up the lid and placed it on the bench. Alisa leaned over his shoulder and peered inside.

"As I said, bones," she declared scornfully.

They were bones, all right, but that's what an ossuary was for. Judging by the size of the leg femur, it was not from an adult. What struck him as odd was the elongated skull and the abnormally large eye sockets. He grinned with excitement.

"These aren't ordinary bones, my dear. The skull is nothing like I have ever seen anywhere. It reminds me of those strange skulls they found in Peru. A dealer I know in the Old City will pay plenty for this."

Without looking at her, he went out and brought back the second ossuary. The lid came off easily, revealing another set of bones...and what appeared to be a small box wrapped in faded brown leather. Seeing it, his mind filled with images of jewels and riches hidden inside.

"Well, don't just stand there. Open it!"

Heart racing, he carefully peeled off the leather to reveal a box

8

swathed in purple cloth. The material felt like fine silk as he un-wrapped it to reveal a container made of rich brown wood that exuded a faint incense fragrance, covered with the same strange symbols as the ossuaries. A thin line ran around the box a centi-meter from the top. He grasped the lid and tugged. It came off easily. Something nestled inside wrapped in white cloth.

"If you're finished staring at it…" Alisa hissed, clearly impa-tient. He snorted and held the little parcel to her.

She hesitated, then took it and fumbled with the cloth. Her breath caught and she gawked. In her hand lay a rectangular pale orange crystal the size of a small smartphone, only thicker. It seemed to glow with an inner light. Every edge was beveled, and a shallow groove ran along both long sides.

"It's beautiful," she whispered, clearly awed. "What is it?"

"I don't know. It's been machined, but I cannot tell if it's a gemstone. Too large to be an ornamental jewel. I know one thing, it's worth a lot of money. I'll take some pictures and make a phone call or two."

"What about the hole in my garden?"

"Fill it yourself!" he snarled and strode toward the door lead-ing into the house.

He swept his eyes across the kitchen, spotted his smartphone on the credenza shelf and grabbed it. Alisa glared at him when he returned, but said nothing, mouth pursed. Ignoring her, he snapped shots of the ossuaries, the bones and the crystal. He walked back into the house and went upstairs to his study. After powering up the tower computer, he hooked the cell to the USB port and downloaded the photos.

Eran was something of an antiquities collector and had some nice pieces. Cheber had seen them and his friend would talk for hours on the subject, lubricated by a glass or two of smooth claret. Although not overwhelmed with emotion at the sight of a cracked pot or misshapen female figurine, Cheber had nonethe-

less accumulated a rudimentary understanding of Israel's tortuous history—from an archaeological perspective anyway.

He scanned the list of Eran's emails in Outlook and finally
found what he looked for. Over a beer one afternoon, discussing
antiquities, of course, and the muddled relationship licensed dealers maintained with the Israel Antiquities Authority—technically,
according to the 1978 Antiquities Law, any artifact found after
passage of the law belonged to the state—Eran spoke of a thriving trade in all types of objects, from pottery, figurines and rare
manuscripts. The IAA wanted to suppress the trade, but it was
helpless as the courts and the Ministry of Tourism upheld the
dealers' right to trade.

Eran's email listed four licensed traders with whom he dealt
regularly. Among its winding lanes and hole-in-the-wall shops,
the Old City had an endless number of outfits selling three-day-
old antiques to gullible tourists. The dealers Eran knew guaranteed that he would not be cheated, but Cheber would have to do
his own bargaining. He never thought he would need a dealer,
but was now glad to benefit from his friend's expertise.

He selected two names, one in the Jewish and one in the Muslim Quarter. After composing a brief email, he attached the photos and sent it off. He wrote another email to Eran and smiled as
he pressed the Send icon. His friend was at work, usually taking
his vacation in June, but Cheber figured Eran would call as soon
as he read the email.

Knowing he faced two hardnosed traders, Cheber started
Googling, wanting to know more about ossuaries and their likely
worth. His face fell as he read the articles. Alisa was right. The
market was flooded with the things. He chewed his lower lip and
pondered the situation. There might be lots of burial chests
around, but he figured his bones ought to be worth something to
a museum or university. However, the prospect of a drawn-out
negotiation process with museum authorities made him wince.
He wanted to sell quickly and rid himself of the things, and Alisa's

nagging.

Trying to value the crystal was much more difficult and turned into a hopeless exercise. Not knowing anything about gemstones, he was stymied. Still, the unique thing had to be valuable. Take it to a jeweler and have it appraised?

His cell trilled and he pressed the phone icon, smiling as he read the caller's name.

"Hi, Eran. That didn't take long."

"You're a bastard, Cheber, did you know that?" his friend replied hotly. "I scratch and scrounge for my collection, and the gods drop two ossuaries in your backyard. I hope you fall into that hole!"

Cheber laughed. "I've got it reserved for somebody else."

"Hah! I keep telling you, old friend. You're clinging to that woman and she's making your life one long torture session. She isn't worth it. Get yourself a new model."

"Like you did?"

"Best thing I ever did. The rabbinical courts these days don't give you a hard time over a divorce like they used to."

"I'll think about it, but it's complicated."

"You're the one who's making it complicated."

"Look, you didn't call to talk about my lousy marriage, and I don't want to discuss it right now."

"No, I didn't. About your find, who did you contact?"

"Yaron and Malek."

"Mmm. Both are fairly honest. I'd buy the things myself, but I've got an ossuary already. As for what they're worth, you may get three thousand for each. There isn't much of a demand for them these days. You could try selling them to an overseas collector, but you'll be buried in government red tape. Not worth it. The unusual bones will be one of your draw cards."

"You want to buy them?" Cheber asked hopefully.

"What do you want for them?"

"Ten thousand, and I'll throw in the ossuaries."

"Sorry, old man. No can do. I'm short of dinero right now. Can you wait until next month?"

"I can't. I have a hole in my backyard I need to fill."

"You've got money stashed away, but I sympathize. That crystal…it's definitely an unusual specimen. Before you talk to Yaron or Malek, I'd suggest you take it to a jeweler for an appraisal. It might be worth a small pile."

"Yeah, that's what I figured. You still okay for dinner on Saturday?"

"Wouldn't miss it. Talk to you later."

Cheber switched off, smiled and shook his head. Eran was a character and his new wife a lovely lady. Alisa liked the younger woman and the two often went shopping in the city together. That's what he needed to do now, shop for a price…and maybe a new model like Eran suggested.

"Cheber! What are you doing up there?" Alisa's caustic voice shattered the atmosphere and he sighed. Will the woman ever give him a moment of peace?

He got up and padded to the master bedroom. After throwing his soiled clothes into the washing hamper, he showered and dressed in beige slacks and a matching short-sleeved shirt. He pocketed his wallet and the ring of keys and made his way to the garage. Not bothering to explain, he wrapped the crystal in its cloth and left Alisa staring after him as he climbed into the Honda Civic. He pressed the button to open the garage door and turned the ignition key. The engine fired and purred. He engaged 'drive' and the car surged forward.

Three hours later, weary and badly wanting some lunch, he pulled into the driveway, waited for the garage door to open, and drove in without bothering to do it in reverse to position the car for an easy exit. He slammed the door and barely glanced at the ossuaries on the workbench.

His cell went off and he dragged it out of his pocket.

"Cheber Shaken."

"This is Jamail Malek. I'm calling regarding the email you sent this morning."

"I appreciate the call, Mr. Malek."

"Please, call me Jamail. You found something very unusual, Mr. Shaken, and I'm not referring to the ossuaries. I have enough of them cluttering my shop. However, I am interested in the bones and, of course, the crystal. Do you want to sell?"

"My price is twenty-five thousand shekels."

Cheber heard a restrained guffaw. "An ambitious price, but one I could not possibly meet. I'm prepared to offer you fifteen for everything, subject to an inspection."

"I had the crystal valued, Jamail. It alone is worth more than eight thousand."

"Perhaps. Without seeing it for myself, I could not say. Think about my offer. If you're willing to sell it at a more reasonable price, call me. I bid you good day."

"Thank you for your call, Jamail," Cheber said, but the line was already dead.

He gazed at the smartphone in his hand and felt a wave of disappointment wash over him. After talking to three jewelers in downtown Jerusalem, each expressed the liveliest interest in the unusual crystal, and all claimed it was not a gemstone. They couldn't tell him what it was, but if he wanted to sell, the highest offer he got was 8,200 shekels. They told him the crystal would have to be cut into smaller pieces suitable for jewelry ornaments. As a single piece, it was a curiosity, but not worth much. Cheber expected to get a whole lot more, but he could not very well argue with experts, albeit thieving ones, no doubt. He had seen the light of greed in their eyes.

Real gem trading in Israel was done in Tel Aviv, and he was tempted to go there to have the crystal examined, but he didn't have the time. Besides, after all the associated travel expenses, he might not get a better price. What he expected to get was more of Alisa's acerbic invective. No, get rid of the thing, fill in the

13

damned hole in the backyard and be done with it.

"Where have you been?" Alisa demanded as he walked into the kitchen.

He placed the wrapped crystal on the table and sat down. "Having the thing appraised."

"And?"

"We'd be lucky to get eight thousand for it."

"Eight? Are you crazy? The thing is priceless!"

Wishing he had never stumbled on that hole, he looked at her. "Maybe. I had a call from a dealer with whom Eran does business. He offered me fifteen for everything: ossuaries, bones and the crystal."

"He was trying to rob you."

"Probably, but at least I now have a better idea what we can expect to make if we sell. Twenty-five thousand shekels, if I can get that much, would come in very handy right now. Don't forget the hole we have back there. It will cost a couple of thousand at least to buy soil and gravel to fill it."

"The crystal alone must be worth more than twenty thousand."

"I wouldn't be surprised. If you can sell it for that, go ahead. I'm already sorry I found the damned thing. Right now, I want my lunch."

About to snap at him, her expression changed. Staring at him, she pushed back a lock of hair.

"What's gotten into you, Cheber? Ever since you dug up that crystal, you've been behaving very strangely."

He stood, walked to the fridge and took out a carton of mixed fruit juice. Pausing, he gazed at her, realizing she was right. He did feel different, the pressing load of her smothering presence gone, and he realized why.

"No, simply coming to my senses. It's like this, Alisa. We either start having a relationship or I walk, and you can keep the house. I never wanted it, but I built it to please you and impress

14

your circle of friends. It's a damn millstone and you're welcome to it."

"Did you expect me to live in an apartment, a crowded hovel? I wanted—"

"I know what you wanted, but you never gave a thought to what I wanted, and that was a wife, not a nagging critic. I always loved you, and still do, but that love is no longer unconditional. I'm not your doormat, and I don't want to be treated like one anymore."

"You don't know how to be a man."

Her words cut deep and he leaned toward her. "Well, you're seeing him now. My lunch."

"Get it yourself!" Cheeks pink, she whirled and stomped out.

He sighed, nodded slowly a couple of times, and got a glass from the credenza. He filled it from the tap and took a sip. She read him right. He didn't know how to be a man. No, he merely kept that part of himself buried for the sake of her love…a big mistake as it turned out.

He sniffed at a pot on the glass top cooker, lifted the lid and peered at the meat stew inside. Fetching a plate and spoon from the cupboard, he helped himself to a large portion, took it to the table, sat down and began to eat, his mind going over what might have been, and of tomorrows yet to be written. He would need to put out feelers for a job in Tel Aviv, he mused as he worked his way through the tasty stew, the ashes of regrets falling around him like dust. He had to say one thing; Alisa knew how to cook. He would miss that.

Done, he washed the plate and spoon and took a last look around the kitchen. It felt cold and alien. He pursed his lips and made his way upstairs into the main bedroom. He dragged a battered cloth suitcase from the walk-in robe and threw it on the bed. Hearing her footsteps, he looked up as she walked in, stopping at the doorway.

"What are you doing?"

"Leaving." Cheber smiled wanly and shrugged. "There is nothing left for me here."

Silence rang in the room as she studied him.

"Not even Neta?"

"Don't start that."

He stood there, wondering what was going through her mind.

"You did it to yourself," she said after a while, eyes bright.

He nodded wearily. "I know."

"I despised you because I thought you were a weakling."

"You wanted someone to dominate you?"

"I wanted a man!"

"You wanted everything, Alisa, and I gave you everything to keep your love, even my self-respect, but you wanted more. Well, there isn't any more. You took all I had. If you want more, you'll have to take it from some other man, otherwise it's time you started giving something back."

She pressed her lips, studying him. After a time, she nodded.

"I deserve that, I suppose. Are you prepared to give me some time?"

"No," he said harshly and felt something tear inside him. Alisa!

"You should have stood up to me earlier, Cheber."

"Perhaps it's too late, but I'm standing up to you now."

"I don't know if I can change. It might be too late for both of us."

"That'll be your choice."

"What about Neta? This would rip her apart."

"You think she doesn't know what's going on?" He allowed his arms to hang at his side. "She'll be hurt, but this is about you and me and where we go from here…if we're going to have a future. We're either husband and wife having a relationship, sharing everything, or we are two strangers living a lie, and I don't want a stranger in my bed anymore."

Her eyes glistened and a fat tear rolled down her left cheek.

Seeing her distress, he wanted to rush to her, embrace her, whisper tender things and kiss away the pain, but he simply stood there. She was very good at playing the psychological warfare game and had pulled the sob routine more than once…and he had always given in. He could not afford to give in this time, even as it tore him up to see her anguish. She had to choose the path she wanted to tread, together or separately. He had trod her path long enough.

She sniffed and wiped her cheek. "This will take time…my husband."

"No," he said gruffly and swallowed hard. "Decide now, Alisa."

Lips trembling, she bit her lip. "I don't know if I can."

He exhaled loudly and nodded. "Draw up whatever papers you want and I'll sign them."

She gaped. "You're divorcing me?"

He opened the suitcase and shrugged. "I guess I am."

Crying openly, she took a tentative step toward him. "Don't leave me."

"I don't want to, but you haven't given me any reason to stay."

"Even if I told you I love you?"

He snorted with disdain. She had played that card before and the words sounded just as hollow this time. He would not allow himself to be manipulated anymore, or let her take what pride he had left.

"Love? I don't know if you're capable of it."

"Cheber! I want you."

As he looked at her wet cheeks, the tragic expression on her face, realizing that a single act would irrevocably change the shape of their lives, he was tempted to give in again. His heart ached for her, but she had bruised it too badly and he did not want to risk more pain. Despite everything, could they make it work?

"Even though my love is conditional?"

"Because it is."

"Come here," he said gruffly.

With a cry of relief, she was in his arms and he kissed her hard. Her mouth opened and their tongues danced. After a time, she pulled back and wiped back tears. She smiled and ran a hand through his hair.

"Wow. It's been a while since you kissed me like that."

"We need to practice more," he growled, and his lips found hers.

"I always loved it when you were strong and manly," she whispered tenderly, smiling into his eyes.

"The old me is back again...for keeps."

His smartphone trilled and he pulled away from her. He brushed her cheek and dug the cell from his pocket.

"Cheber Shaken."

"Mr. Shaken, this is Acaph Yaron. I would very much like to see you and discuss your find. Would three o'clock be convenient?"

He glanced at his wristwatch. It was already after two. "I don't know if I can get to the Old City by then, Mr. Yaron."

"You misunderstand. I want to come and see *you*."

Cheber slowly nodded a couple of times. The old boy certainly seemed keen, which was promising.

"I look forward to it."

"I heard," Alisa said as he pocketed the cell. "It sounds...encouraging."

"Not as encouraging as what we started," he said and pulled her against him.

"The garden..." she mumbled against his lips.

"You are my garden."

* * *

With the space around the ossuaries packed with small cushions, Acaph sighed with satisfaction and shut the back door of his dark blue VW Jetta. He straightened and extended his arm. Wearing a broad grin, Shaken grasped it and they shook hands.

"Thanks for the help."

"Don't mention it."

"Eran taught you well, Cheber."

One arm held around the woman's slim waist, the tall middle-aged man laughed. "I still feel that you got the better of the bargain."

Acaph smiled, admiring the couple, clearly both still very much in love. He'd been divorced for nine years now and missed having Abra's warm body beside him in bed, especially during the crisp winter months. Unfortunately, her love had turned cold many years earlier, and he didn't even know why, not really. They never had children, but he had not held that against her. She wanted a child, but couldn't. One of those things. He often suspected that she blamed him, denying what the doctors told her. Pushing fifty-eight, he was now past such things, but it warmed his soul to see a man and a woman showing affection for each other when too often an argument meant instant separation. The young these days lacked patience to tough it through life's hurdles, he mused sadly. Everything was instant and disposable, even a marriage.

"You are unhappy with the price?"

"Not at all. It was a fair deal."

Acaph chuckled. "I hate to have a customer complain, especially someone who is Eran's friend. I don't want him coming after me. Shalom aleichem, Mr. Shaken."

"Shalom, Mr. Yaron."

Acaph eased his bulging 170-centimeter frame into the car and turned the ignition key. The diesel engine coughed and settled into a soft purr. With a wave at the couple, he eased the Jetta onto the street and pressed the accelerator, eager to examine his purchase more closely. The deal cost him twenty-six thousand shekels, but he'd been prepared to go as high as thirty-five. It was always like that. Somebody digs something up, gets dazzled by thoughts of riches, then comes down with a thud after doing rudimentary research on their own instead of spending time and effort consulting one of the museums or universities for a professional evaluation. Well, Shaken seemed satisfied and that is all that mattered.

Once he hit Hebron Road, Acaph drove quickly through Jerusalem's suburbia, heading roughly north. As always, traffic was brisk, but not too heavy. Patchy clouds streamed across the eastern sky. The afternoon sun hung above the city as if blessing it, still bright. Light classical music whispered from the speakers. Close to his destination, the Old City walls paralleled the road and traffic became heavier, cars competing with taxis, tour buses and reckless tourists scampering across instead of using a proper pedestrian walkway. He passed Jaffa Gate and slowed down. At the intersection, he waited for the light to change and turned right into Sultan Suleiman Street, negotiating the large roundabout near the Damascus Gate. As he turned into Derekh Yerikho Street, he glanced left at the imposing yellow limestone façade of the Rockefeller Archaeological Museum and nodded. He would bleed them for the ossuaries. They would probably be prepared to pay even more for the unusual crystal, but he had plans for that special item.

Before reaching the entrance to the Jewish Quarter at Dung Gate, he turned left into Ma'alot Ir David Street. He had a shop on Hayei Olam Street where he conducted his business, but most cars were forbidden inside the Old City, and what residential parking was available cost a small fortune to obtain. Besides, he didn't want to lug the ossuaries to his shop. They were not for public sale. He slowed and turned left into a narrow driveway of a modest two-story sandstone house, flanked on either side by similar dwellings. Pedestrians gave him dirty looks as they were forced to walk around his car blocking the sidewalk.

He pressed a button on a remote, waited for the beige garage door to roll up and drove in, the ceiling lights automatically flickering on. Sitting on three hundred square meters of land in the middle of the city, the house was priceless, having been in his family for five generations. He'd had plenty of offers from greasy little real estate agents for the place, but he would never sell. Where else would he be within sight of the Dome of the Rock and walking distance from his shop? The garage door rumbled down behind him, which should please the pedestrians no end.

He got out of the small car, deactivated the house alarm system, and strode quickly to a heavy steel door at the back of the garage. He typed in a six digit PIN, pulled the door open and switched on the overhead LED lights, revealing an Aladdin's cave of treasure. The Israel Antiquities Authority would be very interested in his collection if they knew of it—perhaps they did—but Acaph did not fear the toothless bureaucracy. The government more focused on revenue antique traders, legitimate and gray, generated than enforcing an impossible law. Besides, the government already had all the important archaeological sites covered. What kept him and others like him in business, people always found new things of saleable value…or produced them in the back shed. Tourists existed to be fleeced, and Acaph had no moral qualms taking his share.

Breathing heavily, he deposited the first ossuary on the workbench. With the second one safely beside it, he pondered the secrets they held. He had never seen markings like that. They were definitely not old Hebrew or Aramaic, but he couldn't figure out what they were. Anyway, that wasn't important. He lifted the lid off one chest and gazed hungrily at the unusual bones—they were his prize. The skeletal bones themselves did not look remarkable, but the elongated skull with its large eye cavities demanded explanation. Although curious, his only interest was in how much his haul would fetch. Not a professional archaeologist, he knew enough to know that he had something rare, and positive Dr. Kutner would salivate to get his hands on the thing.

Acaph positioned a white screen behind the ossuaries, shifted the camera stand toward him, peered at the display panel and started snapping pictures. Satisfied, he powered up the laptop and transferred the images into his working Pending directory. He chuckled as he composed a brief email, attached several shots and sent it off. As he made his way into the kitchen, he figured he'd hear from old Kutner within the hour.

The burbling percolator gave off an enticing aroma of freshly brewed coffee. Acaph knew how to cook and take care of himself, but most of the time, he ate out. Food cheap and plentiful, which spared him from doing mundane kitchen chores. Tonight, he planned to celebrate at one of his choice restaurants, perhaps Kadosh. Within easy walking distance, and it promised to be a mild evening.

His cell went off and he nodded with satisfaction as he read the caller's name on the screen. Ezrah Kutner was a respected academic at the Rockefeller Archaeological Museum, and Acaph admired the little bird-man's fastidious professionalism. Sporting a disheveled head of white hair, thick brown-rimmed glasses, an old briar pipe perpetually hanging from the side of his mouth, Kutner was everybody's image of an absentminded professor. However, looks can be deceiving and Kutner was far from absentminded. Eccentric a little perhaps, but that only added to his carefully cultivated reputation. He was also a sharp negotiator, receiving constant offers of genuine, and sometimes not so genuine, antiques from all types of operators.

"How do you like the pictures, Ezrah?"

"What's the story?" Kutner demanded without any preliminaries.

"I don't even get a shalom?"

"I'm too busy to bother with trivia. Besides, nobody actually means it."

"Hah! I can see why your circle of friends has stopped growing."

"The young are pragmatic, looking to make a future for themselves, and the old are rooted in a fantasy past. Me, I'm in the middle. I get by."

"That's part of the problem, my friend. We're losing the art of common courtesy. We're losing our humanity."

"The ossuaries, Acaph, you old thief. We'll talk philosophy some other time."

"Like I said in my email, they were dug up in someone's backyard."

"Where?"

"Arnona."

"Ah, makes sense now. I keep telling the city bureaucrats not to release new land for settlement until it's been properly surveyed, but they never listen. Sharron Ibrahim's administration isn't any better, worse perhaps, but I don't want to talk politics and get upset. I want to see the bones."

"Come on over. I'm just brewing some coffee."

"Fifteen minutes," Kutner snapped and hung up.

Acaph smiled, lifted the glass carafe and poured a generous measure into his favorite earthenware mug. He stirred in two teaspoons of sugar as he walked slowly into the garage and his work den. He expected to make a handsome profit from the burial chests and bones, but the crystal could turn out to be even more valuable. Absolutely unique, he couldn't remember seeing anything remotely like it anywhere. When Shaken revealed the thing, Acaph merely stared. Definitely machined—no natural crystal he knew had such dimensions and finish—it had him beat.

He put the mug on the bench, snagged a round stool mounted on four coasters and sat down. He gingerly removed the crystal from its protective box and unfolded the white cloth. Feeling the texture of the material between his fingers, the cloth was another mystery. It felt thick, yet was fine as silk and had an oily sheen.

Uncovered, the pale orange crystal glinted with reflected light. He opened a small drawer in a cabinet that held an assortment of odds and ends, and took out a jeweler's loupe. Acaph fixed it to his right eye and peered at the polished surface, marveling at its transparency, apparently flawless. He sat back and admitted grudgingly that this was something outside his expertise. He knew a lot about antique artifacts, but he was not a gemologist. However, there was someone who could help him—Liam Geffen. Liam was a genuine licensed gem dealer. The only problem, he lived in Tel Aviv, the home of Israel's diamond processing industry, but the crystal's potential value made it worth going there. He would send his friend an email and wait for a reaction.

He wrapped the crystal and locked the box in the safe. As he gulped down the last of the coffee, he heard a car pull up. A door banged and a moment later, the doorbell chimed. Acaph returned to the kitchen, left the mug next to the percolator and strode toward the front entrance. He opened the door and beamed.

"Welcome to my humble abode, my friend," he gushed with open arms.

"Humble? You're bloated, you greasy trader," Kutner declared sourly as he strode in. "Bloated."

"Now you've gone and hurt my feelings," Acaph said and pouted. "Especially since I went out of my way to be nice to you. If you don't want my business, I can always deal with Laske at the Israel Museum."

A ritual they always played and neither took offense.

"Laske is a pretentious fool who thinks he's an archaeologist, which also makes him a dangerous fool." Kutner waved a hand in dismissal, and sniffed as he glanced at the percolator. "That coffee smells good."

Acaph took the hint, smiled and retrieved another mug from the cupboard. He filled it and added sugar and cream, then refilled his own mug. Kutner took a sip and nodded in appreciation.

"You always serve good coffee. Where do you get the beans?"

"I told you before, at Hameel's in the Armenian Quarter."

"Ah, yes. So you did." Kutner stared suspiciously at Acaph. "You weren't serious about talking to Laske, were you?"

Acaph laughed, genuinely amused that his friend thought he was working two angles. "Not yet. It all depends on how much you're prepared to offer," he said smoothly, driving in the barb.

Kutner snorted. "You're a thief, you heretic, but you make excellent coffee." His glasses had slipped down his nose and he pushed them up. "Okay, show me what you've got. I have a meeting and can't hang around too long. Budgets!" he declared with disdain.

"I feel for you."

In the den, Kutner frowned as he examined the burial chests. He peered into the opened one and hissed. He fumbled through his jacket pocket, dragged out a pair of white cotton gloves, pulled them on, and reached for the skull. The tip of his tongue stuck out from the corner of his mouth as he studied the skull, his head darting from side to side.

"Mmm. The cranial cavity is abnormally large and the plate joints are somewhat misplaced. The resemblance to deliberate deformation practiced by the Paracas Necropolis people in southwestern Peru is suggestive, but the bone structure on this specimen doesn't show forced deformation. Most unusual. Most." Kutner glanced at Acaph over the rim of his glasses. "And you say this was dug up in Arnona?"

"The man was hoeing his backyard and almost fell into a burial chamber."

"Interesting." Kutner exhaled slowly, replaced the skull and opened the second ossuary. Head tilted, he stared at the bones inside. "I'll need to get shots of the chamber as corroborative evidence. The skull is somewhat smaller...a child perhaps. Most unusual. Mmm." He stepped back and peeled off the gloves, stuffed them into his pocket and dragged out a worn pipe. He clamped it between his teeth and nodded several times. "Those

symbols…I'll have to examine them more closely. Very strange."
He looked up. "How much?"

"Sixty thousand," Acaph said briskly.

"Sixty! May worms eat your stinking carcass. Robber!"

Acaph folded his arms across his chest, unmoved. "There is always Laske, you know."

The two academics were fierce rivals, but nonetheless got along tolerably well outside their respective institutions. He preferred to deal with Kutner, but this was business. He did not become moderately wealthy by making friendship deals or selling on credit.

"I'll give you fifty, and that's my final offer," Kutner declared.

"Fifty-five."

"Fifty!"

"The Rockefeller Museum is loaded."

"It might be, but it didn't get that way by throwing away its money. I'm being generous and you know it. Without the bones, you wouldn't get a shekel for the ossuaries."

Acaph laughed. Frankly, more than he expected to get. "Okay, fifty thousand, and I'll help carry the chests to your car at no extra charge."

"Big of you." Kutner regarded him with a guarded stare. "You don't normally give in this easily. What are you hiding?"

If he showed Ezrah the crystal, he might want to buy it, but the Museum would never offer as much as Acaph might get on the open market. Still, it would do no harm to slake his friend's curiosity. He wiggled his index finger and stepped to the safe. He retrieved the wooden box, placed it on the bench and stepped back.

Kutner nodded slowly, pushed up his glasses and peered at it. "Same symbols as the chests. Mmm." He took off the lid and unwrapped the crystal, glancing at Acaph from time to time as if expecting the thing to explode in his face. With the shining object revealed, he took the pipe out of his mouth and gave a low whistle.

"Oh my…" After a moment, he licked his lips. "This was in one of the ossuaries?"

Acaph nodded.

"Most unusual. What is it?"

"Damned if I know. I'm taking it to Tel Aviv tomorrow and have Liam Geffen look at it."

"Geffen, eh? Forget him. The Museum will buy it at your own price."

"Eighty thousand," Acaph said immediately, then cursed himself for a fool. He had no idea what the thing was worth.

"Sixty," Kutner replied.

Acaph shook his head, retrieved the crystal and put it back in the box. "Not nearly enough."

"Email me some pictures and I'll talk to the Museum. Don't sell it without consulting me, okay?"

"You have my price, which might change once I talk to Geffen, but I'll call you before I make a deal."

"It would make a fantastic exhibit—once we find out what it is." Kutner finished his coffee and placed the mug on the bench. "The Museum will credit your account for the ossuaries. Now, I've got to run." He offered his hand. "It's been a pleasure, my friend. A pleasure."

Acaph shook his hand and grinned. "Likewise. My regards to Martha."

"You should consider a lifestyle change," Kutner told him seriously. "Even at your age, there are plenty of decent women who'd be glad to marry you. It's not good living alone, and winter nights are cold."

Acaph sighed. "I know, but it's a bit late for that, Ezrah. I'm set in my ways now. Besides, if a woman were to marry me now, I suspect it would be for my money."

"Well, there is always that, but you're overlooking many good ones out there. Many. Think about it anyway."

"Let's arrange dinner one night and we'll talk philosophy," Acaph countered.

"Sounds good. I'll call you. Shalom."

Acaph opened the garage door and helped carry the stone chests to Kutner's red Citroen. He waved as the car accelerated down the street, leaking a thin thread of oily smoke. As the garage door rolled down, he rubbed his hands and grinned broadly.

* * *

Acaph skirted Ben Gurion Airport on his right as he drove along Route 1, he adjusted his shades and shifted his butt. He could see aircraft drifting in for a landing, and others clawing for the sky, engines thundering. The airconditioner purred in the background to the commentary from the morning's current affairs talk show. With the American pullout from Afghanistan two years ago, the Taliban were rapidly reclaiming territory they lost in 2001. It was all so pointless. At least President Walters showed determination in the face of Republican opposition to completely extricate U.S. forces from an untenable position. The event was somewhat drowned out by ongoing diplomatic and economic retaliation against China for inducing a massive land slump of La Palma's Cumbre Vieja's western flank. Had they succeeded as planned, the U.S. eastern seaboard would now be devastated, heralding a new political dawn on the world, or a nightmare.

With formal recognition of a Palestinian state three years ago, things had settled down in Israel, Prime Minster Sharron Ibrahim managing to maintain a coalition government with his right-wing Likud party and Abdon Sayar's Zionist Union nationalists. There was even talk of bringing the centrist Kulanu party into the fold. Acaph approved of any move that would stabilize the Knesset, which for too long was hostage to dozens of ultra-orthodox and single-issue factions who derailed efforts to achieve a settlement with the Palestinians, earning Israel scorn from the international community and the population at large.

The sun shone fiercely through the windscreen, but it was easier to see now that it hung higher in the sky. When he set out around nine, it glared directly into his eyes as he drove along Route 443. Politics forgotten, he glanced at the plastic shopping bag resting on the seat beside him containing the wooden box and crystal. After dinner last night, he spent almost half an hour staring at the magical thing, coffee mug untouched. He was almost tempted to keep it for himself, but he forced down the gush of boyish emotion. He was a trader, not a collector. Sitting in his safe, he had a curiosity, but worthless unless its value was realized. He considered hard cash much more useful...and practical.

The odd nature of the crystal kept him tossing through the night. Get rid of it and be at peace, he told himself sternly. Once he made the decision, he drifted off into deep sleep.

A white BMW overtook him, weaving between slower cars, and Acaph snorted. Everybody was in a rush these days. He figured that was part of the problem with life today; everyone too busy to sit back, relax and enjoy what they had, instead of striving to attain some illusory goal that lay over the horizon. Life had become cold and impersonal, like the unfeeling bureaucrats who controlled them.

As he neared the exit to Route 20—Ayalon Highway—he slowed and joined the queue at the exit ramp. He turned right and headed north toward Ramat Gan, Tel Aviv's Diamond Exchange District, the Bursa. The dashboard digital display read 10:45, which wasn't bad. It had taken him one hour and 35 minutes from his home to get here. Given that the morning rush had not quite subsided, he made good time.

Two years ago, Geffen's nineteen-year-old son collided on this intersection with a driver running a red light. Both were killed outright, the smash producing an unbelievable tangle of twisted wreckage. Geffen took it particularly badly, having hopes that his son would take over his small diamond and jewelry processing factory in the Shimshon Tower. Even now, he didn't want to talk about the incident. His wife maintained a façade of collected charm and decorum, but Acaph had seen her become quieter, devoting more attention to their daughter.

When he approached Ramat Gan, he could see the complex of towers that made up the diamond trading center climb into a clear sky. He exited onto Route 481—Jabotinski Road—and turned left into Zisman Street toward the imposing pink façade of Leonardo City Tower Hotel. He did not bother searching for a parking spot on the first underground level, it was sure to be packed, but drove directly to the relatively empty bottom third level. He grabbed the plastic bag and sauntered toward a bank of two elevators.

In the lobby, squeezed between a souvenir shop and a travel accessories store, the brightly lit Geffen's Dealers sign beckoned visitors toward large plate glass panels protecting shelves of assorted jewelry and watches for the discerning customer. He weaved his way between hotel guests arriving or leaving, dragging carry-on cases on wheels, and bellboys pushing brass baggage carts through a wide entrance beside the revolving door. The hotel always a busy place.

He walked into the store and caught Lila's eye, a pretty brunette attendant standing behind a glass counter. Hips swaying, a tight skirt hugging a trim figure, she walked over and beamed.

"Mr. Yaron! We haven't seen you in a while, sir," she said, friendly, but not inviting.

"Business. You know how it is. Is Liam around?"

"He is expecting you. Please follow me."

At the back of the shop, she knocked once on a heavy wooden door and opened it. "Mr. Yaron, Liam."

"Show him in!" a voice boomed from inside.

Lila smiled at Acaph and stepped back, allowing him enough

room to enter. He returned the smile, smelling light spring perfume as he passed her.

Trim, short, bald, Geffen stepped away from his desk cluttered with paperwork, a laptop at one corner guarded by a white keyboard and mouse, beamed and held out his hand.

"Shalom, my friend! Good to see you again," he gushed as they shook hands.

Acaph winced at the powerful grip and grinned weakly. "Shalom, Liam. You can let go now before you break it."

Geffen chuckled and slapped him on the shoulder. He dragged a soft beige leather chair closer to the desk and waved him over.

"Sit! How was the drive?"

Acaph eased himself down and glanced at shelves of office files, books, a collection of jewelry and mineral specimens.

"Not bad, actually. Every time I come here though, things are different. New roads, skyscrapers, shopping malls. I'm afraid it's not all that different from Jerusalem's lifestyle, changing fast, becoming more hectic and impersonal."

"It's called progress, but I don't know who is progressing. Care for some coffee or something?"

"Thank you, no. And you? Business is thriving?"

"Well enough. A trader these days faces many problems, as you no doubt know, and there are always new government regulations and charges designed to separate me from my well-deserved profits. I tell you, old friend, taxes will nibble away what I worked hard for all these years."

"There is no justice," Acaph murmured dryly, understanding fully. Geffen cocked an eyebrow at him.

"I should go into the underground economy, like you. Sell ten shekels of junk and report five to the government, if anything. It's a great way to run a business—until you get audited."

Acaph stiffened and glared. "I run a respectable business, you bandit!"

After a moment, they both snickered, but Geffen was right. It was getting harder. Progress, like his friend said. He wondered who got the better of it. It certainly wasn't the merchants.

"I heard Chana will be graduating in Business Administration this fall."

"And I couldn't be prouder," Geffen declared with obvious satisfaction.

"Grooming her to take over?"

"I fear she has her sights on the corporate sector. My scrounging, as she puts it, is too much hard work. See what I put up with? I scrimp and save to send her through university and I get repaid with blasphemy. I mean it when I say you're fortunate not to have children."

"That's how the cards of my life were dealt, my friend," Acaph murmured, reflecting on lost experiences. Still, it had not been a bad life, even though no one was there to carry his name. Some things were simply not meant to be.

"Yes…" Geffen locked his fingers and rested his arms on the desk. "About your find…the pictures you sent me were fascinating and I can't wait to see the real thing."

Acaph grinned, placed the shopping bag on the desk, and took out the leather-bound box. He unfolded the purple cloth and slid the box across the desk. Geffen licked his lips, carefully removed the lid, and extracted the wrapped crystal.

"Funny material," he murmured as he pulled back the white cloth, revealing the crystal. After a time, he looked up. "Fascinating. This was in one of the ossuaries?"

Acaph nodded.

"It's refreshing to see something interesting for a change. Staring at gemstones all the time can get dull."

"How you must suffer."

Geffen wagged a finger, reached into a drawer beside him, produced a large loupe and fixed it to his left eye. He frowned, lips compressed into a line, and carefully examined the crystal.

He took off the loupe, lifted the crystal and held it against the light.

"The only time I've seen transparency like this is in a diamond, and I can tell you, this is not a diamond." He stood up, walked to the bench, and placed the crystal on a digital scale. Looking at the readout, he bit his lower lip. "At 390 grams, it's abnormally heavy for what looks like beryl heliodor or topaz. Damned if I know what the thing is."

He walked back to the desk, sat down, reached into a drawer and held up what looked like a silver pointer. He smiled, made an adjustment, and waved a sharp green line at the ceiling.

"Laser," he told Acaph as he held up the crystal.

Alarmed, Acaph sat up. "Hey, I don't want the thing damaged."

"Relax. I had this specially made for checking fake gems. It generates less than one milliwatt."

The laser beam struck the crystal and Geffen gaped as he stared at the fuzzy diffraction pattern on the ceiling.

"What the..." He placed the crystal on the desk, passed a hand over his shining head and exhaled loudly. "This doesn't make sense. That pattern suggests a face-centered cubic lattice like a doped diamond, which is impossible. Beryl has a hexagonal structure, and topaz is made up of connected irregular octahedrons. We should have seen a light central area surrounded by irregular dots."

He frowned, made another adjustment to the laser and raised the crystal. It instantly turned into a mirror when the green beam struck it. Acaph blinked, not believing. After a moment, he closed his mouth with a snap. Geffen switched off the laser and the crystal gradually lost its sheen and became transparent.

"That, my friend, is...fantastic. You've certainly come up with something strange this time. I'll have one of my men look at it more closely. Do you have a price in mind?"

"After seeing this, Liam, I don't know what the thing is

worth," Acaph admitted, knowing Liam would not take advantage of his ignorance. As a respected gem trader, he had a reputation to maintain. Nevertheless, he knew he'd be walking out with the short end of the deal. That's how business was done.

"I'll give you 90,000 for it, and I'm taking a risk on an unknown stone, and I'm not sure that it's a natural stone."

"Not natural?"

"No stone does what that thing just did." Geffen declared. "You're not pushing a piece of plastic on me, are you?" he demanded and immediately held up his hand. "I'm kidding. Well?"

"A generous offer, Liam," Acaph acknowledged, considering whether to hold out for more. Despite its unusual shape and polarizing property, the crystal could be colored quartz for all he knew. "Let me make a call."

Geffen raised an eyebrow. "Who is it? The Israel Museum?"

Acaph shook his head. "Rockefeller." He dragged out his cell and pressed a preset number.

"Kutner?" Geffen asked and Acaph nodded.

"I was just about to call you," the academic replied in a harried voice.

"What have you got for me, Ezrah?"

"Sixty-five is as high as the Museum is prepared to go. Sorry, my friend."

"It's not enough, but I understand. Talk to you soon." He switched off and beamed. "Liam, you thief, you got a deal."

Geffen laughed and extended a hand. "Mazal u'bracha," he said formally, which meant, 'may the deal be with luck and blessing'.

They shook hands, sealing the bargain. That was all it took, no paperwork or weary administrative procedures.

"I'll have the money in your account within the hour," Geffen said. "Call me when you find more unusual crystals."

"You'll be the first."

"You sure you won't have coffee and reminisce a while? We

could go out and have lunch. It's been some time since we saw each other."

"I'll have that coffee now, then I better get back to my shop. I also have customers to look after, and I spent most of yesterday chasing down the ossuaries," Acaph declared with a shrug. "Why don't you and Sarah come up to the Old City sometime? We'll have dinner, talk, and enjoy the sights. She'll like that."

"She would. I'll mention it to her and we shall see," Geffen said and sat back. "Front!" he yelled and waited. Seconds later the door opened, revealing an elfin face framed with cascading brown hair.

"You called, O master?" she asked whimsically.

"Two coffees, Lila."

She smiled and nodded. "I hear and obey."

Acaph inclined his head after the retreating figure. "I could use her at my store."

"She's great, isn't she?"

"She would certainly help move sales," Acaph said and Geffen laughed.

"Dig up your own help."

* * *

Geffen rubbed the stubble on his chin and sighed as he scanned the column of general ledger entries for the week. Sales were down a bit, but they were usually down in August as the tourist season started to wind up. Gold, platinum, and diamond inventories were too high, which he didn't like. Holding inventory cost money and took a slice off his bottom line. Time for an end-of-season sale perhaps? He reminded himself to have a chat with Meyer over lunch and organize something. Meyer did a great job running the hotel store and small diamond cutting workshop, but with business growing, he might be stretched. Geffen noted that they still had a batch of finished diamonds worth US$15 million ready to push through De Beers. He didn't want to hold onto the stuff longer than absolutely necessary. He needed to ask Meyer why he hadn't moved the consignment already. Geffen kept telling everybody, 'Use it or lose it'. Dead inventory was dead money.

The phone jangled and he groped for the receiver, eyes on the laptop screen.

"Geffen!"

"It's Meyer. I need to see you, Liam."

The workshop manager sounded breathless and Geffen sat up. "I was just thinking about you. Anything the matter?"

"Something's the matter, all right. It's that crystal you gave me to check."

"What about it?"

"It's better if I show you."

Geffen frowned, not liking surprises. Perhaps a break would do him some good, and he needed a cup of strong coffee to rev himself up.

"Okay. Come on over."

The line clicked and he replaced the receiver. It would take Meyer at least ten minutes to walk from the Shimshon Tower, plenty of time to have his coffee.

"Front!"

A moment later, Lila walked in, placed a slim hand on her shapely hip and waited.

"Coffee, my dear. Meyer should be around shortly. Show him in and bring him a round."

She grinned and gave a mock bow. "Yes, O master."

Geffen chuckled as the door closed and wondered why his three sales girls put up with him. He did not berate them, nor was deliberately mean, but he did tend to be a bit gruff at times. It didn't seem to bother them.

He only had girls in the store—smart, attractive girls—and for a good reason. Male customers felt flattered when a nice creature batted long eyelashes and hung onto his every word, wafted perfume at him, no matter what his age. It helped lubricate a sale, and women trusted another woman when talking about intimate things like jewelry. He'd had serious men at the counter, all professionals in the game, but the turnover curve climbed when he hired a girl. He didn't need to have the facts of life explained to him.

Lila brought his coffee and undulated out the door, enjoying his admiring look. That's all it was, though. Devoted to Sarah, he never strayed. However, being a devoted and faithful husband did not prevent him from relishing the divine feminine form. He took a sip of the strong black coffee and turned to the laptop.

Sometime later, a knock interrupted his thoughts and he looked up as Lila peered in.

"Mr. Meyer."

"Right."

She stepped back and a skeletal individual strode in wearing black: black shirt, suit, tie, and shoes. Dark hair cut short, a pencil mustache drew attention to his gaunt face. Without saying anything, Meyer removed a wide ruby-red satin jewel case from his jacket, opened it and slid it across the desk.

Lila followed him in, placed a small cup and saucer beside his elbow and withdrew, closing the door softly behind her.

"I don't know what this thing is, Liam, but God didn't make it," Meyer said heavily without any preamble, his voice surprisingly deep. Pulling up a chair, he sat down.

"What are you talking about?" Geffen demanded.

"Watch."

Meyer reached for the letter opener next to the phone and made a small scratch on the crystal's surface.

"What are you doing!" Geffen screamed in outrage and jumped out of his chair.

Meyer grimaced and pointed at the crystal. Not believing, Geffen saw the scratched edges soften and slowly merge, restoring an unbroken polished surface.

"Holy father," he whispered, then wiped his head and sat down with a thump. He picked up his cup, only to find it empty.

Meyer sighed, reached for his coffee and drank without saying a word. There wasn't any need for explanations, if one was possible.

"Where did you get that thing, Liam?" he asked after a while.

"I bought it from Yaron. He claims he got it from a man who found two ossuaries in his backyard. The crystal was in one of them." Geffen peered at Meyer. "A natural gemstone doesn't repair itself."

"Nothing does, and that thing is not a natural crystal. I got ready to do an x-ray when I bumped it against a vise. When I saw the scratch, only about two millimeters, I thought I was dead. You were going to kill me for sure, and you'd be justified. I just about shit my pants when I saw the scratch vanish."

His mind reeling, Geffen swallowed. "You're telling me—"

"I'm not telling you anything," Meyer said and downed the last of his coffee. "I wish I never saw the thing. I won't be able to sleep for a week, if at all. What else was in those ossuaries?"

"Bones, as you would expect. He sold them to the Rockefeller Museum."

"He should have sold them the crystal as well. My nerves won't settle down for a month."

Geffen tapped the desk with his fingers and chewed his lower lip. "Two thousand years ago or whenever, man did not have technology to produce memory materials."

"We don't have such technology today either," Meyer growled. "Not like this."

Geffen studied the strange object, working the possibilities, all of them involving lots of money. Piles of lovely folding cash. Although intensely curious, he didn't really care what the thing was, when it was made, or who made it. That would start him thinking about things he preferred to leave alone, but he knew people who would pay almost anything to get their hands on something like this. The gem market, like with everything else, operated on two levels: the official and the secret network of dealers and collectors. He considered himself a scrupulously honest trader and paid his taxes with a minimum of grumbling, but that did not mean he had to share everything with a rapacious government, and he didn't.

Making up his mind, he looked up. "Not a word to anyone about this. You hear me?"

"What are you going to do?"

"Get rid of it, of course."

Meyer nodded. He knew how the game was played. "I think that's a very good idea. That thing is trouble, trust me." He stood and exhaled loudly. "Thanks for the coffee."

"When are you going to clear the De Beers consignment?"

"Going out today," Meyer snapped and walked out.

When the door closed, Geffen stared at the crystal.

According to the 1978 Antiquities Law, an artifact could not be exported without written approval from the Director of Antiquities. If the artifact was deemed to be of national importance, and Geffen did not consider the crystal had any national significance, written approval must be provided by the Minister of Education and Culture, a tortuous process. What could trip him up was the requirement that all antiquities shipped abroad must be registered with and handled by a licensed dealer. Well, he was a licensed dealer, but not in antiquities. On the other hand, what he had was not exactly an antique. He would let his lawyers argue it if it ever came to that.

"Front!"

The door opened and Lila stuck her head in.

He closed the jewel case and pushed it toward her. "Get some promo shots made." He dug into the drawer and held out the laser pointer. "And one with this. And Lila? Only you get to see what's inside and you don't talk to anybody. Understood?"

"Of course, Liam." Looking puzzled, she took the pointer, picked up the case and made her way out.

He sat back and glanced at the ceiling-high display case. On the middle glass shelf lay a pile of crumpled brown leather, pieces of purple and white cloth, and a wooden box. Those items he meant to keep for himself. After all, business wasn't everything and the soul needed nurturing from time to time with things other than money. It would serve to remind him that the world still held secrets.

He turned to the laptop, pulled the keyboard to him, logged into a special Gmail account he used to run closed auctions, and clicked the New Mail icon. He had contacts with every major diamond clearinghouse and did business with most of them. When looking for a discerning buyer, one cannot simply post a Twitter message or put in a Facebook ad. High end gem trading was transacted more discreetly. Geffen had something unusual, perhaps even controversial, which he hoped would attract only the most discerning collector. He knew several people whom he could contact, but he wanted to cast a wider net for what he had to offer.

He smiled as he pictured Lau Wei's small withered form, eyes darting everywhere, missing nothing. Lau ran an exclusive boutique in Hong Kong's Central District, part of the city's Diamond Federation. Geffen met him during a symposium of international traders organized by the Waldman Diamond Company. They established a firm friendship and traded from time to time. Lau would know people in the Asian arena who would want to buy the crystal, especially the new breed of Chinese millionaires seeking to divest themselves of excess cash.

He covered the European market with an email to Vasily Drotenkov who had a large shop in the TsUM—the Central Universal Department Store—one of the most renowned high end stores in Moscow. A tall, taciturn man with a sprinkling of white hair, totally devoid of humor, Drotenkov's intimate knowledge of the European gem industry unmatched. Normally, Geffen would have picked an outfit in Antwerp to market the crystal, but overregulation had strangled trading over there, Brussels having a finger in everything. If his transaction came to light, he could face serious consequences not only with EU regulators, but the Israel Tax Authority as well, something he did not need at any time.

American high rollers were always on the lookout for the atypical, and what Geffen had definitely fell into that category. Terrence Truscott, owner of the famed Petradi Diamonds store on New York's Broadway, would know who currently sought the exotic. Each company would be paid a flat brokerage fee of US$10,000 for their trouble, but Geffen figured it a cheap investment. Tomorrow, one of them might call him for a favor. It all evened out in the end.

He typed quickly, composing a simple message. The people receiving it knew how these things were run.

Artificial crystal with unique polarizing and self-healing properties available in a closed auction. Bids to start at US$100,000. One bid per participating party only. Auction starts at 12:00 GMT on August 20 and closes at 18:00. No bids will be accepted outside this timeframe.

Geffen checked the text, nodded, and saved the draft. All he needed now were the promo shots. He figured giving everybody three days to make up their mind more than fair.

After passing a hand over his head, he sat back and slowly rocked back and forth, deep in thought. How did a crystal like that end up in an ossuary? Did Acaph lie to him? No, why would he? He lifted his head and gazed at the wooden box sitting on the shelf, wondering what happened in the Arnona hills thousands of years ago.

Chapter Two

"Stone, you're not listening to me," Kevin Morrison hissed, his voice menacing. "I don't care why sales are down. All I see is that they're down. What are you doing about it?"

He heard a heavy sigh at the other end.

"Dr. Morrison, the Chinese have the solar panels market sewn up. We can't compete with them on price."

"For normal PV panels, yes, but they don't have the thin film stuff you're supposed to be pushing."

"Our labor costs—"

"You think my PhD and MBA came out of a Coco Pops box? We've been over this before. I located the new nanograss plant in Bedford for a good reason, and that's to keep our intellectual property. I understand that shifting our production facilities to China would lower our labor costs, no argument there, but we'd be compromising our IP! I'm not about to give them years of my research simply to reduce your labor costs. Which part of that equation don't you understand?"

"Our advertising campaign—"

"Sucks. I've seen your ads. Summer months are a window when we should be raking it in, and you're giving me a song and dance about labor costs. You're the plant manager up there. Whatever it is, fix it."

"I'll get Sales Support on it," Van Rullen said wearily.

"Stone, listen to me. Last year China tried to wipe us out with the La Palma tsunami and most of the country is still sore at them. Play that angle. Tell people to buy American. It shouldn't be hard. We have an unbeatable product the Chinese can't match. Nobody can. You have an airport practically across the street and the plant is a stone's throw from downtown Boston. Exploit our competitive advantage. Who else can sell 26% efficiency panels? Talk to Moore and hammer out a strategy."

"I'll get it done, Dr. Morrison."

"Those sales figure better improve or our next conversation won't be as pleasant," Morrison snarled and jammed down the phone.

Was he the only one who understood the problem? In business, you rip out your opponent's heart and eat it, or he will surely do it to you. He built Solaris Technology from an also-ran to a global player in the fiercely competitive solar roof and window panels market. His patented process to grow vertical nanoscale pillar structures, which some publicity wit promptly labeled nanograss, on an organic polymer thin film substrate able to capture IR and UV light, made traditional crystalline silicon manufacturing methods obsolete overnight, to the dismay of his competition. Only the first step in his business model, and Solaris now held a large slice of the market, which Van Rullen wasn't exploiting!

Having solved the initial teething problems, his next objective was to roll out large scale quantum dot solar cells on continuous sheets of any specified size. The state-of-the-art robot facility under construction in Hanover, Germany, to produce nanograss panels for the rapidly expanding European market should make his company a world leader in the technology. However, everything could be derailed if he failed to generate sufficient cashflow from his existing thin film plants to fund the switchover to QD sheets.

His *real* goal was to develop a pigment able to be sprayed onto any surface: roofs, exterior and interior walls, the old picket fence—anything—from which power could be drawn down across the sun's entire electromagnetic spectrum with a conversion efficiency better than 47%. Imagine having a narrow strip painted on both sides of every road and highway! All existing power generating facilities would be out of business. The tree huggers would build shrines in his honor. However, he understood well the negative social impact such a material could have on a modern industrial society if it were introduced without a carefully thought out transition program. Established vested interests were already fighting him with every weapon at their disposal, legal and illegal, to stop his research. Some were lobbying the EPA and Congress, citing his quantum dot pigment process environmentally dangerous, only because they themselves didn't have a competitive product. Despite these setbacks, a power generating material that could be sprayed onto any surface would have enormous social benefits, especially in Third World countries hungry for energy, a major causal factor limiting their development.

His research team at MIT's Department of Materials Science and Engineering were making progress, but it would be a while before his basic patents delivered a commercial product. Progress might be slow, but he already had a proof of concept pigment. A major problem was enabling the pigment to remain active in an emulsion of coloring agents. Not good telling a customer his whole house would be one enormous electricity generator, and he would not be paying a cent for grid power, provided he accepted having every wall in black!

To make the next leap though, Morrison needed a stable revenue base, which he wasn't going to get by sagging sales statistics. His shareholders continued to support him because he delivered, but research gobbled up money at an unbelievable rate, with no promise of a commercial return anytime soon. A quarter or two of sagging sales figures could see his backers rethinking their investment strategy. He did not relish the prospect of going cap in hand to some cow college looking for a job, or bowing to the government for a grant.

The market appeared ready to embrace cheap solar power, which silicon-based panels simply couldn't satisfy, given poor conversion performance, limited durability, and high installation cost compared to grid power delivered by coal, gas, and nuclear plants. With the introduction of relatively cheap organic thin-film frames, Morrison had given commercial and domestic users a viable alternative. With a plant in Boston and Sunnyvale, California, Solaris should be riding high. Instead, Van Rullen bitched about labor costs. The man knew the solar power industry as well as anyone, and that's why Morrison hired him. Was Van Rullen getting too close to the problem, becoming too involved with operational issues, neglecting sales and marketing?

Morrison decided to wait for August figures to come out before taking action.

He would give the world cheap power, but it would be on his terms. On *his* terms!

He rubbed his eyes and sat back. From his 42nd story floor-to-ceiling window, which took up the entire wall, he gazed past the East River at the majestic Brooklyn Bridge and the suburban sprawl on the other side. Lower Manhattan skyscrapers crowded each other, reaching toward a clear blue sky. It cost him plenty to rent two whole floors with an option for another at 28 Liberty, formerly the One Chase Manhattan Plaza building before the China-based Fosun International bought it and turned it into a choice corporate location. This was not vanity on Morrison's part, but hard business sense. A Manhattan address on the letter-head made people sit up and take notice. Besides, the rent came tax deductible, and he would need the extra floor once the German plant went operational.

He pushed back his chair, stood up, and walked slowly toward the display cabinet. Opening the double doors revealed a Marantz CD6005 player. He pulled out a tray of CDs, picked out Vivaldi's *Four Seasons* and inserted it into the player. By the time he sat down, the haunting strings of the *Winter* movement vibrated softly from the surround system. He leaned back, locked his fingers behind his head and closed his eyes. For a moment, the external business world ceased to exist as his mind drifted in tune with the melody.

A soft *ting* from the computer made him look at the screen. A new email icon flashed and he clicked on Outlook. When he saw the sender's name, he felt warmed. An old friend, Truscott shared Morrison's passion for theater and orchestral concerts, having attended a number of Broadway plays with their wives in tow. When his daughter's boyfriend wanted to buy an engagement ring, Morrison took him to Petradi Diamonds. Thinking about that day, he exhaled slowly. Where have those two years gone? Sandra had a daughter of her own now and lived in Boston. He didn't feel like a granddad, not at forty-eight. Once Stanly marries, Morrison would be free to devote all his energy to business…and Juliana.

His Juliana…

He had been sweating out his PhD thesis in biomolecular engineering at Cornell, and she was going for a master's in business communication. He literally bumped into her at the campus cafeteria and the collision merged their hearts. A tall woman, raven hair framed an exquisitely molded face, large brown eyes that always seemed to sparkle, small firm lips, she smiled at his mumbled apology and invited him to share her corner of a crowded table. Taken aback by this frontal assault, Morrison accepted…and spent the next two hours under her spell, missing a lab session. From there, of course, there was no turning back, and he never wanted to wind back the last twenty-four years they had together.

They had their problems like any couple, but they overcame them. Her teaching job at New York University's Stern School of Business sometimes kept them apart more than he liked, and that required some adjustment by both of them. Quite a woman, his Juliana. He doubted he'd be reaching this high if it weren't for her unwavering support and sharp business acumen. One thing she resisted was work for him. Perhaps she knew him better than he thought, and nodded at the rush of pleasant memories.

Before he forgot, he reached across the desk and pressed a button on his phone pad.

"Allison, please confirm my lunch appointment at Luke's Lobster with Mrs. Morrison."

"Of course, Doctor," his striking, yet stern assistant said, and he smiled. She could probably run Solaris even if he were not around.

Getting back to business, he clicked on the email tag. He scanned the text and frowned as he studied the attached images. A crystal with self-healing properties? Crap. And the polarization garbage? No mechanism existed that could induce a crystal to become totally reflective. No natural mineral he knew of had such properties. If the thing was artificial as the email said, why would the owner seek to sell it? There had to be a catch.

He turned and gazed at a large specimen of rainbow aurora quartz and fluorite encased in glass mounted next to the bar cabinet. The display always went down well with visitors. Crystals held a strange fascination for him as far back as he could remember. He recalled an outing with his dad to a local fair. He could not have been more than five or six, and the visit changed his life. One stand caught his attention, covered with mineral specimens, polished sawn-off rocks, pendants, various trinkets, rock eggs, and broken stones studded with amethyst. His dad bought him a crystal and he used to stare at it in his room, wondering what it was and where it came from. Over time, that specimen grew into a sizeable collection and contributed in no small part to his PhD in biomolecular engineering.

His thesis research resulted in him taking out four basic patents that led him to abandon academic life and pursue industrial application of his ideas. He'd since had offers to buy the rights to his patents, including two he took out later on organic photovoltaic application, from several local and overseas corporations—the Chinese submitting an extremely attractive package—but he would not be bought. Money was nice to have and made life very comfortable for him and his family, but Morrison wanted his ideas turned into marketable products under his direction. If the Chinese wanted to build nanograss or quantum dot solar cells, let them do their own research. He wasn't about to give it to them on a plate for a lousy few million with the industry worth billions. The new generation of solar power generation systems based on his nanograss technology represented a significant strategic and competitive advantage, and Solaris controlled it. *He* controlled it. There would be competitors, but if they wanted to manufacture, they would have to get a license from him or develop a variant of their own, which they would find rather difficult.

Bidding to start on Wednesday, eh? As he stared at the captivating photo of the orange crystal, he wondered whether it was worth $100K. Probably more, as that was only the floor price. As an ordinary mineral, although an unusual piece, it wasn't remarkable and certainly not worth bidding for. The hooks, of course, were its unusual properties, if true. He knew Truscott well enough to know that his friend would not blindside him into a shady deal. Still, he needed to know more before committing himself.

He reached for the phone and tapped in numbers.

"Good afternoon. Petradi Diamonds. Olga speaking."

"Hi, Olga. This is Kevin Morrison. Can I speak to Terry, please?"

"Ah, Dr. Morrison. Let me check. Hold on."

After a moment of easy-listening background music, the line clicked.

"Kevin, I'm not surprised you called," Truscott boomed in a jovial voice. "Still planning to take over the world?"

"It's all scripted. How're you doing, Terry?"

"Well enough. I want to go to Hawaii for a week, but Helen is dragging her heels. She says my timing conflicts with her social program."

"Buy the damn tickets and shove them under her nose," Morrison advised. "It worked for me."

"I just might do that. Hey, what're you listening to?"

"Vivaldi."

"You're running a multimillion-dollar business and you still have time to listen to music?"

"It helps my thinking."

"Well, I collect seashells."

"Those diamonds you peddle don't look like any seashells to me."

"Each to his own. You calling about the auction?"

"You bet I am. Never saw anything like it. What can you tell me?"

"About the crystal? Nothing. You know how these things work. I get an email and pass it to a few select clientele. After seeing your collection, I thought you'd be interested."

"I'm interested, all right. Who's the seller?"

"Now, Kevin. You know I can't tell you that."

"Come on, Terry! You've handed me a hot potato and I want to know who baked it."

He heard hearty laughter.

"It's a gem dealer in Tel Aviv. That's all you'll get from me. The winning bidder will get the details."

Morrison's forehead creased in concentration. "A gem dealer? That means he bought it from somebody. This doesn't ring right, Terry. An artificial crystal with some damn strange properties suddenly falls on the market? What's the catch?"

"I'm only a go-between. I don't make the stuff."

"Somebody did. Tell me. Who else did you send the email to?"

"Kevin! You know better than to ask."

"Sorry. I'll see you on Friday night. Looking forward to that play."

"Me too. How's business?"

"We could be doing better."

"Money is tight everywhere and people are reluctant to spend."

"They spend money on diamonds."

"Go figure. You plan to bid for the crystal?"

"To be honest, I haven't made up my mind, but it's got me intrigued."

"Well, you've got until Wednesday. Catch you later."

"Sure," Morrison said softly and hung up.

He sat back and crossed his arms over his chest. A crystal that repairs itself…why would somebody make something like that? After a while, he licked his lips and rubbed his chin. A memory material—for that's what it had to be—would only be used to preserve an inherent shape. What was so special about the crystal's shape to demand such an ability? No, not shape, but function the shape represented! What possible function did the crystal perform that required maintaining the integrity of a simple rectangular solid? There had to be more.

And the polarization trick? An object polarizes to block out a defined portion of the electromagnetic spectrum in order to limit absorption of energy, like sunglasses that protect eyes from UV radiation. For the crystal to turn into a mirror, it must reflect all radiation, which didn't make sense. There were photos of it under normal visible light. Obviously, the mirror photo was not made under normal light. Terry said a Tel Aviv gem dealer put up the crystal. The man might be an expert in his field, but he wasn't a physicist. Stating the crystal polarizes must be a misnomer, and brought Morrison back to his starting point not much the wiser.

If the thing intended to block a specific part of the EMR spectrum, it followed that becoming a reflector could be a defense mechanism to prevent damage to its internal structure, whatever that might be. It could also be a fancy parlor curiosity designed to glow under a UV lamp or pencil laser. Laser? Was the mirror image made under influence of coherent light?

Speculation might be entertaining, but it didn't give him any answers.

The crystal's self-healing property intrigued him. If he could figure out how it did that, he'd have something extremely valuable. What if he could incorporate that ability into his quantum dot pigment? He would have a material that would never wear out. But why stop there? If *any* material could be made to repair itself, it would transform the entire concept of manufacturing as he knew it. He reeled at the staggering possibilities.

If his photovoltaic QD pigment was deemed radical, releasing self-repairing products on the world would be revolutionary. Not for consumers, of course, but industries that stayed in business selling goods with built-in obsolescence, the process generating ever-increasing demand for energy, diminishing resources, and wastes.

Morrison pursed his lips and nodded. He was extrapolating doomsday after seeing shots of an innocuous crystal? Sobered by the thought, he reminded himself that nothing was innocuous unless buried, and it might not be harmless even then.

This Tel Aviv gem dealer clearly knew he had something unusual on his hands, but he obviously didn't know what, or preferred not to think about it. Did he know where the thing came from? That information might be critical to unraveling the crystal's function.

Morrison rocked slowly back and forth. After a while, he decided he must get hold of it, but what price was he willing to pay? Like Terry said, he knew how these auctions worked. A bidder could bid only once, and no one knew who the other bidders were, or the value of their bids; the transaction executed by their respective intermediary. In his case, Terry. A fair system designed to maintain anonymity of all parties and eliminated potential conflict. However, a single bid also made the process brutal, as a bidder could end up paying an amount far in excess of an object's market value, but that was the nature of the game, requiring a level of knowledge and expertise by the buyer. Anyway, payment was always made on inspection, which safeguarded the purchaser and kept the system reputable.

So, what was the thing worth to him? Worth staking his future on it?

Making a decision, he reached for the phone and pressed a direct line button to his MIT research team. It took four rings before a heavy voice answered.

"Dr. Ferguson."

"Hi, Harold. It's Kevin. Still hot in Boston?"

"Hot and steamy. And the Apple?"

"The same. Still, fall is just around the corner."

"It cannot come soon enough for me. I hope you're not calling about your quantum dot pigment. We're still testing the emulsion stability factors. I'll let you know when I have something."

"You've been promising that for a while."

"Quit griping. If you're worried about expenses, my research is tax deductible."

Morrison smiled. Ferguson looked like a lumberjack, sported awful tattoos on both arms, drank beer like water, and terrorized the faculty. MIT hadn't fired his ass because he was a tenured full professor with two PhDs and a string of honorary degrees behind him, not counting nine patents in his own name. His expertise in materials engineering had industries clamoring for his attention, and the cooperative ventures he'd entered into brought truckloads of money for MIT. Morrison ought to know. His venture so far had cost him better than four million dollars, but it would be breadcrumbs if Ferguson developed a marketable QD pigment, which incidentally would make both of them a trainload of money and bring with it unparalleled personal and political power, all nice things to have.

"I want a product I can sell, not a tax deduction, but you won't be doing any research if I'm broke. Anyway, I didn't call to bug you—"

"That'll be a first."

"I've got a question."

"A question, eh? Make it a quick one."

"Let's say you had an artificial crystal the size of a small smartphone. Normally transparent, it turns into a perfect reflector when exposed to coherent light. To make it more interesting, it can repair itself."

"What do you mean, repair itself?"

"That's all I know."

"I'd say somebody is pulling your leg, Kevin."

"Perhaps, but I doubt it."

"Wait a minute. This thing actually exists?"

"I'm looking to buy it, but before I do, I want to make sure I'm not getting a paperweight. So, what do you think?"

"Could be anything. Mmm. It might be a multifunction oscillator, but those things are normally thumbnail size. Your crystal could also be a photonic resonator. That would explain its odd behavior under coherent light, but I never heard of one that large."

Morrison felt blood drain from his face and his mouth went dry.

"You're talking about a quantum processor bus."

"Hardly! The closest anybody has come to a working qubit processor is the size of a credit card chip. NASA's QuAIL device doesn't count. It's cobbled junk. Nobody I know of has developed anything like a crystal bus, even if we knew how to do it, which we don't. If they had, they certainly wouldn't be selling it. Without studying the thing, there is no way to tell what it is."

"Thanks, Harold," Morrison said softly, his thoughts in total disarray. "Keep this to yourself, okay?"

"Sure thing."

"How's Stan doing?"

"Doing well. He has a couple of ideas that might be patentable. You've got a good boy there, Kevin. Takes after his old man. He should get his master's in nanotechnology this fall."

"I owe you big time for looking after him."

"Getting him to soak up practical aspects of materials engineering at your plant was a great idea. If I had it my way, all undergrads would spend at least a year in the industry before allowing them to apply for a graduate degree, but that's just me."

"If you have someone smart who you think might benefit from some practical experience, let me know and I'll put them to work."

"I'll consider it. A pleasure to talk to you, as always." Ferguson hung up, leaving Morrison staring at the phone.

After a while, he replaced it in its cradle, swiveled the chair and gazed out the window, Vivaldi filling the empty spaces of his mind.

* * *

Although he could not feel the grass of Statue Square beneath his feet, or see the pigeons flutter among people crowding the small park enjoying an oasis of green among towers of concrete and glass, Lau Wei could picture it in his mind and took solace from the images they made. Compassion, moderation, and humility, combined with *wu-wei*—action through non-action—formed the cornerstones of his spiritualism. A practicing Taoist, though not an adherent of its traditional rituals, Lau drew strength from this ancient philosophy, enabling him to exist in a chaotic world beset with the pursuit of materialism. He did not scorn the practice as such, but his business interests were merely one side of *yin yang*, the other firmly anchored in fulfillment of his spiritual needs.

He had seen what happened to men and nations when they lost that balance. Soulless corporations had ravaged mother earth, taking from it what they wanted without any thought for tomorrow as long as their endeavors added to immediate profits. Despite knowing this was unsustainable, the mindless drive for money did not allow them to pause and reflect. Corporations were destroying Earth and their own future, while religious fundamentalism and extremism slowly destroyed mankind. No god, if gods there be, could condone such atrocities committed in his name. Of course, god was merely a convenient shield that hid fanatics bent on gaining personal or political power. Often, the two were one.

A solemn bow to his ancestors and a desire for enlightenment.

Lau sometimes wondered if it would not be better for nature to make a fresh start. Wipe mankind from existence and bring forth a wiser species. Wisdom, however, is gained through learning and experience. He only hoped that man would be allowed sufficient time to gain wisdom before everything vanished in consuming fire. Capable of producing stirring music, moving poetry, art, philosophy, literature, man's nature nevertheless reveled in blood and destruction. He wondered which side would prove to be stronger.

His office had no windows. While working, he wanted to shut out the world and the pressure of its problems. Over many years, life's experiences had endowed him with a small measure of wisdom, allowing him to exist and thrive even when some days seemed mad. And he witnessed madness last year.

Despite the terrible thing that happened at La Palma, causing so much suffering and untold diplomatic damage for Beijing, America setting off a nuclear device over China in retaliation, business went on. Especially the gem business. Governments may fulminate, wage war, conduct summits, but underneath it all, they all relied on their industrial base to project power. Without the capability to sustain a strong economy and military force, a country had to tread carefully when the powers strutted the world's diplomatic stage. Lau abhorred what the two Politburo luminaries had done with revulsion of any sane man, but that did not stop him from trading with the West. Moreover, the West did not stop trading with him. Politicians may wield the guns, but tough businessmen made and sold them.

Lau paid attention to local, national and international political winds, inasmuch as they might affect his bottom line. Student protests through the city, rallies demanding greater autonomy and freedom, press censorship, those things did not worry him much and caused him no loss of sleep. Besides, all freedom was merely an illusion. His exclusive boutique in the Central District had no plate glass front, bright lights, or counters that held gaudy watches and cheap baubles. He catered to discerning patrons, which the emerging mainland millionaires supplied in growing numbers. Politburo heavyweights running state enterprises seeking to wash embarrassing amounts of ill-gotten money often came to him from word-of-mouth advertising. He knew how to be discreet.

He had done well for himself and his family, hoping that one day his eldest son would carry on the business he had built up from a simple corner jewelry store forty-five years ago. Lau had survived invasion, war, corrupt officials, and an authoritarian regime, but he feared he might not survive the creeping encroachment of unfeeling materialism. Compromising some of his principles enabled him to achieve a measure of prosperity—a tree must bend to the wind or break—but he was not prepared to compromise all. He thanked his ancestors for giving him enough wisdom to recognize a point when he had enough, and the realization set him free. He had time for his wife and two sons, both working in the business, and he had time to contemplate the magic of a falling leaf, water tumbling over stones, the tremble of thunder.

Lau had achieved his *yin yang*.

He pulled at his right ear in a characteristic gesture when thinking deeply and read the email again. Liam Geffen up to his practical jokes again. A respectful bow to his friend. A crystal with self-healing and polarization properties? The Mediterranean air had salted his brain. Lau pursed his lips and gazed at the attached photos. They looked real enough and Geffen would not dare play games with something like this. Lau reminded himself to send a note of appreciation to his friend, then pondered. If artificial as the email claimed, why would those who made it want to sell it? He could understand the business driver compelling Geffen to rid himself of the thing. Lau operated under the same imperative. Held inventory was a liability and he had no interest to purchase the crystal for himself. He acted as a pipeline for others, not a collector.

The most likely explanation he could think of, somebody found the thing and sold it to Geffen. Israel was a rich source of all types of antiquities, which set Lau thinking along an unexpected path. Was the crystal dug up at some archaeological site and whoever found it looked to make a quick profit? That would rule out modern manufacture, which he assumed was the case. What if Geffen was mistaken and the crystal wasn't artificial? No, that didn't make any sense. The email said the crystal could heal itself, whatever that meant.

Even Chinese alchemists at the height of their power centuries ago could not produce such an artifact. His friend never dealt with stolen goods, but Geffen might not know he handled suspect merchandise. Some laboratory somewhere made the crystal and an enterprising employee seized an opportunity to retire a wealthy man? This implied that there could be more such things out there. To his knowledge, Israel was not in the business of producing artificial crystals that healed themselves, or any other type of crystal, for that matter.

He could deliberate all day and not get anywhere, Lau reminded himself. Pass it on, collect his commission and forget it.

Whoever eventually bought it can worry about its pedigree. Such an unusual item demanded a most unusual client. He knew several people in Hong Kong who might be interested, and there were a few in Shanghai and Beijing. Lau knew of one special client who would definitely be intrigued. The person only had a Gmail address under the name of Smith, clearly a phony to protect his real identity. Lau suspected the man was a high ranking Party official, but there was no way to tell. Anyway, it wasn't important. He would send him an email and wait for a bid. All his exclusive clients understood how these auctions operated.

Nodding, he stood and made his way to a corner cabinet. He pressed a button on the hotplate and waited for the water to boil in the glass carafe. After making himself a cup of fragrant mint tea, he returned to his desk and started on the rest of his emails. A restful walk through Statue Square later, or perhaps a stroll along the waterfront, contemplating the shifting sea and the deep blue sky, might be in order.

* * *

Doctor Kutner shifted the briar pipe to the other side of his mouth, pushed up his brown-rimmed glasses and stared at the DNA chart, deeply troubled. Earlier in the morning, he received an email from the Weizmann Institute of Science at their Rehovot center, which gave him a carbon-14 date for Yaron's bones at 730 BCE, plus or minus thirty years. Israel and Judah shared a history of blood, and 2700 years ago, not much different. War by King Jehu with Aram-Damascus, defeat by Samaria and the Arameans, conquest of Galilee and Jezreel Valley, deportation of Israelites to Assyria, made for a grim time.

So, what were these strange bones doing there way back then?

No written record existed showing people practicing cranial deformation in old Israel or Judah, although carried out by Proto-Neolithic *homo sapiens* over 11,000 years ago. Disputed by some paleoanthropologists, but evidence from other cultures widely separated geographically and chronologically provided clear proof of the practice.

He knew that deformed skulls were found in Europe occupied by the Huns dating between 300-600 CE. In the Americas, the Maya, Inca, and several North American tribes followed the custom. The Paracas Necropolis culture, occupying what is today the Ica Region of Peru, performed skull deformation throughout their history between 900 BCE and 200 CE. Why was it done? Anthropologists talked learnedly about group affiliation and demonstrating social status, or simply making the skull aesthetically more pleasing.

As a respected anthropologist himself, Kutner did not subscribe to any of these outlandish propositions. If this were practiced in a single isolated social group, he would lend it more credibility, but skull deformation was known to be done the world over. Where did the natural model come from to trigger the practice? No one knew. What also remained unexplained were fetuses with elongated craniums found in mummified pregnant women of the Huancas and Titicacans.

In 1928, a Peruvian archaeologist, Julio Tello, found a massive graveyard of more than 300 elongated skulls in the Pisco Province. What made these skulls unique, they showed no deliberate deformation. The cranial volume was 25 percent larger and 65 percent heavier than normal human skulls. They also had only one parietal plate, not two. The remarkable significance of the find became clear after detailed genetic analysis. Mitochondrial DNA contained sequences not present in *homo sapiens*, Neanderthals or the Denisovans.

Although not accepted by everyone, replication of initial tests made it difficult to fit those skulls into the known evolutionary tree. If the Paracas were so biologically different, they would have had problems interbreeding with the general population. The unanswered question, of course, where did the Paracas come from?

The DNA printout in Kutner's hand only deepened the mystery. The puzzle he faced, according to accepted dogma, 2,700 years ago, Armenian and Euphrates cultures had no known contact with Mesoamerican civilizations. However, bricks found at Comalcalco in Mexico with Roman markings suggested otherwise. Coca leaves and tobacco found in Egyptian tombs, predating the Roman period by several centuries, was further evidence of cultural contact and trade, something that disturbed many anthropologists, preferring not to venture into controversial waters that might threaten their tenure.

Who were the Pisco people really?

Dr. Simon Levin at the Kimmel Center for Archaeological Science who did the DNA analysis on Yaron's bones had asked the same question. What Kutner had done was akin to throwing a grenade into his friend's professional life, and the resulting blast had shattered Levin's demeanor. The printout hadn't done much for Kutner's composure either.

What he had in his two ossuaries was beyond price, and a controversy to be unleashed on the archaeological and anthropological community worldwide. Notoriety didn't bother him. His reputation already made, the two sets of bones would only enhance it. After all, he was presenting irrefutable physical and scientific evidence, not a theory. That evidence might be hard to swallow by some of his erstwhile colleagues, which didn't worry Kutner at all, but it could not be ignored or refuted. He was happy for others to provide interpretation and explanation—if they could.

He remembered wryly how two years ago, Professor Larry Krafter found a 40 million-year-old hand and skull at a Wyoming coal mine. His detractors almost destroyed the young scientist before the scandal that rocked the International Anthropological Society validated his find. Krafter also had irrefutable physical and scientific evidence.

Kutner's situation was somewhat different.

By announcing his find, he realized he'd be shredding several cherished theories and reputations, which he didn't mind doing at all. The only reputation he wanted to maintain was his own and that of the Rockefeller Archaeological Museum.

He shifted his pipe and pushed up his glasses, figuring that the ripples of controversy may have already started to spread. Instead of having a simple historical curiosity, the carbon-14 and DNA results compelled him to make a report to the Israel Antiquities Authority's Artifacts Treatment Department. He had no choice. Finding out about the bones from a newspaper would incur IAA's wrath. Not that they could actually do anything to him, but it would be an irritation he and the Museum did not need. They'd weather it, but deliberately antagonizing IAA bureaucrats didn't have any percentage in it. The problem he had, the IAA were likely to send some busybody and pester him. Why couldn't they just leave a man alone!

What he needed to do was arrange a display of the ossuaries and the bones, and get crowds coming to the Museum. He also needed to write a discovery paper and shoot it off to *Nature* or the *Journal of Anthropological Archaeology*, then sit back as confusion reigned. Meanwhile, he still had to take a closer look at the strange markings chiseled into the ossuaries...and write an article for *The Jerusalem Post*.

Let the battle be joined, fellow gravediggers.

About to get himself a fresh cup of coffee, he frowned. The crystal Yaron showed him...how did that fit into the picture? Not something the Paracas or anybody else were capable of producing. In hindsight, he should have made a better offer when Yaron called, but no use castigating himself over it. It was done, but he could not help wonder what secrets the unusual crystal held. Liam Geffen probably sold it by now to a collector and the thing would be buried in somebody's private collection.

On impulse, he turned to the computer and Googled a search for Geffen's number. He picked up the phone, punched buttons, and pulled the pipe out of his mouth. After five rings, a lush voice answered.

"Geffen's Dealers. Lila speaking."

"This is Dr. Kutner from the Rockefeller Museum. I want to speak to Mr. Geffen if he is available."

"One moment, please."

A click, followed by bland instrumental music. The line clicked again.

"Liam Geffen, Doc. What can I do for you?"

"Thank you for taking my call, Mr. Geffen."

"Just Liam."

"I want to inquire if the crystal Acaph Yaron sold you is now on the market."

"The Museum is interested to purchase it?"

"It might be, for the right price."

Kutner heard a merry laugh.

"I don't know if you have the money."

"That will be my problem, Liam."

"The crystal is on the market, but subject to a closed auction, which by the way, closes at two p.m. today."

Kutner checked his watch. "That still leaves me three hours to put in a bid."

"Mmm. I don't ordinarily do this, but I have no ethical objection seeing the crystal remain in Israel. I'll send you an email with the terms of the auction. If the Museum decides to buy, put in a bid."

"Thank you, Liam. I appreciate this."

"Not a problem, Doc."

The line went dead and Kutner replaced the receiver.

After getting a fresh cup of coffee, he checked Outlook. Sure enough, an email with attachments sat in his Inbox. He opened it and frowned when he read the base bid price. Geffen was a thief, and so was Yaron! Scanning the pictures, he ran a hand through his thatch of white hair, thinking furiously. A crystal that can repair itself, and artificial? It simply wasn't possible for anybody to make such a thing, not even today, let alone by some second period Iron Age tribe, but Geffen would not deliberately mislead potential buyers on something like this.

What the hell was that thing?

The only way to find out was for the Museum to buy it. He picked up the phone and pressed a dial button to the Director.

"Ron Dayan," a gruff voice answered after two rings.

"It's Ezrah. I need to talk to you."

* * *

At precisely 2:15, Geffen rubbed his hands and turned to the computer screen. He logged into his special Gmail account, pleased to see four emails waiting for his attention.

"Front!" he yelled as he clicked on the email from Vasily Drotenkov. The message had a single figure of $290,000, which wasn't bad for an unseen article. Vasily would not have bothered passing on any of the lower bids.

The door opened and Lila peered in. "You called?"

"A cup of your excellent coffee, my girl."

"Immediately, O master," she said brightly and closed the door.

He swept a hand across his bald head and clicked on Kutner's email, not surprised at the bid. The Rockefeller Museum was a wealthy institution, but at $170K, its bid wasn't worth considering. The professor had missed his chance when Acaph called him. Well, that was business, and as an old hand at this, Kutner should have known better.

Lau Wei's email of $340,000 caused Geffen to raise both eyebrows. He never figured the crystal to be worth that much despite its unusual properties. Did one of Lau's clients see something in the crystal he had overlooked? That was more than likely, but the realization didn't bother him at all. His objective was to maximize his return on a 90,000 shekels investment, and it looked like he would do that handsomely.

When he clicked on Terrence Truscott's email, his jaw dropped in disbelief. Four hundred thousand? A small fortune! The buyer appeared desperate to get his hands on the crystal, and the money would give Geffen an opportunity to clear some personal debts and reduce gearing on his business, the diamond trade fickle at the best of times. He looked up at the wooden box resting on blue cloth and wondered again what Acaph had sold him. Nodding in salute, the box would be enough of a memento to fertilize his mind.

A knock on the door jerked him back to reality.

"It's open!"

Lila walked in and placed the cup and saucer beside his hand. "You look pleased," she prompted, holding her trim figure in an ad pose.

"Indeed, my dear, I am well pleased. That crystal you took shots of? I just got an unbelievable price for it. There'll be a bonus for you and the girls."

He operated on a share basis with all his employees, which cost him some money, but encouraged participation and increased productivity, which more than offset the cost.

"I'm delighted to hear that, Liam," she gushed, showing dimples.

"You've earned it. Now, go away and don't bother me." He waved at her and she smiled as she closed the door after her.

Truscott, my friend, you have earned your $10,000 fee and more.

He clicked on the Reply icon and typed a brief email to Terry, telling him that he had a successful bid and his client was to arrange inspection and payment. After dashing off emails to Drotenkov, Lau and Kutner, he sat back, locked his fingers behind his head and slowly rocked back and forth in his chair. After a moment, he picked up the cup and raised it in salute to the enigmatic little box.

The phone rang and he reached for the receiver.

"Dr. Kutner on the line, Liam," Lila announced.

Hell, that didn't take long. Geffen had nothing to say to the old professor. Kutner knew the auction rules. Still, it would not be polite to simply brush him off.

"Okay, put him on." The line clicked. "Dr. Kutner?"

"I just got your email, Liam. I'm naturally disappointed, but I want to know if you'd be open to a better offer from the Museum."

"You know I can't do that, Doc. I'm sorry. I must honor the bidding process. It's nothing personal, you know, but if I were to bend the rules just once, it would come out sooner or later and my reputation would be trashed. I'd be out of business."

Kutner gave a heavy sigh. "Yes, I understand. Well, I want to thank you for giving the Museum the opportunity to bid."

"No problem, Doc. Take care," Geffen said and hung up.

He snorted and shook his head. Governments and institutions were the same everywhere, including Israel's. Wanting everything, but weren't prepared to play by the rules, relying on the old patriotic card to trump the play. They simply didn't understand business.

On the subject of business, should he give his friend Acaph a little bonus? It would only be fair. He thought about it and decided that he'd been more than fair when they made their deal. That the deal turned out to be so spectacularly profitable for Geffen was a stroke of good fortune. He could easily have been thousands out of pocket.

A dinner tonight with Sarah would top off a great day.

* * *

"Ladies and gentlemen, this is the first officer speaking. We have begun our descent and should be landing at Ben Gurion International Airport on schedule. The temperature in Tel Aviv is a pleasant twenty-two degrees Centigrade with clear skies. Thank you for flying El Al and we hope to see you again soon."

The message immediately repeated in rapid Hebrew.

An attractive flight attendant in a dark blue uniform with short sleeves sauntered down the business class aisle holding carafes of coffee and tea. Nolan Trotman wiped his lips with a blue cloth napkin and held up his porcelain cup.

"Coffee, please," he said pleasantly.

She flashed him a smile and topped up his cup. He added cream and one sugar, sipped and sat back, listening to the permeating engine whine. After ten hours in the air, he needed a brisk run to loosen his legs, a shower and some sleep. The lumbering 747 might land on time, but clearing Immigration and Customs a pain everywhere, and he'd be lucky to get out of the airport by eight. At least his body clock would not be scrambled too much, New York being seven hours behind Tel Aviv. It would be a different story on his return flight, having to pay back the hours with no layover stop to recuperate.

Trotman didn't hold this against Morrison, understanding why his boss was anxious to get his hands on the crystal, and he was used to handling rush jobs troubleshooting Solaris' two plants—three, once the German facility was finished—terrorizing their managers. He started working for Morrison as an auditor, but that quickly changed after he sorted out an administrative snag at the Bedford factory, saving his boss four million dollars. The plant accountant lost his job over that fubar and Trotman became Morrison's favorite management accountant and general enforcer. Well, there were one or two other reasons, but they were sidelines really, like this trip, and he did not mind these excursions at all. It beat the hell out of poring over dull accounts.

His flight out of Tel Aviv wasn't until 19:15, and he figured that eleven hours or so gave him plenty of time to pick up the crystal and have a nap at his hotel. The part he didn't relish was getting into JFK International at midnight on the return leg. He normally did not suffer from jetlag and a good sleep after a long flight usually put him together again. Business class or not, a twelve-hour flight back won't be much fun. Understanding about jet stream winds and all would not shorten the flight.

"Handle it," Vivian always told him when he complained, and he grinned as memories chased each other.

That girl was definitely SEAL material, he mused. He met her at Norfolk during a routine physical that Navy regulations insisted everyone must have. A young lieutenant, and she a theater nurse. He pursued her relentlessly and married her reluctantly. Life with an active duty SEAL won't be romantic, he told her, her small hands warm in his big paws. Her deep blue eyes sparkled as she smiled.

"We'll handle it."

Over the last twelve years, they did handle it, all of it. The fact that he was out of the Navy these days had helped, and that wasn't solely because they married. Fortunately, the ghosts of his past had ceased to haunt him…mostly.

Vivian, my soul, will you come to me if I softly call your name?

The seat sagged beneath him as the 747 banked to port, then leveled off. Still wearing a polite grin, the flight attendant pushed a cart down the aisle collecting trays, glasses and odd rubbish. Trotman glanced back at the queue around the two lavatories and didn't try to figure it out. Some people always left things until the last minute.

The heavy jet lined up and nosed down. With an aisle seat, he only caught glimpses of a barren, baked landscape dotted with green patches as the wings rocked. The aircraft steadied up, touched down with a soft jolt and the pilot engaged reverse thrust, which pressed Trotman against the seat. A few moments later the aircraft slowed and turned right onto a taxiway. It took almost six minutes before it stopped at the boarding ramp, the trip made interesting by running commentary from the purser—

elaborately called the In-flight Service Manager—on Immigration and Customs formalities, catching connecting flights, and getting transportation to Tel Aviv for those staying. With only a carry-on case and garment bag, he'd be spared the mind-numbing wait at a carousel to collect luggage.

At the hatch, he said goodbye to the attendant wearing her starched smile and walked out of the aircraft. In the terminal, passengers waited at boarding gates for their flights. Two young boys holding bright orange toy handguns ran screaming among the passengers. As he stared through soundproof floor-to-ceiling reinforced glass panels, the Ben Gurion could be any airport in the world. Trotman had forgotten the sight of soldiers dressed in brown desert fatigues holding short Uzi automatics walking in pairs up and down the terminal. Israel was still an armed camp and the authorities were not taking any chances.

The Immigration formalities were mercifully quick and Trotman strode through the Nothing to Declare door. The public part of the terminal crowded with people waiting for friends or relatives to emerge, or perhaps an enemy or two. New arrivals looked openly relieved to be on the ground again, and those preparing to leave seemed to anticipate the coming adventure. Shops, kiosks, and travel information booths vied for attention in the noisy environment and occasional speaker announcement.

He saw a young woman, perhaps five foot six, wearing a white blouse and black trousers, looking anxiously at emerging travelers, holding a sign at shoulder level with his name in bold print.

He stopped before her and said pleasantly, "I am Trotman."

Both cheeks dimpled in a sunny smile, she gave him an appraising check. At six-two, rugged features, a full crop of thick brown hair, muscled, he was used to getting appreciative glances from women.

"Ah, Mr. Trotman, welcome to Tel Aviv. Mr. Geffen sent me to collect you."

He gazed into her dark oval eyes and returned the grin. "Very considerate of him."

"It's no trouble, I assure you. How long will you be staying?" she asked as they made their way toward the exit.

"I'm flying out this evening."

She pushed back a lock of hair. "So soon? Mr. Geffen looked forward to showing you around the city."

"I appreciate the gesture, Miss…"

"Lila."

"…Miss Lila, but my boss is keen to have me back."

She gave a merry giggle. "After seeing that crystal, I'd also want to have it in my hands as soon as possible."

"You know about it?"

"And the auction? Yes, but I still have no idea what it is. If you don't have somewhere to stay for the day, I can arrange a hotel for you."

"Thank you, but I'm booked at the Dan Tel Aviv."

"A nice place, right on the promenade."

"What's the program, Miss Lila?"

"Program?" She gave him a puzzled look, then grinned. "I can take you to see Mr. Geffen now…and call me Lila, or—"

"Drop me off at the hotel, if you don't mind. I need to freshen up."

"Of course."

As they drove down Route 1 in a neat dark blue BMW 6 coupe, just another car in a stream heading downtown, Trotman admired the way Lila handled the traffic by ignoring it. Vehicles parted in front of her as she pushed the powerful car along the freeway. This in no way distracted from her running commentary about Tel Aviv, Jerusalem, and Israel in general, laughing at Knesset antics, lamenting the suffering people endured in the world's trouble spots, admitting that with the establishment of a Palestinian state, her country enjoyed its moment of uneasy peace. Clearly well educated, smart, confident, and not bashful proclaiming her femininity. As he listened to her dialogue, he didn't have the heart to puncture her enthusiasm by telling her he knew Israel well, having spent three months with the Israel Defense Forces as a liaison officer during the early years of the Iraq occupation.

Once they entered Route 20, the city skyline loomed ahead of them as they headed north. He knew they reached the city proper when every intersection demanded homage to traffic lights. On his left, he caught glimpses of the Mediterranean's deep blue water between buildings, and wondered if the beaches were still littered with tiny globules of oil dumped by ships in the open sea as they flushed their ballast tanks. Probably.

Lila pulled into the visitors slot in front of the Dan hotel and walked with him into the lobby.

"I'll wait for you here," she told him, eyeing the adjoining bar restaurant. "I'll keep myself company with a cup of coffee."

"Fifteen minutes," he promised and strode toward the Reservations counter.

After checking in, he took an elevator to the sixth floor and hunted for his room. A refreshing shower and a change of clothes made him feel immediately better. Mindful of what Lila told him that it would be hot, he still chose to take his jacket. A formal business trip, he didn't want to give Geffen an unfavorable impression of Yanks.

Lila met him in the lobby and steered him toward the car. The air had lost most of its crispness and he could feel the heat soaking through his white polyester shirt. In the car, she turned on the AC and merged expertly into the traffic. On the way to Ramat Gan, she pumped him about his life, which he didn't mind.

"You live in Lower Manhattan?" she demanded, her eyes round in wonder.

"An apartment building on Wall Street," he told her. "A stone's throw from the Brooklyn Bridge."

"It must be grand." She gave a forlorn sigh. "I always wanted to see New York. The statue of Liberty, the Empire State, stroll down Broadway, lose myself among all those skyscrapers…"

"Perhaps one day you will."

"Between you and me, Tel Aviv is bland. No character."

"Oh, I wouldn't say that. Jaffa is interesting, and you have great nightlife. New York doesn't have anything like the Hacarmel Market."

"You've been here before?" she demanded accusingly. "And you let me prattle on like you were a tourist. This is so utterly mortifying."

He laughed at her dejected expression. "I couldn't stop you, and you did tell me things I didn't know."

"When were you here?"

"In 2006. I did some work in Iraq when I was a SEAL."

Her mouth made a large O. "You were in the American Navy?"

"Not anymore. Something my wife appreciates."

"I am sure she does. What made you get out, if you don't mind me asking?"

"Having a wife and a daughter I didn't see often enough. Being a SEAL was fun, and I had a few tight scrapes, but after a while, playing Rambo wasn't all that exciting. There were too many ways to have your account closed permanently."

True as far as it went, and he did not feel Lila would be interested in the gorier details. The pain part he preferred to keep to himself.

She pulled into the Leonardo City Tower Hotel underground parking lot and slid the BMW into the first level reserved spot. Trotman donned his jacket as they waited for the elevator, Lila looking cool and composed. The lobby had people crowding each other, checking in or leaving. Lila marched toward the bright Geffen's Dealers entrance, everybody parting before her, and strode briskly toward a side door. She knocked once, opened it and paused.

"Mr. Trotman, Liam."

"Great! Show him in," a pleasant voice boomed from inside.

She opened the door wide and beamed at Trotman. "I'll take you back to your hotel once you're done."

"Thank you, Lila. That's kind of you."

"A pleasure," she said, giving him another appraising look.

As he walked into the modest office, she closed the door after him. A short, trim, bald man wearing a beige sports suit stood and extended his hand.

"Welcome to Tel Aviv, Mr. Trotman. I am Liam Geffen."

"Good to meet you, sir," Trotman said as they shook hands.

Geffen waved at a leather chair. "Please...coffee, tea, a soft drink?"

Trotman sat down and shook his head. "I'm fine. By the way, I want to thank you for sending Lila to pick me up."

"She is one of my right arms." Geffen looked at him closely. "Dr. Morrison didn't waste any time getting you here."

"You sold him a most uncommon item and he wants to study it more closely."

"Mmm. An unusual hobby for an industrial chemist."

"I used to collect stamps."

Geffen chuckled and nodded sagely. "Yes. Given his background, I can see why he might be interested. I looked him up on the Internet. I know I'm breaking protocol here, but can you tell me what he found so fascinating about the crystal to make such a large bid?"

"I honestly don't know. However, he was very excited about its unusual properties."

Geffen shrugged. "Well, it's not important."

He pulled open a drawer, lifted a red satin jewel case, placed it on the desk and opened the lid. Trotman leaned forward and stared at the strange orange object resting on white velvet. A pretty thing, but he could not figure out why it made Morrison so animated that he had to buy it.

"Definitely different," he murmured politely.

"At one point, I was tempted to keep it for myself." Geffen nodded at his collection as he reached for the letter opener. Without saying anything, he made a small scratch on the crystal's surface and Trotman sat up in alarm, then stared as the scar slowly vanished.

"And it repairs itself, as advertised. Unbelievable."

"Yes, a remarkable property. Like it's alive. That's what made me declare the crystal is artificial. Nothing in nature can do that."

"And the polarization trick?"

Geffen produced a laser pencil and pointed it at the crystal. When the green beam touched it, the surface became a perfect mirror.

"Satisfied?"

"It's everything you said it was," Trotman declared, totally fascinated. "Can you tell me something about the crystal's history?"

"I suppose it won't do any harm. I purchased it from an antiquities dealer in Old Jerusalem. He in turn got it from a man who dug up a couple of ossuaries in his backyard."

"Ossuaries?"

"Stone chests used by orthodox Jews a long time ago to hold bones of a deceased relative. The practice hasn't been followed for centuries."

It didn't mean anything to Trotman, but his boss might find the tidbit useful. "Thank you for the information."

Geffen reached into the drawer, pulled out a stiff piece of paper and held it out. "You'll need this in case airport security or Customs want to check you out. It's an official certificate attesting that you lawfully purchased a rare topaz crystal."

"Topaz, eh? I suppose it could come in handy, thank you." Trotman pocketed the paper, dug into his jacket pocket and held out a white envelope. "A deposit receipt for US$400,000 placed into your Swiss account as per instructions. Please log in for final verification."

Geffen reached for the keyboard and clicked keys. A minute

later, he turned the laptop and pushed the keyboard across the desk. Trotman stood up, scanned the screen and clicked on the red Authenticate icon. It blinked and prompted for a validation code. He typed in a twelve-digit combination and pressed Enter. The $400,000 vanished from the pending line.

Geffen nodded. "A pleasure doing business with you, Mr. Trotman. Are you staying long in Tel Aviv?"

"I'm flying back this evening."

"Well, enjoy your visit. Please extend my regards to Dr. Morrison."

"I'll do that."

Trotman picked up the jewel case and gazed at the crystal, wondering once more what made it worth such a colossal amount.

* * *

A loud knock broke Lau's concentration. He frowned and looked up. "Enter!"

His oldest son opened the door and stood back. "A visitor, father," the young man announced gravely, looking disturbed.

"Oh? And who might that be, Tung?"

A morose-looking individual strode through and glanced at Lau's son, showing no expression. Tung gulped and closed the door.

Lau's frown deepened as he examined the man dressed in a black suit that might have looked pressed when new. Now, it hung on his full frame like a rumpled sheet. His sartorial inelegance did not seem to bother the individual, but it bothered Lau. Something sinister lurked beneath that suave, oily expression.

"Mr. Lau Wei?" the man rasped and Lau nodded.

"May I ask what this is about?"

The stranger reached into his breast pocket and pulled out a familiar red card. When Lau saw it, he felt a flutter of anxiety.

"You recognize this?"

Lau swallowed and nodded. "You're from the Ministry of State Security."

"That's right. I represent…let's call him Mr. Smith. He was most displeased with the conversation you had with him last night. Most displeased." The man clicked his tongue and sighed. "And Mr. Smith is a man you don't want to make unhappy. Believe me, you don't."

Lau winced, remembering the unpleasant call. After sending Smith an email telling him his bid was unsuccessful, the man wanted to place another bid. Lau had to remind him that bidding was closed, having to insist more than once. Lau did not appreciate working with amateurs or sore losers. This client ought to have known better, and was now off his mailing list.

"I regret that Mr. Smith is upset, but he entered into a closed auction. He has dealt with me on a previous occasion—"

"Two previous occasions," the unsmiling man prompted, examining his fingernails.

"—and understands the rules."

"Yes, the rules. He does understand the rules, but I don't know if you do, Mr. Lau, or the gravity of Mr. Smith's displeasure."

"I beg your pardon? This conversation is no longer amusing. Please leave."

"In a moment. If you're not prepared to reopen the bidding, I was sent to do that on your behalf."

"I cannot reopen the bidding. I'm not the seller—"

"Mr. Smith appreciates that."

"—and I resent this haranguing."

The man's shoulders sagged as he gave a long sigh. "Haranguing? That's harsh, and I haven't started that yet. To save everybody a lot of time and needless angst, all I want is the name of the seller, something Mr. Smith is anxious to find out."

Lau sat back as a faint alarm told him to be careful, not liking the man's obnoxious style at all.

"My dear, sir. I cannot possibly reveal the seller's identity. That would be a clear violation of my standing as an intermediary. I could never operate professionally again."

"Regrettable." The taciturn man sighed again. "A most awkward situation…for you." Something changed in the man's expression and Lau felt palpable hostility. "Name and address, Mr. Lau, and I will walk out of here and you can pretend that you never saw me."

"I told you…" The words died when the man produced a black handgun.

Lau could not take his eyes off the sleek weapon as the man screwed on the silencer and clicked off the safety, the sound unusually loud in the small room. Up to now, he thought he had the situation under control, toying with the man, when all along, he was the one being toyed with. The menacing black gun made the situation altogether much more serious.

The stranger leaned forward, his demeanor frigid.

"Your lack of cooperation is making me upset, which is not good for my stomach. I could shoot you right now and get some satisfaction. Unfortunately, I wouldn't get the information I need and Mr. Smith wouldn't like that. Or I could shoot your son and the lady fiddling with the computer. Your wife?"

"No…my office manager," Lau croaked, hoping to wake from what surely had to be a bad dream. He felt his legs tremble and swallowed a lump that had formed in his throat. This couldn't be happening, not over some crystal. His hand strayed toward the silent alarm switch under the desk.

"I wouldn't do that if I were you," the man murmured softly and Lau froze. "Now, about that name."

Lau stared at the gun, his mind in turmoil. Frightened, but he would not be intimidated. "May vipers nest in your bed."

The man gave a barking laugh. "That was good. I like it, but you know something? Somebody already wished that on me and now he's dead. A nice man, too. He also had a family…like you. Yes, a pity." He shifted the gun and his face became stone. "I've got a flight to catch and I can't spend too much time on this. Tell me what I want to know or your family will cease to exist. Oh, I won't shoot them; that would be too quick. How about ten years at a correctional farm? I am told that parts of Inner Mongolia can be particularly harsh. Unfortunately, not many get to come back. You don't want that to happen to them, do you?"

Lau stared at the man in horror. If it were only him, he would bid the man screw himself. He'd had a long life and mostly a satisfying one. Part of that satisfaction came from his family. If he didn't talk, this revolting individual would destroy the Lau line. His ancestors would never forgive him. He could not risk that, certainly not for mere professional pride. Family was everything. He would live in disgrace, but China was a large land where a person can make a new beginning. He had wealth, and that overcame most obstacles.

I am sorry, my honored friend. Lau heard Geffen's booming laugh, remembered his jovial attitude, and mourned. Life stinks, he decided and hung his head.

"Geffen's Dealers, Ramat Gan, Tel Aviv," he murmured, anguish tearing his soul.

"That wasn't so bad, was it? Mr. Smith will appreciate your sacrifice to the state."

The man leveled the gun, his face twisted in an ugly grin. Lau grabbed the chair armrests and felt blood drain from his face.

"No!"

He saw a flash before sharp pain ripped through his chest and darkness descended. He thought he heard the scream of seagulls.

* * *

Major General Tsai Teping dashed off his signature on an order that would banish another dissident to an Uyghur correctional farm, flipped the paper into the Out tray and reached for the slim black cigar smoldering in the ashtray. He picked it up, stuck it between his teeth, and leaned back against the chair. He blew a perfect smoke ring and cleared a rasping tickle in his throat. He smoked too much, his mouth felt baked, and he had a persistent cough that burned his lungs. His doctor told him to have a checkup and an x-ray, but Tsai did not have time for such nonsense. What did those buffoons know anyway? The special herbal tea his wife prepared for him—when he got around to drinking the vile mixture—kept the cough under control, but hadn't stopped it. She also told him to see a doctor.

Across Eandianghang Road, parkland surrounding the Summer Palace provided a refreshing sight beneath a steel sky through which feeble sunshine struggled to penetrate. The damned smog hung everywhere, and on some days, it felt like walking through soup. A westerly wind was supposed to precede a cold front later in the day, which should clear the air a bit. It would definitely help his cough.

The harsh jangle from the phone shattered his revere and he groped for the black receiver.

"General Tsai," he grated and cleared his throat.

"It's Kwang Choi, General," a polite voice announced.

Tsai tightened the grip on the receiver and glanced at a shelf of mineral specimens mounted next to a row of four filing cabinets. He had three very valuable jade pieces from the Tang Dynasty, surrounded by rare crystals of crocoite, a black quartz needle, tanzanite and a nice liddicoatite. His most valuable items were stored at his residence. The Ministry of State Security compound provided everything for high ranking officials and their dependents, but Xiyan was also crowded, being next to the Summer Palace, initially built by the Jin Dynasty emperor Wanyan Liang early in the 12th century, it always teeming with local and foreign visitors. As head of the Second Bureau handling international activities, his spacious two-bedroom cottage more than adequate for his needs. It saved him the daily commuter crush had his job demanded he work downtown near the Forbidden City, for which he was thankful.

What caused him to tense up at hearing the name was expectation of positive news about the bid he'd put in for that accursed crystal. When Lau sent his email advising him that 340,000 American dollars wasn't enough, it sent him into overload. Not possible that someone had outbid him, that someone had clearly thought about the crystal's unusual properties beyond its mere appearance and saw value in it. When he called the little weasel, Lau didn't know who made the successful bid and wouldn't tell him who ran the closed auction. Tsai did not like being thwarted, and definitely not by some greasy capitalist money grubber.

He decided to bid for the crystal not long after he got Lau's email. At first, it was for himself—it would have made a spectacular addition to his collection—but as he studied the attached photos and carefully mulled over the email's wording, he realized he had something extraordinary here. He knew a lot about gems and crystals, but never heard of one that repaired itself. A call to a friend in the Tenth Bureau that handled scientific and technological information confirmed his suspicions. The crystal a definite enigma with unknown potential, and he meant to secure it for the state.

This could also advance him with the Politburo Standing Committee. Minister Lin Jinpan was a doddering old fool, and presenting a valuable artifact to the Committee could get him into the running to head the Ministry of State Security. Of course, if the crystal turned out to be worthless, Tsai would have squandered 340,000 dollars of state money and could find himself off the promotion ladder altogether. Well, one did not advance if one was not prepared to take a calculated gamble.

"What have you got for me?" he rasped.

"Lau Wei cooperated after some positive persuasion, sir, and as per your orders, has joined his ancestors."

"And…"

"The auction was run by Liam Geffen, a gem trader in Tel Aviv. He runs a small diamond processing factory in Ramat Gan's Diamond Exchange District, and has a jewelry store in the Leonardo City Tower Hotel."

"You extracted yourself without any problem?"

"I fear, sir, Lau's CCTV footage will identify me."

"Not important. Return and make a full report."

"Yes, sir."

Tsai replaced the receiver and nodded, taking a puff from his cigar. Head wreathed in blue smoke, he exhaled softly. Pity about Lau, but he could not afford having him alert Geffen. That Kwang was potentially compromised wasn't even an issue. Should Hong Kong authorities pursue the matter, once shown this to be a Ministry of State Security case, the investigation into Lau's death would be filed and forgotten.

The entire episode irked him intensely after receiving the dealer's irritating email at 7:50 last night. The arbitrary rules these traders played by were a tiresome annoyance he could not allow to stand in his way. He glanced at his wristwatch: 10:32. That made it 05:32 in Tel Aviv. This early in the morning, although possible, it was unlikely the winning bidder would have picked up the crystal. Probably still in Geffen's possession, which meant he still had a narrow window of opportunity to get it.

He reached for the green phone and pressed a glowing white button on the keypad.

"Yes, sir?" his personal assistant responded crisply.

"Get me the military attaché's office in our Tel Aviv consulate."

"Right away, sir."

After waiting five minutes, he was seething. Why did it take so long!

The phone jangled and he snatched the receiver.

"I have the duty desk, sir, but most consular staff won't be getting in for another two hours or so."

"Idiot! I asked you to get the military attaché, not the duty desk. If he isn't in, have him called. I want to speak to him in the next ten minutes or he'll be enjoying a change of scenery, and so will you! Got that?"

"Sir!"

Tsai slammed down the phone, reached for the cigar and clamped his teeth around it. The military attaché office should be manned always. After a few breaths, he calmed down and allowed himself a rueful smile. Just because the office was manned, did not mean the attaché himself was there all the time. After all, as a ranking officer, he had a life, not that Tsai worried about disturbing an underling's life.

Twelve minutes later, having chewed the end of his cigar to ribbons, the phone rang and he picked up.

"I have Major Sungan on the line, sir," the assistant said and the phone clicked.

"Major?"

"General Tsai, what can I do for you, sir?"

"Do you have a reliable man who can be trusted?"

"I have such a man."

Tsai issued his orders and hung up. Nothing to do now but wait, which did not come easily to him. He ground the lit end of the cigar into the ashtray and hoped his decision would be vindicated. If things went badly, *he* could end up at that Uyghur correctional farm.

* * *

Huan looked at his image in the bathroom mirror and carefully tapped the stick-on mustache, then added the small beard that covered his chin. He looped the black *agal* twice around the top of his head to hold the black and white checkered *keffiyeh* in place, the mirror reflected a transformed man. Of average height, he wore a light blue tweed suit, white shirt, and dark brown tie. No one would give him a second glance, especially with his reduced epicanthic folds that did not make his eyes look Asian.

He had picked up the accoutrements at the consulate after a session with a testy Major Sungan. The major had not appreciated being woken early to carry out some fool errand for a parasitic Beijing official and then forgot to reset his alarm clock. This caused him to be late getting to work. Understandably, the major took out his frustration on his junior, which Huan bore stoically. It was the way of things. Had he shown any outward resentment, he knew the major would be more than just testy. Besides, he liked the young officer who was ordinarily friendly and considerate, and did not take this morning's dressing down personally.

When he got his instructions, he wondered what all the fuss was about, but orders were orders and he did not anticipate any trouble executing them, however harebrained. Superiors everywhere indulged in their little games, leaving people like Huan to clean up the messes. Silly orders or not, it was better than holding guard duty at the gate, he told himself phlegmatically. Only two more months left in his rotation and he'd be home, in all likelihood facing more fool errands. With his special skills, he hoped to get another overseas posting, and kowtowing to the major to get a good fitness report would likely see that happen.

He patted his left jacket pocket to ensure the silencer for his Glock 19 9mm semiautomatic was there. It would be somewhat embarrassing if he left it behind. He would have preferred to use his Norinco Type 77 standard PLA weapon, but if apprehended, it would be an instant giveaway. Satisfied with his appearance, he walked quickly out of the apartment and tugged the door shut to be certain the latch engaged. When he started his secondment, he was not aware of this quirky tendency by his door, and came home once to find it unlocked. The first time it happened, he thought he'd been burgled. Even when he made sure the lock had engaged, he still suspected that someone had ransacked his apartment once or twice. A Mossad or Shin Bet operative had more than likely nosed around, but he had nothing at his place to incriminate him or the consulate. Just a game, nothing more, although deadly sometimes.

Sungan's assignment something he relished, giving him an opportunity to show off his expertise and superiority. He thrived on generating terror in his victims, feeding on their fear, like the local girls he picked up. He never actually hurt them physically, but their experience with him left them emotionally scarred, and that was good. If it weren't for his PLA training, he would probably have ended up as a hitman in Shanghai's Red Gang. He *was* a hitman now, and got commendations for it. It couldn't get any better. If he finished Sungan's job early enough, he might pick up another girl for the night, the prospect making his loins tingle.

He parked under the Leonardo City Tower Hotel and glanced at his wristwatch: 10:42. He was late, but heavy traffic all the way to Ramat Gan had slowed him down. In the lobby, he spotted the gaudy Geffen's Dealers sign and walked toward the glass entrance, negotiating around hotel patrons. The beautiful young thing, too skinny for his taste, gave him a warm smile. He preferred his women to show meat.

"Can I help you, sir?" she asked pleasantly in Arabic.

"Please tell Mr. Geffen that Mr. Humaidy would like to see him," he replied in Hebrew.

"What is it regarding?"

"An archaeological artifact that might be of interest."

"We don't deal—"

"It's not a pot or an ossuary."

She frowned, regarding him with suspicion. "Just a moment." She walked to a door at the end of her counter, opened it and leaned in. She said something, turned and nodded to Huan. He strode toward her.

"Come in, Mr. Humaidy," a friendly voice declared.

Huan walked into the modest-sized office, swept his eyes around the luxurious fittings, the expensive shelving, lingering a moment on a collection of displayed jewelry and mineral specimens, and turned his attention to the short individual standing behind an ordinary executive desk.

"Thank you for seeing me without an appointment, Mr. Geffen," he said and offered his hand.

"Lila tells me you have an archaeological artifact you want to sell. As she told you, I'm not in that sort of business. The Old City in Jerusalem has many licensed dealers who handle such things. By the way, can I offer you coffee or something?"

"I'm afraid you both misunderstood," Huan said, ignoring the offer. "I am here because of a certain crystal you put up in a closed auction."

He enjoyed seeing the sudden lack of expression on the gem dealer's face, replaced by a degree of apprehension. They all reacted in the same way, he reflected. First, it was confidence and bluster, backed by courage derived from wealth, then concern that this wealth might be threatened, followed by pleading and offers of escalating bribes. In the end, survival and self-interest won out. It always did. Westerners had no morals or honor, and the Israelis were no better, hiding their hypocrisy behind a veil of righteous religious fervor.

Geffen cleared his throat. "Oh? And you represent…"

"An interested party. I'm not here to trick you, and I am not from the IAA. I only want the crystal."

Geffen regained some composure and shrugged. "In that case, you have wasted your time. Your interested party knows how these auctions operate. Incidentally, how did you find out that I am running it?"

"That's unimportant. What is important to you, I am prepared to double the amount of the successful bid."

Geffen's eyes rounded, unable to mask his surprise. Huan had played his card nicely and he could see the gleam of avarice in the Jew's eyes. They were all the same, grubbing capitalists who trod on the needy and the helpless for that extra shekel. Scratch away their feigned morality revealed a greedy thief.

"I must say, that's an amazing offer, Mr. Humaidy. Unfortunately, I could not accept it even if I still had the object. It's not how I run my business."

Huan stiffened. This one may have some principles after all. It would make the game all the more enjoyable. "You don't have the crystal?"

"The successful bidder had it picked up this morning."

That was bad, Huan reflected, but not irretrievable. Time to have some fun and display his skills, anticipating with relish the coming unpleasantness.

"May I ask the name of the winning bidder?"

Geffen scowled. "My dear sir, you know I cannot tell you that."

"Mmm, very regrettable." Huan glanced at a large safe tucked into a corner. "Open it."

"I told you—"

Huan hauled out the silencer and pulled the Glock from his shoulder holster. The Jew immediately tensed, his bubble of confidence burst. Huan enjoyed this part the most, seeing his victim reduced to a sniveling crawler.

"Don't draw attention to yourself, Mr. Geffen. I would hate to see those lovely girls out there hurt in any way." He screwed on the silencer, chambered a round and rested the gun against his chest. "The safe."

Geffen licked his lips, stood and walked to the safe. He knelt, worked the combination dial, pulled back the handle and stepped aside. A glance from Huan was enough to compel Geffen to sit down.

Huan opened the heavy door and looked curiously at an assortment of packages and small boxes. There must have been a fortune in diamonds and gems in there. Tempted to help himself to a sample, he refrained. He had more important things to settle. After rummaging through the packages, he hoped to find a jewel case likely to contain the crystal, but it wasn't there. Huan stood up and resumed his seat.

"Who is the winning bidder?" he prompted.

"As I told you—"

Huan lifted the semiautomatic and pulled the trigger. A soft *thuft* and a black hole appeared in the wall behind Geffen's head. The gem trader lost all color and seemed to shrink, realizing at last the seriousness of his predicament. When he looked up, Huan was surprised to see defiance in his eyes.

"I'll be ruined if I tell you."

"You'll be dead if you don't," Huan told him coldly. "The name."

Geffen's mouth worked, but nothing came out. Huan sent another round into the wall. He didn't mind prolonging this, wearing down his victim in stages until he achieved the final moral collapse.

"Fuck you," Geffen grated.

Huan smiled, relishing his victim's show of misplaced bravado.

"You think if I kill you, I'll have nothing? You're right, but I can hurt you...bad. Then you'll sing to me, you greasy pig."

The Jew yelped when the bullet ripped through his right bicep. Geffen clutched his arm, blood oozing between the fingers, and glared.

Huan nodded, looking forward to inflicting more pain, more suffering. Studying the Jew, this one appeared prepared to last the distance, something he relished. The longer this took, the more pain he would be able to inflict, exacting maximum enjoyment.

"I've got plenty of bullets left," he said pleasantly, tapping the gun barrel against the palm of his hand. "No name? Okay, it's the other arm, then the kneecap. They tell me it's a particularly painful injury and, of course, your leg won't be much good to you afterward. Then again, in your line of work, you don't need legs."

As Huan raised the gun, Geffen spat at him. The bullet caught him in the left bicep and the Jew sagged back against the chair.

Regardless of how much he enjoyed watching the capitalist money grubber squirm, Huan reminded himself that he had a mission to fulfill. He would have his moment of pleasure afterward.

"If you won't talk, let's try something else. Call one of your girls. If you don't, I'll shoot you anyway, and then I'll shoot them. Now!"

"Scum!" Geffen took a deep breath, exhaled, and swallowed, torn with indecision. "The bidder is Kevin Morrison. He is the owner and president of Solaris Technology based in New York."

"Who picked up the crystal?" Huan demanded, disappointed that it ended so quickly. He wanted to see the Jew writhe, clutching a broken knee. Then again, that would probably have generated unwanted noises from his victim, something to be avoided.

"Nolan Trotman."

"And where can I find this Mr. Trotman?"

"He…he is staying at the Dan Tel Aviv Hotel."

"Who else knows this?"

"Ah…"

"Don't tell me. The pretty brunette?"

"I told you what you wanted to know."

"Yes indeed," Huan said and stood up. "You were most cooperative, Mr. Geffen. I'd love to continue our discussion, but I have a meeting with Mr. Trotman."

He leveled his arm and shot the parasitic Jew in the forehead. The back of his head exploded, spattering the wall behind him with splinters of bone, skin and brain tissue. The impact sent Geffen's body and chair crashing back in a tangle. Unmoved, Huan walked to the door and opened it.

Stefan Vučak

The brunette looked up. "Is everything okay, Mr. Humaidy?"

"Can you come in for a moment, please? Mr. Geffen wants you."

She frowned, squeezed past him and gasped when she saw the sprawled body. Before she could scream, Huan closed the door and sent a bullet through the back of her head. She pitched forward and crumpled. Looking at her, he decided she might have been a tasty morsel after all. He unscrewed the silencer and pocketed everything. No one paid him any attention as he made his way out of the store. Once in his car, he removed the *keffiyeh* and settled in. He dragged out the smartphone, pressed the encryption button and called Major Sungan.

With no loose ends, he would now pay a visit to Mr. Trotman and recover the crystal, provided the American hadn't already flown out, however unlikely. If everything worked out, he might even make it back to the consulate in time for a late lunch. Then again, he could eat out, and he did have an expense account, although the bean counters always gave him a hard time when he spent a lousy shekel. The consular heavyweights were free to spend whatever they wanted, but frowned on any perceived extravagance exhibited by their underlings, citing moral corruption and disloyalty to the Party. Occasional moral corruption was good for the body, he decided. As for loyalty, that was for the masses.

Humming to himself, he eased the car into the traffic, pleased with the day's events, looking forward to picking up a girl for the night.

* * *

Trotman heard the knock and came instantly awake. He sat up and glanced at the flat Mediterranean sea stretching toward the horizon. A check of his watch showed 11:55. No wonder his eyes felt gritty. He'd slept less than two hours. He rolled off the queen-sized bed and yawned, slipped his feet into shoes and padded toward the door.

"Who is it?"

"Hotel security, sir," came a muffled reply.

Hotel security? Did someone invade the place?

He rubbed his right eye, opened the door, and immediately took in the neat individual dressed in a blue business suit, wearing a black mustache and beard. He appeared an Arab, but the features didn't quite fit. The man's easy, yet alert stance made the hairs at the back of Trotman's neck rise. The intense slightly almond eyes, face devoid of expression, made him *aware*, a hunter. He had known such snakes in his shadowy past and learned to recognize the signs. As the man moved his arm away from behind his back revealing a silenced handgun, Trotman's training took over.

His body reacting automatically, he lashed out with his right foot, catching the man under the chin, snapping back his head, sending him crashing to the wavy-striped gray carpet. Dazed, the man shook his head and lifted his gun arm. Trotman kicked away the gun, stepped closer and hit him in the right temple with the point of his shoe. The figure slumped. He felt the adrenalin rush and took three deep breaths, all ideas of sleep forgotten. Looking quickly along both ends of the corridor, he bent down, grasped the man's jacket lapels and heaved him up. He glanced at the black handgun. Judging by its distinct square barrel and serrated end, probably a Glock. He scooped it up, shoved it into his trousers and grunted as he lifted the body over his shoulder.

Hell of a business trip when people wanted to shoot him without any explanation.

Teeth clenched tight, he walked toward the emergency stairs next to the two elevators. He pushed open the door and threw the body down the stairs. With some clattering, he heard a crunch as it landed on the middle platform. Trotman leaped down taking two steps at a time and checked for a pulse—nothing. Vacant eyes stared at him from a head bent at an odd angle from the body. He pulled open the jacket and extracted the wallet. Apart from a wad of shekels in various denominations and a driver's license in the name of Kaliph Humaidy, it didn't hold anything.

He pulled out part of his shirt, wiped the card and slid it back into the wallet, then wiped the wallet and shoved it into the man's jacket. Retrieving the gun, he unscrewed the silencer, wiped everything, and slid the weapon into the man's holster. He walked slowly up the stairs, wiped both door handles, and strode down the deserted corridor to his room. Inside, he opened the little bar fridge and helped himself to a shot of Wild Turkey whiskey. He winced as the cheap liquor burned down his throat.

Coming off a high, reaction had set in and a shiver shook him. He stood by the broad window and gazed down at people strolling along the promenade. Beachgoers filled golden sands in both directions. Creamy surf rippled gently over the shallows. It looked hot out there, but he had no intention of joining the bathers and being crisped.

He had killed in the line of duty, but this was the first time someone deliberately wanted to close out his account since he left the Navy, and he found the experience...unnerving. At least his reaction speed was still good, but if working for Morrison meant more of these hairy encounters, he would need to resume his training regimen, which would not please Vivian. He was no longer a hunter.

He raised his arm and studied his hand. The fingers twitched. Mouth pursed, he slowly made a fist until the nails cut into his palm and forced back the images that threatened to overwhelm him. After all these years, they still haunted him. Breathing deeply, he cleared his mind and waited for the images to fade. He opened his hand. The fingers were still.

Settled, thinking clearly, he realized that he should have dragged the body into his room and disposed of it when checking out. Too late now, and he could not risk being seen retrieving the assailant. Had he been a tad hasty killing the man? Arguable, but he wasn't given time to debate the issue. Reflecting, he decided that his initial response the correct one. Storing the body in his room would have left forensic evidence that would have pointed to him. Whether the authorities believed the man stumbled and broke his neck or was murdered did not matter. Nothing must lead them to him, the only thing important here.

With Arabs after the crystal, this dramatically increased the pucker factor of his mission. One thing was clear. He could not remain at the hotel. No, that wouldn't work. When the body is found, it would bring the authorities sniffing, bothering everybody. They were bound to interview everyone on the floor. If he fled now without checking out, they would be after him as a natural suspect. If he stayed, whoever sent the assassin would realize something had gone wrong and maybe send another, perhaps two, to finish the job. He cannot spend the rest of the day fighting off killers. If his identity was blown, would they pursue him to New York? There was no way to tell and no use expending emotional energy worrying about it.

Already up, he decided to get lunch, the airplane breakfast having worn off sometime back. He glanced at the cellphone on the writing desk and pondered if he should call the boss. And tell him what? Waking him after five in the morning to announce that his trusted enforcer had killed an Arab wasn't likely to go down well. Morrison would pause, absorbing the information, then ask what Trotman expected him to do. Of course, nothing his boss *could* do. Handle it, he told himself. Okay, he would call once in the air. There would be time enough for explanations once he got back.

After refreshing himself, he took the elevator to the lobby and handed in his electronic key card at the Reservations counter, then took the stairs to the first floor dining room. When somebody did discover the body, he needed to show that he'd been down here for some time.

After a pleasant lunch of lobster cutlets accompanied by small roasted potatoes and tangy coleslaw, washed down with a crisp Chablis, he went to the bar on the ground floor. No excitement yet. He took his time, downed two shots of very good bourbon on the rocks and nibbled from a bowl of mixed nuts, listening to the wash of conversation around him, watching people coming in and out, trying to spot someone looking for him. At two-forty, he made his way to the Reservations counter to pick up his key card. Two blue-uniformed policemen holding Uzis, warily scrutinizing everybody, flanked a neatly dressed tall individual leaning against the counter chewing a toothpick. Looking bored, the man straightened as Trotman approached.

"May I ask your name, please?"

No 'sir' and no friendliness. It looked like the Israeli police weren't too concerned about their PR image.

"And you are?" Trotman demanded and turned to the girl tapping at a keyboard. "Room six-fourteen."

"I am Detective First Sergeant Hausman," The man did not offer to show identification or shake hands. He shifted the toothpick to the other side of his mouth.

"My name is Trotman."

Hausman checked the name against a list in his notebook. "Nolan Trotman? Where were you during the last two hours or so?"

"I came down to the dining room for lunch—"

"What time was that?"

"Oh, about twelve-fifteen."

"And then?"

"At the bar until now."

"Did you happen to hear or see any disturbance on your floor or anywhere else before coming down?"

"Disturbance? No, the place appeared quiet."

Hausman bit his lip. "I understand you're here for one day only. Is that right?"

"Yes, I'm flying back to New York this evening."

"A business trip?"

Just answer the question and don't elaborate, Trotman told himself.

"Yes."

The detective cracked a feeble smile. "Thank you for your co-operation, and my apologies for detaining you."

"What's going on, Detective?"

"Nothing you need to be concerned about. Enjoy the rest of your stay."

Trotman nodded and strode toward the elevators. The police were off his back—for now. By the time they renewed their interest, he'd be in the States, unreachable. His only worry were the Arabs. Could they identify him? Possible, but he did not consider it likely. Where would they get his photo? Somehow, they found out that he picked up the crystal and were now after him.

Geffen!

The gem trader was the only man who knew about the pickup arrangement, and Lila who drove him to the hotel. God, he hoped they were all right. The image of either of them lying dead somewhere made his stomach churn. Tempted to call Geffen, he resisted the impulse. If nothing had happened, he'd be disturbing him needlessly. If the Arab had gotten to him, there would be no point. The police would surely check all phone calls coming into the store, and Trotman had no desire to get himself involved further, or involve Morrison. The authorities might conceivably confiscate the crystal, wondering why it justified murdering for it, blowing $400K of his boss's money in the bargain.

His instincts screamed at him to get out of this city and this country as quickly as possible and forget about satisfying his curiosity, but if he checked out now, he would be painting a large 'It's me' on his back.

In his room, he tried to sleep, but was too keyed up and kept tossing in bed. Getting up in disgust, he trawled the TV channels, not really seeing the programs, his mind on the damned attack.

At five-thirty, showered and in a fresh suit, he retrieved the crystal from hotel security, checked out and took the complimentary shuttle to Ben Gurion.

No one shot at him along the way.

Chapter Three

Hausman observed two young men wearing casual summer gear, both around 170cm tall, dark hair, round features, no distinguishing marks, emerge laughing from the bar restaurant. He licked his lips, longing for a cold beer. He resented the fact that they were enjoying themselves so openly while his last two-and-a-half hours were spent checking hotel guests. He should arrest and grill them just for fun, which would no doubt dampen their high spirits. He watched as the men strode through the main entrance, turned right and disappeared among the pedestrians.

Chewing on a toothpick, he glanced at the empty white plastic cup beside his elbow. One of the good-looking women behind the Reservations counter had gotten him and his men coffee, but that was sometime back. The cup reminded him of his empty stomach. No beer and no lunch. A crummy way to spend a day. He hoped Karen would have a good dinner prepared.

He gave a sniff, lamenting the lot of a policeman, scribbled a comment beside the last name on the list, and closed the notebook with a snap. The name belonged to a mousy little German man who could not have lifted a chair, let alone murdered the big Chinese bruiser in the stairwell. Everyone on floors four to eight checked out, and they were all guilty as far as Hausman was concerned. If he learned one thing in eight years on the force, there was no such thing as an innocent person. Everyone harbored a misdemeanor, done assault with violence, abused his wife—or perhaps she did the abusing, it happened more often than people suspected—committed robbery in its various guises, or done terminal mayhem.

He had spoken to and accounted for sixty-eight hotel guests, not counting children, and no one had seen or heard anything. If they did, they wisely chose not to get involved. He didn't blame any of them. The frightened little Palestinian bellboy who found the body probably wished he never got out of bed this morning. Hausman shared his sentiment.

Preliminary examination suggested the victim was killed elsewhere and his body dumped down the stairs, the fall breaking his neck and left arm. The medical examiner found two bruises that could not have been caused by the fall: one under the chin and right temple. An autopsy would determine the exact cause of death, but the ME hazarded the blow to the temple probably not fatal.

The young medical examiner peered at him over the rim of his steel glasses. "That took strength, Detective."

"And the bruise under the chin?"

The ME shrugged. "Could be anything. A punch—"

"A blunt instrument?"

"Possibly. Microscopic examination of both trauma points will reveal the means, but I tend to discount a blunt object."

"Oh?"

"The skin discoloration indicates a small diameter impact point. An elongated object would have left broken skin in a line. The same with the temple."

Hausman thought about it for a while. "He was kicked while down?"

"Kicked by someone powerful enough to break bone and probably induce a massive subdural hematoma, although it's unlikely that would have killed him. But as I said, the autopsy will tell us more."

This had not helped Hausman at all. A dozen big men on his list could have committed the crime, and all had unbreakable alibis. The real shock came when they pulled off the man's disguise. A quick fingerprint check by Shin Bet provided the necessary identity. A Chinese military attaché wearing a false mustache and beard, wasn't the type of attire a consular employee would wear going about his lawful occasions. Carrying a Glock semiautomatic also a clear violation of diplomatic immunity conditions. Clearly, there was more afoot here than met the eye.

Why would a Chinese military attaché prowl in the Dan Hotel? Looking for somebody…and presumably found him? Despite a silenced weapon, suggestive in itself as to intent, he ended up the victim. The intended victim, someone strong, according to the ME, who apparently knew how to take care of himself, which only raised more questions.

Perhaps a deeper check should be made on some hotel guests.

Handling an ordinary homicide was bad enough, but when a foreign national—a Chinese foreign national at that—was involved, caused Hausman to think about taking his overdue holiday. Preferably not in Israel. Guns, disguises, murky deals, possible espionage, they all meant trouble and sleepless nights. What made this case worse, having identified the Chinaman, Mossad's Collections Department creeps would probably want to get involved. Relations with the intelligence service were usually cordial, but the Israeli police force resented spooks sticking their noses into purely domestic criminal matters. This, however, did not look like a domestic matter. Well, if they wanted the case, as far as he was concerned, they could take it, but he wasn't likely to have any say in the matter. He would simply be told what to do, like he'd been told to come to the hotel after the body was found.

He glanced at the patiently suffering men beside him, took out the toothpick and nodded.

"We're done for the moment. Thanks for hanging around." Not that they had any choice either. They were also told what to do.

The senior officer grinned. "No problem. I hope you get your man, First Sergeant."

"We'll pin it on somebody," Hausman quipped and watched

them walk off.

His phone rang and he dragged the cell out of his pocket. "Hausman."

"It's Wilson. I'm at the visitors parking lot. We found the Chinaman's car."

"Don't tell me. It's registered to the consulate."

"It isn't, but that's not the interesting bit. We found an *agal* and a black and white *keffiyeh* in the glove box."

"No shit. Anything else?"

"What do you want? A confession note?"

Hausman guffawed. Good news, but it only added to the confusion. Why would a Chinese consular official walk around disguised as an Arab, then dispense with the headgear when he came to the Dan, but not the beard and mustache? Did he intend to visit somebody once he was done at the Dan, or maybe he had already been somewhere that required a *keffiyeh*?

Perhaps Mossad should take over the investigation. He did not relish getting involved in cases with an international flavor. Once the diplomats and politicians got through messing things up, the man on the bottom usually wound up checking parking meters.

"Okay, thanks for letting me know." He switched off and the phone immediately rang.

"It's Inspector Menashe. Get over to Geffen's Dealers at Ramat Gan right away, Yahud."

"Is that Liam Geffen, the gem dealer?"

"That's him. Around eleven this morning, someone wearing a light blue tweed suit, black mustache, and beard, wearing a black and white *keffiyeh*, may have murdered the store owner and one of his sales girls. It was only after you reported the Chinaman's description that we connected the dots."

Hausman rolled his eyes. That was hours ago! What the hell was everybody doing all this time?

"Kehat, have you considered handing this thing to Mossad?

It looks more and more like their type of case."

"If I give this to anyone, it will be to Shin Bet. They're responsible for internal counterintelligence, not Mossad. Until I receive orders to the contrary, this is still a police matter and falls within our jurisdiction. Clear enough?"

"Just asking."

Hausman heard two deep exhales. "Sorry, Yahud. The Superintendent chewed me out because we haven't made any progress."

"Jumping Moses. It's only been four hours since we found the body."

"I know, but a Chinese First Secretary called the Deputy Commissioner, and he called…you know how these things run."

"Yeah. The Chinese want the body?"

"The body and everything else we found. Their man had diplomatic immunity."

"From what you told me, he's also a possible suspect in a double homicide."

"Which I want you to confirm and is the reason why we're holding him. I'm getting a court order to appropriate CCTV footage from Geffen's Dealers. It should provide positive evidence of our man's identity. We want to know what he was doing at Geffen's. It's only a jewelry store."

"You think Geffen was acting as a pipe for some Chinese official and the deal went sour?"

"Anything is possible. Just get over there and talk to people."

"Okay if I have some lunch first?"

"You can drive and have a sandwich at the same time," Menashe growled and hung up.

"Pal," Hausman muttered and pocketed the cell.

This is going to be one long day, he told himself, hoping he wouldn't miss dinner. Karen would not like it and he'd be sleeping in the proverbial doghouse. Still, she understood the demands of his job and the sometimes unusual hours it required, but that did not mean she always took it calmly when he came home late. If he took an administrative job, she hinted more than once, it would make their home life much more congenial. One day, perhaps. Right now, he was a field detective, good at it, and preferred to remain one.

Eyeing the bar restaurant, he sauntered over in the hope of picking up a snack.

He drove toward Ramat Gan more or less on automatic. Too early in the afternoon for traffic to start clumping up, which it would by four-thirty. His mind on the tasty grilled ham, cheese and bacon roll he just finished, he wished he'd bought two. Once accustomed to the invasion, his stomach wanted more, but at 55 shekels—an outrageous price even for a hotel bar—it would have to wait until he got home. He could have gotten something cheaper at a street diner, but he could not afford the time looking for one. Still, the roll left a nice aftertaste in his mouth. Pity he didn't think to get a takeaway coffee to settle it down.

Geffen involved in diamond smuggling? Hausman knew the gem dealer, having run across him on a couple of occasions, but could not accept the idea of the pleasant small man getting mixed up with the Chinese. Working on the theory that everyone was guilty until proven otherwise, he nevertheless conceded the possibility. Geffen must have pissed off somebody real bad to demand his life. To make things foggier, how was the dead Chinese man involved? Tangled, that's what the whole thing was.

Get facts and then start formulating motive, Detective, Hausman told himself sternly, not having to worry about means and opportunity here.

He deposited the toothpick in the ashtray, parked behind a patrol car under the hotel's portico and walked toward the entrance. The rotund man dressed in what had to be an uncomfortable maroon uniform in this heat, guarding the revolving door, pointed at his unmarked car.

"Parking is not allowed here, sir."

"Police," Hausman snapped and moved past him.

The lobby full, but not crowded. Under the Geffen's Dealers sign, a uniformed officer stood watch by the heavy glass doors. Hausman dug out his badge and held it up as he walked into the empty shop. He saw movement on the other side of an open door and sauntered over. Inside, he winced at the gore and blood spattered across the wall. More blood evident on the carpet. The smell didn't do anything for the place.

The skeletal individual inside looked up from the laptop, his black suit, a pencil mustache, and pale expression extenuating his undertaker appearance.

"More police foolishness?" the man demanded truculently. "I told your people everything."

"If you told them everything, I wouldn't be here," Hausman said pleasantly. "Where is everybody?"

"I ordered the two shop assistants to go home. They don't know anything."

They probably didn't, Hausman acknowledged, but he would still check the transcripts of their interviews.

"You must be Meyer."

"Right now, I wish I wasn't. And you are?"

"Detective First Sergeant Hausman."

"I was told to expect you. What do you want?"

"What I want, Mr. Meyer, is to find out why this happened."

"Why does a mad Arab shoot anybody? He was sore at the world and wanted to kill Jews."

"Yes, that could explain it, except the man we think did this wasn't an Arab."

"What?"

"He was Chinese, but I doubt that he'll be of any help to me. He's dead, murdered. Tell me, Mr. Meyer. Do you know if Mr. Geffen had any dealings with the Chinese?"

"The Chinese, Europeans, Russians, Americans; he had connections with most of the world's diamond bourses."

"Is there a particular Chinese he dealt with?"

Meyer frowned and scrunched his face. "He knew Lau Wei quite well. Lau runs a high-class boutique in Hong Kong's Central District, and is an important official in their Diamond Federation."

"Has Mr. Geffen transacted any business with him recently?"

Meyer shifted in his seat. "I was just going over Liam's recent emails to pick up the threads. There is nothing I can see that shows he was in touch with Lau."

Hausman noted the subtle change in the man's demeanor, always a good indicator that something didn't quite mesh. Years of interrogation experience made it easy to spot these things.

"We'll check Mr. Geffen's records, and I must ask you to step away from the laptop for now."

"Do you have a warrant, Detective?"

"Not yet, but I'll get one if you insist. In the meantime, why don't you cooperate and save me getting indigestion. It's been a bad day for everybody. I'm not interested in Mr. Geffen's petty tax avoidance operations or gray deals. I only want to find out why somebody killed him, surely something you'd be interested in."

Meyer sighed and pushed back his chair.

"To help you," Hausman added, "I'm aware of Mr. Geffen's closed auction activities."

"They're not illegal!"

"Like I care. Did he run one recently?"

"You're going to find out anyway—"

"Yes, I will."

"He did run an auction this week, and—"

"Mr. Lau Wei was one of the parties?"

"I honestly don't know. Liam has a special Gmail account he uses for auction emails. I was going over his records to find the password when you showed up."

"Not to worry. One of our tech people will crack it. Now, Mr.

Meyer, and this could be important. Do you know what Mr. Geffen put up on this auction?"

Meyer frowned and inclined his head at the laptop. "You'll understand better if I show you. May I?" He drew the keyboard to him and started typing, then turned the flat screen. Hausman leaned forward and stared at the orange crystal resting on white velvet. Meyer tapped a key and the picture changed showing a perfect mirror.

"What the…"

"That's what Liam probably sold. There is something else you should know, Detective. It's not a natural crystal."

"In what way?"

"You scratch it and the scar disappears. As for the mirror bit, I have no idea how that is done."

"Jumping Moses."

Gazing at the screen, Hausman's mind reeled. What the hell was that thing, and why was it worth killing for?

"Do you know how this crystal came to be in Mr. Geffen's possession?"

"He bought it from Acaph Yaron, a licensed dealer in the Old City."

"An antiquities dealer?"

"That's right. They did business from time to time. Liam told me that Yaron purchased the crystal and two ossuaries from a man who supposedly dug them up in his backyard."

"The crystal was in one of the ossuaries?"

"Apparently."

"What happened to the ossuaries?"

"Sold to the Rockefeller Archaeological Museum."

"Where is the crystal now?"

Meyer pointed at a large safe tucked into a corner. "In there, I assume."

"Can you open in?"

Meyer stood up, walked to the safe and twirled a large dial.

Hearing a click, he pushed down the handle and pulled back the heavy steel door. Hausman saw shelves packed with jewelry cases and small cardboard boxes of various colors. Meyer pawed through the collection, then turned, his face creased in a frown.

"It's not here."

"Are you sure?"

"I handled the jewel case when I examined the crystal."

Hausman fished out a toothpick from his jacket pocket and stuck it into his mouth. The crystal was gone, which suggested that Lau Wei won the bid and arranged with the Chinese consulate to have it picked up—without bothering to pay for it. The deceased probably a courier, but why the disguise, and why kill Geffen and the store assistant? The other thing he didn't understand, once the courier had the item in his possession, why go to the Dan Hotel instead of the consulate? The pieces simply didn't fit.

He had another possibility, of course.

"You were here all alone for quite a while, Mr. Meyer. You didn't happen to procure the crystal for yourself maybe? You did say it has unusual properties."

Meyer gave a scornful snort. "If I wanted to steal anything, Detective, it certainly wouldn't be that crystal. I handle diamonds worth tens of millions. I could have helped myself to a suitcase-full and nobody would have known."

"Okay, you didn't take the crystal. In that case, who did?"

"Open Liam's email account and you're likely to find out."

Hausman wrinkled his nose at the cloying stench of blood permeating the room.

"Go home, Mr. Meyer. I'll have someone check your laptop and have this place cleaned up."

Meyer lifted his chin, his expression stern. "I want to be here when you crack the Gmail account. Geffen has some very sensitive commercial information there which has no relevance to your investigation, Detective, but could be damaging to us if it fell into the wrong hands."

"Like the Tax Authority? I told you before. I'm only interested in emails relating to the closed auction of the crystal. Your permission to access Mr. Geffen's records will be confined to that search, nothing else. If I were to pry further, all information I gathered would constitute inadmissible evidence as it was not obtained under a warrant specific to those emails."

"That's cold comfort if you tipped off the Tax Authority."

Hausman rolled his eyes. Some people required more convincing than others. Then again, given the business Geffen was in, he could hardly blame Meyer for being cautious.

"If you want to hang around, be my guest. It's your shop," he said and shifted the toothpick to the other side of his mouth.

He dug out the cellphone, scrolled down the contacts list and pressed the icon next to Menashe's name. It took three rings before his boss answered.

"What have you got, Yahud?"

"I'm at Geffen's Dealers. Can you send an IT guy to unlock a Gmail account? The emails in it could tell us a lot about what's going on."

"I'll get it done. What else?"

"It appears Geffen sold a weird crystal in a closed auction that may be the Chinese link we're looking for."

"Weird, how?"

"You scratch it and it repairs itself. According to the manager, Geffen bought the thing from an antiquities dealer. We need to dig up an expert who can talk to us about crystals, and I'll arrange to have a chat with the dealer. There are more pieces to this puzzle than we thought, Kehat."

"Get back to the precinct," Menashe ordered and cut contact.

Hausman pocketed the cell and sighed, not looking forward to a lengthy drive along Tel Aviv's tortuous streets with traffic undoubtedly already building. He plucked the toothpick out of his mouth, dropped it on the stained carpet and turned to Meyer.

"When our IT man gets here, I want you to give him a printout of every email that relates to the crystal, unless you want to see a warrant first?"

Meyer broke into a smile. "He'll get his emails."

* * *

Tsai Teping stared unwaveringly at a large stylized image of Mao hanging on the wall behind the minister's desk, sensing Lin Jinpan's eyes raking him. What should have been a simple recovery job had now escalated into a serious diplomatic incident…and a pile of unpleasantness for him.

"Well, General?" Lin prompted softly, his body language openly hostile.

Tsai cleared his throat and swallowed hard. "I…"

"Since you find it difficult to speak, let me enlighten you. One of our military aides was found at a luxury Tel Aviv hotel, neck broken under what can only be termed as suspicious circumstances, and the Israeli government refuses to release the body until they have completed their investigation. Then they hauled in our ambassador and lodged an official protest regarding violation of diplomatic immunity conditions. The Ambassador did not appreciate that and the Tel Aviv Consul General did not appreciate the dressing down he got from the Ambassador.

"I just got off the phone with Dzhang Qishan trying to explain what the Second Bureau was doing in Tel Aviv, and I couldn't. Why? Because I didn't know!" Lin roared and crashed his fist against the polished surface of his huge walnut desk. Pens and stationery jumped. The swarthy minister glared at Tsai, cleared his throat, and composed himself.

"I am aware of your predilection for collecting rare minerals, General, but I want you to tell me that you didn't use state personnel to further your private collection, for that's what the Tel Aviv consular military attaché said you ordered him to do. Not something I could say to the Premier, you agree? Tell me it isn't true, General, and I'd be very careful what you say here."

Tsai fumed, promised himself he'd break Sungan and have him begging his rice from a gutter, the major's call now a distant memory. A dead aide and no crystal. Instead of triumphantly presenting the artifact to the Standing Committee, cloaked in glory, he now stood at the lip of a precipice, with Lin Jinpan ready to push him over. He had not spent the last twenty-three years nurturing a promising career to have it dashed by a doddering Tuanpai fool. The minister may be a fool, but he was also a consummate power manipulator who would see to it that Tsai bore any fallout over this.

He reached into the breast pocket of his uniform and took out two folded color glossies. Face wooden, longing for a cigar, he placed the photographs before Lin.

"That's the object I ordered the military attaché to retrieve, Mr. Minister."

Lin unfolded the stiff sheets and his mouth sagged. When he looked up, his face contorted with rage.

"I'll have you broken for this, General."

"Mr. Minister—"

"Enough! There is nothing more to be said. You're dismissed."

"Sir, you need to listen to me."

"I said you're dismissed. Pending a general court, you are confined to your residence where you'll hold yourself under open arrest."

"In that case…sir, the state will lose an artifact that may be of strategic importance to our country. Do you want to punish me or salvage the situation?"

Lin frowned. "What are you talking about?"

"I wanted the thing for myself, yes, but that was before I realized what it was. Sir, what you have are photos of an artificial crystal supposedly able to repair itself and exhibits unusual polarization properties. I decided then that the state must have it. I did not want it falling into capitalist hands. That's why I ordered the military attaché to get it."

"The military aide was killed because of it?"

"Probably. We did learn one thing. An American industrialist bought the crystal, and it's likely his courier killed our man."

"Before he could kill him," Lin grated. "And now the Israeli authorities are alerted to the existence of this strange crystal and will likely seek to have it recovered if it's as important as you suggest."

Tsai nodded. "That is the probable scenario, Mr. Minister."

"How did *you* learn of this crystal?"

"I, ah, have a network of gem dealers who from time to time make me aware of a rare item coming onto the unofficial trading market. A dealer in Hong Kong offered me an opportunity to bid for the crystal."

"Presumably, he also told you who was selling it?"

"After some persuasion. The man was dealt with."

"That's something." Lin pursed his lips. After a moment, he looked up. "Perhaps the situation is not beyond recovery and maybe we should get this crystal. Tell me, General. Given the embarrassment with the Israelis, how do you propose going about it?"

Tsai's shoulders sagged with relief as he heard the words. He might actually walk out of here with skin bruised, but intact. Of course, by becoming involved, the Minister would ensure that any credit from a successful operation accrued to him. That was the way of things, which meant Tsai needed to manipulate events to highlight his own activities. In the current political climate, with the Tuanpai faction out of favor, that might not be too difficult. Still, he needed to be careful not to overreach himself.

With the Israel situation souring so dramatically, he had to consider another possibility. Everybody who knew of the crystal's existence could now be scrambling to get it for themselves, turning this into a much deadlier game. The amusing corollary was that no one had any idea what the thing actually was or what it did. From being a curiosity, it may have now become an object of international political interest.

"I have a reliable operative whom I could send to the U.S."

"Just like that? And if he is compromised, we risk a major diplomatic incident with the Americans. Very good, General." Lin sneered. "Have you forgotten what happened last year? China is still recovering from the La Palma debacle the former Standing Committee chairman launched."

And Chairman Keung Yang was your friend, Tsai mused.

"I have not forgotten."

"This American industrialist, he must have some inkling as to what this crystal is, otherwise he would not have put in a bid. Correct?"

He nodded wearily. "Yes, sir."

"What if he gets their government involved? If you mishandle the operation, the next American nuclear missile will not be aimed at Lop Nur. Premier Dzhang will likely have me shot, but not before I shoot you. Am I making myself clear, General?"

"With proper planning, I believe we can be successful."

"But you cannot guarantee that."

"Every operation has inherent risks, and this one will accumulate more as other players enter the arena. The Tel Aviv gem dealer undoubtedly offered the crystal to buyers we're not aware of."

"And those buyers may realize the potential of this crystal and might also come after it?"

"Yes."

"They don't have your background information."

"With respect, the information can be obtained."

"In the same manner you obtained yours from that Hong

Kong dealer?"

"Yes, sir. Because of these risk factors, if we want the crystal, we need to move before the situation saturates."

"Can you retrieve the crystal in a way impossible for the Americans to trace it to us?"

"With absolute certainty? No."

Lin Jinpan gave a thin grin. "You're being realistic. I like that."

"Sir, even if the Americans penetrate our operation, we will not be stealing their property, but something from a private individual. Failure would not generate a diplomatic incident."

"Because we'll be stealing an Israeli artifact, and we already have a diplomatic incident with them."

"The incident arose because of the murdered military aide, Mr. Minister. Aware of the crystal's potential importance, the Israelis could mount a recovery mission of their own, but it would be a clandestine operation like ours."

"They could demand the crystal be returned as it's rightfully their property," Lin Jinpan reminded him, and Tsai waved a dismissive hand.

"They could, and they probably will as a gambit, but it's not their property. I doubt the situation would be escalated to an official level."

"It has already been escalated," Lin snapped.

"Only as a criminal breach by our military aide. We can write that off as an unauthorized act by the aide pursuing a piece of private business."

"The Israelis will never believe that."

"Perhaps not, but it would clear us and our ambassador. The underground gem and antiquities trade is a thriving industry in Israel, Mr. Minister, something their government is aware of and tacitly approves. Closed auctions may be a tax avoidance activity, but it nevertheless generates valuable foreign currency for them, which in turn helps their economy. If we blame the incident on the dead aide, it gives us a credible explanation and offers plausible deniability."

Lin raised an eyebrow. "Very impressive, General. You appear to have a deep understanding of this business."

"I learned by doing it, sir," Tsai said dryly.

"No doubt." Lin tapped his fingers against the desk. "Very well. Recover the crystal, but stand warned. There can be no loose ends, and nothing must point to us. Is that absolutely clear?"

Tsai stiffened. "Yes, sir!"

"You have five days before I denounce you. Dismissed."

Outside the minister's office, Tsai Teping's forehead creased in a deep frown as he dug out a cigar and lit it. He took in a deep lungful of smoke and exhaled slowly, relishing the feeling of well-being spreading through him. Ignoring the assistant's disapproving stare, he cleared the tickle in his throat and stomped out.

Easy for Lin to issue orders, knowing he'd remain blameless should the operation fail, which it could at many levels. The American, Kevin Morrison, aware of what happened in Tel Aviv would take steps to protect his investment. Tsai would have done the same thing. To obtain the crystal, he would first need to find out where it was. That meant learning all about the American before penetrating his organization. He also had someone who could handle that side of the operation and not bungle it. There was much to do, and five days didn't give him any time at all, something the minister probably knew.

Should the mission become compromised, despite what he told the minister, the Americans would not appreciate having Chinese operatives messing on their turf. Of course, both sides engaged in active military and commercial intelligence gathering, and nobody got excited provided people didn't get hurt. Getting the crystal could change that status quo. Americans were quick to react and China did not need to give the capitalists another reason to be mad at them. Lin was correct in his assessment there.

However, obtaining the crystal, even if it cost some collateral damage, might be worth wearing the political fallout—if the damned thing did in fact have some application potential.

He told Lin what he knew about the crystal, which was precious little, and he understood the minister's skepticism. With the game assuming a more serious dimension, it behooved him to explore the crystal's peculiar properties further. It would have helped knowing the thing's history, something the murdered aide neglected to find out.

A thought bubble percolated through his turbulent thoughts and burst in a light of revelation, leaving him stunned, wondering why he hadn't seen it before. If one crystal existed, there could be others gathering dust in some museum display or basement annex. A remote possibility at best, he admitted, but one worth pursuing. Time to get his friend in the Tenth Bureau fully on the project. First, he needed to get the American operation underway.

He reached for the phone and tapped numbers. A diffident voice answered after three rings.

"Yes, sir?"

"Kwang, I have a job for you."

* * *

Morrison placed the blue porcelain mug emblazoned with the Solaris Technology logo on the desk and gazed absently at the computer screen, not seeing it, his thoughts on Manhattan traffic. Why is it that on Fridays the number of cars seemed to multiply out of proportion to the number of citizens in any given geographical location? Perhaps a grant to MIT might unravel the conundrum and City Hall could take steps to ease congestion. He admitted it was a fanciful notion, but he still wondered. Fourteen minutes by cab to his office...ridiculous. He could have walked in quicker than that. With 84 degrees outside already and only

8:20 when he started, the walk would have left him rumpled.

He glanced at the barely discernable bulge in his belly and decided that he ought to have walked. Juliana told him more than once that he needed to exercise. Maybe he would hit the gym at lunchtime, hating the idea of turning into another bloated Wall Street plutocrat. Half an hour a day would improve his cardiovascular system, melt off excess baggage and firm up everything, giving him the look he enjoyed in his thirties. Juliana used to tell him during pillow talk how she always liked his craggy physique. Now that he thought about it, the only comments she made about his shape these days weren't complimentary. It amazed him how easily he'd allowed himself to slip into bad habits. Gym...lunchtime, he promised himself. It came with the office rent, so he might as well use it.

The phone rang and he pressed the speaker button.

"Yes, Allison?"

"Mr. Trotman to see you, sir," she announced crisply.

With a flawless English complexion, ash-blond hair trimmed severely short, always dressed in conservative business outfits, she could be a model—had she had an extra foot on her. With him from the start, unless she spent more time hunting for a husband, she was likely to end up an old maid, which would break every male heart who ever met her.

"Show him in," he said with relish, looking forward to seeing his troubleshooter—and the crystal. Two Atlantic flights in two days, the man must be dead, but he was young. He would survive.

The gray ceiling-high door opened and Allison stood back as Trotman strode in, giving her a nod.

"Nolan, you're a sight for sore eyes. Allison, can you bring us fresh coffee, please?"

"Of course."

She retrieved the almost empty glass carafe from the bench hotplate and softly closed the door after her.

Morrison waved at a visitor chair. "Pull up a rock."

Trotman dragged the soft cloth chair closer to the desk and eased himself down.

"I thought you'd still be sacked out," Morrison said pleasantly, eyeing his protégé with approval.

"I had a reasonably good nap on the way over," Trotman replied in his deep sonorous voice. "I'll crash out tonight."

"I'm glad you got the crystal, but your call gave me the impression that things didn't go smoothly. Trouble with Geffen?"

"No, sir. Trouble with an Arab."

"What?"

"He tried to take me out at my hotel."

"Take you out? You mean shoot you?"

"He pulled a gun on me. That didn't leave much room for debate."

Morrison stared at him, digesting the development.

"Are you sure he was an Arab?"

"I saw his driver's license, but that might not mean much. I didn't have time to check him out properly."

"You weren't hurt?"

Trotman cracked a smile. "He's the one who got hurt, terminally. I had no choice."

"Any trouble with the local police?"

"There is nothing to suggest I was involved, but it's possible they may connect me with the murder as the case unravels."

"We'll handle it if and when it comes up. An Arab, eh? Geffen's auction was compromised, that's clear."

"He might also be dead. Geffen and one of his assistants were the only ones who knew I was picking up the crystal and could have told the Arab where to find me."

"This is getting really murky. Any problems with airport security?"

"I always carried it on me and the metal detector portals never twigged."

Trotman reached into his jacket and produced a red jewel

case. He opened the lid and slid the case across the desk. Without touching it, Morrison stared at the orange sheen rippling across the polished surface and felt his stomach flutter with suppressed excitement. Now that he had it, he would need to find out if it was worth the money he paid for it—and why people were so anxious to kill for it.

What are you, my little stone?

"Doesn't look like much sitting there," he said softly. "You're satisfied as to its authenticity?"

"Geffen demonstrated the self-healing and reflective properties." Trotman held out a piece of paper. "Purchase certificate."

Morrison nodded. "Good man. That may come in handy should the Israelis want to play hardball. Give it to Allison."

A knock on the door made him look up. Allison walked in with a carafe of freshly brewed coffee, filled one cup and Morrison's favorite mug. She handed them out and made her way toward the door.

Trotman took a long pull and held the cup in his lap.

"Nolan, I know you must be tired, but I need to find out what makes this crystal worth a life. Get yourself to Boston and give it to Dr. Ferguson. I'll call him to expect you."

"The US Airways Shuttle from LaGuardia?"

"Arrange it with Allison. Once you're done, go home. I don't want to see you until Monday."

"Vivian will like having me for a whole weekend," Trotman said with a smile. "Dr. Morrison, the Israelis would have put the pieces together by now and are probably wondering what all the fuss is about. If they haven't, they'll be doing it soon."

"You mean, they might come after the crystal?"

"They and the Arabs, and perhaps others. We have no way of knowing who participated in the closed auction."

"Our offices and Ferguson's lab have 24/7 security."

"I was thinking of your security and your wife's."

Stefan Vučak

Morrison felt something cold slither down his back. He genuinely had not considered that.

"Mine?"

"That Arab was prepared to kill me for the crystal. If he got Geffen to talk, it's likely he communicated the information and his handler will know you have it."

"I've been threatened before, Nolan," Morrison snapped, not liking what he'd heard.

He exhaled, working the possibilities, none of them pleasant. This was not something he anticipated, but in hindsight, he should have. If the crystal was that valuable, the situation could escalate beyond his ability to manage. He did not relish the idea of being the center of an international squabble. Not if it meant risking Juliana, or anybody else, for that matter.

"Perhaps I should put the thing on eBay and let the Arabs buy it from me, ridding myself of the problem." He stared speculatively at Trotman. "If anybody is going to come after the crystal, you could also be the target."

"I am conscious of that possibility, but I'm in a better position to handle such a situation."

"Perhaps, but I don't want to put it to a test. I'll talk this over with TriCon. Did you ask Geffen about the crystal's pedigree?"

"He bought it from an antiquities dealer in Old Jerusalem, and the dealer got it from somebody who dug up two ossuaries in his backyard."

Morrison pulled at his chin. "That means it's old, very old. Jews stopped using stone chests centuries ago as convenient places to dig burial caves ran out and customs changed."

Trotman frowned. "But—"

"I know. In those days, it should not have been possible to make such a crystal. We don't know how to make one now."

"What do you think it is, sir?"

"I have no idea, Nolan, but I have my suspicions. That's why I want Ferguson to run some tests. Somebody in our past had

116

the technology to make the thing, which only begs the question. With those peculiar properties, what was the crystal supposed to do? That is something I hope to find out, because I don't believe it's simply an ornament. Somebody else also thought that or he wouldn't have sent that Arab after you." He closed the case with a snap and held it out. "Get this to Ferguson, and take care, hear me?"

Trotman placed the cup and saucer on the desk, stood and reached for the case.

"Vivian will bust me up if I don't," Trotman said and his mouth twitched.

Alone, Morrison sat back as he held the warm mug between his hands, deep in thought. His nanograss and QD pigment work had exposed him to threats, but they were confined to manipulating his share price and hostile takeovers, with the exception of the in-your-face government approach. The idea of Juliana hurt because of the crystal was something he refused to contemplate. However, with an attempt on Trotman's life, he had to acknowledge the grim possibility.

He could hand the thing to DARPA and defuse the situation, making it the government's problem. He'd be free and safe, but it wasn't a palatable solution. They would classify the crystal and despite any written agreement, he'd probably lose all commercial rights under the umbrella of national interest. He knew how these things worked. DARPA tried to get the quantum dot pigment off him for military use, as did the DOE's Office of Intelligence and Counterintelligence. Their objective was more insidious, hiding their demand behind a gauzy veil of identifying strategic energy sources. Every time he recalled Crawford's visits and the wheezing man's repellant attitude, the day soured for him. He held out, but could not guarantee that either agency had not simply gone ahead with their own research using processes described in his basic patents. He wished them luck, but if they trotted out a product based on his work, the government would find itself before the Supreme Court for breach of intellectual property. He did not believe the Walters administration would relish that experience, but it might be prepared to wear bad publicity for a short while until another scandal took over the headlines. It wasn't a pleasant thought.

Knowing he was getting ahead of himself, he needed to apply a methodology to the problem, and he had already taken the first step—find out everything about the crystal, which he hoped Ferguson would be able to do. Second, review security across the board. TriCon managed security for his Massachusetts and California plants using subcontracted personnel. Despite the scandal two three ago involving the firm and the International Anthropological Society over some 40 million-year-old human bones and rumors of shady operations, he liked how they did business. He would arrange a meeting with TriCon's CEO and work out an approach. Lazars will know what to do.

If some fucker wanted the crystal, he would have to pay for it with blood.

His anxiety level reduced, he reached for the phone and pressed a direct line button.

"Dr. Ferguson," a grumpy voice answered.

"It's Kevin. Got a minute?"

"A minute."

"Remember that question I asked a few days ago about an artificial crystal? I'm having Trotman fly over and deliver it to you. Run some tests and tell me what it is. Not a detailed analysis, just the basics."

"You actually have the thing?"

"There is a downside, Harold. People may want to get hold of it. Notch up your security protocols."

"What's going on, Kevin? You're not mixed up in anything shady, are you? Because if you are, count me out."

"Nothing shady, but that crystal cost somebody's life, perhaps more than one. I want to find out why."

"You have me intrigued, I'll give you that."

"I would like you to handle this yourself, if you don't mind. Don't talk to anybody and don't show the crystal to anyone. One more thing, if you lose it or damage it, I'll come over and personally shove a lit Bunsen burner up your butt."

Ferguson chuckled. "That's been tried before, my boy, but I get the picture. I assume you want an answer yesterday?"

"Or sooner."

"I'll get back to you on Monday, okay?"

"Don't spend the whole weekend on this."

"I won't. By the way. I thought you'd like to know the accreditation committee has accepted Stanly's thesis."

"Say, that's great news. Thanks for the heads-up. I always knew the boy had it in him. Does he know?"

"You want me to tell him?"

"If it's not breaking any MIT regulations. Has he talked to you about going for a PhD?"

"Isn't that something you'd know?"

"He was still undecided last time we discussed it."

"A PhD behind his name would carry a lot of weight if he decides to file for a patent, and I'd be happy to be his thesis advisor."

"I don't want to push him, Harold. He already thinks I'm controlling his life—"

"You are."

"—but a word from you could help him decide."

"Leave it with me. Interesting to talk to you, but not always a pleasure," Ferguson said and hung up.

Still holding the receiver, Morrison scowled as he pressed a white button. "Allison, get me Mr. Lazars at TriCon Security, will you?"

"Just a moment."

Getting a master's was great, but Morrison wanted his son to get a PhD, and maybe a business or law qualification. These days more than ever a person had to be properly armed to venture into shark-infested corporate waters. He grinned and rubbed his hands with satisfaction. He would ask Juliana to arrange a family celebratory get-together. This was a milestone in Stan's life and he deserved to bask in the limelight.

* * *

Fridays always gave Yahud Hausman a keen pain. Apart from some stores and restaurants, most businesses and public institutions were closed. However, that did not include the police department, something Karen regarded with ominous silence. What made Friday worse, with the exception of Arab countries, the rest of the world had weekends off too, which meant he couldn't get in touch with anybody until Monday at the earliest. A war could break out and nobody would know about it!

Checking Geffen's Gmail entries proved easy once the IT man obtained the laptop's IP address, which enabled him to access Google's email server using an application not available to the general public. In effect, Geffen's account was hacked, but done in the cause of righteousness, Hausman reminded himself wryly. He got his emails, that's what counted, and very interesting they proved to be. Instead of regarding the whole episode with suspicion, Meyer should be grateful; he got the account's password and access to all his boss' secrets.

Lau Wei definitely received an invitation to bid for the crystal, which established the Chinese connection, but did not help identify the party who initiated action against Geffen. Hausman knew how closed auctions worked and the methods used to protect the anonymity of all parties. What could not be protected, of course, was the identity of brokers used to promote the auction to their clients. As it turned out, one of the brokers was a Russian. Would one of Drotenkov's clients start chasing the crystal? Since the buyer was an American, the prospect didn't worry Hausman at all. They could shoot each other for all he cared.

Unfortunately, as Wilson found, that is exactly what appeared to have happened. Lau Wei was found shot in his store, which directly linked a Chinese official sufficiently powerful to order a hit on Geffen. He failed to get the crystal, which meant he might try again. Hausman did not want to be in Morrison's shoes right now.

Regardless of how interesting, his focus extended to one American, Nolan Trotman, the man who picked up the crystal and stayed at the Dan Tel Aviv Hotel where the Chinese military aide happened to meet with an untimely end. He did not believe in coincidence. In one of his James Bond books, Ian Fleming said: 'First time, happenstance', 'Second time, coincidence', 'Third time, enemy action'. Hausman always cut to the enemy action part right away. He hadn't been proven wrong yet.

He recalled the tall, powerful man, and had no doubt that he killed the Chinese attaché. Given the circumstances, probably in self-defense. He had no forensic evidence to prove that Trotman was the murderer, but the American was a loose end he wanted tied up. Pity Trotman wasn't still here. Call Solaris Technology and arrange an off the record phone interview? If Trotman was in any way involved, Morrison would probably just brush him off. Should he make an official request through the American embassy to seek Trotman's extradition? He would need to sound off the Inspector about that, but without evidence, he probably wouldn't get very far.

The talk with Professor Laske from the Israel Museum proved disappointing. The academic was a recognized expert in anthropology and turned out to have a deep understanding of crystals, but could not add to what Hausman and Menashe already knew. What they needed was a physicist versed in the subject, which he left to his boss to sort out. It was an opportunity for the Inspector to earn his bountiful salary.

Hausman pulled into Acaph Yaron's driveway, got out of the

car, stretched his arms and sniffed. Jerusalem's air did not smell of lilacs, but then, neither did Tel Aviv's. He could hear the rush of traffic along Derekh Yerikho Street, the golden Dome of the Rock gleaming in morning sunshine. Before locking the car, he made sure the prominent blue police sticker was visible on the dashboard. It wouldn't do to find some city busybody had towed the car away. His boss would not be amused.

He walked to the heavy wooden front door and pressed the bell button. When he called Yaron, the dealer told him he didn't know anything and the detective was wasting his time coming. Hausman agreed, but it was his time to waste. Menashe wanted to know everything about the ossuaries and the crystal, and Yaron happened to be an important part in a sequence of events that led to bodies everywhere.

The door opened and Hausman was confronted by a man of average height, past his prime, stomach bulging, dressed casually in brown slacks and black T-shirt. He dug out his badge and held it up.

"Detective First Sergeant Hausman."

That did not seem to impress Yaron. "As I told you on the phone, Detective, you've squandered a trip. Come in anyway."

Inside the cool kitchen that also served as a small dining room, the dealer didn't offer Hausman a chair. A percolator burbled on the breakfast bench. He could have used a cup then, but it looked like he wouldn't be getting it here.

"When we spoke on the phone, Mr. Yaron, you told me you purchased the ossuaries—"

"From Cheber Shaken who lives in the Arnona hills. He came across a burial chamber while digging up his backyard. The crystal was in one of the chests. He sent me an email with an offer to sell and I bought the lot. I sold the crystal to Geffen's Dealers at Ramat Gan, and the ossuaries to the Rockefeller Museum."

"So you said." Hausman dug out his notebook and flipped a page. "You sold the chests to Professor Ezrah Kutner."

"That's right. You want to know about the ossuaries, talk to him. I don't do archaeology."

"I'll do that. There is one thing that has me puzzled. Why did he buy the chests? I would have thought the Museum had enough of them."

"The bones. Didn't I tell you?"

"You didn't."

"Both chests held bones, presumably child bones judging by their size. What struck me as unusual as soon as I saw them were the skulls. They were elongated, not normal. I knew Kutner would want them."

"You've dealt with him before?"

"I sold him an occasional piece."

"Was there anything else unusual about the ossuaries?"

Yaron frowned. "Well, they had strange markings. Nothing I recognized. Kutner seemed excited when he saw them."

"Tell me about the crystal."

"He made me an offer when I showed it to him, but I wanted Geffen to check it first before I committed myself. I never saw a stone like that and Geffen seemed particularly fascinated by it. When he shone a green laser at it, the diffraction pattern didn't match what he expected from a topaz or beryl stone. He did something to the laser and the next thing, I saw the crystal turn into a perfect mirror. Talk to Geffen, Detective. He'll confirm what I told you."

Hausman mulled over the information, got a toothpick out of his pocket and stuck it into his mouth.

"Unfortunately, I can't do that. You see, he was murdered yesterday, together with one of his store assistants."

Yaron turned pale. "Liam is dead?"

"That crystal you got is more than it seems. Tell me. You bought two ossuaries, but there is only one crystal. That seems strange. Are you sure there weren't two crystals?"

Yaron composed himself and took a deep breath. "Two crystals? No. Shaken told me he found only one."

"He could be lying."

"You'll have to take that up with him, Detective. Now, if you don't mind…"

Hausman pocketed his notebook and held out a business card. "If you think of anything else, call me."

Yaron took the card and nodded, but his mind was elsewhere.

In the car, Hausman went over what the dealer said. Everything hung together, with the exception of the bones. Definitely something he would need to check with Kutner. He glanced at his watch, figuring he would miss his appointment with the professor by about five minutes.

He parked in the museum's almost empty lot—the place only open until noon on Fridays—toothpick sticking out of the corner of his mouth, he nodded in appreciation as he gazed at the impressive yellow stone structure. A trickle of people walked in and out, stoically bearing up in the late morning heat. As he neared the wide entrance, two rows of chattering children rushed out, kept in a semblance of order by harried teachers, and plowed through everybody in their path. He waited for the tide to sweep by and strode into the cool interior.

He announced himself at the security desk and surveyed the glass exhibits. Footsteps echoed on the dark gray marble floor and he turned. The little bird-man, a pipe stuck in his mouth, a mop of untidy white hair that needed a comb, pushed up his brown-rimmed glasses and extended a hand.

"Detective Hausman?"

"That's me."

"Doctor Kutner."

They shook hands, the smaller man's dry grip surprisingly strong.

"Thanks for seeing me, Doc."

"Always glad to help the authorities." Kutner removed the

pipe and tapped it against the palm of his hand. "You know, young man, you're the second government official to see me."

"Oh?"

"Yesterday, I had a visit from a rude fellow in IAA's Artifacts Treatment Department. I sent him packing in short order. I hope you're not going to be rude, Detective?"

Hausman smiled as the professor led him down a corridor lined with doors.

"I need your cooperation, Doc. That means I must be polite."

"Hah! And once you get your information…"

"I can arrest you."

Kutner let out a bellowing laugh, stopped beside a plain white door and walked in. The cramped office cluttered with overflowing bookshelves, piled up periodicals, and variously colored folders. Paperwork covered the small desk tucked into a corner, tower computer perched at one end. The professor removed a stack of books off a metal chair and pushed it closer to the desk.

"Have a seat, Detective," he offered as he walked behind the desk and lowered himself with a grunt, completely at ease in his little world.

Hausman sat down and dug out his notebook. "What did that annoying IAA man want, if you don't mind me asking."

"The same thing you do, Detective. The ossuaries. Acaph called me a few minutes ago about Geffen. I can hardly believe it. Are you sure he was murdered because of the crystal? It could be a robbery gone awry."

"Except it wasn't a robbery, Doc. An inventory check by the manager did not reveal anything missing."

"So, it had to be the crystal. An absolutely amazing thing. It hardly seems possible that somebody 2,700 years ago could have carved and polished such a thing."

"Jumping Moses. Two thousand seven hundred years ago?"

"That's the carbon-14 date I got for the bones. Of course, the crystal itself could have been produced much earlier than that."

"The IAA official," Hausman prompted.

Kutner pushed up his glasses. "Yes. The individual had the effrontery to demand that I hand over the ossuaries and the bones. I threw him out, of course. The Antiquities Authority has no legal claim on the chests or their contents, and the Museum's ownership is uncontestable."

"Why the interest?"

"The strange symbols carved on the chest, Detective. Nothing like I have ever seen, and nobody I talked to has seen anything like them either. All my research to identify the symbols has proven futile. I wish I had the box that contained the crystal. It was covered with those symbols. Absolutely covered."

Hausman's forehead creased as a memory teased him. It surfaced and he lifted a finger. "I saw a little wooden box in Geffen's office."

"Made of brown wood?"

"Dark brown, yes."

"I need to get hold of it!" Kutner declared and Hausman shrugged.

"Talk to Meyer, the store manager."

"I will, I will."

"You were telling me why the IAA wanted the ossuaries."

"It wasn't only because of the symbols, but the bones. Yes, the bones."

"What's so special about the bones?"

"According to DNA analysis, they represent an unknown branch of *homo sapiens*. Strictly speaking, I should not call them genus *homo* as the bones don't fit into our evolutionary tree."

"They're not human?"

"They have human genome sequences, all right, but they also have sequences not present in any other mammal species. Most puzzling."

"Would those sequences explain the elongated heads?"

"The elongated heads are merely one physical manifestation

of the DNA makeup. You have heard of elongated heads found in Peru?"

"I've seen some TV programs."

"Well, what Acaph sold me are skulls that appear to be naturally elongated, which is absolutely astonishing. Very."

Hausman tried to grapple with concepts not in his sphere of expertise. "And that's why you think they're a different species?"

"That's right." Kutner leaned forward, eyes sparkling with excitement. "You don't appreciate the significance, do you?"

"I'm afraid not."

"Evolution does not produce a species isolated from other population groups. It doesn't. There must be a common link somewhere, and interbreeding would gradually create a single uniform species that contains DNA from every contributing branch. This is not the case with my skulls. They and others found in Peru are unique! I wonder what happened to those people to make them vanish," he mused and pushed up his glasses.

Fascinating as this was, Hausman needed to steer the discussion relevant to his investigation.

"Doctor Kutner, do you know if anybody else has dug up anything like the crystal Mr. Yaron sold you?"

Kutner frowned and tapped the pipe against the desk. "Not that I know of. I could run a check for you with some of my Peruvian colleagues and people in the Mesoamerican community."

"I would appreciate that. Instead of simplifying my job, you just made it more complicated."

"What is so special about the crystal, Detective? As a piece of topaz or beryl heliodor, it's an attractive specimen, but hardly worth murdering somebody over it."

Hausman rolled the toothpick in his mouth. "Like your bones, Doc, it's not what it seems. It can apparently heal itself and exhibits a strange property under laser light."

"Yes, Geffen's email mentioned that, but I discounted it as

fanciful advertising on his part."

"You must have realized the crystal was unusual or you would never have made your bid."

"What do you know about that?" Kutner demanded, instantly on guard.

"We got hold of Geffen's auction emails."

"Am I in trouble over that?"

Hausman laughed. "Hardly. The Museum did nothing illegal."

"Tell me about the crystal."

"You scratch the surface and the surrounding material will flow into the scar, repairing the damage."

Kutner gaped. "You have to be kidding me. No natural…" he trailed off as the realization struck him. "It's not natural," he whispered in awe.

"Apparently not. Now you see why somebody was prepared to commit murder to get it."

"But…it wasn't possible to produce a crystal like that 2,700 years ago."

"No, it wasn't…that we know of. Makes you wonder who did make it. Your mysterious species?"

Kutner stared through him, then blinked. "It's not a question of who, Detective, but of why."

Hausman nodded and sighed. "There is that. Come on, Doc. You must have known the crystal was unique, otherwise you would not have urged the Museum to make its bid."

"Well…"

"Never mind. Did you discuss the crystal with the IAA man?"

"No, the subject never came up."

"Keep it that way."

"Do you know who bought it?"

"I do, but I can't tell you. Maybe it will come out in the wash one day and you'll know."

"What are you going to do now?"

Hausman stood up and sighed. "Hand this to my superior and

let him worry about it while I enjoy a day off."

He walked toward the exit and glanced at his watch: 11:42. He would probably make it home by two, by which time Karen would have done her house chores and they could have the afternoon and evening to themselves. Perhaps dining out might be in order, making up to her for a couple of long days. His cellphone shrilled and he reached into his pocket. He frowned as he read the caller's number. Didn't the Inspector have a life?

"What's up, Kehat?"

"You still in Jerusalem?"

"Getting set to drive back."

"Anything new I should know?"

"I got a lot more information about the ossuaries, which only deepens the mystery surrounding the crystal's origins, but that's about it. I planned on seeing the man who dug up the ossuaries, but decided against it. We won't get anything useful out of him."

"Agreed. As of now, Detective, you're off the case. See me when you come in."

"Off the case? What are you talking about? We got three bodies and a killer still on the loose."

"The real killer is not the American, but the Chinese aide. Our own ballistics tests proved it."

"We'll let the American walk, Inspector?"

"We won't, but our priority is recovering the crystal. After talking to a physicist from Tel Aviv University, the Commissioner had a chat with the Ministry of Foreign Affairs North American Division, asking them to contact the American ambassador with a request to return the crystal, a national treasure illegally appropriated by one of their citizens."

"Geffen *sold* the crystal to Morrison. There is nothing illegal about the transaction. Not directly anyway."

"It doesn't matter. We want it back and we're prepared to offer Morrison compensation. If he baulks, we'll threaten to charge Nolan Trotman with multiple murders."

"That's playing dirty."

"Whatever is necessary to get it back."

"What's so special about the crystal, Kehat?"

"Apart from its obvious characteristics which you already know, it could be a photonic resonator—a computer that uses light instead of electrons. That's what our physicist claims."

"Jumping Moses."

"If Morrison has that figured out, and he might have or he wouldn't have made such a high bid, it's likely he won't part with it willingly, but we're working on a contingency plan to recover it."

Hausman grimaced at the thought of Mossad's spooks getting involved. "Inspector, if things go wrong, this could turn very ugly."

"It's already ugly, First Sergeant."

* * *

"You're absolutely sure about this?" Sharron Ibrahim demanded sharply.

"Absolutely sure? No, but I had sufficient information to act," Abdon Sayar said, the Harvard accent clearly distinguishable behind his Hebrew.

He projected an aura of calm and confidence that always irritated Ibrahim, making him feel provincial. There was no getting around it; the man had a presence and a level of sophistication that commanded attention. Childish resentment, but that's how it was.

"Without consulting me," he grumbled sourly. If only the man didn't look so...regal.

Sayar frowned and sat up. "I am your deputy and Foreign Minister. I thought by now that you could trust my judgment...as I trust yours."

"Trust my judgment? Every time—"

"Peace! Let's not start another war."

Ibrahim sighed heavily and raised a hand. "My apologies. I didn't mean it to sound like that." He tapped his fingers against the desktop and shook his head. "I hate it when stuff like this comes across my desk."

"What's the matter? Being Prime Minister is getting weary? Can't handle the tough ones?"

Ibrahim glared. "I thought you didn't want to start another war."

"Sorry. I couldn't help it."

"My day hasn't begun well and your news doesn't make it any better."

"You're hung up on the China Free Trade Agreement negotiations?"

"Not really. The Gulf Cooperation Council is threatening to derail our talks on ideological grounds. For the Chinese, the equation is simple. They need cheap energy the Gulf states can provide and they don't want to risk upsetting the Arabs for a lousy six billion or so we spend on their imports. What's to get hung up about?"

"Get yourself a tougher negotiator as your point man to handle them. I told you before. Kleiner isn't up to this. He is a good Trade and Industry minister, but he doesn't know how to close a deal."

"It's not him, exactly. The whole thing is a farce," Ibrahim mused with a scowl. "We'll keep trading with the Chinese whether our Arab friends like it or not and everyone knows it."

"And they'll keep selling weapons to people who are trying to wipe us out."

Ibrahim glared. "And that's news? We're doing the same thing, you know. Everybody is. It's just business."

"And posturing, I know. So, if it's not the Chinese, what is it? Iran?"

"What makes me lose sleep is the idea of Pakistan taken over by the Taliban, and all the signs are there that it will be. Can you imagine them, Deobandi Sunnis, in control of nuclear launch codes? I'm not surprised that a predominantly Shi'ia Iran asked North Korea for those warheads. They're worried that one day the Taliban will lob a nuke at Tehran. Not that I'd weep or say this in the Knesset, mind you, if we weren't affected."

"You're telling me their test in the Dasht-e-Lut's southern plateau was a message—"

"Aimed at Pakistan, not us, despite what the General Staff want us to believe."

Sayar shrugged. "The General Staff want to expand the *Tzahal*, even though we don't face a credible threat to warrant an armament buildup. That's nothing new. They always want more tanks, field pieces, planes, and ships."

"I can handle the General Staff, but you've given me a more immediate problem, potentially much more serious. In the short term anyway. You did the expedient thing going after Trotman, but I fear it will only tip the American's hand. This industrialist—"

"Dr. Morrison."

"—must know what he has or he wouldn't have made the bid he did."

"As did the Chinese."

"Ah, our Chinese friends. Little yellow bastards. Haul in their ambassador and tear a strip off him. Tell him I want a formal apology and reparations. Having diplomatic immunity does not give them a license to murder our citizens."

"That won't stop them from going after the crystal."

"Probably not, but that won't be our problem."

"You can't be dense, Sharron. This *is* our problem."

"How?"

"The American State Department will go through the motions and ask Morrison to return the crystal, which he is likely to refuse. He has no reason to give it back. Given its importance, we have to take more positive steps."

Ibrahim stared at the Zionist Union leader, wrestling with the implication of his words as the hairs on the back of his neck prickled.

"You know what you're saying?"

"If the crystal is a genuine quantum computer and we have it, Israel could control the world's IT industry for decades to come, which would give our country an incalculable and badly needed economic boost."

"If we can exploit it."

Sayar shrugged. "There is always that, but we won't know if we cannot study it."

"If we fail, we'll have the U.S. and everybody else mad at us again."

"Even if we succeed, I imagine the U.S. will be mad at us. More so, quite likely."

Ibrahim raised a finger in warning. "I don't want to repeat the angst we endured three years ago. We'd be lynched."

"Sabotaging that Galveston refinery was a rogue Mossad operation. This will be different."

"Because it will be an authorized operation? I doubt President Walters would be overly sympathetic with that interpretation."

"The crystal belongs to us, Sharron. It's our heritage."

"Claiming it's ours would work if Morrison stole it."

"That's lawyer talk and you know it. We have to get it back, and what's more, it's what you want to do."

Ibrahim banged his fist against the desk, making the stationery jump. "Not by creating a diplomatic incident!"

"We let the Americans have it, is that it? Let them reap the benefits? The thing belongs to us!"

"Perhaps it shouldn't belong to anybody." Ibrahim leaned back and crossed his legs. "Fighting Hamas and the Intifada was much simpler."

Sayar smiled. "We've had an interesting three years, all right.

For a while there, I didn't think our shotgun marriage would last."

Ibrahim nodded. When the Valero Texas City Refinery scandal broke, his Kadima-led government faced oblivion. Entering into coalition with Sayar's Labor Party snatched a political victory from the ashes of defeat and staved off serious disruption within the country. He lost the prime minstership to Sayar, but working together, the two parties held enough seats in the Knesset to implement President Walters' demands: creation of a Palestinian state, withdrawal from the West Bank, and abandoning most of the illegal settlements. There were the inevitable marches and protest rallies, but the population at large was tired of waging a street war and welcomed peace on any terms.

Predictably, a number of Kadima and Avoda Knesset members were outraged at the deal forced on Israel by the Americans, as were the ultra-orthodox fringe parties, supported by the right-wing Likud, which resulted in a number of resignations and by-elections. Under Abdon Sayar's skillful management, the coalition survived, but Ibrahim had created too many enemies in his own party for his position to remain tenable and he resigned. This satisfied some, but the Kadima Party was too fractured and no longer a viable electoral entity. To save their political careers the remnants created the Hatnuah centrist party. With Labor, they formed the Zionist Union, saving the government from becoming hostage to the orthodox elements and sliding back into ineffectiveness.

"It lasted long enough to do some good," Ibrahim said moodily.

"When you got ousted, I thought your life in politics was over, but the coup you mounted against Kalman caught everybody flat-footed."

"And you." Ibrahim nodded fondly at the memory. "I was his deputy before I took over the Kadima. Kalman's increasingly radical policies were becoming uncomfortable even for the

Likud. I convinced enough of their members that a coalition with your Zionist Union would ensure stable government, and more importantly, safeguard their seats in the Knesset if I were elected leader. Pragmatism won over ideology, at least with enough of them for me to pull it off."

"It was always dangerous to underestimate you," Sayar said ruefully.

Ibrahim squinted at his deputy. "You wouldn't have shed any tears had I failed."

The foreign minister spread his hands in capitulation. "You lived to fight another day."

"Bastard. Talking about living to fight another day, I heard rumors…"

"Of dissent in my ranks? I face similar dissatisfaction in my party that you had. The morally outraged resigned after Valero, but there are enough diehards who would love to turn back the clock."

"I doubt that will happen. The general elections a year ago gave us a clear mandate and an absolute majority," Ibrahim pointed out. "The people approved the changes and now enjoy a relatively peaceful coexistence with the Palestinians, marginalizing the single-issue parties. Your Avoda diehards can't complain about that."

"They adjusted to the new reality, but they haven't forgiven me for entering into coalition with your Likud party."

Ibrahim looked incredulous. "They want to have policies controlled by the right-wing and ultra-orthodox minority? Those parties helped promulgate the war with the Palestinians."

"Don't worry. I have a solid caucus majority, but I have to be careful how I handle new members and assign portfolios. Come the next elections, the old guard will not be endorsed and they'll be eased out."

"And you'll be the PM again."

"We rotate the office between our parties, that was the agreement. You don't like the arrangement?"

"It's working fine, Abdon, and maintains stability."

Sayar shifted in his seat and bit his lip. "What are you going to do about the crystal?"

Ibrahim's shoulders sagged in resignation. "Life can be a bitch when your options are eliminated. I'll talk to Joakim."

Sayar stood and patted down his jacket. "You're doing the right thing, Sharron."

"Perhaps, but I don't like this. I cannot help feeling that I should call Walters and tell him everything."

Sayar gaped. "You can't be serious!"

"I am perfectly serious. Provoked, there is no telling what he will do. We may have a solid claim on the crystal, I'll grant you that, but once the Americans learn what Morrison has, if they haven't already, they'll want it for themselves, and who can blame them. Talking to Walters might defuse a potentially grave backlash if we fumble our recovery operation."

"How?"

"We enter into a three-way cooperative partnership with Dr. Morrison."

"Would this partnership include the Chinese? When this breaks, and it's bound to, do we cut in the Russians? Why not simply hand it to the UN, or post it on eBay!"

Ibrahim snorted at the absurdity. "Better still, let's smash the thing and give everybody a piece to play with."

"Very amusing. The way to defuse this is to negotiate from strength, and the only way that will work is if we have the thing in our hands. Talking to Walters will leave us with nothing."

"Let me think about it," Ibrahim said heavily, seeing dark clouds on the horizon. Prodding an eagle, one has to be mindful of its claws.

"While we're on the subject, I came across an interesting article in *The Jerusalem Post* by Professor Ezrah Kutner, an academic at the Rockefeller Archaeological Museum," Sayar mused.

"Oh? I didn't know you were into such stuff."

"Keeping an open mind, that's all."

"What made the article so interesting?"

"Remember how the crystal was found? Professor Kutner claims the bones might not be entirely human."

Ibrahim felt a tingle of apprehension run down his spine and the hairs on the back of his neck bristled. "You know what you're saying?"

"I'm not saying anything, only commenting on an interesting article. Don't do anything radical."

"Count on it. Shalom."

Sayar wore a concerned expression as he nodded and walked out.

Ibrahim stared at the closed door, figuring that his friend had cause to be concerned, but Sayar's concern was focused on the wrong objective. If what he'd been told was true, the crystal—without delving into its mysterious origins—represented a revolutionary computing device, but like all revolutions, it also meant blood and upheaval, and Israel had just weathered a major revolution. He doubted the country would survive another. Yet the benefits Sayar alluded to could potentially ameliorate any backlash from the Americans should recovery of the crystal create a major diplomatic incident. Possession does give the holder a strong bargaining positon.

Nevertheless, Ibrahim did not want to underestimate President Walters again, or be humiliated. Vigorous, at the height of power, the young president was reelected with only token Republican opposition. In control of both Houses, Walters would not hesitate to vent his wrath on Israel. This is where Ibrahim feared Sayar had lost focus. A bungled recovery would lead to inevitable finger pointing within the Knesset, which could result in dissolution of an agreement that had survived through some turbulent times. That in turn could fatally fracture the government, allowing emergence of new coalitions where the minor parties held the balance of power again, effectively strangling any progressive policies. Ibrahim would not allow Israel to slide back into the hands of the radical orthodox fringe.

Still, his friend was right about one thing. Negotiating with the device in his hand, he could dictate the terms.

He rocked slowly back and forth and realized that he had no choice. He never had. The crystal belonged to Israel.

Alien bones?

Damn me if it wasn't easier fighting Hamas.

He reached for the white phone and punched a direct dial button on the keypad. Two rings later, Natan Joakim, Mossad's director, answered.

"Good evening, Prime Minister. What can I do for you?"

Chapter Four

The cellphone jangled, sounding unnaturally loud, shattering Morrison's pleasant dream, and scattered the images it made. He jerked awake, momentarily disoriented. Beside him, Juliana mumbled something and turned over. He glanced at the electronic clock display and wished curses on the caller. Groping for the cell, he glared at the displayed name and clamped the cold instrument to his ear.

"Harold, you better have a good reason for doing this to me," he whispered fiercely.

"Sorry for the late call, Kevin."

"It's one goddamn thirty in the morning!"

"You don't have to tell me what time it is. Do you want to hear what I have to say or chew me out?"

"Both. It's Saturday, for Chrissake!"

"I know what day it is."

Morrison swung his legs out of the bed and slid his feet into lined slippers. "Talk while I grab some juice."

"I've been looking at that crystal you sent me—"

"You're at the lab?"

"You wanted to know what it is."

"I didn't mean you had to spend the night at it," Morrison said peevishly, walking into the kitchen lit by an emergency downlight.

"Once I started, I couldn't let it go."

Morrison opened the fridge and hauled out a carton of mixed fruit juice. He admired Ferguson's dedication, but whatever he had to say could have waited until Monday.

"What did you find?"

"Remember what you said that the crystal could be a quantum processor bus? Well, my boy, it seems that's exactly what the thing is."

Still not fully awake, Morrison gulped down some juice straight from the carton, his thoughts scrambling to grapple with what Ferguson told him, the implication hardly believable.

"Give it to me straight."

"The self-repair function has me beat, but I suspect it's performed by internal roaming nanobots."

"Wait a minute. How can nanobots move through a solid object? Movement implies shifting of atoms."

"Quite right. That's what got me beat. I think we've been misled into thinking the thing is a mineral crystal. A natural enough assumption given what you knew about it. With its reflective property, I didn't dare subject the thing to an x-ray, fearing it might damage the internal structure."

"It would be interesting to know if the thing is opaque in the high energy photon ranges," Morrison mused, "but you were wise to be cautious."

"Just protecting your investment. However, low level laser light produced a sufficiently clear diffraction pattern to suggest the object could be composed of quantum dots embedded in a matrix of organic photonic crystals. It's not a fixed solid. As you know, electron-hole pairs in such a structure are confined and the energy levels can be manipulated by laser light. The problem with all such structures is that they suffer from decoherence as quantum dot states are disturbed by the surrounding nuclei. In our attempts to stabilize qubit points, we used complementary QD pairs. The thing you gave me probably has eight QD pairs in a 3D matrix, effectively circumventing decoherence of qubit states. You've heard of Controlled-NOT gates?"

"I know about them."

"Well, your crystal, and I might as well call it that, could be a 3D matrix of quantum dots, each acting as a control qubit."

"A machine of C-NOT gates," Morrison whispered, sleep forgotten.

"C-NOT gates that operate at picosecond speed using single photons emitted by interconnected QDs able to execute multiple simultaneous logic operations. A lot of this is still conjecture on my part, but the tests I ran so far tend to support my hypothesis."

"Harold, all experimental quantum processors I ever heard of look like standard chips. The crystal I gave you is the size of a smartphone! The processing power of such a device—"

"Would be staggering, I know, but I don't think the whole crystal is a quantum computer. A lot of the structure would contain input/output buffers, memory buses, and interface junctions. You would need to couple the device to something capable of feeding it programs and data and extract output. By itself, the thing is a paperweight, to use your quaint terminology."

Morrison pulled back a round stool beside the breakfast bench and sat down, his mind reeling. Absolutely incredible and the possibilities beyond comprehension. He did not believe the Israelis have figured out what the crystal was, but they may have worked out enough of the physics to want it back, and perhaps want it badly enough to use any and all available means. Trotman could be more right than he knew about his warning.

He placed the carton of juice on the bench. "Is there a way to confirm your hypothesis?"

"I'll have to set up specific tests and evaluate the data. This could take a while, as the lab doesn't have the necessary equipment. Tell me, Kevin. Where did this crystal come from?"

"Somebody in Jerusalem dug it up in his backyard."

"Dug it up? But—"

"Who made it, right? An ancient civilization?"

"No ancient civilization I know of had the technology to produce a quantum computer, and further speculation would not be good for my sanity. I'll tell you one thing. I fear the wrath of the gods, my boy."

"What are you talking about?"

"Look what happened to Prometheus when he stole fire from the gods and gave it to mankind. Whoever buried this crystal knew what they were doing. Instead of a boon, you could be holding a key to the gates of chaos."

Morrison frowned. "You're talking like a mystic, not a physicist. What the hell's the matter with you?"

"Simply reflecting on the danger of unleashing a far more dangerous fire."

"Look, I asked you to do an objective analysis, not give me a lecture on metaphysics."

"You're young, and I guess you'll have to learn some things the hard way."

"Remember what you told me when Solaris was just another startup?"

"The critical national industries of the twenty-first century will be energy and information processing. I remember."

"You bent my ear telling me that fossil fuels and nuclear have reached their use-by date and the world needs sustainable alternatives. Thorium reactors will be the next wave, but they have long rollout times. People want cheap, reliable power now, especially those in the Third World. My QD pigment will give them that, and the crystal will give them information processing, allowing us to tackle questions beyond our ability to solve now."

"You have vision and a drive to achieve it, I give you that. I hope it's enough. What do you want me to do?"

"As a scientist, I'd love to study the crystal thoroughly, but that would require putting together a new team. You'd be the logical man to run the group, but I cannot spare you, and you told me what I wanted to know. We have to finish work on the quantum dot pigment first and get a marketable product out. I need more money coming in, Harold, before I get sidetracked by something that's likely to cost heaps to evaluate and may yield nothing for a long time, no matter how exciting its potential prospects."

"Always thinking about dollars and cents, eh?"

"We can't do science if I allow the Solaris share price to slide and my balance sheet goes into the red. You know how these things work."

"Have you considered a joint venture? We could get MIT involved under a nondisclosure agreement. They foot the bill for the research and we cut them in on a piece of the pie. I've done this deal before."

"Mmm. Let me think about it."

"Even if we do have a genuine quantum processor on our hands, it may be impossible to reverse engineer it."

Morrison scratched the stubble on his chin. "That's what I'm saying. I don't want you spending too much time on this, but if the thing behaves like a neural network, why not simply hook it up to an existing interface, pump it full of photons and see what comes out. Work at it from first principles. My home computer is run by some very sophisticated software, but I don't need to understand Windows to run BIOS or DOS commands."

"I haven't considered that, and it's a good suggestion for a proof of concept. Just goes to show you I'm not thinking straight. If we could get the crystal to actually accept instructions and provide meaningful output—"

"We'd have a supercomputer able to solve anything, and a service worth charging a premium for."

Ferguson laughed. "I can hear the cash register clanging already, but like you said, we're a long way from anything like that, my boy, and remember my warning."

"You worry too much. When you're tinkering with it, I don't want you using high-powered lasers, x-rays, or particle irradiation. If the thing is a QD matrix infused with nanobots, exposing it to high energies would scramble it like you said."

"Aren't you glad I didn't run that x-ray?"

Morrison was also glad that Trotman carried the crystal on him when going through airport security. A luggage scanner might be powerful enough to damage the crystal and he could indeed have ended up with a very expensive paperweight.

"When we do get a team on this, you and I will draw up an agreement how this is going to work, and how we'll share papers and any patents we apply for."

"There could be a problem with that, Kevin. We may not be able to file any patents at all, not if the crystal operates on already demonstrated theoretical principles."

"If we can understand how the thing repairs itself, that alone would be worth a patent or two. But we're getting ahead of ourselves. For now, we need to understand how the crystal is put together, which means understanding its structure. Do you know somebody we could bring in to help you run some tests? Under your supervision, of course."

"I'll need to look into that," Ferguson said and paused. "I almost wish I never saw the thing."

"The Pandora's box is already open, Harold."

"And look what she has done to us. Keep one thing in mind. Governments and corporations will do a lot for power, and this crystal represents a lot of power."

"I considered that, and I already spoke to TriCon to beef up surveillance of all Solaris facilities, including your house."

"I wonder if TriCon *can* protect us."

Morrison did not understand why Ferguson was so troubled. Most of his work had military classification or was commercially sensitive. The crystal was simply another item requiring careful handling. Morrison was ready to give the world free power, and he now had an opportunity to give it unparalleled computing power, but he needed firm men around him to do it. He started to wonder if Ferguson had the necessary mettle for this.

"This is no more controversial than our QD pigment."

"And everybody is still after it, you know."

"You're exaggerating the risk."

"I've been doing this shit far longer than you have, my boy. You'll see. Have you considered getting the government involved?"

"The thought had crossed my mind," Morrison said, "but I don't want DARPA or any other predator anywhere near this. I want to guarantee IP ownership before I consider sharing it with somebody."

God, he sounded like one of those unfeeling Wall Street traders!

Ferguson gave a heavy sigh. "Well, if things start getting grim, I can always return to teaching."

"If you want out, Harold, now's the time to say so and there won't be any hard feelings."

"I'm not abandoning you, but that doesn't mean I can't worry a little."

"We'll all worry a little, but trust me. We'll get this thing licked in due time. Get some sleep, and thanks for the call," Morrison said and switched off the cell.

After reaching for the juice carton, he took a couple of long swallows, Ferguson's words still buzzing in his head. Why couldn't the old fool see the bright sparkle of opportunity the crystal represented instead of souring everything with prophecies of doom? He looked up and saw Juliana standing in the doorway hugging her patterned blue silk nightgown.

"Spying on me, my *chère?*" he said with a broad grin.

"I heard you talking. What's going on, Kevin? It's that crystal, isn't it."

"Ferguson ran some tests—"

"In the middle of the night?"

Morrison shrugged. "You know Harold, a one-track mind. Once he gets going, there is no stopping him."

"Good news, bad news?"

"I'll tell you in bed," he said softly and stuffed the carton into the fridge.

Arm around her slim waist, they walked along the polished floor toward the bedroom. Lying on his back, hands locked behind his head, Juliana rested her head on his shoulder, her fingers marching playfully across his chest.

"What's got you spooked?" she demanded, and Morrison realized she was right, partially anyway.

"Not spooked exactly, but I have what perhaps might be the most revolutionary object on the planet. If I could harness its power, it would transform computing as we know it, but as always, there are dark clouds."

"Isn't setting off one revolution enough?" she murmured.

He smiled and brushed a lock of hair off her face. "My quantum dot pigment has some very powerful people trying to stop the project, but it's only because they don't control the technology and won't be reaping the profits. What's more, there are now others who will fight just as hard to get the crystal."

"Why are you worried?"

"Who said I'm worried?"

"I heard you talking to Ferguson."

"You hear too much."

"So, why are you worried?"

Morrison let out a long sigh, gathered her in his arms and held her close. "It's Ferguson. I've let loose a genie and he thinks I should be careful what I wish for."

"He could be right." She lifted her head and looked at him. "You know what they say. When the gods want to punish us, they grant us our wishes."

He stared at her. "I'm surprised you believe such irrational nonsense."

"And you don't?"

"Knowledge, like energy, cannot be destroyed. The crystal represents knowledge and I aim to exploit it fully."

"No matter what the cost?"

"What cost? The little stockholders who'll lose everything if existing computer companies collapse? It'll be a long time before I'll be able to roll out a product based on the crystal's underlying technology. The market will have time to adjust, as will the people."

"You're talking like a hardnosed businessman, Kevin, willing to trample over anybody who stands in your way. While you're pursuing your grand vision, don't forget the human dimension."

"I'm not, but I'm damned if I'll allow the government or some big corporation to steal the thing like they're trying to steal my QD pigment."

"Have you considered defusing the situation? Put an international team on it. That way, everyone gets to benefit and no one is left behind."

Morrison stroked her back. "Always the practical one, my *chère*, but that would not be a solution at all. Everybody would have the results of the research, that's true, but not the means to take advantage of it. Powerful countries with a broad industrial base would be the ones who'd benefit, leaving the small players holding out their hands for any crumbs we'd care to throw their way. If I can work out how the crystal works and replicate the process, I'll make sure the end product is available to all without any strings attached."

"You'd give it away?"

"Not quite, but I need to figure out how to share it without losing control."

"I didn't know you were a humanitarian, Kevin," she murmured.

"Did I surprise you?"

"Not really. I always knew that behind your hard businessman façade stood a kind and considerate man."

"Unfortunately, my little butterfly, the people who'll be coming after the crystal won't take that into account, and they'll come. Because of that, I'm a little worried for all of us."

She stared at him. "You mean, those people could target

you?"

"Not only me, but you, Stan, and Sandra."

Juliana threw an arm across his chest. "It might be better if you simply dropped the thing down the drain."

Morrison chuckled. "Perhaps I should, my *chère*."

"Just don't let this crystal come between us, okay?" she muttered sleepily and suppressed a yawn.

Startled, he heaved himself up on one elbow and gaped at her. "What on earth made you say that?"

She smiled faintly and stroked his cheek. "You have a compelling force that drives you. That same force swept me into your arms, which I never regretted, but like any force, unless controlled, its effects are indiscriminate." She pulled his head toward her and cradled it against her breast. "Your crystal is another indiscriminate force and I fear it might take you from me."

His emotions churned, torn between her thinly veiled concern that the crystal was clouding his judgment, and the rational, calculating part of him that dismissed her words as mere women's sentimentality. He had a possible product to market, the process governed by cold business rules, that was all. Those who stood in his way would be dealt with using those same rules. Determination and drive got him what he had, but he never deliberately trod on others to get it. He bent down and kissed her forehead.

"If you ever see me neglecting you, tell me and I'll drop the thing down the drain there and then."

"Mmm."

After a while, her breathing slowed and she went limp. He kept stroking her back, disturbed by her words. Had he been neglecting her?

He remembered their evening walks along Broadway, pausing to stare at glittering store displays, oblivious to people rushing by, alone in their private universe, her hand locked in his, afraid if he let her go, she'd be swept away in the tidal crowd. She cooed when they paused in front of Petradi Diamonds, pointing at rings, necklaces, and bracelets. That was where he bought her the engagement ring, but he didn't tell her that. He never did. Her radiant smile when he slipped it on her finger was all the reward he needed. He remembered eating hot dogs in Central Park, smeared with rich yellow mustard, onions, and relish. They sailed little boats on the Conservatory Pond, giggling and carrying on like teenagers. There were serene walks in the Carl Schurz Park, allowing the thick silence to envelope them, being close without the need for words, intimate without touching.

It seemed eons ago since they shared such togetherness. He had his world of business, power and ambition, and she wasn't in it. He could not remember when they last had a walk, and the thought disturbed him.

He stared into darkness and allowed his mind to drift. It took him a while before his eyes closed.

* * *

The black Camry switched on its lights, pulled away from the curb, and accelerated down Cleveland Street. Kwang Choi nodded with satisfaction as it turned left into Harvard Street. The two men inside were probably heading for Samba Bar & Grille on the corner of Somerville Avenue. He'd been there himself yesterday, relishing a hot pastrami on rye while scouting the area, mildly wondering what the General would think of him succumbing to decadent indulgence. In the privacy of his opulent office, the General probably allowed himself more than a few indulgences, unconcerned about breaking silly Party rules. Life of a Second Bureau operative on assignment did have its few compensations, and Kwang never hesitated to enjoy them, or worried about rules. As far as he was concerned, only the General made the rules.

Eliminating the parasitic Hong Kong gem dealer was fun, but something of an anticlimax, and the rush wore off too quickly.

149

He preferred a deeper challenge. The hot rice pudding he'd been handed with this assignment definitely a challenge, one that could very well turn out to be terminal. Karma, he thought, giving a mental shrug. So far, everything had fallen into place as planned and he saw no reason why the rest of the operation shouldn't work out as well.

He had watched the Camry for most of the day, working out a pattern of movement by the surveillance team. They had to be surveillance, and the only thing worth watching was Professor Ferguson's residence. A quick check by the consulate of people living in Cleveland Street revealed a mixture of occupants, most of them with unimposing occupations. Two academics worked at Harvard, and they definitely did not rate a protection detail.

The surveillance team appeared to work in shifts of four hours, sometimes parking in front of Ferguson's house, at other times farther down the street, but no more than three houses away, not bothering to mask their presence. Such a blunt approach would deter most intruders, but did nothing to discourage a professional. On the contrary, it made things easier for him. Kwang doubted they had a watcher inside the house, not having seen any strangers enter the premises. For his plan to work, he had to get rid of the team on duty, preferring to do it quickly and cleanly with a bullet in each head, but bodies always complicated an operation and the General was insistent about limiting collateral damage. Not out of squeamishness, but simple tradecraft imperative. Kwang reluctantly admitted that in this case the General was probably right.

By leaving their post, the surveillance team had opened a window of opportunity for Kwang to execute his mission cleanly. If they left to pick up a snack, he had perhaps twenty minutes before they showed up, more than enough time for what he needed to do. He was always suspicious when things appeared too easy, but that did not stop him from taking advantage of an offered break. If his luck held, he could be in Beijing by tomorrow.

Recruited from the elite Snow Leopard Commando Unit as a young lieutenant after serving only two years, he completed his training as a foreign operative at Shanghai's National Intelligence College. They taught him well how to apply Sun Tzu's strategies and tactics, including how to inflict pain to a victim, something he relished. Kwang took quiet satisfaction at the ease with which he outmaneuvered his Western opponents—amateurs really, lacking any finesse. Well, that was okay with him.

Hands on the steering wheel, he turned to the heavyset individual sitting beside him.

"No mistakes, Mr. Payne."

The mercenary smirked, glanced at one of his men in the back seat and they both climbed out. Kwang watched them cross the street and make their way toward Ferguson's modest two-story weatherboard house indistinguishable from other houses along the street, the front porch lit by four dimly glowing globes. The men climbed the steps to the porch and Payne pressed the doorbell button. A few moment later, Ferguson opened the front door and immediately stepped back when the two men showed their guns.

The individual in the back seat grunted. "Piece of cake."

Kwang didn't say anything, ready to spring into action should the surveillance car show up, his eyes scanned the street for something unusual.

Two minutes later, Ferguson walked out, glanced at the burly man behind him, and stepped down to the sidewalk. Kwang switched on the engine and waited for his passengers. Ferguson opened the back door and climbed in, followed by his escort. Kwang immediately steered the Ford Fusion toward the intersection. At the corner, he turned right. Three blocks later, he turned left onto Somerville Avenue and merged into evening traffic. So far, everything had gone as expected. He recalled his tradecraft instructor saying patiently, 'Keep the number of variables to a minimum and your operation should succeed, barring random events, which thorough planning should mitigate.' His experience to date had reinforced that maxim.

"What's this about?" Ferguson demanded, having overcome his shock at being waylaid by two gunmen. "If you're after money—"

"I only want the crystal, Professor," Kwang said mildly in perfect American English. "You cooperate and we'll fade out of your life. On the other hand, if you don't cooperate…"

He did not have to explain why Payne stood guard over the professor's wife. If something went wrong with the ops, the woman would not be harmed, but Ferguson did not have to know that. Kwang had no interest exacting hollow retribution. He liked to make his victims suffer, but this was a simple recovery operation.

"What are you talking about? What crystal?"

"Professor, I know the work you're doing for Dr. Morrison. So, let's cut the blustering, shall we?"

"And you'll simply let me and my wife go?"

"Once we get to your lab, my two colleagues here will take the crystal off your hands and that'll be the end of your unplanned adventure."

Nobody said much during the rest of the trip. Concentrating on his driving, Kwang figured Ferguson wasn't in the mood for small talk. Running down Massachusetts Avenue, he slowed as he reached the MIT complex and turned into the well-lit small parking lot on the corner of Vassar Street. The man next to him immediately stepped out and waited for his partner and Ferguson. Kwang watched the three of them head for Building 41 shrouded by tall trees. Yellow lights hung from concrete poles cast milky pools on the surrounds. An occasional car whispered by, its headlights bright. Several pedestrians were taking advantage of a warm evening to indulge in a stroll. If everything went according to plan, he should be in his apartment by eleven, which suited him just fine.

He wanted to get the crystal himself rather than rely on hired help, and despite checking MIT security, working through possible risk factors, there was always the chance element impossible to anticipate that could derail the seemingly simple operation. One thing he had to avoid at all costs was getting apprehended, providing U.S. authorities a link to China. He would have preferred using consular operatives, but the General wanted to restrict official knowledge of the operation. The three men he hired were professionals, all of them former SEALs and Army Rangers, and he'd used two of them before. They would not compromise him, but even if they talked, all they had was the name Kim and that he looked Asian. The American authorities may have their suspicions, but without proof, that is all they'd have. The concept of a soldier of fortune was not foreign to the Chinese mindset, demonstrating how easily certain types of men could be corrupted by wads of dollars for the opportunity to ply their trade, even to betraying their country. Kwang wasn't moralizing. He understood human nature and used that knowledge to achieve his objective.

He switched to FM 107.5, sat back and allowed tension to seep out of his body as the soothing classical piece washed through him. Having spent three years in America doing covert intelligence—military and commercial—he had developed a taste for Western classical music, among other things, so different from Chinese compositions. The music he'd grown up with had subtlety and played on the listener's moods and passions, but most Westerners found its alien sounds unsettling. The piece he listened to, Mozart's *Eine Kleine Nachtmusik*, had a stirring, direct tempo that was emotionally satisfying. Not everything the West produced was decadent. That could not be said for young artists these days who gyrated almost naked in an attempt to mask their shrill voices devoid of any artistry.

He glanced at his wristwatch: 9:25. A ripple of unease made him switch off the radio. His men should have been out by now.

The sound of approaching police sirens made him frown and he buckled on his seatbelt. Two MIT police cruisers, their red and blue lights flashing, pulled up in front of Building 41 and armed officers rushed toward the entrance. Realizing the mission was blown, he immediately switched on the engine, eased the car into Vassar Street and drove past the cruisers. He dug out his cell-phone, scrolled down the contact list and pressed the direct dial icon.

"Identify," Payne's heavy voice demanded after two rings.

"Kim. Mission abort," Kwang grated and cut contact.

He stopped the Fusion beneath a dark elm, pulled the SIM out of the cell, stepped out of the car and crushed the little chip with the heel of his shoe. Reaching for the plastic bottle of water in a slot behind the gear lever, he placed the cell on the road and soaked it. The device crackled as the circuits fused, effectively scrambling the phone's operating chip. Picking up the cell, he wiped it to remove prints and tossed it down the storm drain.

He got into the car and navigated back onto Massachusetts Avenue, wanting to know what went wrong. Mulling over the possibilities didn't give him any answers and only drained his energy. He crossed Harvard Bridge and headed for Bay Village. His mission potentially compromised beyond retrieval—Morrison would undoubtedly tighten security all around after this—the assignment might not be doable anymore. He would need to review the risks before admitting failure, something he did not want to do.

Sleep did not come easily.

Monday turned out to be sunny, still, and invigorating. The TV weatherman said it would probably rain in the afternoon, but that did not spoil Kwang's morning. After the usual regimen of exercises, a quick shower and light breakfast, he jumped into his car and drove toward the meeting point, the TV news clip about a shooting at MIT forcing from him a grim smile.

Kwang stared absently at moored boats and motor cruisers

tied along Commercial Wharf, an ugly three-story building casting a black shadow across Joe's American Bar & Grill, and downed the last of the cappuccino as he glanced at his watch: 7:55. Throwing down a ten dollar bill, he pushed back the plastic chair with a scrape and strode toward the entrance, ignoring patrons tucking into enormous breakfasts—the sight turning his stomach—others lost in a newspaper or vacantly watched aircraft coming and going from Logan International across the bay.

Outside, a cool breeze ruffled his long black hair. Seagulls perched on black bollards were taking in the sun's warmth. Gentle waves slapped against the boats, making the hulls sway. His nose wrinkled at the rank smell of iodine coming off the water. He strode to the back of Joe's Grill and slowed as he entered the Christopher Columbus Waterfront Park. Spotting Payne's bulky form in the small clearing surrounded by tall trees, he composed himself, preparing his body for action. The Glock G43 9mm with a fitted silencer tucked against his spine forced him to walk without slouching.

Payne straightened as Kwang strode toward him.

"You extracted yourself without difficulty?" Kwang demanded.

"No problem, Mr. Kim. I left the professor's wife tied up and gagged. The surveillance car was there, but nobody saw me when I got out through the side gate."

"They were careless."

"They weren't careless at MIT. I lost two good men last night."

"Ferguson must have tipped them off," Kwang mused, rubbing his chin.

"I don't see how."

"Not important now. You have men for a follow-up mission?"

"How many and for how long?"

"Three, including yourself, for three days."

"Doable."

"I want you all in New York before noon. Find a hotel in Lower Manhattan and call me. We'll have a briefing there at two this afternoon." Kwang extracted a bulky white envelope from his pocket and held it out. "For last night."

Payne took the envelope and allowed himself a small grin. "A pleasure doing business with you, as always."

Kwang nodded, turned and walked quickly out of the park past Joe's Grill and stopped beside his black Ford Fusion parallel parked beside other cars on the wharf. Last night, sipping good vodka, he went over every aspect of his mission and, despite the setback, decided that his original plan was still feasible—with one modification. He would make the target bring the crystal to him. This time, everything had to work out. Failure was not accepta-ble, not with the General.

* * *

Morrison stepped out of the elevator and faced another bank of three elevators running through the building's core. He turned right and marched quickly toward a frosted glass wall with the Solaris Technology logo etched into two door panels. They slid out of his away as he approached.

Joanne looked up from her reception desk workstation and smiled brightly.

"Good morning, Doctor."

He nodded to her and headed for his office. Mouth set in a tight line, he glanced at the open plan bullpens that allowed nat-ural light to stream across the floor, in his opinion, creating a more conducive working atmosphere. Some of his senior staff disagreed and felt they rated a private office. As president and majority stockholder, he had the only office on the floor. He ran a lean organization and looked critically at anyone seeking more staff or special consideration, which in his view only added to administrative overheads and bureaucratic procedures. Besides, offices broke down group cohesiveness, making the environment impersonal and clinical, alienating people.

As Solaris grew, the organizational complexity would invariably grow with it, and would warrant additional staff at all levels. Provided those overheads contributed to core business—research, development, manufacturing and sales—he accepted the need for extra staff. What he did not want to see, as happened to many industries, principal business functions replaced by accountants and legal weenies bent on expanding the bureaucracy, forgetting what contributed to the bottom line, riding on obsolescent products. Most of the time, that led to stagnation, slow decision making, and ultimate decline as more vigorous enterprises captured the marketplace; IBM being a textbook example.

He reminded himself to talk to Moore. As general manager for Solaris' three plants, he should be formulating a sales strategy with Van Rullen, putting together marketing tactics to improve throughput. The solar panels business demanded hard men to prosecute it. Men who knew the business and were not bashful about killing a competitor. Perhaps he should get rid of Van Rullen without waiting for the monthly sales figures. The man simply hadn't been pulling his weight.

Trying to put last night's events into perspective, his gut still twisted at the thought of what could have happened. None of it should have happened if TriCon were on the ball. He paid them a hefty retainer to mitigate such an event and they were looking elsewhere when the shit started. The only thing they got right was giving Ferguson a remote alarm device, enabling them and the MIT police to set up an ambush. Then they screwed up by fatally shooting the two assailants, which left everybody starved of vital information.

What if Ferguson had *not* activated the alarm?

He did not blame his friend for walking away from the project, but the incident highlighted dramatically the dark portents

157

gathering over the crystal. How many others were likely to be killed because of it? Ever since his weighty talk with Juliana, he'd been figuring angles to inject some sanity into the whole thing, if that was even possible. Last night only added urgency that he do something to stop this madness. One thing he would never do though, was give up the crystal.

The sound of his feet absorbed by tightly woven industrial pile, he kept telling himself that he was not morally responsible for those deaths.

At least Ferguson's tests showed the crystal was capable of accepting and processing photon binary bit streams. Without an input/output interface, the results were incoherent, but patterned, showing that logic operations did take place. Lack of an I/O bus might scuttle the whole effort to turn the crystal into something he could analyze more fully. Still, it was early days and he had his proof of concept.

Allison quickly stood up as he approached her open glass-walled cubbyhole. It wasn't exactly an office, but as his personal assistant, she rated more than a desk enclosed with dividers.

"Dr. Morrison, Dr. Ferguson has been trying to reach you."

He did not like how Ferguson fell apart on him at the first sign of trouble. Last night probably wasn't much fun, but the man knew what he got himself into. It wasn't the first time one of his projects became the subject of corporate espionage and some strong-arm handling. Well, what happened was not exactly espionage, Morrison allowed. Anyway, he was off the project, which should have settled his nerves. Morrison hoped the incident would not interfere with his work on the QD pigment.

"Bring me some coffee, then put him through."

He closed the door to his office, walked to the desk and sat down. Soothing sunshine streamed through the floor-to-ceiling window wall. For once, the Manhattan skyline crystal clear, but the weatherman said to expect rain later. Set in a neat pile in front of him were papers Allison had passed on from his plant managers. He scowled as he glanced at a letter from Sleeman. Scheduled completion of the new factory in Hanover threatened by an electrical trade union strike unless Solaris upped the weekend bonus rate, never mind that such a demand was in breach of an agreement entered into before construction began. It was blatant extortion.

Allison came in carrying a carafe. She filled his mug, added cream and sugar, and placed it at his elbow. He shook the letter at her.

"Why am I seeing this? This is Doug Moore's baby."

"Sir, Mr. Moore is down in California for two days."

Morrison frowned. He'd forgotten about the management love-in. If Ethan Joelson could not keep the Sunnyvale plant humming, Moore should be looking for somebody who could. This hand-holding crap from head office had to stop.

"And because of that, I'm supposed to do everything around here?"

Face expressionless, Allison cleared her throat. "Please refer to the attached email, sir."

Feeling stupid, he flipped to the second page and quickly scanned the email Moore sent to Sleeman, which basically quoted chapter and verse of the contract, including the one about invoking penalties for any breach. If the union wanted to strike, he authorized Sleeman to engage contract labor and sue the union for damages. Mollified, he flipped the letter onto the desk.

"Remind Moore to see me about this when he gets back. He should not have allowed the situation to deteriorate to this point," he added peevishly.

"Yes, sir. Dr. Ferguson is on line two."

Watching her walk out, he shook his head. With her executive ability, she should be sitting in his chair. He took a sip of coffee, savoring its warmth, and picked up the phone, his sour mood somewhat pacified.

"Harold?"

"Kevin, thanks for getting back to me. Look, I was quite upset last night and said some things in haste."

"Under the circumstances, an understandable reaction."

"That's kind of you to say so. If you still want me, I'd like to keep working on the crystal. It would be a shame to abandon my tests just when I'm making progress."

Morrison pursed his lips, sorting through his options. "I should have listened when you called on Friday night, but I thought I had all the answers. The crystal's been buried for quite a while. It can remain buried for a little while longer."

"Don't tell me you're walking away?"

"Not exactly, but I'm suspending all research. We need to focus on our business priorities. Solve the problem with the QD emulsion stability factors. Once we have a product we can market, we'll revisit the crystal."

"Makes sense, but the emulsion problem won't be easy to crack."

"You've been working on this for more than three weeks and haven't gotten anywhere. I thought we had the theoretical framework resolved."

"Nothing wrong with the theory, it's the engineering that's driving me nuts. Despite computer modeling telling me it should work, every binding agent I tried degrades the pigment's fill factor and quantum efficiency below expected levels. The pigment doesn't like carrying paint molecules."

"What's the degradation factor?"

"Up to 16%, reducing the overall efficiency to 32%."

"Not good. If we can't roll out a pigment with an efficiency of 45% or better, we're wasting our time."

"I know. Part of the problem is that I can't get more time on the university's Pleiades computer to do more modeling."

"Have you considered using ionic nanoballs to stabilize the emulsion?"

"Ionic nanoballs as a binding agent? That's a creepy idea, Kevin. I would never have thought of it, and it just might work."

"Set up some tests. I want results, Harold."

"I'll crack this one way or another."

"Call me when you have something."

Replacing the receiver, the phone immediately rang and Morrison picked up.

"Yes, Allison?"

"Mr. Lazars from TriCon, sir."

Just the man he wanted to take a strip off. "Right...Mr. Lazars?"

"Good morning Dr. Morrison, although you might not think so."

"I don't. One question, Mr. Lazars. Why did it happen? Dr. Ferguson's residence and his lab were supposed to be under surveillance 24/7. I outlined the risk factors for you."

"A momentary breakdown in procedures, Doctor. The two men on duty were relieved."

"Relieved? They could have gotten my principal researcher and his wife shot!"

"I can only offer my apologies and guarantee that this will not happen again."

"Offer your apologies to Dr. Ferguson and the MIT guard who got wounded. I trust the measures you have in place for my family won't have to test that guarantee, Mr. Lazars."

"I assure you, sir, there will not be a repeat of this embarrassment."

"I hope not. This might escalate and I need to be confident that TriCon can handle it."

"Additional resources were assigned, Doctor. With your permission, I want a man at Solaris offices as additional security. There will not be an extra charge for that."

"Approved. Good day, Mr. Lazars."

He reached for the mug and frowned when the phone's jangle

shattered the momentary silence. What the hell was going on this morning?

Fluffy clouds had started to crawl across the sky and it looked like the forecast might be right for once. Rain would settle the dust and freshen the air for a while before the sun broke through and it became steamy. Well, September was nearly here and things should start to cool down. He sighed, set down the mug and pressed a glowing white button on the phone's keypad.

"Yes, Allison?"

"There is a Mr. Jesse Lipman from the State Department to see you, Doctor."

He blinked and gave a sour smile. The State Department had meddled in his affairs before, worried about technology transfer with his German plant, but the starched shirts usually made an appointment. Something unexpected must have come up for them to send someone unannounced and he suspected he knew the reason. Figuring he'd have to deal with them sometimes...

"How is my schedule?"

"You have forty-five minutes before the sales and budgets meeting. Conference phone links to all plants are on standby. All plant managers, including Mr. Moore, are linked in."

"Good. Show Mr. Lipman in."

A moment later the door opened, admitting a youngish man wearing a dark black pinstripe suit and navy tie. Balding on top, he strode in with confidence many government officials assumed when dealing with the public and Morrison took an instant dislike to him. Just because the weenie was a minor official did not rate him automatic deference. Civil servant did not translate into civil master, which they seemed to forget. Lipman stopped before the desk, dug into his pocket and held out a business card.

"I'm from the local Office of Foreign Missions, Mr. Morrison, and I appreciate you seeing me without notice."

Without looking at it, Morrison took the card and placed it

next to the phone. "Have a seat, Mr. Lipman, and call me Doctor."

The youngster eased himself down and crossed his legs. "I was sent by the Assistant Secretary for Near Eastern Affairs...Doctor. We have a rather delicate situation on our hands..."

"Oh?"

"Our embassy in Tel Aviv received a somewhat unusual request from the Israeli government regarding a topaz crystal you purchased from one of their local gem dealers. Ordinarily, this would not be a matter for the Department, but this case has sensitive international implications."

Morrison held his face expressionless and leaned back against his seat, unmoved by the boy's blunt approach. It hadn't taken the Israelis long to sort things out, but he wondered how much they actually knew and what they passed to the embassy. They would not have revealed a whole lot. It didn't make any difference. The web threads were expanding.

"And what is this request?"

Lipman locked fingers over his lap. "The Israeli government would like to have it back. It appears the crystal, which apparently has significant cultural importance, found its way to a dealer trafficking in illicit artifacts and unfortunately ended up on the underground gem collector's market."

Significant cultural importance? Morrison didn't doubt it.

"I purchased the crystal in a closed auction, that's true, the transaction perfectly legal from a licensed gem dealer. It's not my concern how he got it." He waved a hand at the display case. "As a collector, I thought it would make a fine addition."

Lipman glanced at the cabinet and nodded. "You have some nice specimens there, Doctor, but I don't see the crystal."

"Not everything I have is here. Some specimens are too valuable to be left unguarded."

"Like the crystal?"

"Like the crystal."

"Given the awkward situation, the Israeli government is prepared to compensate you for any expenses incurred if you return the item."

"I appreciate that, but I have no desire to relinquish it."

"I see." Lipman uncrossed his legs and leaned forward, his features stern. "There is something far more serious, Doctor. Something you might not be aware of. The Israelis want to charge Mr. Nolan Trotman with multiple cases of culpable homicide. Our embassy was told that after picking up the crystal, Mr. Trotman shot the gem dealer and one of his shop assistants. Later that afternoon, it appears he may have been involved in another altercation that resulted in the death of a Chinese consular aide."

Morrison raised an eyebrow. Chinese? Where the hell did they come from? He pressed a button on the phone keypad.

"Allison? If Trotman is downstairs, have him come up right away."

"Yes, sir."

"Tell me, Doctor. In what capacity is Mr. Trotman employed by Solaris?"

"He is the firm's management auditor and troubleshooter."

"Troubleshooter?"

"He sorts out procedural and administrative problems that sometimes come up at one of my plants."

"Our records show he is a former Navy SEAL. Unusual background for an accountant, wouldn't you say? Is that all he does for you, clean up bookkeeping errors? Why did you send him to pick up the crystal?"

"I sent him because he is a trusted employee who can take care of himself," Morrison said mildly, not minding this rain dance. It was amusing pulling the youngster's chain.

"It appears, Doctor, your trusted employee may have placed you in some difficulty."

A knock on the door and Trotman walked in, casting a brief

glance at the visitor.

"You wanted to see me, sir?"

"Mr. Lipman here is from the State Department, Nolan. He claims the Israeli government wants to charge you with three counts of murder. They allege you killed Geffen and one of his girls—"

"That's crazy! When I left, Geffen was very much alive, and one of his assistants drove me back to my hotel. That's not something she'd do if I simply shot up the place."

"And the murdered Chinese?" Lipman prompted.

Trotman scowled. "What Chinese?"

"The local police found a dead Chinese consular aide at your hotel," Morrison said, studying his protégé.

"I never saw any Chinese man, and I don't see what that has to do with me," Trotman said and glared at Lipman.

Morrison suppressed a smile. Trotman had handled the evade nicely, telling the literal truth. He had proven himself again to be a major Solaris asset. The whole mess was likely to get exposed in due course, but there was no need to bare his soul to a minor State Department jerk looking to score easy points with his superior.

"Tell me, Mr. Lipman. What is the evidence behind these charges?"

"The Israelis have not provided us with any details. However, the situation is grave enough for the Department to enter into possible extradition proceedings."

Trotman snorted. "Extradition? For what? Picking up the crystal? Tell your embassy to get CCTV footage from Geffen's Dealers. It will show me leaving Mr. Geffen very much alive. As for the dead aide, I have no idea how I can possibly be involved, and I can prove it."

Lipman looked up in surprise. "You can?"

"I was having lunch in the hotel's dining room. Afterward, I spent some time at the bar. Before going back to my room, I was interviewed by a local detective. Hausman, I think. Now I know why. I couldn't have been eating lunch and murdered that Chinese man at the same time."

Lipman clenched his jaws. "We'll look into this further, Doctor."

"You do that."

"Regarding the request by the Israelis—"

Morrison stared hard at Lipman. "Tell them I won't hand over the crystal, cultural curiosity or not."

"Doctor, it's only a mineral specimen. You can always buy yourself another. In the interest of furthering a cordial relationship with a friendly foreign government, the Department would appreciate your cooperation in this matter."

"As you say, Mr. Lipman. It's just a mineral specimen, but one I happen to like. I regret pouring sand into your diplomatic machinery, but I cannot see what cultural importance the Israeli government attaches to the stone."

"It's not up to us to question their motive," Lipman said archly.

"My respects to the Assistant Secretary, but I can't help him."

"The extradition proceedings—"

Morrison slowly rose and placed both palms on the desk. "If I don't cooperate, you'll grant Mr. Trotman's extradition?"

"In the interest of maintaining friendly—"

"You've said enough. Get indictable evidence before you start making hollow threats, and then show me an arrest warrant. Unless you have something else…"

Lipman glared, stood up and nodded stiffly. "You'll be hearing from the Department, Doctor."

"No doubt. I'm sure you can find your way out."

When the door closed after the irritating individual, Morrison sat down and exhaled. "That didn't take long, but I suspect this was only a ranging shot. The next move by the Israelis is not likely to be through diplomatic channels."

"Them or somebody else," Trotman said.

"Mmm. If the man you encountered was from the Chinese consulate, the person who wanted the crystal may be more than an ordinary mineral collector."

"Sir, has Dr. Ferguson figured out what the thing is?"

"What we have Nolan, is a quantum computer, and I was tossing and turning all weekend trying to figure out what to do with it."

Trotman raised both eyebrows. "That's very sophisticated technology to be dug up in somebody's backyard."

Morrison nodded. "Very sophisticated indeed. Before you ask the obvious question, don't. I prefer not to know where it came from or who made it. One thing is certain. I won't give it to the Israelis or anybody else."

"Has TriCon beefed up security?"

"They have two men hovering around Ferguson and his lab—at least they were supposed to—and they've assigned extra personnel to watch the office and our residence."

"May I ask what you intend doing with the crystal?"

"For now, nothing. It's too big to handle piecemeal and I cannot afford to set up a proper research team. Ferguson suggested a joint venture with MIT, and it's something I'm prepared to consider, but not right now. In view of Lipman's visit, I think we need to take extra steps to ensure the crystal's safety." Morrison peered quizzically at Trotman.

"There is another reason why I want the thing secure. Last night, four men tried to snatch the crystal. One held Ferguson's wife hostage while the others drove him to the lab. TriCon's people foiled the operation, but an MIT security guard got shot. He'll pull through."

"And Mrs. Ferguson?"

"After receiving a call on his cell, the man left her bound and gagged and disappeared. MIT police called the local precinct and she was set free."

167

"Where the hell were TriCon's guys while she was held captive?"

"Good question, Nolan. Lazars apologized, but I put him on notice. He's assigning more men on everybody."

"That'll be handy. Anything on the abductors?"

"According to Ferguson, all three were Caucasian, but there was a fourth man who drove the car to MIT and did all the talking. An Asian. Ferguson never got a good look at him, but he sounded American."

"Doesn't mean much. How did they figure out that Dr. Ferguson had the crystal?"

"My research program is in the public domain. It would not have taken much to work out who Ferguson is and what he's doing for me."

"Using information my assailant obtained from Geffen."

"More than likely. To forestall another attempt, I'll remove the object of everybody's temptation. Are you up for another trip to Boston?"

"Of course."

"I'll arrange for one of TriCon's people to meet you when you land at Logan and accompany you to MIT. Get the crystal, bring it back here and take it to JPMorgan Chase on Park Avenue. I'll call Donohue to expect you. The TriCon man will stick with you until the crystal is safely banked." Morrison opened a drawer and took out a key. "For the safety deposit box."

Trotman nodded, pocketed the key and stood up. "Very good, sir. I'll call in when the job is done."

The phone rang and Morrison pressed a button on the pad.

"Sir, an FBI man is here to see you. Something to do with a break-in last night at Dr. Ferguson's lab."

Morrison winced, not totally surprised by the visit. "Show him in." He glanced at Nolan. "Hang around. The FBI wants to talk to me."

Trotman resumed his seat as the door opened.

"Special Agent Earle Fisher, sir."

"Thank you, Allison. A fresh cup, if you please."

"Of course."

The lanky FBI man wearing a dark brown suit and gray tie, black hair combed straight back, clear blue eyes noting everything at a glance, walked to the desk and extended his hand. Morrison stood up and grasped the proffered hand.

"Welcome to Solaris Technology, Mr. Fisher. Please, have a seat."

"Thank you, Doctor. Nice place you've got here."

"May I introduce Nolan Trotman, one of my executive assistants."

"Mr. Trotman…"

"How can I help the FBI?"

"I'm here on behalf of the Boston Office who is looking into last night's attempted break-in at MIT's Building 41, the Fuel Cell Laboratory. Incidentally, I saw Jesse Lipman leaving as I came in. He didn't see me, but it left me wondering why the State Department was interested in you, Doctor. Any connection with last night?"

Morrison exchanged glances with Nolan.

"There might be a connection."

"I see. I understand Professor Ferguson is conducting research into advanced solar energy application for Solaris."

"That's right. We're developing a pigment to extract energy across the sun's spectrum based on the quantum dot theory."

"The factory you're building in Germany is designed to produce this pigment?"

"No. The plant will turn out conventional panels and sheets using our nanograss technology."

"Not so conventional, I understand. You were approached by DARPA to form a joint venture to develop your pigment."

"More than once, and you know that I turned them down. I don't like my research exploited by the military."

"The strategic significance of the pigment would help maintain our national security and competitive advantage."

"DARPA and the DOE will get the pigment once I have it developed, but they will have it under license like any other customer."

"I see. I understand that a Chinese consortium—a government front actually—also made a bid for the pigment."

Morrison nodded. "You seem to have done your homework. You think the break-in was an attempt to steal the pigment's secrets? Now that you mention it, it's more than possible."

"But you don't think so, Doctor?"

"What did Harold tell you?"

Fisher's expression hardened. "Let's dispense with this fencing, Doctor. Ordinarily, the FBI is not interested in an apparent break-in by local thugs looking to steal drugs or chemicals, except that Dr. Ferguson's lab doesn't carry any chemicals. Solaris is at the forefront of strategically vital technology, which foreign interests tried to acquire—"

"As did the U.S. government."

"That's your problem, but when four men attempt to steal sensitive research and two of them get shot, that makes it an FBI problem. Were these men after your research, Doctor?"

"Is the FBI now acting as a front for the Department of Energy, Mr. Fisher?"

"The men shot last night were identified as former Army Rangers. Both were guns for hire...mercenaries. We have some knowledge of this particular group and we're looking into their activities. However, we don't believe snatching Dr. Ferguson was their idea. Mercenaries don't think that way. I ask you again, Doctor. What did those men want?"

Morrison stared at the FBI agent, debating what to tell him. Trying to cover things up would be futile and potentially counterproductive, especially if there were further attempts. He might need the FBI if things escalated.

"The men weren't after my QD pigment, although attempts were made. They wanted to steal a certain crystal that has come into my possession."

"That's not the information Dr. Ferguson provided to the MIT police department."

"He was not in a position to divulge it."

"I see. Tell me, Doctor. Why were these men interested in this crystal?"

"Because it represents technology that could revolutionize computing as we know it."

"A computer using crystals?" Fisher waved a hand. "Never mind. How did you come into possession of the thing?"

"I bought it from an Israeli gem dealer who got it from a man digging up his backyard."

Fisher gaped, then shifted in his seat and cleared his throat. "Are you pulling my leg, Dr. Morrison?"

"I couldn't be more serious."

Fisher bit his lower lip and nodded. "Let's say I believe you. Presumably, the Israelis have figured out what this crystal represents and want it back? Is that why Lipman came here?"

Morrison smiled with genuine warmth, liking how the man connected the dots. "And because the Chinese might be involved."

"Involved how?"

"It's likely that a Chinese consular aide killed the gem dealer and the Israelis want to pin it on Nolan if I don't give them the crystal."

"How did the Chinese come to learn of this crystal?"

"The gem dealer put it up in a closed auction—"

"And one of the collectors figured out what it was and made a bid for it. When you beat him to it, he didn't take no for an answer."

"A likely scenario."

"He must be somebody high up in the food chain to command consular help."

"Probably, which doesn't make my life any easier."

Allison walked in with a cup and saucer. "How do you like your coffee, Mr. Fisher?"

"Black, one sugar, please."

After handing him the cup, she made her way out. Fisher took a sip and nodded in appreciation. "Good coffee." He held the cup and saucer in his lap and looked up. "What does Lipman know about the crystal?"

"Only that it's an Israeli artifact. In view of what happened last night, I dare say I'll be seeing him or somebody else from the Department quite soon."

"And the Israelis, no doubt." Fisher snorted. "I must say, Doctor, you've got yourself a situation. Too bad your TriCon people killed the two men at the lab. I would have liked to hear their side of it. The other two have disappeared. However, knowing the identities of the two dead men, we're hopeful it will lead us to the others. You realize, of course, having failed once, whoever organized last night's snatch might try again."

"I'm taking steps to neutralize future attempts to steal the crystal."

"May I ask what you plan to do?"

"Mr. Trotman will fly to Boston, retrieve the crystal and have it taken to the JPMorgan Chase Park Avenue branch. Anyone looking to pry it loose from there will find it somewhat difficult."

"That won't do anything to neutralize the situation. Whoever wants it won't have to go after it directly. Not when you can simply give it to them…under suitable inducement."

"By taking my wife or me hostage? I'm aware of that possibility. That's why I have TriCon looking after our security."

"They're professional, all right, but that might not be enough. Tell me, Doctor. Is any other government agency aware of the existence of this crystal?"

"Apart from the State Department, you mean? I couldn't possibly tell you, but nobody else has come calling."

"Yet." Fisher gave a fleeting smile. He stood up and placed the cup on the desk. "I have enough information for now, Doctor, but the Bureau will be in touch." He dug out a business card and held it out. "In case you need to call."

Morrison took the card. "It might come in handy."

"Thanks for the coffee," Fisher said and strode toward the door.

When the agent left, Trotman heaved himself up. "Fisher is an interesting man."

"And he might know more than he is telling, is that it?" Morrison said. "The thought had crossed my mind."

"If I may, sir, he was right when he said that securing the crystal will not be a deterrent."

Morrison exhaled loudly. "I know, but it narrows options for whoever wants to take it."

Trotman got up. "I'll be on my way."

Alone, Morrison swiveled his chair and gazed at dark clouds filling the sky. A warning of things to come? Perhaps he *should* get rid of the crystal. He understood the negative economic impact an advanced quantum computer could unleash if released suddenly, he faced the same dilemma with his QD pigment. He may be underestimating the international dimension and the price Israel and China might be prepared to pay to get the crystal. No, he understood, all right, but he had treated this like a chess game, an intellectual exercise. He wondered how many people got Geffen's email and who else would come knocking on his door.

They can knock, but after last night, he was determined to make the crystal work, and nothing was going to stand in his way.

The business world laughed at him when he switched production from advanced silicon-based PV panels to untried nanograss sheets, but no one laughed now. Solaris had carved out a respect-able market niche and his competitors were sitting up, taking no-tice. When he announced development of his QD pigment, it set off a ripple of consternation across the industry and takeover bids started coming in. Well, when the world learns about his crystal, it would generate more than just consternation, and he would be the one controlling it.

Juliana's words echoed in his mind.

Chapter Five

The US Airways Airbus A319 shuttle landed with a crunch and reversed thrust, pressing Trotman against the seat. The narrow-body jet slowed and turned onto a taxiway, which gave him a glimpse of Logan International's sprawl of terminals surrounded by parked aircraft. The flight from LaGuardia took forty minutes, but getting to the airport and clearing security, the whole trip consumed almost two hours. His New York return flight wasn't until 14:00, which should give him plenty of time to get the job done. Actual flying did not wear him down. It was the hassles in between and the sheer tedium waiting to board. He often wondered whether it would be quicker driving to Boston. Considering the traffic along the way, perhaps not.

The aircraft pulled into the Terminal B south building, his business class seat allowed him to exit quickly, beating the crush of coach passengers. In the arrival/departure lounge, people were already standing at gates waiting to board, most of them wearing business suits, some clutching briefcases for moral support. Those fortunate to get a plastic seat buried themselves in newspapers studying the financial pages or pounded away on laptops. A pleasant female voice announced boarding of US Airways Flight 2159 for Washington DC at Gate B19, and would all passengers please have their boarding pass ready for inspection. A scramble followed the announcement and a gaggle formed at the entry counter, most wearing mixed expressions, wishing they were already there.

"Mr. Trotman?" a heavy voice inquired and Trotman turned. The tall young man sported a marine crewcut, wide shoulders, narrow waist an ad for any gym, which his light gray suit couldn't hide. He smiled and extended his hand. "Shaun Kogan, TriCon."

"Glad to meet you," Trotman said as they shook hands, the kid's grasp hard and dry. "You don't look like your picture."

"Better or worse?"

"Better."

Kogan chuckled. "Your picture doesn't do you justice either, sir."

"Since we'll be glued to each other for the duration, call me Nolan."

"Suits me. Do you have any luggage?"

"Only you," Trotman said wryly and the youngster laughed.

"I know the feeling."

After navigating their way through the crowd, they exited the terminal and confronted cars, cabs, and buses lining the approach road, and a wave of hot air laced with humidity. Harried cops blew whistles and waved arms at double-parked cars to move off. A jet took off with a roar and the air trembled, heavy with the stink of avgas, diesel, and petrol fumes. Kogan walked to a dark red Chrysler 300 parked under a blue Reserved sign. Trotman was surprised to see a driver. His young minder opened the back door for him and climbed in after him. The driver started the engine and pulled the heavy car away.

"That's Mike," Kogan told him.

"Nice to meet you, Mr. Trotman," the driver said with a nod.

As Trotman buckled up, Kogan took out two slim semiautomatics from the door's side pocket and held one out.

"Just in case," he said with a straight face as he slipped his under the jacket.

Trotman stared at the weapon, not wanting to touch it. It all came flooding back. Men clad in black brandishing Kalashnikovs spraying bullets everywhere. His men falling around him as he stood under the cloak of night, his Heckler & Koch UMP mowing down the attackers, mixed with fire from his team. Then it was all over and silence swallowed everything. Seeing blood flowing down his left side, he realized he'd been shot and the pain hit. He stumbled and found himself face down in the warm sand. They put him together again, but they never managed to find all the emotional pieces, leaving gaping holes he still sought to fill. All things considered, they had not done a bad job.

He pushed back the memories, bit his lip and took the gun, checked the slide, chambered a round, flicked on the safety, and tucked the weapon behind his back, relieved to see TriCon taking this seriously, but not necessarily this seriously. Carrying hardware implied they might need to use it, which kind of spoiled an otherwise nice day. It came with the territory, but he wondered if he could still handle it, the incident in Tel Aviv fresh in his mind.

They drove through Sumner Tunnel and turned right onto expressway 93 North following a stream of traffic heading for downtown Boston. The airconditioner whispered in the background. They took the second exit to Storrow Drive and followed the canal to Harvard Bridge, turning right onto Massachusetts Avenue. Trotman didn't say anything along the way, letting his mind wander, thinking about a missed lunch, noting how Mike kept glancing at the rearview mirror from time to time. Probably checking if they picked up a tail, which increased his confidence in TriCon's professionalism. Of course, real pros would not be caught out committing such a simple gag. Still, it was all part of tradecraft, even if sometimes it didn't make any sense. Just a game…however deadly.

They parked in front of Building 41 guarded by a thick stand of trees and got out. Mike stood beside the car at parade rest looking at traffic and passersby. Cars cruised along the narrow street in both directions. Inside the Fuel Cell Laboratory, Trotman approached the security counter guarding two electronic access portals.

"Please notify Professor Ferguson that Nolan Trotman is

here."

The security guard's fingers flew over the keyboard. He nodded and looked up.

"Can I see some ID, please?"

Trotman pulled out his Solaris access card and held it out. The guard matched faces and reached for the phone. "Professor Ferguson? Security desk, Doc. A Mr. Trotman...right." The guard replaced the receiver. "The Professor will be down shortly."

Trotman stepped away from the counter and scrutinized people leaving and entering the building, ID tags pinned to their clothing. Most were young males and females, probably students. The older ones were doubtless faculty staff or technicians. Nobody gave him or Kogan a glance.

"Ah, Nolan, good to see you again!" Ferguson boomed as he exited the security portal. Dressed in a white lab coat, pens crowding the breast pocket, the large man exuded a jovial attitude.

"How are you, Professor?" Trotman asked as they shook hands.

"Glad to have this thing off my hands, my boy," Ferguson said and held up a small metal box the size of a lunch pail. "It's all yours. I don't like the excitement that seems to follow it."

"I heard about last night," Trotman said as he took the box.

He opened it and lifted the familiar red jewel case from its foam lining. He slowly raised the lid and peered at the enigmatic pale orange crystal looking so innocent sitting on a bed of white velvet. He snapped the lid and placed the case into the metal box.

"We're locking it up. That should stop the excitement."

"I doubt it somehow, but I'm just a rambling old man. Give my regards to Kevin." He shook his head, turned, and swiped his badge against the access portal's sensor. The thing gave a beep and a red panel turned green.

Watching the elderly professor stomp down the wide corridor, Trotman smiled, not doubting Ferguson's sincerity to rid himself of the crystal. He glanced at Kogan and nodded.

"We got what we came for."

"What did he mean about excitement?"

"Certain people have been after what's in this box. Long story."

"And it's none of my business. Right, we better get going, then. I want to grab a snack at the airport before we lift."

That suited Trotman just fine. Outside, he froze when two men in dark blue suits got out of a black GMC Yukon SUV parked behind the Chrysler leaving the doors open and walked toward him. Both had short cropped hair, serious faces, and exuded a readiness to explode into instant action. Senses alert, Trotman recognized the type and wondered whose side they were on.

The leading suit reached into his jacket pocket, extracted an ID wallet and flipped it open showing a gold badge. Several passersby stopped to watch the development.

"Special Agent Lester, Diplomatic Security Service. I'll take that box, Mr. Trotman."

After an initial jolt of adrenalin, Trotman scowled. They must have tailed the Chrysler to appear on the scene so conveniently, but why wait for him? They could have waylaid Ferguson without bothering with street dramatics, a much smarter move.

"Did that shit Lipman send you after me?"

"Our instructions came from the Assistant Secretary of State. You're charged with possession of stolen goods belonging to a foreign country and three counts of culpable homicide."

Lester's steely eyes gave nothing away, but Trotman sensed a wariness that went beyond confronting a target. This didn't smell right.

"Show me your arrest warrant."

"We hoped you would cooperate without the need—"

"Without a warrant, Agent Lester, you have no authority to detain me or remove any item in my possession."

"All we want is the box."

Trotman turned to Kogan. "Let's get out of here."

Lester reached into his jacket and pulled out a semiautomatic. "Hold it right there!"

Someone screamed and the onlookers immediately scattered, diving for the sidewalk or crouched behind trees.

Mike whipped out his gun and leveled it at Lester. "Drop it," he snarled.

The second blue suit drew his weapon and shot Mike in the chest, flinging the lithe man against the Chrysler. Without hesitating, Kogan pulled out his piece and squeezed off a shot. The blue suit yelped and clutched at his upper right arm, the gun clattering into the gutter. The sharp cracks generated more screams. His reaction on automatic, Trotman tossed the metal box at Lester and clawed for his gun. Not expecting this, Lester instinctively grabbed it with both hands, allowing Trotman time to level his weapon.

"Put the box down, nice and easy," he grated, finger tight on the trigger, fighting to keep his breathing even.

"I am a federal law officer, Mr. Trotman. Don't make this any more difficult than it already is," Lester hissed.

"You're the one making it difficult, Mister. The box."

Mouth set in a tight line, Lester slowly crouched and placed the box on the sidewalk.

"And the gun."

Lester dropped the hardware, stood up and shifted his left foot forward.

"If you move again, I'll shoot you," Trotman said. "Relax until the police get here and we'll check your pedigree."

He saw the Yukon driver reach for the door handle, then froze as Kogan traversed his gun at him. The momentary distraction enough for Lester to take a step and lash out with his right leg. Trotman felt a stab of pain in his wrist and his gun went flying. Reacting instinctively, he sent his foot crashing into the agent's chest and Lester's arms flailed as he staggered back. Trotman lunged at him and they both fell, Lester's head making a dull thump as it struck the sidewalk. The agent Kogan shot dove into the Yukon and the SUV immediately pulled from the curb. It screeched up the street leaving a trail of stinking black rubber.

Kogan lowered his gun and swore softly.

Trotman stood up and looked down at Lester, but the agent was out of it. He retrieved his gun and slid it behind his back. He massaged his wrist and exhaled loudly, surprised to find himself calm and unmoved. He was also surprised to see Mike picking himself up apparently unharmed.

"Bulletproof vest," he said as he rubbed his chest. "Rough neighborhood."

"I got the Yukon's license plate," Kogan said brightly.

Seeing the action was over, people slowly started getting up, glancing around uncertainly as if expecting more bullets to start flying as they dusted themselves off.

"Hold it right there!" a voice bellowed behind him and Trotman turned. The building's security guard stood crouched, holding his revolver in a two-handed grip. "Drop 'em."

The crowd ran for cover again.

"We're the good guys here," Trotman said peevishly, reaction setting in.

Another security guard came running, weapon held ready. "What happened here, Marty?"

"Beats me, Fred. I heard shooting. By the time I called the police and came out, it was all over."

Trotman took a step forward and retrieved the metal box. "They were after this."

"And what is that?" Fred demanded as his arm came down.

"Property of Solaris Technology. We just picked it up from Professor Ferguson."

"That's right, Fred. I was there," Marty confirmed.

The crowd slowly moved in again, waiting curiously to see

what would happen next.

Sirens wailed coming closer and Trotman sighed. This would take some explaining, and he did not relish what was about to happen. Two white cruisers with MIT Police logos plastered on their side pulled behind and next to the Chrysler, their blue and red lights flickering. Officers in black uniforms piled out, revolvers held ready, looking eager to shoot somebody. Seeing that nobody moved, they slowly lowered their hardware.

A burly black man wearing a gray suit holstered his weapon and approached the two security guards.

"Fred…Marty. What's going on here?"

Trotman stepped forward. "My name is Nolan Trotman, Detective. My colleague and I were picking up an item inside the lab when two men claiming to be Diplomatic Security Service agents got out of a black GMC Yukon SUV and started shooting at us."

"It's Lieutenant." The man gave him an appraising stare, then glanced at Lester's sprawled form. "And him?"

"He wouldn't take no for an answer."

"I see." The lieutenant scowled when he saw the two semiautomatics still lying on the sidewalk and pointed at one of the uniformed cops. "Evidence bags, and call an ambulance to have that guy checked out. Then we'll have a talk with him." His hard eyes turned on Trotman. "I don't see any Yukon SUV."

"It took off when Mr. Trotman tackled Lester," Kogan said easily, seemingly enjoying the whole incident.

"And you are?" the lieutenant demanded.

Kogan pulled out his wallet and held it out. "TriCon Security, Lieutenant."

"TriCon, eh? I heard of you guys. And you, Mr. Trotman? You're also TriCon?"

"Solaris Technology."

"The man picking up the item. Must be something damn important to cause all this fuss."

"Call Special Agent Earle Fisher at FBI's New York office.

He'll explain the whole thing to you."

"And why should I want his explanation when I have you right here to explain things for me?"

"Because this is a federal matter and you have no jurisdiction. We acted in self-defense—"

"We saw the whole thing, officer!" somebody shouted and others joined in. "The men jumped out of the Yukon and started spraying bullets."

Traffic had slowed as drivers gawked at the packed onlookers, police cruisers, and armed cops. Two officers strode briskly onto the road and shouted at drivers to move on.

Trotman dug out a business card from his breast pocket and held it out. "This has my number if you want to call. Now, if you don't mind, I have a flight to catch."

"Not so fast," the lieutenant grated as he took the card and frowned. He hauled out a cellphone and, after a clipped conversation, slowly nodded. "Fisher confirms your story, Mr. Trotman. Since this is an FBI case, I can't hold you, but you have a lot of explaining to do to somebody."

"I am sure of that, Lieutenant. Now, can you have someone move your car out of the way?"

Kogan scribbled on the back of his business card and held it out. "The Yukon's license plate, Lieutenant."

The cop glowered, pocketed the card, and barked an order. One of the officers reversed the police cruiser, which enabled the Chrysler to get out. Kogan held the back door open for Trotman and they clambered in. The heavy car immediately pulled away from the curb and headed for the Massachusetts Avenue intersection.

"I thought the clown was going to bundle us away," Kogan remarked brightly.

Trotman ground his teeth. "I want to get hold of Lipman and bundle *him* away!"

"Who is Lipman?"

"A jerk from the New York State Department office who may have arranged this reception."

"I'm not sure I like him. That Lester guy…government agents don't usually come at you with drawn guns."

"Yeah," Trotman said and dragged out his cellphone.

"Calling your boss?" Kogan asked.

"He needs to know what happened."

"Sound like a hardass to me."

Trotman didn't bother to comment. In many ways, Dr. Morrison *was* a hardass, but he figured the business he was in demanded a tough executive. Shareholders wanted a solid return on their investment, not a nice guy who ran the company into the ground. His boss did have a human side though, having given him and Vivian a luxury apartment at 95 Wall Street, the same building where the Morrisons lived. He also paid for his little girl's schooling at Lehman Manhattan Upper School, one of the most prestigious New York private schools. Growing up in sky-scraper canyons was a terrible environment for a girl who needed to see wild flowers, trees, animals, and running water, but Petra seemed well adjusted.

Trotman was not the only one to benefit from Morrison's largesse. According to the office grapevine, at least four other employees were equally well taken care of. When Trotman asked his boss why he was doing this, the doctor merely laughed, saying it was all tax deductible. Perhaps, but Trotman did not believe Morrison was in it to minimize his tax liability or buy loyalty. Whatever the reason, he was prepared to do almost anything the boss asked of him.

"Allison, if Dr. Morrison is available, I have to talk to him."

"One moment…putting you through."

"What happened, Nolan?" Morrison demanded harshly.

Trotman blinked, always taken aback by how swiftly his boss connected small bits of data. Knowing he must still be in Boston, the call meant a problem.

"After I picked up the crystal, we were confronted by agents from the Diplomatic Security Service. At least that's what they claimed to be. Shots were exchanged and one of their men was wounded. I disabled one and the MIT police have him in custody. The lieutenant in charge let us go after I suggested he talk to Fisher. I'm on my way to the airport."

"The crystal—"

"Is safe."

"Thanks for the heads-up, Nolan. See me when you get back. I want to get a full story on this."

"Yes, sir."

He pocketed the cell, exhaled loudly and leaned back against the seat. Holding the box in his lap, he listened to the purr of the engine and traffic noises outside.

* * *

Mouth pursed, Morrison cradled the phone and stood up. What the hell was going on today! Did he lose objectivity, his preoccupation with the damned crystal turning into an obsession? He did not think he was obsessed, but people who were after it certainly seemed to be.

Controlling his breathing, he stood before the ceiling-high window wall with hands clasped behind his back and gazed absently at Manhattan's bleak skyline. Soft, misty rain shrouded the concrete and steel towers, blurring outlines. In the east, broken clouds allowed shafts of golden light to stream through.

Instead of being carried away by emotion, reacting to developments, he needed to insert some methodology into the situation. He calmed down and began working the scenarios.

Trotman said the men were Diplomatic Security Service agents, an arm of the State Department. It looked like Lipman hadn't wasted any time trying to recover the crystal, relying on his men to overawe Trotman. He was not surprised the gambit hadn't worked. His protégé knew how to handle himself and the State Department weenie had underestimated his opposition. Always fatal in any confrontation, but what happened to Trotman was nothing short of blatant assault.

On the other hand, it might not be Lipman at all, and he doubted the State Department would have taken such drastic action merely to recover a mineral specimen, no matter how peeved off at being thwarted. They were bound by the rule of law. Weren't they? How much did they actually know?

Lipman said the crystal had cultural significance, a nice play on words. If that was all the Israelis told the American ambassador, it did not make sense for Lipman to send his goon squad to recover an ordinary rock. Why would they follow Trotman to MIT? They could not possibly know he was going there to pick up the crystal. Trotman could have gone there for any number of genuine business reasons.

The only person who knew everything was Earle Fisher. The thought of Fisher colluding with Lipman simply didn't wash. If the FBI wanted the crystal, they could have obtained a warrant and gotten the thing themselves. The problem Fisher had, there were no legal grounds to issue a warrant. Trotman said there was a shootout, which could mean Lipman's men may not have had a warrant either. Even if they did have one, it's unlikely Trotman would have handed over the crystal simply because someone asked for it.

Morrison pushed the pieces around, but they refused to form a coherent picture.

Anyway, the FBI would sort out who those men really were.

He scowled, strode to his desk and sat down. He picked up Fisher's card and dialed.

"Special Agent Earle Fisher."

"This is Dr. Morrison."

"Ah, Doctor, you were the next man I was about to call."

"We have a meeting of minds, then."

Fisher sighed. "You were told about the incident in Boston?"

"Trotman called me a few minutes ago."

"The MIT police are very unhappy, Doc, and so is my boss. However, he became less unhappy when I told him the State Department denied any knowledge of the incident."

"You spoke to Lipman?"

"I spoke to Lipman. Of course, he could be lying, but I don't think so. He is an officious weasel. Men like him prefer to exercise the government apparatus to get what they want. Employing a Diplomatic Security Service detail to do his mopping up is not something that would occur to him. Besides, he doesn't have the authority."

"But you do, Mr. Fisher, and you knew why Nolan went to Boston."

"If I wanted the crystal, Dr. Morrison, I would not be hiding behind another agency's skirts. I'd be in your face."

"That was my conclusion," Morrison said softly. For a few moments, he heard nothing.

"You figured it out, eh?" Fisher said at last. "The FBI took the man Mr. Trotman disabled into custody and we'll check his legitimacy."

"Whoever waited for Nolan knew exactly why he was there. Lipman certainly did not and had no legitimate reason to tail him."

"You believe the people who tried last night made another attempt?"

"It's possible, and it's also possible that we may have a new set of players joining the game."

"We'll talk to our guest and do some sifting. A useful grain may remain after we get rid of the chaff. We did establish one thing, or the MIT police did. The license plate number your Tri-Con man gave them belonged to a stolen car. It doesn't look like those men were Diplomatic Security Service agents after all."

"Presumably, you'll be following this up with the CIA?"

"Have you considered joining the Bureau? We could use a man like you."

Morrison laughed, amused at the thought. "In another incarnation perhaps. I want to thank you for running interference for Nolan with the local authorities."

"The MIT police chief had a few things to say, but the FBI had clear jurisdiction, although it wasn't all that clear to him. Given that we have one of the assailants, my boss will now be less inclined to fire my ass. Was there anything else, Doctor?"

"There is. Can you arrange for a couple of men to meet Nolan when he lands at LaGuardia and escort him to JPMorgan Chase? I would prefer the FBI waiting for him than some third party."

"Mmm. I'll need to bounce this with my boss."

"I'll have my assistant call you and give you the flight details."

"Given the trouble this crystal has caused everybody, Doc, perhaps you should drop it down the drain."

"You know, my wife suggested I do exactly that."

"Sounds like a wise woman."

Morrison slowly nodded. Juliana *was* a wise woman, he decided, and maybe he should follow her advice. If it were anything else, he would consider it, but he was not ready to give up the crystal just yet. Not after spending $400K to get it. Whoever wanted it would have to fight him for it, no matter what the cost. He had never shied away from a challenge and was not about to start now.

"I do have one more request."

"Oh?"

"The people who attempted to snatch the crystal today and last night might try again."

"This time targeting you or one of your family? It's a predictable gambit we already discussed—"

"But one that could still work."

"I thought you said TriCon Security looked after you."

"They are, but that might not be enough."

"Leave it with me and I'll see what I can do. By the way, may I ask what security measures you have in your office?"

"TriCon has a man on my floor and they've installed a panic button under my desk."

"I hope you don't have to use it. I'll be in touch," Fisher said and cut contact.

Morrison replaced the receiver and sat back. What if Stanly were taken and he got a call to hand over the crystal or else? In the movies they always got the bad guy, but what they didn't say, in the majority of real life cases the hostage was usually found dead. A cold prickle ran down his spine and he gave an involuntary shudder. It might be a good idea to make his son take a vacation somewhere until things calmed down. A graduation present from his old man. The boy didn't need to know about the crystal—unless Ferguson already told him, which was possible. That left Sandra. She and her husband had careers and would demand to know why he wanted them to uproot for a couple of weeks or so. Even if Fisher arranged something, could he rely on TriCon and the FBI to protect his family? Did he want to find out the hard way?

However unpalatable, he may be forced to hand over the crystal to the government. It wasn't worth seeing his family harmed because of it.

Patches of blue showed through broken cloud and sunlight streamed across Manhattan.

The phone jangled and he pressed the speaker button. "Yes, Allison?"

"Mr. Crawford from the Department of Energy to see you, Doctor."

He furrowed his brow, not sure he wanted to spoil his day further. He'd met the DOE's Office of Intelligence and Counterintelligence ferret before and neither enjoyed the experience. He wondered how many times he had to say no before the government got the hint. First, DARPA got nosy about his QD pigment, then the Defense Security Cooperation Agency started making intimidating noises if he didn't come across, hinting he did not have the interest of his country at heart, which cracked him up. Seeing they weren't getting anywhere, he suspected they loosed Crawford on him as another gambit, although the DOE denied all knowledge that they were pursuing him. Senior officials might not be aware of what went on, but knowing how these agencies worked when upset, Morrison didn't believe it. The IRS investigation that followed soon after a nuisance, but they walked away empty-handed.

"You can tell him he's wasting his time. I'm not giving him the pigment."

"Ah, he is not here about the pigment, sir."

He didn't want to see the obnoxious pest, but it could give him an opportunity to be rude.

"I'll give him five minutes."

The door opened and Allison ushered in the small bald individual carrying a slim black briefcase. Crawford carried his rotund bulk like a bulldozer carving through anything standing in his way. His round face, jowls drooping, appeared congenial, until one looked at his small, piercing brown eyes buried in cavernous sockets. They were chips of ice devoid of any human warmth. The man had never learned to accept a setback and Morrison's refusal to cave in made him an enemy.

"Dr. Morrison…" Crawford grated sonorously, exhaling with a wheeze. "Thank you for seeing me."

Morrison's eyes opened wider. The DOE weenie had never shown any courtesy before, which immediately set his alarms clanging. Was this a softening up tactic before steamrolling over his victim?

"Please sit down, Mr. Crawford. My time is rather limited—"

"You may want to give me more than five minutes once you see what I have," Crawford said comfortably as he sat down, placing the briefcase on his lap.

"Oh?"

"By the way, I want to extend my congratulations to your son for getting his master's. You plan to keep him at your Bedford plant?"

Morrison carefully digested what he'd heard, not liking any aspect of it. Why would the DOE want to spy on Stanly? A psychological prelude to another assault on his pigment?

"Please come to the point, Mr. Crawford."

"Very well."

Crawford opened the case, held up a small, flat blue plastic box and slid it across the desk.

"Take a look." A faint smile of satisfaction creased his corpulent face as Morrison stared at the box.

Wary of a possible trick, he flipped open the lid and peered at a piece of broken orange crystal encased in white foam. He felt blood drain from his face and his mouth went suddenly dry. For a wild moment, he thought it was his, that Crawford had somehow managed to pry it loose from Trotman, breaking it along the way. Realizing how absurd the idea sounded, he let out a slow breath. This specimen roughly two-thirds the size of the original, the broken end looked clean like it was made yesterday. Morrison swallowed hard, licked his lips and closed the box.

"Where did you get this?" he rasped, fighting for control.

Logically, he should have expected something like this. With one crystal, a strong possibility existed that there could be another. The assumption did not necessarily mean it was true. In this case, however, logic seems to have prevailed.

"The same place you got yours, Doctor. From an antiquities dealer. Except ours lived in Cusco, Peru, purchased sixteen years ago. That one crystal should be in Cusco and another in Jerusalem makes for an interesting discussion in itself, don't you think?"

It certainly did, and Morrison had entertained some of the

more outlandish possibilities as mental forays. He collected himself and cleared his throat.

"As an ordinary mineral specimen—"

Crawford winced and raised a hand. "Please, Doctor. Even if your startled reaction hadn't given you away, we know all about your quantum processor device and how you got it."

Several things fell into place. Glaring, Morrison jabbed a finger at him. "*You* sent your goons to ambush Trotman?"

Crawford looked genuinely surprised. "I beg your pardon?"

"I sent Trotman to MIT to collect my crystal and he was waylaid by persons claiming to be Diplomatic Security Service agents."

"Dr. Morrison, I give you my word. The DOE knows nothing of this. It could be the Israelis. They do have an interest, you know."

Mollified, Morrison nodded, inclined to believe him. "It's possible, and the matter is being looked into."

"Yes, the FBI investigation should clear things up."

"How—"

"You are a person of interest, Doctor. More so now than ever and we have our contacts."

"Tell me, Mr. Crawford, how did you find out about my device?"

Crawford's mouth twitched. "Our office specializes in the unusual. Sixteen years ago, one of our employees picked up a crystal at a local bazaar. He was a small-time collector like you and thought it looked interesting enough to buy. Unfortunately, he didn't take good care of his purchase, and in the course of his travels, he broke it. Given what it is, that was most regrettable," he said and glanced at his watch. "My five minutes seem to be up."

Morrison laughed, developing a degree of reluctant admiration for the man's stalking approach.

"You got yourself an extension."

"I thought I might. Anyway, about two years ago, while messing with his mineral collection, he scratched the crystal. After fifteen minutes...well, I don't have to explain his reaction. Even though the thing was broken, the self-repair function was not totally disabled. He brought it in and we've been trying to figure out the device ever since. We understand it's a quantum processor of some kind, but broken, the most we could get out of it was random signal noise.

"We examined a minute shard under a tunneling electron microscope to try and understand the repair mechanism, and found molecular structures that were some type of nanobots, which I suspect you already know. Unfortunately, the scanning electron beam appeared to deactivate them. An attempt to x-ray another piece did the same thing." Crawford gave a thin wheeze. "We were more careful after that, but it severely limited what we could do. As to how the crystal's C-NOT gates matrix was fabricated is a complete mystery. It could have been constructed atom by atom in a lattice or grown organically. As you're aware, the thing is not a mineral in the conventional sense. However it was done is beyond any technology we have today or are likely to have for a long time to come."

Morrison understood that irradiating a broken crystal would damage it, but he still suspected that an intact device should be impervious to high energy radiation to protect its internal functions. The laser mirror image he got from Geffen suggested this. He was not prepared to run a test though, merely to prove himself wrong.

"What happened to the other piece?"

"Our man has it in his private collection."

"A lot to think about isn't there, but you still haven't told me how you found out about my crystal."

"As I said, Doctor, we specialize in the unusual, and the device we had definitely belongs in that category. Once we discovered its properties, we undertook an extensive search program to procure another specimen, preferably whole. Unfortunately, information about Geffen's closed auction surfaced too late for us to put in a bid. Before you ask how we know all this—"

"You don't have to tell me," Morrison said dryly. "NSA spied on the world long before it got around to spying on American citizens."

"Not guilty this time, although they do advise us on developments pertinent to our activities. No, this was purely an internal bungle."

Morrison had a startling thought. "The other piece—"

"Before you ask the obvious, we tried to fuse them. Without success, of course. Otherwise, I wouldn't be here."

"I see. Now that you know about my specimen, you don't expect me to simply hand it over in a gush of patriotic fervor, do you?"

Crawford's eyes glittered. "We attempted that with your pigment, remember? It didn't work. I doubt it would work with the crystal."

"Damn right. If you're planning to threaten me with another IRS investigation, go ahead."

"No, I'm not here to threaten you, Doctor. Our Israeli and Chinese friends will probably take care of that. I would hate it if they succeeded, hence my reason for seeing you. As a businessman, I appreciate the commercial possibilities inherent in the crystal and your desire to exploit them, if you can make it work, which is something I doubt. In a decade or two when the technology matures, perhaps. I don't know what Professor Ferguson's research has revealed, but it cannot be more than we already know. However, I must be sure, and he might be persuaded to help us, in the national interest, of course. You see, he is a tenured academic and some of his projects are highly valued by MIT…and the government. He enjoys the benefits and prestige of his position and I believe he would want to maintain them. Should he refuse…but never mind.

"Let me say that life for the good professor could become less comfortable, which wouldn't do your pigment project much good either. I understand your investors are already questioning the wisdom of pursuing the project and the enormous outlay you're putting into it. Negative information about the pigment's viability could have undesirable consequences for its release. Sadly, the stock market is not driven by facts, but perception, something you know very well. By the time you debunked a rumor or two, the bright future you envisioned for Solaris Technology might sink into the proverbial sunset." Crawford waved a hand. "Just speculating, of course."

Morrison forced himself to breathe normally, even though he wanted to jump over the desk and physically punish the repulsive man, and tried to remain calm. The officious prick was a worm, quite prepared to use all the tools at his disposal, legal or otherwise, to get what he wanted. Well, there were ways to counter such tactics, which Morrison had been reluctant to use…until now. If the little shit thought he would be intimidated, he was due for some attitude adjustment.

"I don't know if this is a personal pet project you took on yourself because you failed to get my pigment, or you're acting under higher authority, it doesn't matter. You're a government organ, but you're not the government. As a citizen, I have rights and I shall exercise them to expose you and your department. Now if you will excuse me, I have given you more than enough of my time."

Crawford clicked his tongue and shook his head. He heaved himself up with a wheeze, slid the plastic box into his briefcase and snapped it shut.

"I tried to do this the friendly way, Doctor, but I guess some people need more convincing. You're playing with forces you hardly understand and I shall enjoy stepping on you."

"Get out before I step on *you*!"

"Enjoy your moment of victory, Doc. It won't last long. By

the way, I haven't given up on your pigment. You'll be hearing from me."

Morrison waited until the horrid figure left, then slammed his fist against the desk. Everything that could possibly go wrong over the last three days had gone wrong. Three days, that's all it took to scramble his life. No, that was not quite right. If his life were scrambled, it meant he'd lost control, which was definitely not the case. He still had options.

Playing with forces, was he? The little government shit would personally experience one of those forces.

He took a deep breath and touched a button on the phone keypad.

"Allison? Get me Senator Randal Lockhart."

* * *

"There is nothing to worry about, Mr. Keller," the young Indian doctor announced cheerfully without a trace of accent. "Mild concussion and the CT scan shows no evidence of subdural bleeding. However, it does not mean there wasn't some damage when you took that fall. I would like to keep you here overnight for observation, but…"

Meir Keller kept his face expressionless and nodded. Understandably, the FBI were anxious to get their hands on him and start their interrogation, something he could not allow. They also knew his name, not altogether a revelation. Whoever handled his case worked fast to identify him. The fact they knew who he was meant he needed to disappear quickly or the ripples of his capture could disrupt a delicate political situation, not to mention making his own life decidedly uncomfortable. However, escaping could be problematic. He had seen the beefy black cop standing guard outside when the medic walked in. Undoubtedly, there were others.

He should have carried his diplomatic ID card!

"Thank you, Doctor. By the way, where am I?"

"Massachusetts General Trauma Center. The MIT police brought you in." Plunging a hand into his white lab coat, the medic held out a small plastic bottle. "One a day for the next three days. Preferably after breakfast. It's to offset any possibility of mild seizures."

Keller took the bottle containing three dark brown pills. "I appreciate this."

"You can get dressed now." The medic cleared his throat, uncomfortable having to deal with an FBI prisoner, gave a polite nod and walked out.

When the door closed, Keller threw the bottle into the waste basket, the movement causing his headache to flare. He touched the lump on the back of his head and winced. Still sensitive, it could have been much worse. To be taken out so easily by someone he figured to be an amateur...

He strode to the open window, squinted at the harsh sunlight and glanced down at cars rushing in both directions along Cambridge Street, the Charles River dividing the city. MIT's jagged campus skyline clawed toward a clear sky on the other side. Three floors up with no visible ledges, an obvious, but impossible escape route. Besides, clinging to the wall in a hospital gown was bound to generate some comment.

He sat on the bed and pouted. It was supposed to be a simple operation! Unfortunately, no one bothered to tell him about Trotman. The way the man moved, he had to be military. He had the bearing and command presence. They should have told him! Instead, he walked into a situation without adequate preparation, but failure was failure no matter what the reason. Time enough to dissect the mission once he got out of here.

Keller looked up as the door opened and recognized the youthful looking Greenfield, face freckled and carroty hair in total disarray. Dressed in a dark gray suit, the FBI agent stood aside as another man entered, setting off Keller's internal alarms. Some

180cm tall, solid build, hair graying at the temples, his swarthy appearance could not hide the coldest black eyes he had seen for some time. Keller recognized the guarded way the individual swept the room with those remote eyes, taking everything in, then turned those x-ray projectors on him. He was such a man himself.

Greenfield pulled back a chair with a scrape and sat down. The tall man clasped his hands behind his back and remained standing, a piece of machinery ready to spring into instant action. Keller stared into the bottomless black eyes, interested to find who would blink first. Stupid really, but he was good at playing these little mind games. After about a minute, his blink reflex kicked in and he fancied he saw a shadow of a smirk on the man's granite face. Definitely a hard character.

"Mr. Lester, or should I say, Meir Keller. I want to introduce you to Mr. Rohan Chester from the Boston CIA office," Greenfield said, appearing to enjoy the situation. "He has taken a special interest in you and your activities in the United States. You were read your rights, but Miranda doesn't apply to foreign intelligence operatives disguising themselves as trade attachés, even when they come from Mossad's Special Operations Division, which we all fondly know as Metsada."

"I want to call my embassy," Keller said flatly, forcing his voice to remain even despite an increased pulse rate and hammering heart.

"You don't seem to appreciate the gravity of your position, Mr. Keller," Chester grated in a deep voice that could have come from a tomb. "Impersonating a federal agent carries a penalty of up to three years imprisonment. As a foreign intelligence operative, we could keep you incarcerated forever."

"I have diplomatic immunity."

Chester grinned. "As Keller, perhaps, but you entered the United States as Karl Lester. He does not have diplomatic immunity—"

"That's a technicality."

"—and he is certainly not a Diplomatic Security Service agent, which is no technicality. The State Department does not use stolen SUVs to conduct its operations, and it doesn't kill people to procure a valuable artifact that belongs to one of our citizens. You see, Professor Ferguson explained everything."

Keller wished someone had explained everything to him! He was only told to get the crystal and don't ask questions.

"I haven't killed anybody," he protested, the image of the Tri-Con man shot in the chest vivid in his mind. The whole thing had turned into one smelly mess for everybody concerned.

"Not directly, but you're an accessory. Even if your diplomatic status were recognized, it doesn't cover murder. You appear to be in a shitload of trouble, Mister." Chester glanced at Greenfield and gave a small nod. "Strictly speaking, this is still an FBI case, but given your pedigree, we agreed to pool our resources. Shall we talk?"

Chester did not have to state the alternative. Keller wasn't sure what the CIA wanted, but hoped his men had managed to get away. However, he feared the worst.

"Talk about what? You seem to know everything already."

"Well, if I knew everything, we wouldn't be having this chat, and I *do* want to know everything, Mr. Keller. We may even discuss some of Metsada's activities in this country. I would find that particularly fascinating, and believe me, so would you. What happens to you afterward will depend on what you tell us."

The enormity of Chester's demand made Keller turn pale.

"I don't know anything. Like yours, our operations are compartmented. You must realize that."

"You may know more than you think and we'll know what questions to ask."

"If you force me to talk, it will come out sooner or later and we'll do the same thing to your people. Do you actually want to go down that path?"

Chester smirked. "What's there to come out? As I said, you disappeared. If you're worried about betraying your country, think of it as an exchange of information between friends. You have us infiltrated already. At least you think you do. After all, we're all on the same side. Or are we? Aren't we pals?"

Keller stared into the man's frozen features devoid of warmth or expression and pursed his lips.

"We'll retaliate."

"You already retaliated when you blew up one of our Galveston refineries three years ago, making it look like the Iranians did it, which almost dragged us into a war."

"And we paid a heavy price because of it."

"Allies don't do that to each other, but then again, Israel has never been a true ally. You're users, takers, with relationships of convenience, as your operation to retrieve the crystal vividly demonstrates. You think rules don't apply to you, but you want everybody else to play by them."

Keller forced himself to breathe evenly, wondering if he would live to see tomorrow.

Greenfield rose and patted down his jacket. "Get dressed and then we'll take a ride downtown." He glanced at the open window and gave an ugly smirk. "You're free to jump if you want."

The two men walked out, the click as the door closed echoing in Keller's mind. The prospect of jumping not outside the realm of available options. He simply could not allow himself to be interrogated, which would only serve to prove Chester's accusation.

He'd heard about the Galveston black ops stage managed by Colonel Matan Irian. Everybody did. It raised enough hell, costing Namir Bethan, Metsada's director, his job and a prison term, and toppled Sharron Ibrahim's Kadima Party ragtag coalition out of office. Keller never worked for Irian, but knew of the man's reputation as a fastidious stage manager.

He regretted not having someone like Irian plan his mission

to retrieve the crystal and wondered what made it valuable enough to risk America's wrath, which his capture would likely bring down on Israel. Yanked out of the comfortable Washington embassy, he told the First Secretary that one day was not enough time to plan a complex mission even with most of the required research on his target already done for him, but the starched shirt remained unmoved. The resulting fumble wasn't of his making alone, which forced from him a wry smile. He suspected the First Secretary not likely to be so understanding. Regardless of any future consequences, his job was to get out of here, happy to leave the political fallout to his superiors. The bottom line: he was an intelligence operative in the hands of a foreign power with a duty to escape.

He worried the problem as he dressed. He could not simply stroll out, not with that big bruiser waiting outside. The obvious solution was to bring the cop in away from prying eyes. If there were others out there, his plan would need some real-time revision.

One problem at a time.

He picked up the plain white wooden chair and smashed it against the window, shattering the single glass panel. Still holding the chair, he sprang behind the door outside its swing radius and waited. The cop rushed in, revolver held in his right hand. Keller brought the chair down on the cop's head, bringing the big man down. Not subtle, but it did the job. The second cop managed to point his weapon when Keller's shoe caught him under the chin and snapped back his head. He folded like a fallen trunk. Keller shifted the body out of the way and peered up and down the corridor. The commotion had apparently not disturbed anyone. He exhaled softly, closed the door after him and strode toward the emergency exit stairs. An elderly nurse pushing a bare gurney barely glanced at him.

They should have had a cop inside the room watching him, he mused as he hurried down the stairs. Sloppy procedure. He was sure Greenfield's boss would have something to say about it, as would Chester. When he reached the ground floor, Keller paused, then continued down to the basement, smiling coldly. He pictured himself appearing in the main lobby walking into the hands of waiting FBI men. That would have soured things properly.

He emerged into the gloomy parking lot sprinkled with cars, which smelled of oil and exhaust. The door gave a hollow booming sound as it closed behind him. Once outside, surrounded by a comforting press of pedestrians, he patted down his jacket and strode toward the Charles River Plaza mall. Cabs waited for customers and he walked to the first one in line. As he took the back seat, the cabby started the engine.

"Where to, buddy?"

"Boston Park Plaza Hotel."

The cabby glanced at him in the rearview mirror and nodded. "Park Plaza, got it."

As the cab pulled away from the curb, Keller sat back and exhaled softly. Successfully extracting himself was but the first step. He needed the safety of the Israeli consulate, a stone's throw from the Plaza Hotel. However, this was such a predictable move, it was possible the FBI might try to stop him from entering the consulate. Once he got to the hotel, he would ring in and have a car pick him up under the full cloak of diplomatic immunity. Getting him out of the country would be somebody else's problem, including the inevitable repercussions.

His headache flared as the cab bounced over an obstruction. *Screw you, First Secretary.*

Chapter Six

"The power has gone to your head, Manfred. Just because you guys won the elections and control of both Houses doesn't give you a license to ride roughshod over every Republican citizen who shows some backbone. You get this fixed or I'll initiate a special Senate hearing directing the FBI to start corruption proceedings!"

Exasperated, Manfred Cottard sighed and rubbed the underside of his bulbous nose in a characteristic gesture. When he got up this morning, he thought he was going to have a regular day, as far as that was possible. He had an overflowing meeting agenda and Lockhart's call had thrown it into total disarray, not that he expected his daily schedule to last more than ten minutes.

"For the third time, Senator, I told you I'll look into it."

"See that you do. The President campaigned for open government, transparency and accountability. Well, what you're doing doesn't sound like open government and transparency to me. If the White House is behind this program of intimidation, I will raise a stink. If someone is doing this on their own, it means you have lost control over your own government organs, and that smacks of irresponsibility and incompetence. The President may enjoy unprecedented popularity, but that could vanish if I go to the papers with this."

"You don't want to be playing that game with me, Senator," Cottard growled, tired of having his ear bent out of shape. "Some of your party's laundry isn't pristine white either, you know."

"Are you threatening me?"

"No more than you're threatening me. I told you I'll take care of it."

"You've got until close of business tomorrow. If I haven't heard from you by then, the Administration will wish it lost the elections."

Cottard winced as Lockhart crashed down the phone. He exhaled loudly, gently replaced the receiver, bit his lip, and sat back. If what Lockhart said was true, somebody had not only grossly exceeded his authority, but also opened himself to possible criminal proceedings. He wasn't too concerned that Lockhart would go to the papers, but he couldn't be sure. The old buzzard was capable of anything.

Vice chairman of the Republican Senate Budget Committee with two terms behind him, the man had a reputation for being a hard charger who did not suffer fools gladly, especially fools from his own party's right-wing Tea Party religious ideologues. A pragmatist, he was one of a growing number of Republicans prepared to work with the Walters administration in the national interest. Playing partisan party politics on principle cost them three elections and the enmity of many Republican voters, which the last elections demonstrated vividly, returning Walters into the White House with a sixty-four percent margin. After seeing more House and Senate seats lost to the Democrats, the old Republican leadership were quietly ousted, replaced by more progressive visionaries who did not relish having the GOP decimated by pursuing electorally poisonous policies dictated by radical special-interest groups.

The electorate liked Walters and his reform agenda. Unless the administration stumbled badly along the way, the Democrats were likely to retain the White House in four years' time. If Lockhart went public, it would hurt the president and the administration in the short term. Would it matter in the long run? Cottard doubted. Voters had a notoriously short memory. However, in politics nothing was certain.

He didn't care, not really. He'd be retired by then, relieved to be out of the pressure cooker, even though he walked into it him-self, eyes wide open. He promised he would remain chief of staff as long as the president did not slide into complacency, which many of his predecessors had done during their second term, worn down by Congressional infighting. In Sam's case, that was not likely to happen. Walters enjoyed one of the highest approval ratings of any president before him, earned by pursuing and im-plementing policies that reflected everyone's needs, Republican and Democrat. That earned him enemies from labor unions, cor-porate, and military-industrial complex camps, not counting the religious far-right, but he almost halved the deficit, trimmed gov-ernment bureaucracies, and gave business confidence, reflected in the Dow Jones topping 20200.

Cottard decided that he didn't mind if Lockhart went to the papers. It would be a momentary irritant, but threatening to un-leash a Senate hearing was another matter, which would distract the administration from its legislative program. Not seriously, but he did not want to give the Republicans any fuel he didn't have to.

He exhaled loudly. What Lockhart dumped in his lap required thorough investigation, and if proven true, had very grave impli-cations that went beyond simple abuse of official power, and an-other potential confrontation with Israel just when everybody was getting over their previous fiasco. That something like this had surfaced was not all that startling. The U.S. government was the largest employer in the country, operating more than 400 agencies and fifteen executive departments. This provided a lot of scope for unscrupulous individuals to abuse their position and authority. In theory, department secretaries and agency directors were responsible for direct management and supervision of their staff, but that was simply not practical on an individual level. The bureaucracy was too large.

It might be too large, but Cottard did not accept that as an excuse.

"Chapelle!"

His formidable personal assistant opened the door and peered in.

"Get me the Secretary of State on the phone, will you?"

"Mr. Tanner is in Beijing—"

"I didn't ask you where he was. I asked you to get him on the phone."

She nodded and closed the door.

He did not need her to tell him where Tanner was. As chief of staff, he knew what every departmental secretary was doing and where they were. He did not micromanage them, but it was his business to keep a finger on the administration's pulse. If asked a question by the president, he wanted to make sure he could answer it, or raise an issue of his own before it became a problem. Technically, department secretaries reported to the president, but Cottard ran them.

His phone rang and he picked up.

"Mr. Tanner is on line three."

He pressed a button on the keypad. "Larry, sorry to get you out of bed—"

"It's four-thirty in the morning, Manfred, for Chrissake!"

"You would probably be up shortly anyway," Cottard said without sympathy. His day wasn't going to end anytime soon either.

"I barely had two hours of sleep. The session with Dzhang Qishan finished after midnight."

"Did you suck him dry?"

"I got the little shit. In return for lifting our sanctions and putting China back on the most favored trading nation status, the Premier agreed to stop product dumping and clamp down on outfits copying name brands. They also agreed not to lobby for establishment of a basket of currencies to replace the dollar as the de facto medium of international trade. That's a big concession for them, Manfred."

"Superficially, but with four trillion in currency reserves, they're still in a strong position to manipulate the world's bond market."

"Our bond exposure is not as bad as it used to be, and they can't use that lever against us anymore."

True to a certain extent. After the Global Financial Crisis, China bought billions of U.S. Treasury bonds to underwrite the bank bailouts. This gave them an enormous economic advantage, which Walters in his first term largely negated by buying back most of the issue. The attempt last year by Keung Yang, the former Standing Committee chairman, to set off a massive tsunami by collapsing La Palma's Cumbre Vieja western flank, which would have devastated the American eastern seaboard and sent the country into recession, probably relegating it to Third World status, raised the ire of the international community. China paid a heavy price for that act, but not so heavy as to plunge the global economy into another crisis.

Tanner's trip, the last of three, was designed to bring China back into the global economic and political fold, but on U.S. terms. Walters had to tread carefully by not pushing them into a corner. Clipping the dragon's wings in substantive retribution told the Chinese they were not free to do what they wanted, not if they sought to be part of the global community. There was no denying they achieved remarkable economic and social progress, but progress was bought on the back of cheap international trade. As a global power, it enjoyed privileges, but with that also came responsibilities, which President Zhou Yedong recognized. He understood the Western mindset, having received his MBA from Stanford. Once China allowed itself to be ensnared in the global economic web, it was also constrained by that web.

Although in a strong position, the U.S. nevertheless needed to handle this delicately. If the administration demanded curtailment of their navy, reduction of weapons exports, and insisted on liberalization of human rights and implementing the rule of law, Zhou would simply laugh and continue what they were doing. The administration could not afford to forget that China was run by a communist dictatorial regime, which the trappings of a liberalized free market economy could not disguise.

"What else did they want?" Cottard demanded.

"A seat on the IMF Executive Board. Last year was a setback when we blocked them—"

"And we'll block them again if they don't stop building artificial islands in the South China Sea!"

"—but they take the long view, and an IMF seat is but one piece in the puzzle of their Go Global Strategy. Nothing will deter them from achieving economic and political domination the world over. Establishing bases in the South China Sea is merely one visible example of that policy."

"Perhaps, but to get there, they'll have to turn themselves into democratic capitalists, and I don't know whether their leaders are prepared to pay that price," Cottard said.

"I think President Zhou is prepared to pay some of it. He might be a progressive by our standards, but he will never allow reforms that would undermine the Politburo's authority, I'll give you that," Tanner acknowledged.

"What about enforcing their labor laws? Part of everybody's problem are the cheap goods their sweatshop factories churn out. That gives them a significant competitive advantage. If they want to deal with us, they'll have to do it from a level playing field."

"This could be a deal breaker, Manfred, and might hurt some of our own corporations if we push it. Besides, a level playing field is only level if we say it is."

Cottard grinned. "Yeah. The thought of Apple or Nike losing a few million because they're turning a blind eye to how their products are made won't cost me any sleep. The President is keen to get this one wrapped up, Larry."

"I know, but there is only so much we can ask for in one round of talks."

"There won't be a better time."

"I'll have a chat with Dzhang. Anyway, what did you want to talk to me about?" Tanner demanded.

"The mess George Brooks may have created for this Administration!"

"Brooks? Assistant Secretary for Near Eastern Affairs?"

"That's our man. I'd rather you sort this out, because if I talk to him, I'll rant and rave and his next appointment will be to Iceland."

Tanner gave a heavy sigh. "If I didn't have enough problems already. Okay, what's he gone and done?"

Cottard sketched out the situation with a few pithy sentences.

"The shit started when he directed the New York Office of Foreign Missions to accost Dr. Morrison with a demand to hand over the crystal or else the State Department would initiate extradition proceedings against Trotman. This is not how we execute our foreign policy, Larry."

"What are you leaving out, Manfred?"

"Randal Lockhart."

"Christ! How did *he* fall into this picture?"

"The DOE and the Defense Security Cooperation Agency— damn little cooperation, if you asked me—are leaning on Morrison and the guy called Lockhart. I'll deal with the agencies, but I want you to sort out Brooks and the Israelis. Haul in Ambassador Caplan if you have to, but get it done."

"And the Chinese?"

"I'll have Mark Price do some digging before we sound off officially."

"Is the President in the loop on this?"

"Not yet, and I don't want him bothered unless this gets out of hand."

"I hate to tell you this, but it looks to me like the situation is already out of hand. You've got China, Israel, *and* our own agencies after this crystal. He'll need to know sooner or later."

"He'll be briefed once I have a clearer picture of what everybody is doing," Cottard said.

"If Mossad tried to take out Trotman, Sharron Ibrahim must have authorized the ops. If he didn't…"

"We could be facing another rogue operation. You don't have to tell me. This time though, I don't believe it. That's why I want to keep the President out of it until I have all the pieces sorted out."

"If this crystal is a quantum computer, the economic and national security implications, not to mention the international dimension, shouldn't be left in the hands of an amateur like Morrison."

"Agreed, but we won't be winning him over with intimidation and threats."

"What are we doing to protect him?"

"The FBI is on the case. Get things rolling, Larry. If we don't handle this right, it could blow up in our faces from several fronts."

"I should have taken that Senate seat when I had the chance," Tanner grumbled and Cottard grinned.

A former Boeing executive and ambassador to China in the previous Republican administration, no one questioned Tanner's administrative competence or expertise in international affairs. When he put forward a position, it left little room for disagreement. His abrasive style tended to rub some people the wrong way, but these days, he took pains to couch his deliveries in language that did not offer obvious offense, but he did not brook dissent either. His views often clashed with the president's—the two were after all on the opposite sides of the political spectrum—but it was more in the nature of a patient teacher instructing an irascible student. With Tanner in the room, no one doubted who was the teacher. However, when Walters made a decision, Tanner accepted it with grace and implemented the policy with detached efficiency.

After four years serving a Democrat president, viewed by some of his Republican colleagues as betraying the Party, Tanner was approached to take the Maine seat in last November's partial Senate elections. It took all of Cottard's skill and several lengthy fireside chats with Walters to convince the fiery SecState to stay on at least until the midterm elections. If by then Tanner decided he'd had enough, the administration would let him go with no hard feelings by anyone. Tanner acquiesced, but never lost an opportunity to rub it in how he missed his big chance in politics, a hollow protest and everyone knew it.

"You could have, but you wouldn't be having as much fun. The Senate is a stuffy place as we both know."

"You call getting up at four-thirty fun?"

"Stop crapping. You like formulating foreign policy for the free world."

"Policy, yes, but not skullduggery by unfriendly intelligence operatives."

"They're all unfriendly, even ours."

Tanner gave a fruity laugh. "You got that right. I'll be talking to you."

Cottard hung up, sat back and chuckled, although there was nothing funny about this situation. Far from it. This was serious as it could get. Tanner was certainly right about likely international fallout even if he took the Israelis out of the equation. After Valero, he'd have thought they had smartened up. Apparently not. Still, if the damned crystal was genuine, and he had no reason to doubt it, otherwise all this fuss would never have come up, he could understand why they wanted it back. However, there were other ways of going about it than shooting people up, diplomatic ways. Allowing Mossad onto the stage had needlessly soured the whole situation.

"Chapelle!" he yelled. A moment later, she opened the door. "Get me the DCIA on the line."

She nodded and closed the door. When the phone rang, he

reached across the desk and picked up the receiver.

"How are you, Mark?" Cottard heard a groan and grinned.

At forty-seven, Price was one of the youngest CIA directors in the agency's troubled history. Walters liked how he managed the Valero Texas City Refinery incident. Price's input into streamlining the Department of Homeland Security got him the posting of DCIA with a directive to clean up the agency, emphasis being on intelligence rather than information interpretation. Price delivered, proving himself during the North Korean crisis when Admiral Pacino bombed their Yongbyon nuclear facility. The president paid attention when Price said something, seeing a lot of potential in the younger man.

"You only call when you have something smelly for me," Price complained.

"I have no reason to call you otherwise. Besides, the CIA is supposed to handle smelly things."

"Nice of you to clear that up for me. Right, what can I do for you?"

Cottard outlined his problem without wasting words.

"Talk to Tanner for his take on the situation and have your Boston office plugged into the FBI if the Bureau hasn't done that already. Have a word with Natan Joakim. If Mossad is involved, we want them to know that we know and they're to pull their people out before I talk to Sharron Ibrahim and things get messy."

"Well, crap! I'd say they were already messy, Manfred."

"Yeah, that's what Tanner said. Containment, Mark. That's the objective here. The Chinese situation might be a tangled web and potentially far more serious. Have somebody sniff around. This could be an officially sanctioned black ops or someone over there is pushing a private agenda. Frankly, I don't care either way, but I need to know for sure before we escalate. After what they did to us last year, I doubt they want to play rough with us right now."

"If this thing is as important as you say, escalation might be the order of the day. While we're spending our time sifting through the pieces, Morrison could find himself in some deep shit."

"I always enjoy your insightful analyses, Mark," Cottard remarked dryly. "You're right, of course, but right now, all I have is Senator Lockhart's input and I need verification. The Administration would look pretty stupid if we started accusing Israel and China of an unfriendly act without proof."

"I'll get things moving at my end."

"Positive reports only, Mark."

"You'll be hearing from me."

Cottard replaced the phone and tapped his fingers against the desk. He would enjoy doing this one.

"Chapelle!" he bellowed, rubbing his nose.

She poked her head in and waited.

"Get me Bertrand Ulesky."

"The DOE Secretary?"

"That's the miscreant."

It did not take long for the phone to ring. He suppressed a growl of irritation and picked up.

"Bert, what the hell is going on in your department?" Cottard demanded, knowing it wasn't the most conciliatory way to get Ulesky onside.

* * *

Kwang Choi relaxed against the soft leather upholstery and absently watched cars inching down Liberty Street, the one-way traffic filling the narrow thoroughfare. Pedestrians on either side, most of them wearing conservative business suits, some clutching briefcases, made their way toward the surrounding Lower Manhattan towers where their day would begin. He wondered mildly why the mad rush to get to work consumed these people.

Westerners were like that, he reminded himself. Preoccupied with money, power and control, failing to notice a gauzy cloud high in the sky, the perfume of an orchid, or words in a stirring poem.

A shapely creature wearing a dark blue skirt and white blouse, blond hair cascading across her shoulders, walked by and Kwang forgot the poem's stirring words. When she disappeared in the flowing throng, he imagined holding her supple form in his embrace, lips firmly attached to hers as his hands explored her curves. A discrete cough shattered the illusion and he glanced at the bulky form beside him.

"I wouldn't mind having *her* for breakfast," Payne drawled.

Kwang frowned and the man's lewd smile faded. He never indulged in levity with hired help, even though the same thought had crossed his mind.

His cellphone trilled and he dug it out of the jacket pocket. "Kim."

"We have the package."

Kwang cut contact and nodded to Payne. "We're set."

The former SEAL scowled. "About time. I thought they were taking in the sights."

Kwang got out of the black Buick Regal, slammed the door shut and headed for the tower entrance at 28 Liberty. Inside the spacious lobby, he strode briskly toward the nearest alcove housing the elevators. Walking in like this, he realized he was exposing himself to internal surveillance cameras, but if this didn't work out, he wouldn't need to worry about compromising himself. He'd be dead at the hands of American security or eliminated by the General. Given those unpalatable scenarios, he had to get it right this time.

He winced as he recalled yesterday's conversation with the caustic individual. From the General's agitated voice, he figured he wasn't the only one working to a deadline. Kwang cringed and simply took the abuse and threats pouring over the phone. The

General was not interested why the Sunday's operation failed. He expected results and Kwang better deliver. No need to state the obvious corollary.

A lush automated voice announced the 42nd floor. The elevator doors opened with a hiss and Kwang stepped out. He turned right and strode toward a frosted glass wall with the Solaris Technology logo etched into the door panels. They slid out of his way as he approached. Ignoring workers at their open plan desks, he stopped before the reception bench. An eye-catching brunette looked up from her workstation, her dark eyes appraising him with detached friendliness.

"Welcome to Solaris Technology. Can I help you?"

"I would like to have a few moments with Dr. Morrison."

She glanced down and frowned. "Can I have your name, please? I don't seem to have you in my appointment book."

"It's because I don't have an appointment."

"In that case—"

"Tell him it has to do with a certain crystal he purchased recently. I'm sure he'll see me."

Looking uncertain, she picked up the phone and spoke rapidly. She nodded, replaced the receiver and got up.

"Please follow me."

After a short walk along a corridor created by bullpen dividers, they stopped before a ceiling-high gray door. She knocked once, opened it and walked in, closing the door after her. Appearing a moment later, she stepped aside to let him in. Kwang walked through, scanning the sparsely furnished office. His eyes lingered on the mineral specimens in a glass cabinet as he stopped before an executive desk, giving the man behind it his full attention.

Morrison did not look his years despite a small bulge around the middle. The little frost at the temples added dignity to his full crop of black hair. What held Kwang's interest was the man's aura of authority, the dark eyes lively with curiosity. Under ordinary circumstances, this was someone who would not be manipulated easily. Then again, everybody had a vulnerable pressure point and Kwang had Morrison's. Skin tingling, he looked forward to the coming confrontation, anticipating seeing the pain in Morrison's eyes, watching the capitalist squirm, stripped of his superiority. He enjoyed these moments when they came his way.

"Thank you for seeing me, Doctor," he said conversationally as he dragged a visitor chair closer to the desk and sat down without waiting for an invitation. It was important that he assumed dominance here.

Morrison smiled faintly and leaned back. "Comfortable?"

"Quite."

"You mentioned a crystal, Mr..."

"Kim."

"One of your many names?"

Kwang chortled, pleased at the man's perceptiveness, not bothering to answer the obvious, appreciating the byplay. He dug out his cellphone and pressed a direct dial icon. A heavy voice answered after two rings.

"The package is ready."

Kwang activated the speaker and placed the cell on the desk.

"Kevin?"

Color faded from Morrison's face, his eyes turning to ice. "Juli? Where are you?"

"I don't know. They took me in front of the Washington Square Park—"

The line went dead.

"Juliana!"

Kwang stroked the cell with his thumb and crossed his legs. The capitalist had lost his aura of assurance, giving Kwang pleasure, feeding his ego. Not so superior after all.

"Proof of life, Dr. Morrison. You give me the crystal and your wife walks. In case you have some heroics in mind, if I don't call a certain number every hour…well, I'm sure you understand."

"I don't have the crystal here."

"Where is it?"

Morrison hesitated. "JPMorgan Chase branch on Park Avenue."

Kwang sighed and flipped open the cell. Too easy. He had hoped for a *little* fun.

"Yes?" the same heavy voice answered after a single ring.

"JPMorgan Chase on Park Avenue."

"Right."

Kwang pocketed the cell and gave Morrison a speculative stare. "I must say, you're taking this with surprising calm."

Morrison placed both hands on the desk and slowly pushed himself up. "If you harm her—"

"Whether you believe me or not, Doctor, I have no wish to see your wife suffer. She is merely insurance. However, should you do something foolish, that insurance will be canceled and she could be harmed…badly. It won't come to that if you're reasonable." Kwang stood and extended a hand at the door. "Shall we?"

"Release my wife and you'll get your crystal."

"I don't doubt your word, but things have a way of getting out of hand, if you know what I mean. She'll be freed once I have it secured."

Morrison pocketed his smartphone, then reached down to open a drawer. Kwang raised a finger in warning.

"Careful…"

"Key for the safety deposit box."

Kwang waited for Morrison to precede him out of the office, then closed the door after him with a soft click.

"Cancel my appointments for the morning," Morrison told Allison looking at them with large eyes from a small glass-walled office, her face wrinkled in a frown.

"Is everything all right, Doctor?"

"Everything is fine. I have some business to finish with my

guest."

A hard-looking man sitting in a bullpen behind Allison slowly looked up and Kwang felt momentary unease wash through him. Some inner sense had reared up warning him of danger. He could not see how he was threatened, but he never discounted the feeling that had saved his butt more than once. Pushing back the warning, he watched Morrison stride deliberately toward the frosted glass doors.

Still, something did not feel quite right. For someone whose wife was abducted and about to lose a prized possession, the American, although distressed, had taken this far too lightly. Kwang pushed his concern to the back of his mind. So far, everything had progressed as predicted, and Morrison had not done or said anything to the blonde that hinted of trouble. Perhaps the man was simply a cool customer.

The elevator ride down done in stony silence.

In the spacious lobby, Kwang cast a probing look at everybody around him, searching for telltale signs that he might be under surveillance, but nothing stood out. Of course, if he were stalked by professionals, he would never spot them. His inner alarm stopped clanging as they took the steps down to the sidewalk. Car horns blaring everywhere, the sight of hurrying humanity, the clammy warmth, it was suddenly all too depressing. He walked quickly to the Buick and opened the rear door. Morrison slid in without having to be prompted.

"JPMorgan Chase on Park Avenue," Kwang told Payne and the sedan pulled away from the curb with a surge of power.

"What happens when we get there?" Morrison demanded woodenly without moving his head.

"Nothing dramatic, Doctor. You retrieve the crystal—I'll be right beside you when you do it—you get your wife back and I walk out of your life. Play it smart and no one gets hurt."

As the driver negotiated the moderately heavy traffic as they wove their way toward Upper Manhattan, Kwang reflected on what looked like a successful conclusion to his mission. If the local consulate clowns did their part, he'd be on his way to Beijing on the afternoon flight. The General would be pleased.

He dug out his cell as they crossed 42nd Street and clicked on a number.

"Yes?" a soft voice answered in Mandarin after two rings.

"Approaching," Kwang said and hung up.

As they turned left onto 47th Street, the towering JPMorgan Chase building rose into a blue sky in a canyon of towers. Making a right at Park Avenue, the car slowed as Payne searched for an empty slot. On the other side of the broad boulevard, Kwang nodded when he saw a parked black E-Class Mercedes with tinted windows bearing a consular 'C' license plate. Payne pulled up opposite the bank's entrance and Kwang stepped out. He walked to the back of the car, opened the trunk and lifted out a slim brown leather briefcase. Without saying anything, he followed Morrison into the building, hearing the Buick speed off.

Their footsteps echoing on the gray marble floor, they passed somberly dressed men striding purposefully toward or out of a bank of four elevators, as Morrison headed for the round security desk.

"Can I help you, sir?" a burly uniformed guard demanded politely.

"Please inform Mr. Donohue that Dr. Morrison from Solaris Technology is here to see him."

After a brief conversation on the phone, the guard looked up and held out two visitor badges. "Mr. Donohue is expecting you. Nineteenth floor."

"Thank you."

When they got out of the elevator, Morrison led Kwang to Donohue's office, the floor well-lit in the open plan environment. He knocked once on a gray ceiling-high door and walked in. An elderly man wearing a dark blue pinstripe suit stood up, grinned, and extended his hand.

"Glad to see you again, Kevin."

"Thanks, Keith," Morrison said as they shook hands. "My associate, Mr. Kim."

Donohue nodded to Kwang and gave Morrison an appraising look. "What brings you to our end of town? Another operating loan?"

Morrison forced a smile. "Afraid not. I need to retrieve the package Trotman deposited yesterday."

"No problem," Donohue said and swept an arm at two soft chairs. "Take a seat and I'll have your box brought up. Care for a coffee or something?"

"No thanks. Next time."

Donohue gave him a searching look. "Is something wrong, Kevin? You look preoccupied."

"Labor problems at the Hanover plant. I may have to go there to sort them out."

"Unions!" Donohue snorted. "Pests," he growled and reached for the phone. "Jack? Keith. Have security box 3782 brought up...Right." Cradling the receiver, he leaned back. "How's business treating you these days?"

Morrison shrugged. "Sales are down a bit, but I'm looking into it."

"Yeah, that seems to be the story from everybody. Poor EU performance is dragging everything south. Mr. Kim, new in town?"

"Tidying up some unfinished business," Kwang said softly and glanced at Morrison.

"China!" Donohue declared. "That's where you should shift your focus, Kevin. Despite the recent slowdown, it's still the place to be. Right, Mr. Kim?"

Before Kwang could answer, a knock and the door opened. A youngish man walked in carrying a standard metal safety deposit box. An armed heavyset guard hovered behind him.

"Ah, Jack. You know Doctor Morrison?"

"Sir." Jack nodded and placed the box on Donohue's desk.

Morrison stood up, dug out the key and opened the box. Kwang noted an assortment of papers, slim brown envelopes, and a small ruby-red jewel case. Morrison took out the case and locked the box.

"Thanks for the personal touch, Keith."

"Glad to be of service," Donohue said. "Let's have that coffee next time you're around."

"Count on it. My regards to Leonora."

Donohue escorted them to the elevator and more handshaking. In the lobby, Morrison held out the jewel case. Kwang hesitated, took it, and opened the lid. He stared at the pale orange rectangular crystal with interest, wondering what made it worth killing for. Not his problem. It looked innocent enough resting on a bed of white velvet.

"Satisfied?" Morrison asked.

"You did your part." Kwang closed the case and locked it in the briefcase.

As they returned the visitor badges at the security desk, a tall, grim individual dressed in a light gray business suit walked casually to Kwang and held out a brown briefcase. With the exchange made, the tall man strode toward the exit. Kwang smiled at Morrison's startled expression and extended a hand.

"After you."

Outside, city noises assaulted his senses, and he was glad to see the consulate car waiting at the curb. He walked toward it feeling a warm glow of satisfaction. This had turned out to be one of his better jobs and atoned for Sunday's bungle. He had picked the wrong target, that was all.

The rear door opened and a heavy man stepped out, his Mongoloid features expressionless as he waited for Kwang to get in.

"Not so fast," Morrison grated and spun him around. "Where is my wife?"

"Like I told you. She'll be freed once I have the crystal secured."

"You son of a bitch!"

Morrison swung at him. Kwang easily blocked the clumsy punch, countering with a sharp jab to the man's sternum. Morrison gasped, clutched his chest and staggered back. Without saying anything, Kwang slid into the car. The security guard pushed the door shut, walked around the car and got into the front seat.

A sharp squeal of tires made Kwang look up as three black sedans surrounded the Mercedes. Dark-suited men scrambled out, guns held ready as they approached the car. He recognized fellow professionals, which was bad news. One of them, bulky, with a jagged scar running down the left jaw, pointed at Morrison and two men ushered him toward the JPMorgan building.

"He doesn't have it! Understand me? He doesn't have it!" Morrison protested.

Kwang watched him being marched off and nodded. He didn't know how Morrison managed to alert his TriCon minders, but he had clearly done it somehow. No wonder he looked calm and collected. Well, he did not look calm and collected now.

The Merc's doors were jerked open, accompanied by energetic shouting.

"Everybody out! Out, out!"

Eyeing the naked barrels, Kwang didn't move.

"This is an official vehicle belonging to the Consulate General of the People's Republic of China," he told Scarface staring at him. "As such, it and its occupants enjoy diplomatic immunity."

"You can shove your diplomatic immunity, Mister!" the man snarled and pushed his handgun into Kwang's face. "Get out under your own power or be dragged out. Take your pick, but decide right now."

Kwang slowly stepped out.

Scarface grabbed his arm, spun him around and shoved him against the Mercedes. After a quick patdown, he reached into the car and held up the briefcase.

"You may enjoy diplomatic immunity, buddy, but this certainly doesn't!" He placed the case on the car's roof and opened it, then snapped it shut. "Where is it?"

"Where is what?"

Disgusted, the man gestured to the others. "Search the car."

"Your State Department will be receiving an official protest at this unwarranted harassment!" Kwang blustered.

"Be my guest."

One of the men looked up, lifted his arms and shrugged. Scarface snarled in frustration and banged his fist against the Merc's roof.

Curious bystanders stood on either side of the street observing the proceedings.

A black SUV pulled up in front of the leading sedan. A lanky individual wearing a dark suit and navy tie, black hair combed straight back, stepped out and walked quickly toward the group. A shorter, stockier man followed him out.

"Not in the case, and the car is clean," Scarface explained.

"Morrison?"

"Inside." The man hooked a thumb at the JPMorgan building.

Kwang watched the lanky individual stride toward the tower and allowed himself a mirthless smile. Less than a minute later, the man emerged and approached the Merc. He stopped and dragged out a black ID folder.

"FBI Special Agent Earle Fisher. Can I see some identification, please?"

Kwang pulled out his wallet and extracted the Diplomatic Identification Card.

Fisher glared and nodded. "Where is Mrs. Morrison?"

"She'll be freed once I'm safe. Was there anything else?"

Teeth clenched, Fisher glared. "You and your party can go, but get this straight. If I don't hear from her in half an hour, you'll need more than diplomatic immunity to see another day. Are we clear?"

Kwang gave the FBI agent a smirk and stepped into the Mercedes. With nothing to show for his efforts, and despite his threat, Fisher had no choice. Kwang's diplomatic shield was inviolable, and presumably, Morrison must have told Fisher about having to phone in. Even if Fisher was prepared to ignore Kwang's diplomatic status, he could not ignore that precautionary measure.

"The consulate, sir?" the driver asked diffidently.

"No. Bobby Van's Steakhouse on Park Avenue. You know it?"

"Yes, sir. Next to The Helmsley Building, two blocks up."

Kwang leaned against the upholstery and relaxed as the car pulled away. When they reached the East 46th Street intersection, he got out and watched the car continue down the narrow street. The tall man standing beside the restaurant's entrance showed no expression as he pocketed his cellphone.

"Where is the briefcase, Payne," Kwang demanded, knowing he was in serious trouble. This cursed assignment had been nothing but one long string of troubles.

"It happened a couple of minutes ago. Two guys jumped me. Before I knew what was going on, one of them jammed a gun against my spine and demanded the briefcase." The man shrugged. "I had no choice, Mr. Kim."

Kwang ground his teeth and exhaled slowly, his mind churning. He'd been tailed, and it wasn't only by Morrison's TriCon people. Another player joining the game? Not totally unexpected, but right now, most inconvenient. Without the crystal and no idea how to retrieve it, he did not relish giving the General another round of bad news. Well, he could always ask the Americans for asylum.

"Your job is done. Release the package."

The former SEAL gave a nasty grin. "Not so fast, Mr. Kim. It looks like we're holding a very valuable item here. That's got to be worth something extra."

Kwang pursed his lips and shook his head. Westerners had no sense of honor, always seeking to exploit a situation.

"You don't want to be doing this, Payne."

"What's it to you if we make a little profit on the side?"

"You were recommended to me because you are profession-als."

"This is merely an exercise in pragmatism."

"You want to see an exercise in pragmatism? Your associates won't be impressed when I go after them—once I tell them who is putting the squeeze on me."

"I don't think that's gonna happen. You got problems of your own. I watched you get into that consulate limo, Mr. Kim, and saw the shakedown the TriCon people gave you. I figured I better cut my losses before more of my boys get hurt. I lost two already. Too many players in this game and I'm folding. Give my regards to your commie friends in Beijing." Payne snickered and strode down 46th Street.

Kwang stared after the retreating figure, thinking dark thoughts. He bit his lip and scowled. So, Payne wanted to play, eh? Doing a quick Google search on the phone, finding what he wanted, he tapped in numbers. After completing the call, he slid the cell into his pocket and nodded with satisfaction. He wasn't averse to an occasional game himself, and there were lots of ways to inflict suffering on a victim.

He glanced at the restaurant's glass entrance and decided to indulge himself. It could be his last meal.

* * *

With two TriCon men flanking him, Morrison could only stand and fume as he watched Kim getting the treatment. The crystal gone and Juliana with it. All the security surrounding him had turned out to be totally useless. He wanted to lash out at somebody, preferably Kim, but the pain in his chest reminded him that resolving his predicament demanded a different approach. What that could be, he had no idea.

Not knowing what happened to Juliana churned his guts. All sorts of worst-case scenarios flashed through his mind, which didn't help. The thought of her hurt, lying in some dark room, screaming for help, and the fact he was responsible, riddled him with guilt. Intellectually, he knew he wasn't responsible, but that did not stop his ravaging emotions.

Ignoring the steady stream of people in the now crowded foyer, most of them making their way toward the elevators, his spirits lifted when he saw Fisher get out of the black SUV. He didn't blame TriCon for what happened. Kim clearly a professional, he hoped the FBI would be able to retrieve the situation.

As Fisher strode through the entrance, Morrison called out, "He switched briefcases!" The remark caused several people to stare at him as they passed by.

Fisher pursed his lips, paused, then turned around.

Morrison saw Kim get into his car and drive off, which left him nonplussed.

"What the hell is going on?" he demanded when Fisher returned.

"He has diplomatic immunity, Doc. I had to let him go."

"Diplomatic immunity? He is a Chinese spy? I don't believe this!"

"Intelligence operative."

"I don't give a crap what you call them. Kim has my wife!"

"His real name is Kwang Choi—"

"Who the hell cares! What are you going to do about getting her back, and my crystal? By the way, how did you happen to be on the spot so quickly?"

"When you activated your alarm, TriCon got in touch with us."

The heated exchange had not gone unnoticed. When Morrison looked around, he found he had an audience. Fisher pulled out his badge and glared.

"FBI. Move on!"

After some clearing of throats and sheepish grins, the gallery dispersed.

A bulky man, scar running down his left jaw, walked toward them and stopped.

"Doctor Morrison? I am Pollard, TriCon. I couldn't help overhearing. Don't worry about your wife, sir. Our men are on the case."

"On the case?"

"The kidnappers tasered Mrs. Morrison's bodyguard when they took her. It was an expert snatch. Your wife was bundled away before anyone realized what happened."

"Get to the point, Mr. Pollard," Morrison growled.

"She had her cellphone with her."

Morrison exhaled loudly and nodded. When he engaged Tri-Con, one of the things they did was install a tracking app on his phone and on everyone else's deemed to have a security exposure.

"You know where she is?"

"Andaz Wall Street hotel. That's the location of her phone anyway."

Morrison felt a wave of relief wash over him, the situation apparently not so hopeless after all.

"Now I know how you managed to get your team here so fast," Fisher growled.

Pollard pursed his lips. "Doctor, the people who have your wife may know about tracking apps."

"I understand."

"I must tell you, sir. A hostage recovery is inherently danger-ous. Your wife could get hurt."

"Kim has my crystal, which means she is now a liability to

him. If we know where she is, I want to go after her. Let's go."

Pollard glanced at Fisher and raised his hand. "Ah, you better leave that to us. One of my cars can take you back to your office."

Morrison chewed his lip and thought it over. Although he desperately wanted to physically strangle the men who took Juliana, he could be in the way, a possible impediment.

"I appreciate that, but I'm coming with you."

"I think our Hostage Rescue Team should handle this," Fisher said after giving Morrison a long look. "TriCon doesn't have authority for something like this, but I don't mind having you tag along."

"When can they be ready?"

Fisher glanced at his wristwatch. "We can be at the hotel in half an hour, 10:20."

Pollard nodded. "Good enough. I'll see you there. Come with me, Doctor."

As the car pulled away, Morrison sat in the back seat, absently watching the traffic and the swarm of pedestrians filling the sidewalks, not really seeing them. He felt detached from the bustle outside. It was another world out there; cold, indifferent, impatient, seemingly aimless as it carried the anonymous faces toward an unknown destiny. And where was *he* being carried?

Gazing out the window, his thoughts churned.

He reminded himself to call Stan and Sandra. With the crystal gone, he could probably lift their security blanket. He would need to talk to Lazars about it.

The car pulled up opposite the imposing Andaz hotel Water Street entrance. Morrison got out and the city sounds assaulted his senses, magnified by the street's canyon of buildings. He clenched his teeth and stared at the hotel's orange façade. Pollard slammed the car door shut and stood beside him. If the TriCon man was right, Juliana was somewhere in there. Something made him turn and he saw Fisher walk toward him.

"The gods are smiling on you today, Doc."

"I know, but it's with mischievous glee."

"Hardly. I received a very interesting call from Mr. Kwang, but that doesn't mean I suddenly like him." Fisher glanced at Pollard. "They're holding Mrs. Morrison in room 809."

Pollard frowned. "What's the deal?"

"I don't know. Kwang didn't say. A falling out perhaps, or a case of professional courtesy? The important thing is that we have her location, which makes this a lot more doable."

"Your men?"

"Waiting in the lobby." Fisher turned to Morrison. "You stay here, Doc, and no arguments."

Morrison was about to protest, then clamped his mouth shut and gave a jerky nod. This wasn't a time for hollow heroics.

"Don't worry. We'll get her out." Fisher gathered Pollard with his eyes and they started to cross the street.

Morrison watched the two men walk into the hotel and felt tension knot his stomach. He expected to see an FBI assault van double-parked and black-clad agents brandishing rifles. That's how these things were shown on TV. He didn't know and didn't particularly care what made Kwang call as long as it helped free Juliana.

He looked at his watch. The second hand seemed to crawl. Unable to stand the strain, he cast a quick glance at the traffic and sprinted across the narrow street. He caught his breath and stopped beside one of the heavy white columns guarding the double entrance doors. An elderly couple emerged, squinted at the sun and casually walked toward Wall Street.

After what seemed like an eternity, a wailing siren made him turn his head toward the sound. Seeing the approaching ambulance, watching it pull up sharply beside the hotel, his mouth went dry. Pedestrians stopped to gawk at the development. Two medics wearing heavy black outfits scrambled out, opened the rear doors and pulled out a gurney. Fisher emerged and spoke quickly to the medics. He spotted Morrison and his shoulders sagged.

"Your wife—"

"What happened?"

Fisher raised a hand. "She's hurt, but it's nothing serious. We shot the man responsible and have his accomplice in custody. It's all over."

"Like hell it is!" Morrison snarled. "I want to see her."

"When they bring her down."

A second ambulance, its siren winding down, braked behind the first. Morrison watched the medics wheel another gurney into the hotel.

"Any of your men injured?" he heard himself say.

"Only your wife, Doc."

"Figures."

Pollard stood in the doorway, saw Morrison and walked over. "I'm sorry, sir, but one of the bad guys shot your wife before we could do anything."

"I'm glad that no one else got hurt."

"We'll have someone watch her at the hospital—"

"Surely there is no need for that now?"

"Sir—"

"I'll talk to Mr. Lazars."

Pollard pursed his lips, not liking it, but Morrison didn't give a damn. He had enough of everything, especially security. The medics appeared, pushing a gurney with a body covered by a thin white blanket. His heart melted at the sight.

"Juli!"

She turned her head and gave him a small smile. "Kevin…"

He knelt beside her and brushed her cheek. "My *chère*…"

"One of those things."

He glanced at the medic. "How bad?"

"She was lucky. The bullet went clean through above the left kidney. We stopped the bleeding and she's stable, but we need to get her into surgery."

Morrison brushed Juliana's cheek, stood up and stepped back, allowing the medic to load the gurney into the ambulance. Before getting in, he glared at Fisher.

"This isn't over."

"I believe you, Doc."

Morrison climbed in and the medic closed the door with a clang. The ambulance started its siren and pulled out. Morrison grasped Juliana's hand and squeezed lightly as the medic hooked her to a drip.

"Are you in pain?"

"It's okay…now. They gave me something." Her voice sounded tired.

"I'm sorry about everything," he said brokenly, wanting to be in her place, to take away her hurt. Because of him, because of his pride and arrogance, she was made to suffer. He stroked her cheek. "Love you, my *chère*."

She sighed and her eyes closed. Morrison looked at the medic in alarm.

"We had to sedate her."

Morrison was surprised to see the ambulance pull up a few blocks later.

"Where are we?"

"New York–Presbyterian Lower Manhattan Hospital," one of the medics replied as he stood up.

Things happened quickly then. They wheeled Juliana into Emergency, leaving Morrison to handle the admission details, made more complicated by the fact that she was a gunshot victim. After fielding a call from Allison, he spoke to Doug Moore, telling him he was temporarily in charge and hung up without giving any details.

After an anxious hour, a surgeon dressed in a green operating gown assured him that Juliana was fine and her wound treated without any complications.

"I want to see her."

"She is still recovering from anesthesia. It might be better if you came back in a couple of hours when she is lucid."

"Just tell me where she is."

The surgeon frowned and capitulated. "Room 312."

"Thank you, Doctor," Morrison said curtly and strode toward the elevators.

As he stood before the gray door, he took a deep breath and walked into the room, his eyes on the still figure on the hospital bed. Her raven hair framed a delicately molded face, angelic as she lay there, eyes closed. Her arms rested on a thin white blanket covering her body. The room smelled faintly of antiseptic. A large LED TV stood mounted on the wall opposite the bed. Beige gauze curtains hid a double window.

He pulled up a chair and sat beside the bed. Groping for her hand, he stroked the soft skin. He smiled faintly and brushed away a lock of hair from her forehead.

"My *chère*..."

There was so much he wanted to tell her, but he struggled to find the words in the jumble of his thoughts.

"You were right. I should have thrown the damned thing down the drain. Because I didn't listen, you were hurt, and it's my fault." He lifted her hand and kissed her palm. "The irony, it was all for nothing. The crystal is gone, and with it my misguided dreams. Perhaps they were merely delusions, but I have you, which is more important than any dream. Even my pigment may be an elusive phantom, thinking it would give me what I wanted, when all along, I had it in you, but was too blind to see it. I hope I haven't lost you because of it, like I seem to have lost Stan. Is there still a chance for us?"

Her eyelids fluttered and her large brown eyes focused on him.

"Kevin?"

"Juli—"

"You haven't lost any of us, silly man," she whispered and he swallowed hard.

"You've been listening."

"I didn't want to stop you, and I've been awake for a while. It's not often I get to hear what you're thinking these days, and you've been keeping long hours lately. We need to take time to talk. Business isn't everything, Kevin, and don't worry about Stan. Give him room to make his own decisions. He wants your approval, not advice, but I think he would welcome it if you just talked to him."

"Just talk?"

"He is a grown man, still uncertain, but desperate to please you. More than anything, he wants to control his own destiny and be successful, like you. Tell him that you'll be there for him, no matter what. That's all he needs."

"Like you were there for me," he murmured, "and I wasn't there for you."

She shifted her body and winced.

"Are you okay?" Morrison demanded, immediately concerned.

"I can move. Just pulled the stitches a little." She reached with her free hand and stroked his cheek. "You're a driven man, my dear. You always were. I sensed that force in you the first day we met when you bumped into me at Cornell—"

"You remember that?"

She nodded. "I loved listening when you talked about conquering the world, letting nothing stand in your way. I was caught up in your vision—"

"And because of it, you got hurt."

A frown creased her forehead. "I don't blame you for what happened today, my dear. We were both swept up in something that might be too big for you. I think the world is far more cruel than you believe…" She closed her eyes, her breathing slow and even. When she opened them, they were kindly.

"The crystal, Kevin. It's surrounded by death. It represents power, and that's why men seek to possess it, but you don't want that kind of power."

"What are you trying to tell me?"

"Let it go before it darkens your soul and turns you into somebody I don't know. Maybe that's why somebody buried it."

"Even if I wanted to, getting it back might not be possible," he said softly and a stifling load rolled off his shoulders. She was right, and he was better off without the thing. The guilt he felt dissolved and he breathed easier.

She grasped his hand. "I'd like to rest for a while. Will you be here when I wake?"

"I'll be here, my *chère*. I will always be here."

* * *

"The situation is still retrievable, Mr. Secretary," Keller insisted, trying hard to mask his exasperation. Bureaucrats! Interested only in greasing themselves to make sure nothing stuck.

"Retrievable? You were declared *persona non grata* by the American State Department and Ambassador Caplan is asking me some very pointed questions regarding something he doesn't want to know. Your incompetence has caused me an unwarranted degree of embarrassment, and you have the gall to suggest that we continue the mission? Your actions have generated a serious diplomatic incident for Israel, something your superiors will be made aware of, and I don't relish complicating matters further by permitting another foolhardy attempt."

If he were given the support he requested, they'd have the damned item in their hands, but Keller didn't say that. Descending into acrimonious diatribe would not be productive for anybody.

"Mr. Secretary, do you want to nail me to the wall or get the crystal? You have nothing to lose and my diplomatic immunity will shield me if something goes wrong."

He waited for almost a minute before hearing a heavy sigh.

"Very well. I will speak to the Consul General to extend you his full cooperation, but I wash my hands of this, and you better make that flight tomorrow evening. Once your twenty-four hours expire, so will your diplomatic immunity. You'll be on your own," the First Secretary declared and hung up without even a parting *lehitraot.*

"And a goodbye to you too," Keller muttered as he replaced the receiver.

He'd been on his own during this whole sordid mess and had not expected things to change. Besides, there wasn't any down-side for the surly First Secretary and both of them knew it. If Keller pulled this off, the Washington weenie would get a 'well done' from the ambassador, and Keller's involvement would be just another classified file in Mossad's archives. In case of a screw-up, Keller would be eating with the dogs. Life of a Metsada operative rarely reflected the debonair James Bond image, and there weren't any commercial breaks when things got difficult.

The greasy First Secretary was correct about one thing. Twenty-four hours did not give him much leeway to carry out his hastily cobbled plan, such as it was. A desperate gambit at best, but he lacked time for subtlety. He needed a telling lever to compel Morrison to give him the crystal. He considered taking the man's son, but negotiating between Boston and New York would not be personal enough. Keller was sure that Trotman had the crystal in New York by now, and that was where he needed to be.

He picked up the phone, dialed the Israeli New York consulate, identified himself and demanded to speak to the Mossad desk. He then called American Airlines and purchased two international tickets.

During the shuttle flight to LaGuardia, Keller worked on his notes, refining the coming ops. He disliked the brute in-your-face approach—look what that got him at MIT—but he was out of options…and time. The plan looked simple enough on paper; they all did until implementation. Its virtue lay in the simplicity of execution and should be doable. He would run with it unless his Mossad colleagues came up with something better.

At LaGuardia, his business class seat enabled him to leave the aircraft quickly without going through the tiresome wait of people stuck in coach. As always, the departure lounge a crush, crowded with arriving passengers. Those waiting for flights sat stoically in gate lounges reading papers, staring at laptops, tapping on tablets or phone pads, or simply gawked at nothing. Apart from a small carry-on bag, he wouldn't have to wait for luggage, which sometimes took longer to show up than did the flight itself! Outside the US Airways terminal, Keller winced at the noise, the press of cars, buses and pedestrians everywhere, the pervasive stink of oily exhausts, and stepped into the first cab waiting at the taxicab rank. He gave the driver instructions and sat back as the cab pulled away, merging with the traffic stream.

The drive along the Queens Midtown Tunnel, packed with cars—where the hell were all these people going—with the Manhattan skyline glowing in evening light, it didn't take long to reach the Israeli consulate on Second Avenue, a stone's throw from the UN building on the East River. He spotted the Hilton tower on 42nd Street squeezed between soaring towers, and thought it would make a good place as any to spend his last night in America.

Inside the consulate, a thin undertaker type met him, his bald head shining under fluorescent ceiling strips.

"Shalom. Essel Nehim, Mr. Keller," the individual rasped, offering his paw. "We spoke on the phone."

Keller blinked at the man's strong grip and nodded. There was more to Nehim than showed in the plain dark suit.

"I'm glad to have the Collections Department on my side. Is there somewhere we can talk?"

"Do you want to freshen up or anything before we get

started?"

"Let's get our ops sorted out first."

Nehim opened a white door along a corridor with several doors and waited for Keller to get in before following. A young man, his blond hair slicked back, stood up.

"Yuri Benning," Nehim announced as Keller shook hands. "One of my more reliable operators."

"He always says that, but doesn't really mean it," Benning added with a wry smile as he sat down.

Keller dropped his carry-on on the floor, swept the bare room with a glance, pulled back a metal chair and sat at the head of an empty black-laminated table.

"What have you got?"

Benning dug out a map from his jacket pocket and spread it out.

"Mrs. Morrison teaches at New York University's Stern School of Business. We had her followed when she headed home. She walked down West 3rd Street, past Mercer Street and flagged a cab at Broadway, which took her to Wall Street. Traffic being what it is here, she elected to walk to her apartment building. Since this is the first time we tailed her, we had no way to tell whether this is her normal movement pattern." Benning looked directly at Keller. "She had an escort. Presumably someone from TriCon."

Keller pursed his lips and shrugged. "We'll simply have to get rid of him."

"We don't know how she gets to work," Benning added. "Broadway is a one-way street. She had a clear run home, but going uptown, there are any number of ways to get to NYU. Without an established movement pattern, we could easily miss her if we waited for her there."

"Only one entrance into the Stern building?"

"Most people entering and leaving use the main entrance, but it's not the only one. Before you ask, she used the main entrance to get out."

Keller exhaled and nodded. "We'll assume that she'll use it tomorrow and take her there."

"Why not take her as she leaves her apartment?" Nehim demanded.

"We could, but getting away would be a problem." He pointed at the map. "Wall Street also goes one way. It's narrow and bound to be clogged with traffic that time of morning, not a place where we can scoot off in a hurry. Besides, her TriCon people will be at their highest alert there. No, we'll snatch her at NYU. Once you have her, I will confront Dr. Morrison." He stared at Nehim. "No one is to get hurt here. Is that absolutely clear?"

"Not a problem. Yuri will play like a student, which will allow him to get close to our targets and shoot them with a hypo gun. The stuff reacts almost instantaneously."

Keller took off his jacket and leaned over the map. "Sounds good and I like it. Let's talk contingencies and extraction scenarios."

It was long into the evening when the meeting broke up, leaving Keller in a buoyant mood as he checked into the Hilton Manhattan East hotel. After ordering a light dinner from the room service menu, he showered and went directly to bed.

He slept well, but naturally enough, his mind played what-if games with him, conjuring worst-case slipups to derail his plan. Everything that could be done within the given timeframe was done. Worrying about random possibilities would merely wear him down. The ops would either work or it wouldn't. However, he was serious about no one getting hurt and made sure Nehim got it. Bodies always complicated things, something he did not need right now. The First Secretary would relish taking strips off him, and the Americans would raise hell.

After a breakfast of mostly fruit, juice, and yogurt, ignoring the sumptuous buffet laid out in the dining room, he walked to the consulate, picked up a car and drove to 28 Liberty, parking himself opposite the building. All he had to do now was wait for his team to do their part, and waiting was the only aspect of his work he didn't particularly care for.

At 8:20, a black Buick Regal pulled up three spaces in front of him. At 8:28, a tallish Asian, possibly Chinese, stepped out and walked toward the 28 Liberty entrance. Keller's phone trilled and he activated the speaker.

"It's Nehim. Someone else read our mind and snatched Mrs. Morrison before we could get to her. Do you want us to follow them?"

Keller clenched his teeth, hissed with exasperation and banged the steering wheel with the palm of his hand.

Just once, O Lord, things could break my way!

Thinking furiously, he made a decision. "No, stay put. Dr. Morrison is still our prime person of interest. The kidnappers need him to get the crystal, and that's what we're after."

"What if he has the thing in his office and simply hands it over?"

"Possible, but I doubt it. Morrison will want an exchange. I would."

"And if you're wrong?"

"My day will get a whole lot worse," Keller admitted and heard a snort. "I'll call you."

All the contingencies they covered last night, he never figured that another party would be after the crystal, a serious oversight, especially when he knew the Chinese were probably that party. He should have confronted Morrison last night!

He had blown it...again.

With wild ideas churning through his mind, he saw Morrison and the Asian come out of the building. Perhaps the situation could still be recovered. He dug out his cell.

"Essel, Morrison just came out accompanied by someone I assume to be a Chinese agent. I'll follow them. Keep this call open and I'll give you updates."

"Standing by."

The Buick pulled away. Keller waited for three cars to pass by and followed it. The traffic wasn't bad and moved steadily, but he had to be careful. Whoever drove the Buick was likely to be a professional and might spot a tail. What Keller needed was two or three cars changing places as they kept the target vehicle in sight. Well, he didn't have three cars.

"Entering Bowery Street. Looks like they're heading uptown."

"If they keep on Bowery, we could intercept them as they run past East 4th Street," Nehim pointed out.

Keller considered it. "It's worth a shot. Set yourselves up." A few minutes later, he nodded. "Passing East Houston Street."

He gave Nehim the Buick's description and license plate number. At East 4th Street, he saw Nehim slide in behind him. Keller pulled back, allowing the other car to overtake him. When they hit 3rd Avenue, he changed places. Twenty minutes later and two more swaps, the Buick made a left turn at 47th Street and a right into Park Avenue. Keller nodded when he saw the looming tower claw into the sky.

"I think they're going to the JPMorgan building to pick up the crystal. Park yourself as close to the entrance as you can."

"Got it…Dr. Morrison and the Chinaman just got out and the Buick has taken off. The Chinaman is carrying a brown leather briefcase."

As they drove past, Keller saw a black E-Class Mercedes bearing a Chinese consular 'C' license plate and grinned. His opposition had executed their plan flawlessly. Getting the device now seemed a remote possibility at best. He parked the car and waited, watching the JPMorgan entrance across the street. He had no good reason to linger, but he didn't have a reason not to either. An instinct…

Twelve minutes later, he saw a tall, heavyset man dressed in a light gray business suit come out carrying a brown briefcase.

"Essel, see the guy with a briefcase who just came out?"

"I see him."

"Follow him and get the case. I think our Chinese friend made a switch. I'll wait to see what happens here."

"Got it."

With a consulate car and protection of its diplomatic immunity, was the Chinese agent finessing something? Shortly afterward, Morrison and the Chinese man emerged and walked to the Mercedes. He saw Morrison throw a punch at the agent, which the other blocked easily. Tires smoking, three black sedans rounded the corner and surrounded the Mercedes. Keller saw dark-suited men with drawn guns approach the car and figured it was time to do a fade.

"It's Nehim. We got the briefcase and the item."

Keller felt a release of tension wash through him. He wondered what happened to Mrs. Morrison, but it was only detached curiosity. He got what he came for.

"Well done! I'll meet you at the consulate after I check out of my hotel."

Now that he had the crystal, there was a small matter of getting it out of the country. The Americans had a special interest in him, and would make sure he left within the allocated 24 hours. They were likely to search him when he made his appearance…and anything he carried. Would that extend to a diplomatic bag? The things were supposed to be inviolable, but countries around the world broke the Vienna Convention when it suited them. He was certain the Americans were prepared to risk a minor diplomatic row with Israel to get the crystal.

If he couldn't carry it out, someone else would have to. Basic tradecraft.

Nehim met him wearing a broad grin, and took him to the same nondescript room they used last night. Nehim pulled out a red jewel case from his jacket pocket and held it out. Keller slowly reached for it. Resting on what looked like white velvet, the pale orange rectangular object seemed to have a glow of its own, probably a reflection from the ceiling lights. There was a certain compelling quality about it that made it hard to look away. He glanced at Nehim.

"I hope it was worth the fuss."

"What the hell is that thing?"

"I don't know, and frankly, I don't care."

"How are you going to get it out?"

Keller explained his problem. The Mossad agent nodded, the plan tickling his sense of humor.

"I like it."

"It should work," Keller said indifferently. "We'll drive to the airport in separate cars. No need to give the Americans ideas."

"When is your flight?"

"I have a 5:29 p.m. with American Airlines."

Nehim whistled. "That's shaving it close. Half an hour before your diplomatic immunity expires. You haven't left yourself any wiggle room at all."

"I shouldn't need any. Make sure you're there to slip me the jewel case. I'll contact you if I get detained." Keller looked around, reached for his carry-on bag and extracted an envelope. "Your e-ticket and boarding pass. You'll need them to get into the departure lounge. Don't forget your passport."

"It's risky and they'll be watching you," Nehim said, pocketing the envelope. "Wouldn't it be better if I took it to our embassy in DC and got them to courier it through normal channels?"

For a moment, Keller was tempted to reconsider. What Nehim said made a lot of sense, but the plan meant he would need to involve the caustic First Secretary, nominally in charge of all Mossad activities in the U.S., and the twitch had already expressed his disdain for the operation. Keller felt he was compromising the mission on purely personal grounds, something that did not sit easily with him. There was also the question of time.

"No, we need to do this quickly while the Americans are still disorganized."

"Mmm. I wouldn't place too much stock in them not being organized," Nehim mused. "Still, it's not a bad plan, provided they don't spot me giving you the jewel case."

"Slide it into my pocket as you brush past me. Remember, have the case wrapped in lead foil, and don't forget to put a diplomatic label on the thing."

"Why lead?"

"Despite your credentials, airport security may want to x-ray the jewel case. I don't want them to know what you're carrying. They might be alerted to watch for it. If for any reason you cannot make the transfer, take the package to DC."

Nehim shook his head and sighed. "It's too elaborate. Even if everything goes smoothly, the Americans may figure out that you have it and intercept you when you land at Roissy. Remember, you'll be in the air for seven-and-a-half hours. Plenty of time for them to run through airport surveillance footage and tag me."

"Leave that to me." Keller glanced at his wristwatch. "I better shower and change and grab some lunch. This is your turf. When do you suggest we leave?"

"If you want to get to JFK by four, we should be on our way by three-fifteen. I'll have your car ready at the front. I'll leave ten minutes earlier."

Keller liked Nehim's unflappable competence and slapped him on the shoulder.

"I appreciate what you're doing."

Nehim laughed. "Tell it to my boss when you get to Tel Aviv. I wouldn't mind a change of assignment."

Keller grinned and nodded. "I'll do that."

At three-fifteen, he walked out of the consulate. As promised, a car waited at the curb. He threw in his carry-on and a slim silver metal briefcase, and climbed in. The driver pulled away without saying a word. Keller preferred the silence as he absently watched the traffic and the shifting skyline. He doubted he would be allowed into America again, but he didn't mind. The world was large and Metsada made sure its operatives were not bored. A job somewhere in Europe would make a nice change. He liked working there. It spelled culture and sophistication, something the Americans were still to master. Business there conducted with a certain cordiality without having to resort to unpleasantness as the first and only option.

Keller sat back against the upholstery, looking forward to seeing Tel Aviv again. He'd been away for too long and missed the familiar sights, sounds and smells, and would relish a hot *cholent*.

When the car slid to a stop at American Airlines Terminal 8, Keller got out, picked up his carry-on and case and pushed the door shut. The car moved off, leaving him gazing at the terminal's glass panels, the crowded sidewalk, hearing the sounds of a busy airport. A heavy jet took off, making the air tremble with its warble.

Not having to check in, he headed directly for security. He placed the carry-on on the rollers and watched it disappear into the x-ray machine's black maw. Briefcase in hand, he approached the metal detector portal. The guard on the other side frowned and pointed at the x-ray machine. Keller lifted the briefcase to show the diplomatic bag stripe and was waived through.

"Can I see your passport, sir?" the guard demanded diffidently.

Keller handed it over. The guard flicked through it and held it out.

"Thank you, sir."

Keller nodded, picked up his bag and strode toward passport control, ignoring the bars, restaurants and curio shops waiting to separate travelers from money they didn't need.

He approached the glass cubicle after waiting in a queue for some ten minutes, feeling completely at ease. At the counter, he slid his passport and boarding pass toward the immigration officer. The man glanced at his computer screen, gave Keller an appraising look and handed back the documents.

On the other side before getting into the duty-free area, two dark-suited heavies walked up to him. One reached into his pocket and flashed open a badge folder.

"Mr. Meir Keller? Airport police, sir. Would you mind coming with us?"

"Is there a problem?" Keller demanded, not altogether surprised to see them.

"If you don't mind," the man prompted and extended an arm.

With the other taking station behind him, Keller was marched off. Standing before a plain gray door, the first man opened it and waited for Keller to get in.

"Take a seat. Someone will be with you shortly."

"I demand an explanation!" Keller blustered to a closed door.

He pulled back a black plastic seat tucked under a bare metal table, sat down and glanced at his watch: 4:42. He hoped this nonsense would not make him miss his flight, but looked forward to confounding his opposition.

At 5:14, the door opened. The lanky man who strode in, black hair combed back, clear blue eyes taking in everything, nodded and dragged out a chair. He sighed and flashed a badge folder.

"Special Agent Earle Fisher, FBI. Apologies for taking this long to get here. JFK is a warren and we didn't know where you would make your exit."

"Mr. Fisher, you probably made me miss my flight," Keller growled good-naturedly. "You better have a damn good reason for detaining me. You are aware that I have diplomatic immunity?"

"I know who you are, Mr. Keller. That's why I was so anxious to meet you." Fisher sat back and guffawed. "That was a very slick move you made this morning."

"I beg your pardon?"

"Our Boston office clued me in. After what happened at MIT, we never figured you'd try again, but when your security photo came up on a US Airways Shuttle flight, we guessed that MIT hadn't been enough fun. By the way, getting yourself out of Massachusetts General the way you did was neat. Caused us no end of headaches. Having you declared *persona non grata*, we didn't expect to see you anymore. Happily, you managed to prove us wrong, and I admire your persistence. Now, if you would hand over the crystal, I'll brush myself out of your hair."

"What crystal?"

A pained expression crossed Fisher's face. "Kwang, that's the Chinese agent we intercepted at the JPMorgan building, doesn't have it. He told us that, and you know something? I believed him. In case you were wondering, we got Mrs. Morrison. Now, Mr. Keller. The crystal."

"You don't dare search me, Special Agent Fisher."

Fisher stood up. "Barry!"

The door opened and a compact man strode in. Of medium height, his expressionless features held unmoving black eyes. Without saying anything, he dragged out a Glock and chambered a round, the sound very loud in the small room.

Fisher picked up Keller's carry-on bag and pawed through it. He placed the metal briefcase on the table and studied the central numbered lock and two side latches.

"Unlock it."

Keller pursed his lips, produced the key, and unlocked the latches, then set the four combination lock wheels. Fisher opened it, glanced in and held up a handgun.

"Now, why would a peaceful diplomat carry a Beretta 70?"

"To protect himself from the not so peaceful world?"

Fisher snorted in disbelief, replaced the gun, closed the case, and jerked his head.

"Against the wall."

After a quick, but professional patdown, Fisher shoved Keller into the seat.

"Okay, you don't have it. You're free to go."

"Just like that, eh? No apologies? No explanation?"

"Your government can seek an apology from our State Department. As for explanations, you already know everything."

"And my flight?"

Fisher reached into his jacket and threw down a business class boarding pass. "Your Air France flight leaves at 19:05 from Terminal 1. Technically, you'll be in violation of your *persona non grata* status, but seeing that it wasn't your fault, we'll look the other way. You'll be a little late getting into de Gaulle, but you'll have time to catch your planned 10:25 to Tel Aviv. By the way, I will make sure you get on your flight, in case you get lost or something. JFK is a large airport."

Keller smirked and picked up the boarding pass, taking it for granted that Fisher would have done his homework.

"I feel reassured. Since I have some time on my hands, care to have a drink and talk over old times?"

Fisher shrugged. "Why not."

Chapter Seven

Major General Tsai Teping stood rigidly at attention, swallowed hard, his eyes riveted on the cheap Mao print hanging on the wall. He could not bring himself to look at the grim features of the man who sat behind a wide desk strewn with papers, computer screen, and keyboard. To do so would risk meeting those terrible eyes he was sure were fixed on him ready to pronounce judgment.

His throat burned and he desperately wanted to cough, the effort to suppress the impulse made him clench his fists. When he saw the flecks of bright blood on the tissue this morning, it caused him to reflect that perhaps getting that chest x-ray might not be such a bad idea after all. Depending on how this meeting went, he might not need an x-ray...or anything else, for that matter. Should he somehow survive, Tsai promised himself to make Kwang suffer.

"You're saying the Americans don't have it," Lin Jinpan, Minister of State Security, prompted softly.

Wishing he never heard of the damned thing, Tsai allowed his eyes to drift down, taking in the man's imposing form. Dressed in a dark blue suit, the swarthy features bore an ominous scowl, always a bad sign for somebody. Lin might be a fool, but still a dangerous and powerful one...and he never allowed someone else's mistake to touch him.

"That's what my operative reported, sir."

"Ah, your operative. One of Second Bureau's finest, no doubt. Enlighten me, General. Who *does* have it?"

Unable to hold back any longer, Tsai coughed to clear the rasp in his throat.

"Most probably the Israelis."

"Our friends the Israelis, yes, but you're not certain."

"No, sir."

"I see. A reasonable assumption, but it's only an assumption after all. What you're telling me is that anybody could have it. Is that right?"

A damnably simple question, leaving Tsai no room to throw blame on somebody else. Kwang had been outmaneuvered, which sometimes happened despite rigorous preparation and planning. The problem with fieldwork was that the opposition rarely cooperated with his plans, and his own people would be the first to carve up the carcass of his failure.

He squared his shoulders.

"Yes, sir."

"We don't have the crystal and your operative has stripped off our cover of deniability, something I expressly ordered you to maintain. In addition to a diplomatic incident with Israel, your quest to procure the device has now generated a much more serious incident with the Americans. You are aware why I wanted to avoid such an incident, General?"

Seeing himself accused, convicted and sentenced, Tsai glared at the minister. If he were to be sacrificed on the rack of expediency, he would not go down alone.

"Five days. That's all you gave me to execute a mission that ordinarily needs a week merely to plan! Under the circumstances, the mission was prosecuted with initiative."

He was actually surprised to hear himself say that, grudgingly admitting that Kwang *had* done a creditable job under the most adverse conditions. Admittedly, Tsai had not given his operative any slack for contingencies either.

"It wasn't your mission to embarrass this government!" Lin roared, slamming his fist against the desk.

Tsai swallowed hard. "Perhaps we should not have involved New York consular staff in the second attempt, but your rigid timeframe did not allow for a transparent operation. After trying to obtain the crystal in Israel—"

"And failed!" Lin rasped.

"—the Americans knew we were after it. So what! There were no official casualties, and I doubt they will escalate this because two mercenaries were killed…killed by local police! I warned you that it might not be possible to provide total deniability. You ran the Second Bureau yourself, Mr. Minister, you must be aware what can happen in the field."

Lin showed no expression as he reached across the desk and pressed a yellow button on the phone's keypad. The door flung open and a uniformed guard holding an AK-47 copy at port arms strode in. Lin pointed a stiff finger at Tsai.

"Arrest—"

Tsai whipped out his Type 64 semiautomatic and shot the guard in the chest, the impact throwing the figure against the wall, his rifle clattering to the floor. Gun in hand, Lin's assistant rushed in and gaped.

"Sir…"

Tsai stared at the minister's ashen face and slowly holstered his weapon. The stink of cordite hung heavy in the large room.

"Put that thing away and get rid of the body," Lin snarled with a wave of his hand.

Clearly uncertain as to what just happened, the assistant hesitated.

"Sir, perhaps I should—"

"Do as you're told!" Lin bellowed.

The assistant blanched, pocketed his weapon, grabbed the guard's arms and dragged him out, leaving a thin trail of blood on the floorboards. Retrieving the rifle, he softly closed the door after him.

Lin sat back and slowly nodded. "You're obviously not going to go quietly, General. It is clear why I thought you worthy to head the Second Bureau. Had you pointed that gun at me…but you hadn't, although you still could."

"I will not be made a scapegoat, Mr. Minister," Tsai grated. Whichever way he cut it, he was damned, but he might walk out of this alive after all.

"That is altogether evident. However, we still have a situation with the Americans, which your…our…operation precipitated, and one we need to resolve." He twitched a finger at a cushioned chair beside the desk. "Sit down and let's talk how we can save both our hides. Premier Dzhang will get to hear about this latest development and I want to be in a position to placate him. I'm not keen to be made a scapegoat either, General, and he is less forgiving than I am."

Tsai sat down, crossed his legs and leaned back, studying the elderly man. The minister could still have him shot, but that would leave Lin to answer some very awkward questions. By authorizing a clandestine operation in the U.S. in a climate where China was still repairing damage from last year's La Palma debacle, the minister had opened himself to possible retribution if things went wrong, as they obviously had. Lin was right when he said he needed a plan to save both their hides.

The Tuanpai faction out of favor, and Tsai was sure the premier would use this incident to ease Lin out. He once had an ambition to sit in the minister's chair, but right now, merely getting through the day would be an achievement. Like it or not, both needed each other…for now. As for tomorrow, something to be considered later.

"If I may, Mr. Minister?"

Lin nodded. "Go ahead. Tell me what you think."

"I suggest you defuse the situation with the Americans."

"And how am I supposed to do that in an atmosphere where they might not be predisposed to listen?"

"Arrange to have a quiet talk with Ambassador Sawyer and tell him everything, using an appropriate slant, of course. You became aware of a covert operation to retrieve the crystal and tried to stop it. I'll be disciplined and forced to retire due to, ah, health reasons."

Lin Jinpan scowled. "A delicate way of putting it, General."

"But not altogether without some truth. I may have a serious lung problem that could require lengthy treatment."

"Presumably not at a correctional facility," the minister quipped with genuine humor.

"No, sir."

Lin turned serious and pursed his mouth. "A preemptive talk with the Ambassador has merit. Whether he believes my story or not is another matter, but as you pointed out, there were no official casualties, for which you have to thank your operative. The line being that China was attempting something the Americans themselves were already doing, as were their Israeli friends. We did nothing to threaten relations between us regardless of possible political and economic advantage possession of the crystal would have given us. However, I doubt that would need to be mentioned. Sawyer can read between the lines." Lin slowly nodded. "Yes, an excellent suggestion, General. However, appeasing the Premier might not be that easy."

"He is aware of the attempt to retrieve the device?"

"I sketched out the scenario for him."

"After you talk to Sawyer, play the same hand, sir. We seized an opportunity to advance China's position and the authority of everyone involved. The Americans may still lodge a protest, but I suggest it would be done informally. They will quietly tell us not to do it again and the whole thing will go away, for us anyway. I doubt that President Walters will want to jeopardize Secretary Tanner's mission here. What they intend doing to get the crystal from the Israelis, if they have it, is not our concern. As for any steps we might take, that will be in the Premier's hands, and his responsibility."

"And if you're wrong, General?"

Tsai shrugged. "Then I'm wrong."

"Mmm. Dzhang could still hang me out to dry."

"For what? For exercising initiative?"

Lin gave a sour laugh. "Initiative is only rewarded when you succeed."

"Things don't always break the way you want them to, sir."

"A reality the Standing Committee often doesn't appreciate." Lin stood and placed both hands on the desk. "General, as of this moment, you're relieved and on sick leave. I will not take further action against you. If you are questioned, which is likely, and you attempt to compromise me, you and your family will be liquidated. Do I make myself perfectly clear?"

Tsai stood at attention and saluted. "Perfectly, Mr. Minister!"

"Dismissed!"

Only when he marched out of the minister's office, giving the assistant a challenging stare, did Tsai Teping allow his shoulders to sag with relief. He was under no illusion that he bought his safety, but after expecting to face a firing squad, a wary truce was more than he hoped to get. His career may be in ashes, but the prospect of idleness no longer daunted him, given the alternative.

Throat sore, he longed to light up one of his cigars, wanting to savor the fragrant smoke deep in his lungs. The image sent him into a coughing spasm. When he pulled away his hand, he could see smears of blood. Perhaps his days of idleness may also be numbered, but he refused to drink any more of his wife's revolting brew.

He didn't trust Lin, certain the feeling was mutual. What he needed was insurance. A subtle message to the minister? That could be dangerous, though. One hint that Tsai considered taking direct action, he would find himself in front of that firing squad, or worse. The thought of spending his remaining days at a Mongolian labor camp made him shiver. If he went down, he needed to make sure the minister did not have time to savor his victory. Of course, the minister was likely to be thinking the same thing.

He would talk to Kwang and work something out.

253

In the meantime, he would need to check with his Tenth Bureau friend for news of another device. If one is found, he may yet sit in Lin Jinpan's chair.

* * *

"Abdon Sayar requested our help to recover a national treasure and Ambassador Koffel staffed it out." Larry Tanner said, his voice weary.

Manfred Cottard wasn't too concerned if the secretary of state was tired. His day had not been song and light either.

"Didn't it seem unusual to receive a request from the Foreign Minister? If this was a criminal matter involving one of our citizens, I'd have thought their police commissioner would have called."

"I guess Sayar wanted our ambassador to appreciate how seriously Israel took the matter."

"When you say Koffel staffed it out—"

"He got somebody over there to call the Assistant Secretary for Near Eastern Affairs in DC—"

"And George Brooks called the New York Office of Foreign Missions—"

"And they assigned Jesse Lipman to the case. Koffel told me that Sayar didn't demand Trotman's extradition, although it was hinted if we did not cooperate. Looks to me like Lipman was out to score points with the Secretary and got too enthusiastic."

"The way it looks to me, Larry, there was far too much enthusiasm shown by everybody over this," Cottard growled sourly. "What have you done?"

"As far as the State Department is concerned, Trotman has no case to answer. The Israelis have no evidence that he was involved in any criminal activity and Koffel should have sniffed a scam right away."

"I hope you gave him a blast."

"I did. As for their request to return the crystal, that is somewhat more complicated. Dr. Morrison bought the thing legally and we cannot compel him to hand it over."

"Especially if the thing is a quantum computer and he knows it," Cottard added dryly. "I want somebody to call Morrison and apologize."

"Already told the Assistant Secretary to do that. Manfred, you know this won't be the end of it. Having failed officially, the Israelis could mount a covert operation. If they haven't already."

"As could the Chinese. Mark Price is digging into the possibility."

"He told me. The situation has matured, but I'll let him fill you in. This has the potential to turn very ugly, you know. Whoever has the crystal and can make it work would control the computing industry for centuries. That's worth fighting for. Worth risking a confrontation with us."

"Tell me about it."

"Do you still want me to talk to Caplan?"

Cottard pursed his lips and rubbed the underside of his nose. "No, I'll have a quiet chat with our eminent Israeli ambassador. This has gone too far and I want him to know that the White House has taken notice. Then I'll ream the Chinese ambassador."

"I'm your SecState. You should really let me handle him. Since I'm already in Beijing, I could have a chat with Premier Dzhang, which would be more effective."

"Mmm. I don't want you distracted from your mission, but talking to Dzhang might not be a bad idea. Okay, do it. Tell him to stop playing games with us or we won't be pals anymore. You can go back to sleep now."

"At three in the morning? You have a low sense of humor, Manfred," Tanner sounded outraged.

Cottard chuckled. "Give Dzhang my regards," he said and replaced the phone in its cradle. He took a sip of tepid coffee, exhaled loudly, and sat back in the chair.

A mess. That's what this was.

If it weren't enough to have foreign intelligence agents involved, the administration's own agencies turned out to be no better. The Department of Energy operated under the rule of law. They did not make it, not that another apology was likely to make Morrison forgive and forget. Nevertheless, a formal White House acknowledgment might go a long way to placate his feelings when the administration sought his cooperation. The QD pigment Solaris Technology was developing needed to be in government hands. Not so easy to do without some legal basis, which he didn't have.

Nibbling a fingernail, he reached out, pressed a direct line button to Langley and activated the speaker.

"I was just about to call you," Mark Price answered cheerfully.

"What have you got on the Morrison thing?"

"Not even a good day or how are you?"

"You're alive and that makes it a good day," Cottard answered callously, not in the mood for banter.

"You're heartless," Price quipped.

"I can live with it."

"Since you want to be mean…have you talked to Tanner?"

"Just got off the phone. He said the situation has matured, his words."

"I'd say it's matured. The man Trotman disabled turned out to be a Metsada agent. We were holding him at the Massachusetts General Trauma Center for a checkup. Before we could have a chat with him, he gave us the slip."

"How the hell did he manage to do that? Sprout wings?"

"The two cops guarding him were careless, but we can't blame it all on them. We underestimated our man. He was declared *persona non grata* and the Israeli embassy told he had twenty-four hours to leave the country or he's ours."

"And why did I need to know all this?" Cottard demanded and heard a snort.

"Well, crap! Because it's probable that this morning, he snatched the device from a Chinese Second Bureau operative."

"Snatched the crystal? How?"

"The Chinese kidnapped Dr. Morrison's wife and used her as a bargaining chip. Without getting into details, the operation didn't quite work out as planned for them."

"Jesus, Mark. The thing could be out of the country by now."

"Granted, whoever has the crystal will want to get it out, and the safest way to do it would be under a diplomatic cover. We can do something about that when our boy tries to leave."

"He could hand it to their embassy and that would place it outside our reach."

"It's not over yet, Manfred."

"You told Tanner?"

"We just put the pieces together ourselves."

Cottard exhaled loudly, venting frustration. "I don't want to know what you're doing to get it back, just get it. Clear?"

"We're on it."

"Keep me updated." Cottard rubbed the underside of his bulbous nose in a characteristic gesture and fumed.

In one stroke the ground had fallen from under his feet. Morrison's dream to create a new computer industry, one that would have given America an unbeatable economic advantage, was now a vanished puff of smoke. Not much point talking to the Israeli ambassador now, or bending the Chinese out of shape. Without the crystal, all he had were violations by their intelligence operatives. He would have to update Tanner.

He bit his lip and decided to hold off. The Chinese didn't have the device, but they could not say who did, not definitely. For now, it might be advantageous to have them think it was still in American hands. Dzhang would be forced to abandon his operation, or at least reevaluate it, leaving the field less muddied—he hoped. Given the crystal's potential value, China would probably not give up so easily, but they would know that they were on notice and penalties would be applied if they persisted. What those penalties might be, he would have to discuss with the president.

The tangled web we weave…

"Chapelle!"

His assistant knocked once and peered in.

"Call Ambassador Caplan and ask him to come over. I'll see him in the Roosevelt Room. Then call Senator Lockhart."

She nodded and closed the door.

In some respects, he would rather deal with the Israelis and the Chinese than the fiery Republican reactionary. Fiery or not, given what the administration had done to Morrison, the senator had cause to vent vitriol.

As he stared at the computer screen, he found it difficult to focus on the myriad issues clamoring for his attention. He scrolled through the Outlook Inbox, not seeing the messages. From the look of some, he could delegate them to Howard. Might as well keep the deputy chief of staff busy, he mused wickedly.

After a knock, the door opened and Chapelle stuck her head in.

"Ambassador Caplan is on his way over and Senator Lockhart is on line two."

"Thanks," Cottard said and punched a glowing yellow button on the phone pad. "Senator?"

"Okay, Manfred. What's going on?"

"There are aspects of this situation I cannot get into right now—"

"Because of the Chinese and the Israelis?"

Cottard smiled briefly. Lockhart was nobody's fool and attempting to treat him like one would be dangerous.

"That's right. They have added an extra dimension that goes beyond Dr. Morrison, but I'm sure you have that figured out already."

"I have. Although I'm interested and I hope you'll fill me in once the dust settles—Congressional leadership has a need to know—my immediate concern lies with the Administration haranguing Morrison."

"Crawford was disciplined and shifted into a less demanding position with a reprimand in his file, which is a career stopper. If he hasn't already, Bertrand Ulesky will call Dr. Morrison offering a personal apology on behalf of the Department of Energy."

"Ulesky is a weasel."

"Between the two of us, I agree, but he is a very good DOE Secretary."

"Does this mean the Administration will stop hounding Morrison?"

"You have my word. However, given what's at stake, we will continue to secure his cooperation in the national interest."

"As long as you don't try something sneaky, which I presume is what the Israelis and the Chinese were doing?"

"There have been, ah, developments."

"Okay, I won't press you. What about Israel's demand to extradite Trotman?"

"They never made that demand…directly, and the matter is closed."

"So, that shit Lipman took it on himself to threaten Trotman?"

"He was counseled for it."

"To Madagascar, I hope. Is that it?"

"Someone from the State Department will call Dr. Morrison with another apology."

"You kept your word, Manfred, but if I have to call you again, I won't be as friendly next time."

"Always a pleasure, Senator."

"Hah!" Lockhart snorted and cut contact.

"Asshole," Cottard growled as he stabbed the speaker button. He scowled and pushed back a stack of papers to clear the desk a little. It had been a while since he'd seen the polished brown surface. His fault, really. He should be more organized. Too damn many pieces to juggle and not enough time to look at each one in detail, but that is exactly what he had to do. If he didn't, the president would have to eat into his already diminishing free time. Cottard wanted Walters focused on policy—domestic and foreign—without being distracted by administrative minutiae.

Sooner or later though, he would have to update the president on the latest problem. Perhaps he should have done so already. The international ramifications could get out of hand, something he would not allow, but it was not his job to decide how to handle it. Not directly anyway. He would talk to Walters in the morning—after hearing from Price. Things may sort themselves out by then.

He sighed and pulled at his nose. Work was slowly killing him and he knew it. It had certainly aged him, and the president now bore new lines around his eyes that took the shine off his smiles—not that he smiled often these days—and Cottard did not want to give him new ones. The downside, of course, is that *he* had more lines!

He needed a long vacation, but realized glumly that it wouldn't happen for at least three years until a new president sat in the Oval. Not feeling sorry for himself, not exactly, he knew very well what it meant when he agreed to serve a second term, but wished for just one day where he would not be getting another gray hair.

Suck it up, he told himself sternly, and turned to the computer screen. If there were gray hairs to be had, he saw no reason why Howard shouldn't get some.

At four o'clock, Chapelle told him Ambassador Alon Caplan waited in the Roosevelt Room. Having passed on the most irritating emails to his deputy, Cottard felt more pleased with himself and in a better mood to face his important visitor.

LEGITIMATE POWER

After the Valero incident and a change of government, Caplan had taken over from Israel's former ambassador, replacing the haughty and arrogant Lucila Hannakah. In essence, she represented Israel's old image: confident, dismissive of international opinion, demanding unconditional support for its flawed policies, refusing to do the moral and sensible thing vis-à-vis the Palestinians and settlements building. Walters had forced their hand, which resulted in creation of a Palestinian state, ushering in relative peace. It did not generate peace in the Knesset, the orthodox and far-right parties condemning the coalition agreement the newly appointed Prime Minister Abdon Sayar hammered out with Sharron Ibrahim, but Cottard lost no sleep over it. Perhaps the Holy Land had not become holier after all. What mattered, Caplan was a statesman of the old school and, more importantly, a pragmatic realist. He did much to repair the frosty atmosphere that had lingered between Israel and the U.S.

Cottard would test that pragmatism now.

He walked into the large Roosevelt Room and found his visitor standing at the corner of a long polished conference table surrounded by leather padded chairs. The orange walls and floor made the room appear spacious and airy. He fixed on a diplomatic expression and extended his hand.

"Thank you for coming, Mr. Ambassador."

"It is not a summons I could ignore, Manfred," Caplan said easily in good American English as they shook hands, a twinkle of amusement lighting his brown eyes.

Only five-foot eight, a slight bulge around the middle pressing against his jacket—a diplomatic posting tended to fill out a person—Caplan's grip strong and dry. He exuded calm and assurance, both valuable skills in his position. He also played a mean game of chess and never gave any quarter.

Cottard swept a hand at the elaborate chairs on the opposite side of the table. "Make yourself comfortable. Can I get you anything? Coffee, tea, or perhaps something stronger?"

Caplan shook his head and sat down. "No, thank you, but I appreciate the offer. Later, perhaps."

Cottard picked up the subtle hint and smiled as he settled himself in, watching his relaxed visitor across the table. If their meeting went well, sharing a drink would seal whatever understanding they might reach. Otherwise, their parting would be more somber.

Caplan leaned forward. "This meeting, only the two of us?"

"For the moment. The President will get involved...subsequently."

"I see. Please extend him my regards."

"I'll do that. You may also give Prime Minister Ibrahim my respects...and a message."

"A message? Is that why I'm here?"

Cottard crossed his legs and leaned back. "I have come to have a lot of respect for you, Alon—"

"Thank you, Manfred. You know the feeling is mutual."

"—and a lot of respect for your country. Israel has done a fine job repairing its reputation after the Valero incident. Your government has managed to hold a stable coalition in what is frankly still a hostile and fractured Knesset. As long as the Prime Minister maintains his coalition, Israel's international reputation will continue to grow, as will your trading position. My message, Alon, is that Israel would be wise not to undermine those achievements by embarking on a questionable course of action."

Caplan brought the tips of his fingers together in a pyramid. "I am not quite sure what you're getting at," he said cautiously, his eyes wary.

"Very well. I shall spell it out for you. This concerns Mossad's activities to procure a certain computing device, which it has managed to do, and which you're undertaking to return to Israel. Mr. Ambassador, there were any number of better ways the Prime Minister could have handled this, but he chose expediency over diplomacy, repeating the mistake made with Valero."

After a moment, Caplan nodded. "I will not resort to hollow denials, Manfred. I know about the crystal Dr. Morrison purchased through a closed auction and what it represents. I'm not in a position to comment on the Prime Minister's action, that was his decision, but I can confirm that we have it and that it's being returned to its rightful owner."

"What you have done, Alon—"

Caplan raised a hand. "Let's stop posturing. We both know what this is about. The crystal represents a revolution in computing, which you wanted to exploit—"

"No less than you."

"Do not forget the Chinese and whoever else realizes the importance of that device. The auction disseminated information to some very powerful people in several countries. You're sore at us for snatching it, to use your quaint vernacular, because we're denying America the ability to develop a multi-billion dollar industry that would have controlled computer hardware for decades to come."

"The industry that Israel now wants to control."

"That's business, but we don't pretend that anything will come from having it, not for a very long time, if at all. It is technology we barely understand, let alone be in a position to replicate. There is something else for you to consider, Manfred. We did nothing that you would not have done, and have done. No one got hurt, except your wounded sensibilities."

Cottard shrugged. "I admit that my reaction can be construed as a case of sour grapes, but there is something else." His face turned grim. "By involving Mossad, Israel has demonstrated once again its proclivity to treat allies as instruments of convenience, to be discarded when they get in the way of pursuing what you see is your perceived national interest."

"Again, I cannot comment on the Prime Minister's motives," Caplan said. "Tell me. What would you have us do?"

"I'm sure the President will have a comment—"

"He doesn't know?"

"Not yet, but this has progressed too far for him not to know. Speaking personally, you should have been open with us. Prime Minster Ibrahim was wrong to assume that the United States would seek to exploit the crystal to gain a singular economic and political advantage. A moment of reflection will make you realize the thing is too big for any one country. If there is any advantage to be gained, it must be shared by the whole world. What you and the Chinese have done by your respective actions will alienate everybody when existence of the device becomes known, which it will. This has set into motion forces likely to badly damage Israel and China. What is regrettable, you could have avoided all this."

Caplan sighed and shook his head. "I'm disappointed at your attitude, Manfred. The United States shrugs off criticism when you violate some other country's rights, but you're ready enough to preach to others how to be a correct moral citizen. This is realpolitik, and I defend my country's right to gain any advantage in its fight for survival—"

"Surrounded as you are by Arab hordes ready to annihilate you," Cottard added wearily, tired hearing the worn rhetoric. "You're posturing now, Alon."

The ambassador pursed his lips in annoyance, then smiled. "I guess I deserve that. If I may, what will you advise President Walters to do?"

Cottard rubbed his nose. "I haven't decided. The situation is still fluid." He didn't have to elaborate. The crystal wasn't in Jerusalem yet.

"I understand. Was there anything else?"

"I think both of us have enough to think about," Cottard said and stood up. "A piece of gratuitous advice. Prime Minister Ibrahim should prepare himself before the President calls."

Caplan stood and offered his hand. "I shall let him know."

"Thank you for seeing me, Alon." Cottard shook hands and

steered his visitor toward the door.

The Israeli ambassador paused. "You are aware that we're holding a function this evening?"

"And the Chinese ambassador is attending. Your Free Trade Agreement negotiations. Enjoy yourself," Cottard quipped without elaborating. He, of course, would not presume to tell Caplan what he could or could not say to the Chinese ambassador.

Caplan laughed. "You're very devious, Manfred."

Back in his office, Cottard asked Chapelle to bring him fresh coffee. Hoping to get to his Georgetown residence by ten, he spent some time marshalling the available facts and his approach for briefing the president. The facts skimpy. The implications huge. He wished that he never heard of the damned crystal, figuring that Morrison probably felt the same way.

At 8:20 p.m. the Langley direct line button glowed yellow and the phone jangled. He pressed the speaker button.

"I hope I have some good news for me, Mark."

"A mixed bag, Manfred. You know, an occasional hello would do wonders to bring the CIA into your corner."

"You're already working for me, which can change if I don't start getting some results."

"Well, crap! Perhaps Homeland Security would take me back."

"Don't count on it. They also work for me. So, what's new?"

"I've got an update for you on that device. The good news is that we may know for sure who has it."

"The bad news is that we don't have it," Cottard grumbled.

"We still might. Our favorite Metsada agent had a flight booked for Paris this afternoon. The FBI man on the case had him searched."

"By violating his diplomatic immunity?"

"Do you want to know?"

"I don't. Let me guess. He didn't have the crystal."

"He didn't, and that's where it gets cute. He pulled something so simple, we may add the gag to our dirty tricks list. Before boarding his flight, we established that another Mossad operative slipped him the device, and the FBI man with him never saw a thing."

"And you know that how?"

"After being searched, our man made a call on his cell. Obviously to arrange a meet. We monitored the JFK CCTV system and spotted the other operative near the boarding gate. What is interesting and why we believe a swap took place, he left the terminal directly afterward, even though he was also booked on an earlier flight to Paris."

"How does that help us?"

"We intercepted him and had him searched. Now that we know our favorite Metsada agent definitely has the crystal, we'll take care of him when he lands at Charles de Gaulle."

"Another violation of diplomatic immunity?"

"I thought you said you didn't want to know."

"Keep me posted, Mark, and thanks. You get to keep your job for another day."

"Big of you," Price said and the line went dead.

Cottard nodded with satisfaction, stood up and strode to the bar cabinet. He poured himself a finger of 18-year-old Wild Turkey and raised the tumbler in a salute.

"In your eye, Alon."

* * *

"It could be a blessing in disguise, Kevin," Ferguson said gently. "Remember our weighty talk on Friday night?"

Morrison sighed, feeling drained and despondent, adrift in a world he no longer recognized. Up to now, it had all been an exciting game, anticipating moves by his competitors and countering them, never believing that anyone would be hurt. The attempt on Sunday to get the crystal off Ferguson should have been a poignant warning. He didn't ignore it, not exactly, but it was something remote, happening to someone else. Even the death of two mercenaries never really sunk in. They were merely pawns swallowed by larger pieces.

The shock of having Juliana wounded still hadn't worn off. It wasn't a game, and he now recognized the brutal reality within which he had so carelessly moved. Would that reality also swallow his quantum dot pigment, in many respects far more dangerous to corporate vested interests than the nebulous potential of an alien computing device? It wasn't worth it if it meant risking Juliana again, or anyone else.

"I remember, but think what we could have done with it!"

"I've been thinking, all right. I couldn't help it. It's gone and I believe we're better off without it."

"Somebody else has it now, though," Morrison pointed out.

"And all Pandora's ills that came with it."

Morrison chuckled. "You paint a vivid, but gloomy picture, Harold."

"I told you before. I've been doing this shit for a lot longer than you, my boy, but I guess you had to learn the hard way. I'm glad the lesson came so cheap."

"Cheap? Your wife threatened and Juli shot? You call that cheap?"

"Take it from me, Kevin. It was cheap."

Morrison exhaled loudly. "I suppose. Now that we're no longer distracted, have you made any progress to stabilize the pigment emulsion?"

"As a matter of fact, I have. Your idea to use ionic nanoballs as a binding agent did the trick. All the Pleiades simulations were stable across the electromagnetic spectrum. Initial tests show an average conversion efficiency of 62%, and it doesn't degrade across the color range. Your customers can have any shade they like."

"Say, that's great. Have you stressed samples in weather models? I'd hate to have the emulsion dissolve in a shower, or peel off under direct sunlight."

"We're setting up the environmental scenarios, including biologics."

"What's the timeframe?"

"Two, three months. It could take longer."

Morrison didn't like it and gave a soft hiss. "I guess it can't be helped."

"Not if you want it done right. The bonding agent that provides surface adherence for the pigment is reactive, but once dry will require a solvent to remove it. The photon conversion emulsion itself is chemically inert, which should clam up the tree huggers."

"And the EPA. I don't want the federal approval process to hit a pothole or risk a lawsuit down the track. There will be enough pressure put on the EPA to knock us back."

"I *have* done this once or twice before, Kevin."

"I know you have, Harold, and I'm sorry if I sound like a nervous freshman—"

"But you have a lot riding on this. Relax, I'll make sure your ass is covered. Remember, I have a stake here as well. Things look promising, but there is still a lot of work to be done before we have a viable commercial product. Besides, you don't have a production plant yet."

"Already thought about that. There is enough vacant land at Bedford and Sunnyvale sites to set up a pilot facility. I would like to use Bedford as it's close to you, but I cannot move until we work out the manufacturing process and design machinery needed to run it."

"Which will be complicated, but I'm happy to leave the business end in your hands, and Bedford sounds good. You know, I would love to write a paper on this," Ferguson mused. "Ionic nanoballs...such an ingenious idea."

Morrison blanched in horror. "Are you out of your mind? The ionic nanoballs make the pigment possible. You might as well email my competitors all our research notes."

Ferguson laughed. "Don't worry, Kevin. Wishful thinking on my part. I *am* a tenured professor at MIT and they expect me to publish an occasional paper. You know, it's too bad that you gave up the academic life, selling your soul for the dollar. You have a visionary and penetrating mind, which is rare even among us."

"Your bank account isn't doing too badly either last time I checked." Morrison pointed out, amused by his friend's distracted attitude.

"I'm getting the best of both worlds: scholarly acclaim and commercial recognition. You, on the other hand, have only achieved a measure of commercial success. The QD pigment will enhance that success, but at what personal cost? The government is after you, as are the conglomerates, and you live in the shadow of TriCon's security. Is that how you want to live your life?"

Over the last few days, Morrison had pondered that same question, brought to a sharp focus by the crystal. He no longer had that hanging over him, but Ferguson was right. It might not be worth the price, disturbed by a vision of a dark future where he and his family lived under constant protection, denying him the basic freedom of movement. What good was wealth and power if he could not walk along the street like the next guy without having to worry that someone would kidnap him or his loved ones? He was not sure he liked that future.

"You and I spent four mind-wrenching years and more millions than I care to think about on this, Harold, and I will be forever damned if I'll simply give away the pigment for the asking. Besides, how would I justify it to the stockholders? If I tell them that I am a great humanitarian and I'm doing it to benefit mankind, Solaris stock wouldn't be worth the printed certificate."

"Ah, my boy, you just proved my case for remaining an academic. And no, I was not suggesting that you give it away."

"Damn right I won't. I may be the majority stockholder and immune from takeovers, but I need external investment to finish the Hanover plant and build a pilot for the pigment. Don't think I haven't considered the possibility, but you said it yourself. The manufacturing process is bound to be infernally complex, which would make any released information on it useless to most countries, except those who already have an advanced industrial base. It would be like giving Nepal blueprints for a nuclear reactor and telling them that their power needs are solved.

"I want to retain the IP and distribute the technology as I see fit, and don't tell me that's hubris on my part. Once the prototype plant is working properly—there are bound to be engineering problems to iron out—I will sell the pigment at a markup to recoup the initial investment, and I'll be able to charge whatever I want."

"It sounds like you're not planning an initial wholesale release."

"Corporate and government customers only, with a general release six months later after I have gauged market reaction."

"You *have* considered what the pigment is going to do to your existing product lines? Once it's out, nobody will want to buy your current panels. Your two plants will be out of business, not to mention the millions you sunk into Hanover. Doesn't strike me as a sound business strategy."

"It will be two years at least before we can start producing the pigment on even a limited scale. When everything is working properly, I'll convert the existing plants to produce the pigment and the growth in demand will be such that I will probably need a fourth plant. In the meantime, my current nanograss lines are still better than anything that's out there. I am prepared to sell the panels at a loss, but I'll offer any buyer a free pigment upgrade on release. Don't worry, my plants will be running for some time yet."

"Once you make the initial product release, where will that

leave energy-hungry countries who cannot afford to buy anything now?"

"Let's face it. One of my largest customers will be the U.S. government. I won't have any valid reason not to deal with them. However, I will have a rider on our contract. They will have to use their Third World political and economic contacts to set up pipelines to distribute the pigment, which those governments would purchase from Solaris. I am willing to make a loss on those accounts to see cheap power available to all."

"What is to stop those governments from profiteering, selling the pigment to their people at a rate only the affluent can afford? Keep in mind that most of those governments are rife with corruption and nepotism."

"Not sold, but given away under a means test mechanism. There are ways to get this done."

"I suppose. You do realize that Washington won't be happy until they get their hands on the manufacturing process, or develop a pigment variant of their own, and I'm throwing your competitors into the mix. The fact that we filed patents won't stop them."

"You think I don't know that? If the government sets up a plant and rolls out a QD pigment of its own, I'll take them to the Supreme Court and raise a public stink. Senator Lockhart would relish a brawl with the Administration. Remember Crawford?"

"The weasel from the Office of Intelligence and Counterintelligence who tried to get the pigment off you?"

"That's him. I made the same thing clear to him, but I don't believe President Walters will risk a damaging scandal he doesn't need to have."

"How will you get the Administration off your back?"

"Offer them a deal they will not be able to refuse."

"Hah! Why try to develop a pigment of their own when they can buy it from you at a discount, saving taxpayers millions in original research and setup costs. You know, of course, a variant

of the pigment is bound to surface sometime, patents or no patents."

"Coming up with a totally new photovoltaic molecular theory
won't be easy. I'm sure somebody out there will do it, but it won't
be for a long time. By then, Solaris should be the major industry
player."

"I like your enthusiasm and optimism, Kevin, but I deplore
your naiveté. Preserving our manufacturing IP won't mean a
thing to an industrial spy or software hacker. How do you imagine China came by its prosperity boom? It certainly wasn't
through original research. It took the Western world 150 years to
get there, and they did it in fifty. Admittedly, we helped them by
being greedy and stupid when we set up advanced plants to take
advantage of their cheap labor, which they immediately reverse
engineered, ignoring whatever contracts they signed to guarantee
IP, but they also got there by conducting sophisticated cyber pi-
racy. They will do the same thing to the pigment."

"Only if we set up a plant there, which we won't," Morrison
countered, "and we can safeguard ourselves by implementing security protocols. We did it with the Bedford and Sunnyvale
plants."

"The stakes are much higher this time, my boy."

"Look, I know the world is a rotten place and everybody
wants to rip my heart out. I had a taste of it with the crystal. For
the QD pigment, we'll have to set things up so that nobody can
reverse engineer it or discover how the thing is made by snapping
pictures inside the factory. You worked on such protocols yourself in your shady past."

Ferguson sighed. "You'll have a fight on your hands, that's all
I've got to say. Anyway, how is Juliana?"

"The doctors tell me two or three days and she'll be home. It
will take longer for her to heal completely, but at least she'll be
out of the hospital."

"Give her my best wishes next time you see her."

"I'll do that. By the way, you won't believe what happened this afternoon."

"Oh?"

"I got a call from the DOE, Secretary Ulesky himself."

"No shit."

"Well, it looks like my call to Senator Lockhart actually did some good. Crawford was canned, which should put a plug into his department's meddling."

"Don't count on it."

"I'm prepared to work with them, but it'll be on my terms."

"Good luck with that. Talk to you later, Kevin," Ferguson said and the line went dead.

Morrison switched off the speaker button and allowed himself a small smile. Ferguson was a starched ass who couldn't see a good thing when it landed on him. No, that wasn't quite fair. His friend bore the scars of government agency fires and was naturally wary. Morrison got singed, but he had one equalizer Ferguson lacked—political pull.

He reminded himself to call Lockhart and thank him. A donation to his reelection war chest would not be out of order either. Having Crawford off his back good, but he appreciated that Trotman was also in the clear and Lipman got his comeuppance, the little creep.

Morrison pulled at his chin, still feeling an emotional hole left by loss of the crystal. Even the news that Ferguson made a breakthrough with the pigment did not generate the anticipated excitement he knew he should be enjoying. Both had worked on the concept for years and the prospect of bringing cheap power to the world would ordinarily call for a celebration, but it left him unfulfilled.

Get your head out of your ass, Kevin!

He shrugged and decided his inner voice was right, as was Ferguson. He was better off without the damned thing hanging over his head like the sword of Damocles.

Morrison glanced at his wristwatch: 5:40 p.m. He shut off the computer and walked out of the office.

"Allison, tell Doug Moore that I want to see him tomorrow at eleven. I also want to see Trotman at 10:30. I won't be in until then."

"Going to the hospital?"

"Yes. I'm heading there now in case anyone wants me." Looking around the floor, most of his staff had already left for the day.

"Please give Mrs. Morrison my regards."

"I'll do that. Good night, Allison."

"Good night, Doctor."

The New York–Presbyterian Hospital only a few blocks from 28 Liberty and he decided to walk, giving him time to think. His TriCon minder maintained several discrete steps separation between them. As he strode along Nassau, cars and pedestrians crowded the one-way street, the afternoon crush well underway. Bright sunshine made deep shadows, but the air was warm, although filled with the stink of car exhausts and rumbling engines.

When he reached the hospital, overshadowed by the soaring gray slab of Beekman Tower, he took the elevator to the third floor in the west wing. He stopped before Juliana's room, knocked once and walked in. Her eyes lit up when she saw him.

"Kevin! You're a sight for sore eyes."

He leaned over her, planted a kiss on her forehead, and pulled a chair closer to the bed. Taking her hand in his, he squeezed it lightly. Her color was back and she appeared alert.

"You look marvelous," he told her, and her brown eyes shone.

She patted down her raven hair and snorted. "I'm a mess."

"My *chère*, you're gorgeous and you know it."

"I bet you say that to all your women, Mister."

"You're the only woman in my life, my love. How is the side?"

"A little sore, but as long as I don't move too much, it's okay. And you?"

Morrison didn't pretend not to understand. "A little over-whelmed by events."

She lifted her arm and ran soft fingers across his cheek. "Shat-tered dreams, Kevin?"

"Somewhat, but it's not the end of everything. You're safe, which is far more important than any quantum computer."

"Perhaps it's better this way."

"That's what Ferguson said. He sends you his regards, as does Allison."

"Thank them for me, will you?" She looked at him specula-tively.

"Stan and Sandra are coming to see you tomorrow," he said.

"I know. I talked to them. They were more than a little wor-ried."

"Well, getting shot will do that. By the way, I called your boss and told him what's going on. He said he'll ring."

"Thanks, Kevin, although I don't know how he'll cover my classes."

"His problem. When you're better, feel like taking a trip?"

"A trip? Where?"

"Germany. I want to see my plant in Hanover and smooth out some construction snags. We could cruise the Rhine and take in the sights. It would do both of us good to get away for a while."

"It would do me good and it sounds lovely, but can you afford the time?"

Morrison cocked an eyebrow. "Didn't you tell me that we needed to make time to talk and be together?"

"I was doped up, and it's mean of you to remind me."

"No, you knew what you were saying, and you were right. Be-sides, Moore will handle things in his usual efficient manner. He wants my job anyway, and he just might get it. It will take a long time to prepare the pigment for the market. Ferguson made a breakthrough."

"I'm pleased for you, darling. You sweated over the thing long enough." Her brow furrowed in a frown. "They'll try to take it from you, you know that."

He patted her hand. "I know. I'll work something out. Don't worry yourself about it."

"Losing the crystal, it has hit you hard. Hasn't it?"

"Yes, it has," he told her honestly. "More than I thought it would. You have no idea the plans I had for it."

"That's just it, I do. You didn't realize it, but the crystal was changing you into somebody I didn't know. You can try and deny it, but I could see its influence taking you away from me."

Morrison stared at her. She said that before. Could she be right? The crystal's fascination and the potential it promised certainly captivated him, but he did not believe that it changed him. Had it?

"Well, it's gone now and you have the old me back...with a few changes."

Her face broke into a radiant smile. "That is all I ever wanted. Still, I can understand how it came to absorb you. A computer from a distant past...It makes me wonder who built it."

"I thought about it. The Indian Vedas, the Tibetan Kanshur, and the Book of Enoch, they all say that we had a civilization that could have been capable of producing the crystal." He gave a short laugh. "Unless little green men left it behind."

"Is that so far-fetched?" she asked softly.

"I honestly don't know, my *chère*. It makes me question many of our beliefs, though."

* * *

After almost eight hours in the air, Meir Keller sat relaxed in his comfortable seat as the wide-body jet touched down with a jolt, knowing he was almost home. Under reverse thrust, the aircraft slowed quickly, turned onto a taxiway and bumped its way toward the sprawl of terminals of the enormous Charles de

Gaulle airport. Having finished the spiel describing the airport's facilities, baggage collection area and transfer options, welcomed silence filled the cabin.

Flights out of JFK and LaGuardia were always unpredictable, and this one had not disappointed. After a delay pushing the aircraft back, jolting on the taxiway to reach the runway, and then waiting in a queue for their slot, he lost almost forty minutes. If there were delays getting down, he could miss his 10:25 to Tel Aviv, which would mean rescheduling, transfers and hanging around the airport totally bored. Fortunately, it appeared that he had adequate time before his flight out.

Some twelve minutes later the aircraft mated with the air bridge at Terminal 2E, which spared him a tedious and lengthy bus trip normally used to ferry people between terminals, his flight departing from 2E. Keller had endured more than one such ride and never enjoyed it, wondering why an airport such as this could not service all its aircraft with boarding bridges.

When they came to a stop, everybody scrambled out of their seats and reached for overhead lockers to retrieve bags and duty-free items. With only his metal briefcase and carry-on bag, he didn't move, waiting for the main door to open. The first class passengers finally exited and he followed the business class throng past a pert Air France attendant dressed in a knee-length skirt, her dainty neck wrapped in a thin white scarf. She smiled at him as he said goodbye.

"Bonjour, monsieur."

As he stepped off the aircraft, he felt completely comfortable. He took a chance calling the Paris embassy using the aircraft's satellite phone. Probably monitored, but by the time someone got around to checking the call, it should be all over. What he feared was interception before he got off the aircraft.

Inside the modern terminal with its rounded roof and spacious interior, he checked the signs for his boarding gate. He glanced at his watch, figuring he could indulge in a coffee before his scheduled departure, his stomach still processing an excellent in-flight breakfast.

His inner alarm clanged when he saw a colorless individual in a dark suit wearing a David Niven mustache, accompanied by two gendarme with an FAMAG G2 assault rifle slung on their shoulder, standing beside the gate. The tall thin man exuded a readiness to explode into instant action. Keller recognized the type, having experience with these things.

Where the hell was his embassy escort?

"*Monsieur* Keller?" the civilian grated in a reedy voice. "Please come with me."

"And you are?"

"Pierre Arnauld. Airport Security. We need to ask you some questions."

Keller stared hard at the expressionless face, black eyes returning his gaze without blinking. As he suspected, the Americans had tagged Nehim, and that meant they knew he carried the crystal.

"You're aware that I have diplomatic immunity?"

Arnauld pursed his lips, looked at the gendarmes and nodded. Both of them immediately reached for their holstered guns, but did not draw them.

"This way, *monsieur*."

The walk didn't take long, but attracted more than one curious look from people around them. Along the way, Keller unobtrusively reached into his jacket pocket, extracted the briefcase key and dropped it to the brown carpeted floor. A short walk later, they stopped before a plain white door marked *Administratif.* Arnauld strode in and waited for Keller and the gendarmes to get in before closing the door after him. The two men inside the plain room, both wearing dark gray suits, pushed back their chairs with a scrape, stood away from the table and gave Keller a measured look.

"Your man, *monsieurs*," Arnauld announced with a sweep of

278

his hand.

"Thanks, Pierre," the heavier of the two said in American English and gave what he considered a disarming grin. "You can call me Adam, Mr. Keller. Nicolas here doesn't say much, but he is very useful to have around." He pointed a finger at the briefcase. "On the table."

Nicolas, eh? Keller figured him to be French DGSI: General Directorate for Internal Security. Jaws clenched, he pushed the case across with a scrape.

Adam glanced at the numbered lock and two side latches and looked up. "The combination and key."

"What you're attempting is illegal and violates my diplomatic immunity," Keller declared calmly, although his fluttering insides betrayed him. These guys looked mean.

Adam glowered. "You either open it voluntarily or I will open it by force, and I don't give a shit about your diplomatic immunity. Now, open the damn case!"

Keller said nothing and crossed his arms. After searching his bag, they shoved him against the wall and frisked him, not being gentle about it.

"No key. He could also have passed the item to somebody as he got off," Nicolas hissed with a distinct French accent, looking amused.

"No shit!" Adam snarled, not amused at all. "And most of the passengers would have left the aircraft by now." He turned to Renauld. "Did anyone go into the air bridge as the aircraft mated?"

Renauld spread his hands in a typical Gallic gesture. "Airport personnel, *monsieur.*"

Adam looked disgusted. "That means it could have been anybody, if that's what he did. You checked the IDs?"

"*Oui.*"

"Well, check the crew, ground staff and everyone who was near that plane."

Stefan Vučak

Renauld nodded, gathered one of the gendarme with his eyes, and the two filed out.

Adam kicked back a chair. "Have a seat, Mr. Keller," he said and glanced at his companion.

Keller sat down, not relishing what was to come as Nicolas produced a slim case from his pocket and held up a syringe containing a pale yellow liquid, probably one of the barbiturate derivatives, sodium pentothal or amatol. These two were hard professionals prepared to do whatever was necessary.

Damn the embassy chair warmers!

Adam plunged his hands into his pockets and sat on the edge of the table, his face an ugly mask.

"If you played it cute and slipped the device to somebody, it will be a temporary setback at best. Your man won't get away. This airport has excellent face recognition software and we've tagged all your embassy people, but never mind that. I want to talk about your briefcase. To make things clear, you don't exist and I can do anything I want to you. If you're thinking of making a break for it, the cop behind you will shoot you before you're out of that chair. Feel free to try it.

"Nicolas is going to give you something to help stimulate your memory. It takes about five minutes to work. If you cooperate and tell me how to open the case, you get to walk out. If not, they'll be sending you home in a body bag, that's a promise, and I'll still have the case. As you may have gathered by now, I'm not a very nice person. Being nice doesn't get the job done, which you should know. Do we understand each other?"

Keller stared at the syringe as Nicolas held it up and pressed the plunger. A thin squirt of liquid shot up from the needle. Nicolas leaned over him and jabbed the needle through the jacket into his left arm. He felt a sting and winced as the liquid rushed into his flesh.

Five minutes, Adam said. That would be about right. Feeling the drug take effect, he relaxed and settled into the chair, waiting for the minutes to tick over.

The door flew open and Renauld strode in, accompanied by a balding little man in a dark brown pinstripe. Keller wondered who he was, but with detached interest and of little importance. Content to sit there, he waited for someone to ask him a question, anything.

Renauld gave him a long look and turned to the DGSI man.

"This no longer concerns Internal Security, *monsieur*."

"You have no authority—" Nicolas began, but his protest died when Renauld twitched a finger and the gendarme in the corner lifted his rifle. Glancing at Adam, he shrugged and walked out.

"What's going on?" Adam demanded. "I was told that I would have full cooperation."

"No longer." Renauld turned to the little man and swept a hand at Keller. "Your man, sir."

"Who is *he*?" Adam demanded.

"First Secretary Doron from the Israeli embassy."

"Are you all right, Mr. Keller?" Doron asked, looking genuinely concerned.

A question at last!

"I am well, I think," Keller said, having to drag out the words.

Doron turned to Adam. "What has been done to him?"

"Nothing drastic. He'll recover."

The First Secretary stared hard at the American. "Your government can expect to hear about this brutal treatment of an accredited Israeli national, sir."

"Accredited national, my ass!" Adam snarled and pointed at the briefcase. "He is carrying stolen property. Property belonging to the United States. That doesn't fall under accredited behavior, Mister."

"I suggest you leave, *monsieur*," Renauld said and stepped away from the door.

Seeing the gendarme ready to use his weapon, Adam pursed

his lips and, after giving Keller a glare of hatred, stormed out.

Doron stood by the chair and helped Keller to stand. "You're in no condition to travel. Mr. Renauld will put you in a room at the airport Sheraton where you'll have time to shake off whatever they gave you. Do you understand?"

Keller felt mild annoyance at having his sanity questioned. He was lucid, but without any willpower.

"When is my flight?"

"We have you on an El Al at 14:35 for Tel Aviv," Doron said and glanced at Renauld. "Thank you for your help, sir."

"I have taken precautions, Mr. Secretary. Two of my men will be guarding his room."

Renauld picked up the briefcase and carry-on bag and motioned to the gendarme who helped Keller as they walked into the terminal.

Keller did not remember getting into the hotel room and felt disoriented when he sat up with a jerk, taking everything in at a glance. The room could have been in any hotel anywhere, cut from the same mold. He then heard the incessant jangle from the bedside alarm clock. He reached out and shut the thing off. 1:15, the clock read. It gave him time for a quick shower before heading for the departure gate. He noticed the black shape of a standard Sig Sauer P2022 beside the clock. Renauld wanting him to feel secure? He picked up the weapon, ejected the clip and checked the chamber—empty. He slipped in the clip, chambered a round and placed the gun beside the clock.

He threw back the single sheet, finding that he still had his pants on. Wearing a crumpled suit, he was not going to look his best when he boarded. He managed only a few movements of his calisthenics when he heard the familiar soft *thuft* and the lock splintered, which sent him diving for the Sig. The door crashed against the wall and Nicolas crouched, holding his weapon in a two-handed grip. Keller shot him in the chest with a double tap, the crack of the pistol hurting his ears.

Adam sidestepped the body and let fly two shots. Keller felt a searing pain along his upper arm and ducked as another sharp lance ripped through his guts. He managed to shoot Adam in the stomach and saw the CIA man stagger and sag to the carpet, a dark red pool of blood making an ugly stain. Keller figured the cleaning lady would be pissed. Looking down, he had a nice red stain of his own spreading across his shirt. It looked like the bullet went through his right kidney. It could have been worse.

He clamped a hand on the wound and felt something wet slide down his back from the exit hole. He staggered toward the bed-stand phone, lifted the receiver and punched nine.

"Réception," a nice female voice answered. *"Puis-je vous aider?"*

"Yes, I need help. Room...Room..."

The receiver slipped from his hand and he sagged across the bed. God, his side hurt. It did not look like he would make this flight either. Appreciating the humor of it, he tried to laugh, but the effort defeated him. The last thing he heard were running footsteps.

* * *

"I endured Secretary of State Tanner's veiled tongue lashing because I could not refute anything he said. Polite and respectful, his warning came through clearly enough," Premier Dzhang Qishan said softly, forcing Lin Jinpan to lean forward, putting himself in a position of supplication.

He sat in a brown leather padded chair that could have taken two of him, his delicate fingers tapping lightly against the polished surface of an elaborately carved desk, Dzhang turned to the tall windows and the immaculately sculpted grounds surrounding the South Sea Lake. The Zhangnanhai compound, an imperial retreat for Jin and Yuan emperors, nestled against the Forbidden City's western wall, now served as headquarters for the Com-

Stefan Vučak

munist Party and State Council administrative arms. It also provided residences for high ranking Party officials, which included
the premier and president of China's Communist Party. The arrangement solved many security problems—tourists and the general public not permitted inside the compound—and made life
very comfortable for those living there.

The population at large was also doing well enough, Dzhang
told himself phlegmatically. Under President Zhou Yedong's Go
Global Strategy and limited liberalization of the financial sector
that supported an increasingly open market economy, ordinary
citizens were allowed to exercise their natural bent for business
and private enterprise to enrich themselves, and many had done
so spectacularly. For the common peasant working the land, life
was still harsh, but far better than the terrible years endured under
Mao's Cultural Revolution, although he would not say this openly
to some of his diehard *taizidang* colleagues.

The elitist princeling coalition held power now and were likely
to be the dominant force inside the Politburo for some time to
come, their position strengthened immeasurably by Keung
Yang's spectacular dismissal as chairman of the Standing Committee following the diplomatic La Palma disaster. The Tuanpai
populists were slowly being weeded out of Beijing's corridors of
power, although they still enjoyed considerable support in the
provinces. Perhaps not such a bad thing, he reflected moodily.
Yin and y*ang*...

Dzhang turned to look at the tense figure sitting before him.
The Fates have handed him an opportunity to sweep another
populist faction thorn from the Politburo. Lin Jinpan had shed
his mantle of vigor and competence long ago, enjoying a sinecure
post in his twilight years. The State Council did not want that
type of man to run the vital Ministry of State Security.

"Tanner has come to know us well, perhaps too well, for any
misunderstanding. Is it true, General?"

Lin sat back and squared his shoulders. "I relieved Tsai

284

Teping from duty and placed him on indefinite medical leave, Mr. Premier."

"That doesn't exactly answer my question. When you first informed me of this magical computing device, you cloaked the operation as an opportunity for China to become the dominant force in information technology, and an opening to consolidate your own position under the assumption that I would also gain considerable prestige in the State Council. Laudable goals—had you succeeded—but you did not succeed."

"I authorized a simple retrieval, nothing else!"

"Knowing full well that if something went wrong, Tsai Teping would make a convenient shield for your failed ambitions." Dzhang lifted his hand to forestall a protest. "We have all played these games before and I'm not castigating you for it. Without knowing all the facts, I allowed the operation to proceed, given your assurance of minimal exposure risk. Playing with the Americans turned out to be very risky, something as minister for our foreign intelligence arm, you should have appreciated. Tsai Teping is an opportunist who also sought to enhance his personal standing, and perhaps even gain your job," Dzhang added.

"Don't look surprised, General. I am aware of his ambitions. Had he managed to retrieve the object, as a loyal princeling coalition supporter, he might have gotten it, and China could have bargained with the imperialists from a position of strength. In his haste to get the device, his operation exposed us to the Americans and raised their ire with the kidnapping of Dr. Morrison's wife. You have also compromised the government and me, and damaged efforts to repair our relationship with America."

Shafts of golden light slanted in from the windows to splash against the polished floorboards, setting off their grain. For once, the Beijing sky was clear, taking on a deep blue afternoon hue, a pleasant change from the blanket of gray pollution that normally hung over the city.

"Mr. Premier—"

"You have something to say, General?"

"Granted, the operation failed, but I maintain it was worth undertaking despite the obvious risks. Possession of the device—"

"Would have made us an IT giant, I know. But when? In ten or twenty years, if at all? From what you told me, we don't even understand the theoretical principles underpinning the crystal's function, let alone be in a position to build anything vaguely similar. For some uncertain future gain, you have set this country on another possible collision with the West, one that's probably already happening, and whose outcome is by no means certain, but definitely unfavorable for us! This is something I cannot ignore. You allowed your vision of greatness to override your judgment. If you sought to benefit the State, you should have submitted your action proposal to the State Council for proper deliberation."

"I had your approval, Mr. Premier," Lin said evenly, evidently not caring if he was insubordinate.

Dzhang smiled without humor. "An error on my part, for which I still might suffer the consequences. Effective immediately, you're relieved of your post and confined to your private residence pending a review and possible action against you. You are dismissed, General."

Mouth set in a tight line, Lin Jinpan stood up, came to attention and marched out, the heavy ceiling-high door making a hollow boom as it closed behind him.

Dzhang reached for the phone and pressed a button on the pad.

"Yes, sir?" his confidential personal secretary answered.

"Can you come in, Leijang?"

"Of course."

Tall, slim, young, and alert, Weng Leijang strode in and stood respectfully before the desk. A new breed of bureaucrat who genuinely believed in the value of the rule of law and government accountability. With mentoring, Dzhang intended for the young-ster to have a posting in the Central Military Commission on a ladder to power.

"General Lin has been relieved. Make sure he reaches his res-idence and does not stray from it. Monitor any calls he makes."

"Relieved? Yes, sir."

Dzhang gave his protégé a bleak look. "A sordid plan that went wrong. I'll fill you in later. Call Zhou's office and ask them if I can see the President at his convenience."

"Of course, sir. Will there be anything else?"

"No, thank you."

Alone, Dzhang got up and faced the weathered windows. He wanted to stroll beside the two lakes, enjoy the relative peace of the soothingly landscaped gardens and clear his mind. At sixty—how the years have flown—he realized he was still young for his position, which left room for advancement, and the only position he could now aspire to was the presidency of the communist party. Zhou, of course, was aware of his ambition and appeared to foster it, but it would not happen for some time. Dzhang had to be careful not to overreach himself or he would find himself back in the Xinjiang Uyghur Autonomous Region handling the rebellious Uyghurs who sought to overthrow the ruling Hans, seeing them as long-standing invaders.

Technically, the president's office was supposed to be largely ceremonial without power to intervene directly in matters of the State Council, which made the premier the most powerful figure in the government. Under Zhou though, that changed when he started to exercise executive authority. Not every State Council member approved of the change, seeing it as erosion of their power, which it was, but several judicious transfers and retire-ments silenced the dissenters.

Dzhang did not mind the shift in authority, being more a shar-ing of responsibilities, and he knew how to be patient while giv-

ing Zhou his undivided support. It would all come with the waiting, he thought comfortably, but it did no harm to contemplate
how it would feel to be the Paramount Leader. Right now, China
did not need internal disruption, still consolidating itself from the
La Palma disaster. He would not last long if Zhou discovered that
his loyal supporter and trusted confidant plotted against him. By
unmasking his aspirations, Dzhang had defused the threat, while
tacitly acknowledging that should the president stumble…but
that is how everybody played the game.

In the meantime, he must neutralize the hot dim sum Lin
Jinpan had thrown in his lap, thanking his ancestors that Mrs.
Morrison wasn't seriously hurt. Had she been, he was certain the
young reactionary American president would not hesitate to
bring the might of his country's economy and military to bear on
China in retaliation. Shooting an opposition's operative now and
then—rarely done these days—was the price everybody paid to
be a player, but countries frowned on collateral damage.

By talking to Ambassador Sawyer, Lin Jinpan handled the situation well, he admitted grudgingly. Dzhang would eat humble
yum cha and apologize to Tanner while maintaining an accepta-
ble political façade, both knowing this was not the end of it. He
found nothing inherently wrong with Lin's plan, except that it
failed, and Dzhang understood what the device could mean for
China, albeit in some future. If the Israelis had the thing now,
there had to be a way to pry it from them.

A germ of an idea surfaced and he slowly nodded. The Israelis
badly wanted a Free Trade Agreement, but how badly? Enough
to form a joint venture to study the strange device and develop
any offshoot industries? It was worth putting out feelers to them.
He always had the clandestine approach if diplomacy failed, and
China would not be concerned about economic or political sanctions, not from the puny Jews—unless the Americans intervened,
which he did not consider likely. They were bound to be sore at
Israel for having the crystal snatched from under their noses.

Dzhang could not be too high-handed, though. Israel had supplied and continued to supply China with advanced military
equipment and sophisticated technology—American technology—it could not acquire elsewhere.

Of mild concern were the Arabs and their threat to shut off
oil supply if China entered into any formal trade agreement with
Israel. Trade was happening now, and expanding, but everybody
looked the other way because nothing was official. If the Arabs
wanted to play tough, he reminded himself that they were not the
only source of energy for China, certain the Russians would be
happy to expand their oil pipelines eastward across the taiga in
return for fat profits.

How the mighty have fallen, Dzhang mused. Russia, the bas-
tion and father of socialist communist doctrine reduced to capitalist profiteering. The dollar would also placate the prickly Arabs, he thought comfortably. Withholding supply would not be
in their long-term interest with OPEC no longer the unified force
it once was, always bowing to Saudi policies. There was also Australia with their seemingly endless abundance of gas and iron ore.
Anyway, China was already weaning itself off polluting coal and
aging nuclear plants. In a few years, modern thorium reactors,
and an expanding renewable energy program, would provide all
the energy China needed.

However, oil had a more strategic use than merely powering
cars and trucks. It served as an irreplaceable feedstock for many
vital industries. Disruption of those industries could be very damaging to planned growth projections and prosperity. Too many
things to consider in an increasingly tangled web of international
trade. Running a closed economy used to be so much simpler.

He straightened and exhaled slowly. He would present his arguments to Zhou and get things moving. In case of difficulties,
they would cover each other, or both would end up enjoying early
retirements.

He glanced across the tailored lawns and decided the gardens

Stefan Vučak

really looked lovely…

Chapter Eight

A light drizzle softened the harsh outlines in the canyon of sky-scrapers as the tires whispered on the glistening road. Not cold, the rain had washed out some of the smog, refreshing the air. When the clouds cleared, the sun would bake the city, making it humid and sticky.

The TriCon driver slowed the car and turned into New York–Presbyterian Hospital's west wing visitors' parking lot, the Beek-man Tower across the street lost in low cloud.

"I'll be waiting here, Doctor."

Morrison nodded to the driver and stepped out. On the side-walk, people huddled beneath umbrellas, hurrying to wherever they were going, mostly to work. He waited for Stan and Sandra to get out and made for the entrance. Both had flown in late yes-terday afternoon, a TriCon car picking them up from the airport. He disliked the security blanket hovering over him, but Lazars was right when he insisted that it be maintained, the focus having shifted to his QD pigment. This aspect of his business had defi-nitely soured some of Morrison's days and he wondered how long he would have to put up with it.

Having Stan and Sandra with him gave them all an oppor-tunity to catch up on the latest family gossip. Although Stan tried to shrug it away as unimportant, he looked pleased when Morri-son congratulated him on getting his master's. In a quiet moment when Sandra left to attend to some personal business, he asked Stan if he considered going for his PhD. With Ferguson as his thesis advisor, he would get his degree in a year, unless the thesis required extensive research. He was glad to hear that Stan would consider it, but not right away. Although his son looked wary as though he expected an argument, he was obviously relieved when Morrison told him he would help him no matter what he decided. At that moment, he felt closer to his son than he'd been for some time, especially after Stan started gushing about ideas he wanted to test that might lead to a patent or two. If the research required money, Morrison told him he would square it away with Ferguson.

In the entrance foyer, they headed for the elevators. On the third floor, as they walked toward Juliana's room, Morrison glanced at Sandra carrying a large bouquet of assorted flowers. Slightly apprehensive, she gave him a tight smile.

"You're sure she's all right?" she demanded, something she had asked more than once already.

He patted her arm. "She is fine. Seeing you will make her feel even better."

When they reached 312, he knocked once and entered, then gaped when he saw the empty room. Something cold coiled in his stomach. Stan pushed past him, looked around and their eyes met.

"Where is Mom?"

"What is going on, Daddy?" Sandra asked, a frown creasing her forehead.

"I don't know, honey. Maybe they had her transferred. We'll check with the Outpatients desk."

"They would have told you, wouldn't they?" Stan prompted.

That was it, Morrison agreed. They *would* have told him. His emotions under control, banishing the demons in his head, they headed for the front desk. Just finishing with an elderly woman pushing a walker, the nurse behind the counter looked up.

"Can I help you?"

"I am Dr. Morrison. I just went up to see my wife and she wasn't there."

"Room?"

"Three-twelve."

She tapped on her keyboard, mouth set in a pout of concentration, then gave him a mechanical grin.

"She was checked out this morning by two FBI men. Witness protection they said."

"She wasn't well enough to be discharged," he exploded.

"Her doctor authorized the discharge on condition that she didn't exert herself, and the FBI would have proper facilities. I thought you knew all this, Doctor. We were told that you were informed."

"Well, I wasn't. The two men who took her, do you have their names?"

"Their IDs were in order and we didn't record their details."

Morrison hissed in exasperation and slapped the counter, making the nurse flinch.

"Daddy? What is happening here?"

He turned to Sandra and tried to wipe the concern he knew showed on his face.

"I don't know."

"What's this witness protection thing, Dad? You told us the FBI got the men who kidnapped her."

"They did. Let me clear this up." He dug out his cell and selected a preset number.

"Special Agent Earle Fisher."

"Mr. Fisher, this is Dr. Morrison. We have a problem."

"Another problem?"

"My wife is gone and I was told taken by two FBI men."

Fisher cleared his throat. "I don't know anything about this, Doctor, but I'll look into it."

"Call me," Morrison ordered and cut contact.

He should have listened when Lazars recommended that Juliana be kept under guard. With the crystal gone, he figured there wasn't much point. *Stupid!*

His cell trilled and he pressed the receive button. The screen showed 'Unknown number'.

"Dr. Morrison."

"Listen to me, Doctor, and listen well. The crystal for your wife." Heavily disguised, the menacing voice made Morrison's hands go clammy.

"I don't have the crystal."

"Eleven o'clock in front of your building. You'll see a blue van. Hand the item to the driver and I'll call you later where to find your wife. If you try anything tricky, you'll never see her again."

Juliana hadn't talked, or the caller did not believe that he did not have the crystal.

"I told you—"

"Play it smart and both of us walk away happy."

Before the line went dead, Morrison heard what he swore was a faint wheeze and he froze. Could he be mistaken? No, he had heard that wheeze often enough to recognize the caller. After staring thoughtfully at his phone, he made another call.

"Dr. Morrison, I'm good, but you're pushing what is possible even for me," Fisher declared good-naturedly.

"It's Crawford. He just called demanding that I hand over the crystal." Morrison gave him the details.

"You're positive it's him?"

"Positive enough. He's been after me for a while. After getting demoted, I guess he took it personally. I tried to tell him that I didn't have the crystal, but he wouldn't listen."

"You have given me something definite to go on with, Doc. Make sure you keep your rendezvous. It's unlikely that Crawford would be foolish enough to drive the van. When the handover takes place, we'll be ready."

"Mr. Fisher, you do know what Crawford was doing in his job?"

"I am aware of his training and he will undoubtedly take precautions, but there are ways to get around them."

"They won't help me if the driver decides to open the package. I cannot give him a brick."

Fisher chuckled. "We'll get you a facsimile crystal, Doc."

Morrison did not like any of this, but there weren't any options to pick from.

"Thank you, Mr. Fisher," he grated, ready to do anything to have Juliana back safe.

"Of course, it might not be Crawford at all."

"I know that, but like you said, you have something solid to work with."

"Hang in there, Doc," Fisher said and the line went dead.

Morrison pocketed the cell and clenched his teeth. He should have had her guarded!

Sandra grabbed his arm. "Daddy, if you don't explain what is going on, I'll…I'll never speak to you again!"

He sighed and his shoulders sagged.

"A DOE agent could be the one holding your mother, and Fisher, the FBI man I've been dealing with, has a plan to get her."

"You didn't seem all that confident on the phone," Stan said.

"I'm not, but I have to trust Fisher. Look, I must get back to the office, but I'll tell the driver to drop you off at the apartment. You'll be safe there, okay?"

Looking at the two, it was definitely not okay with them.

Sandra glanced at Stan. "Drop us off at Broadway," she said. "We'll make our own way to the apartment."

Morrison bit his lip. "I don't like the idea of you two wondering around alone."

"Oh, for heaven's sake, Dad!" Stan erupted. "We don't need a TriCon minder holding our hand."

Morrison smiled and capitulated. "Hopefully, this will be all over by lunchtime and then we can celebrate. I have reservations for us at Luke's Lobster."

Outside, the drizzle had stopped and the clouds were breaking up. An occasional flash of sunlight made the puddles glitter and the city noises sharper.

Allison looked up as he walked toward his office.

"Good morning, Doctor. I trust Mrs. Morrison is better?"

Things appeared darker and the load pressing on his shoulders heavier.

"Someone took her, and I think it was Crawford."

Her face crumpled. "That horrible DOE man? I'm so sorry!"

"The FBI is on it. Keep this to yourself, okay?"

"Of course. If there is anything—"

His mouth twitched and he nodded. "Thank you." Straightening, he fixed on his CEO face. "I'll be leaving at eleven and I don't want an escort. Give the TriCon man the word. Anything I should know?"

"Mr. Moore wanted to see you."

"Send him in," he said as he walked into his office.

He barely had time to power up his computer and log in when a knock interrupted his thoughts and Moore strode in. A little on the corpulent side and balding, that did not interfere with his crisp can-do attitude.

"How are you, Kevin?" Moore asked, not meaning it as he pulled back a chair and sat down. "How is Juliana?"

"Somebody kidnapped her, Doug."

"Again? Shit. That somebody wants the crystal?"

"And I don't have it. Keep this under the lid. So, what's up?"

"Are you sure you want to be here? I mean…"

"There is nothing I can do and the FBI have all the facts."

"Okay. I had a talk with Stone Van Rullen, and I hate to say this, but I think you're right. He should go. He is a terrific operations guy, but he doesn't have the big picture killer instinct we need to push sales. In a way, I feel responsible for not seeing this—"

"And I'll make you pay," Morrison said with a grin.

"I know you will. I sent Trotman up there to check things out, but I doubt he'll come up with anything we don't already know.

I hope you don't mind."

"You're the general manager and Trotman is an employee to use as we see fit. Why would I mind?"

"Well, you seem to use him as your confidential asset, and I thought—"

"I use him because he is capable, and that's how you should use him."

"Suits me. Van Rullen was right about one thing, Kevin. The Chinese make most of the world's PV panels, like they make LED TV screens. Our competitors value-add with proprietary electronics and slap on their brand label. We produce our own nanograss thin film panels, but there isn't much variation in electronics where we can value-add. I cannot see how we can cut costs further to boost margins. Maybe we can offer cheaper inverters."

Morrison shook his head. "We stick with SMA, Fronius, and ABB. We built our reputation for excellence, reliability, and quality. I will not erode that simply to lift margins. Marketing, Doug. That's the key. Run promotional ads where we offer periodic specials. Give customers two free roof panels if they buy more than fourteen or a free window. A discount if they display our logo somewhere. Look into it."

"Already in the pipeline. There is something else. Some of the corporate customers are bitching about our thirty-day payment demand. If we offered sixty, even ninety—"

"Forget it. Their own invoices read thirty days. I'm not about to give anybody sixty days or more free credit. That's a cost to us and impacts our liquidity management."

"Just thought I'd mention it."

"You have somebody in mind as a replacement for Van Rullen?"

"Keith Laumer."

"The GE guy?" Morrison demanded and Moore nodded.

"He doesn't know squat about PV panels, but he could write

a book about eating your competition. I already sounded him out. He is open to an offer, and he won't be cheap, half a million base, but with bonuses and options, that will push him well over $600K. He'll be making more than I'm getting," Moore growled and Morrison laughed.

"We're just paper shufflers, Doug."

If Laumer was as good as Moore said, and he had no reason to doubt it, he could be the right man to take on the QD pigment program: plant development, trials, marketing plan, the lot. Taking over from Van Rullen would give him time to learn the business, which for someone savvy shouldn't take long. PV panels were just another commodity with a different set of competitors.

"Laumer is okay moving to Boston?"

"He is already there."

"I forgot. GE has its new global headquarters there. Get him on board. Once he lets you know when he can take over, make it clear to Van Rullen that we don't want to lose him, but he will be more effective looking after the plant without the executive responsibilities weighing him down. If he is honest with himself, he will accept the demotion. If not, he is free to go."

"Got it," Moore stood up and pulled down his jacket. "I hope things work out with Juliana, Kevin."

"Yeah."

When Moore left, Allison brought a carafe of fresh coffee and filled his mug.

After taking care of some emails and calls, signing papers, Morrison checked the time: 10:30, and began to wonder when the FBI would deliver the fake crystal. On cue, Allison walked in trailing a familiar figure. She nodded to him and closed the door.

"Take a seat, Mr. Fisher. I was wondering when someone would show up."

"Traffic. Glad to see the clouds go."

The FBI man sat down and placed a red jewel case on the desk. Hesitating, Morrison reached for it and opened the lid. He gazed at the transparent object, and for a moment, he thought it was his crystal, which was impossible. Picking it up, it felt warm and heavy like the real one.

"This thing is amazing. How did you guys manage to make it this quickly?"

"We didn't. This is courtesy of the DOE. When you mentioned Crawford, I had the Special Agent in Charge of the New York office give Secretary Ulesky a call. It turns out they've been playing with a broken crystal for some time and they made several lookalikes. This is one of them. We had it flown in by helicopter from DC."

"That was great, and I know about their broken piece. Crawford brought it in the other day. One problem. He will scratch it and that'll be it."

Fisher gave him a nasty grin. "If we had the real thing, we wouldn't risk giving it to Crawford."

"Just to save my wife," Morrison added grimly.

"Look, Doc. I didn't mean—"

Morrison raised a hand. "Don't worry about it. I understand."

"If he does scratch it, stall him until we get there."

"That's comforting. Can you tell me how you intend to handle this?"

"We cannot risk following the van. No matter how sophisticated a tail, a professional might spot it. We will follow it with a drone, moving my men into position from a safe distance. When the van makes contact with Crawford, or whoever is putting the squeeze on you, we'll get him. Before you say it, he will know that you have spoken to us, but since he didn't mention it, he feels confident enough in his plan to foil us. He could, you know, but having a drone watch everything is a killer and hard to beat." Fisher glanced at his wristwatch and stood up. "You can buy me lunch when you get the real thing back."

Morrison laughed. "We will both be starving if I wait that long."

"Then dinner once we get your wife."

"Deal."

Morrison escorted his guest out and returned to his desk. He fondled the replica, looking so real the pang of loss hit him again. Better that it was gone, he told himself. Standing before the window, gazing at the washed city, he made a decision. He sat down, glanced at his watch and pressed the phone speaker button.

"Allison? Please call Senator Lockhart's office and ask him to call me when convenient."

"Yes, sir." A few moments later, she called back, sounding surprised. "Sir, the Senator is available now."

Morrison raised an eyebrow. He had not expected such a quick response, knowing how everybody wanted a piece of his friend's time.

"Put him through...Randal, thank you for getting back to me so promptly."

"A pleasure, my boy. I had several free minutes when your call caught me. By the way, did that creep Ulesky call?"

"He did, and apologized handsomely. I owe you big time for that, and for sorting out the Department of State, but it looks like Crawford isn't done with me yet. I went to see Juliana at the hospital this morning and she wasn't there. I got a call from somebody soon after demanding that I turn over the crystal and I recognized the voice. It was Crawford. It sounded like him anyway."

"Shit! That thing has caused you no end of troubles. The FBI is on it?"

"I'm about to head out and make an exchange using a facsimile crystal the FBI gave me, but that's not why I called. I need your help again."

"Name it. Us Republicans have to stick together."

Morrison allowed himself a small smile. "I want you to set up a press conference and announce the existence of the computing device, including attempts to steal it."

"That won't help you get it back, and I cannot see the Israelis giving it to you."

"No, but I want everybody to know what's been going on and the lengths China and Israel were prepared to pursue to get it...as did our own government."

"You could be drawing others out of the woodwork with this."

"I know, but I'm hoping that under the glare of publicity, we may inject some rationality into the situation."

"You won't be doing the President any favors with this, my boy. It galls me to say it, but he has been a good president to us, even though he is a Democrat, and I sort of promised the White House chief of staff that I wouldn't go public on this."

"I regret if this will cause you or the Administration some embarrassment, but this is no longer only about me. Things have escalated and could potentially get out of control. The crystal is far too important to squabble over. Can you do it?"

"It will be on the twelve o'clock news."

"Thanks, Randal. I appreciate this."

"Keep me updated on Juliana."

He checked his watch, scrambled to his feet and hurried out. As he stood outside 28 Liberty two minutes short of eleven, a blue van rolled to the curb. Staring at the ancient contraption, he slowly walked toward it. The driver wound down the window. His hard olive features, black hair neatly combed back, a cigarette hanging from the corner of his mouth, gave nothing away as he jerked his head.

"Get in."

Morrison frowned, not liking this development. "The package for my wife. That was the arrangement."

The figure jerked his head again. "In."

The passenger door opened with a squeal and Morrison's nose crinkled at the stale smell permeating the dirty, dusty interior. He banged the door shut and the van pulled away. The driver did not look at him, concentrating on the traffic.

Probably looking for a tail, the driver made random turns into narrow streets, sometimes doubling back. Totally disoriented, Morrison did not have a clue where they were. As he listened to the clatter of the van's engine, it was a wonder the ancient thing actually moved, a testament to German engineering. The van rounded a corner and jerked to a stop beside a warehouse that had seen better days. On the right, the East River glittered in bright sunshine. Across FDR Drive, a cluster of tall brown tenement buildings formed the foreground.

Without saying anything, the driver got out and walked toward a small door cut into the warehouse's looming, paint-flaked side. Morrison gave a mental shrug and followed. Inside, he blinked to adjust his sight to the pervasive gloom. The massive interior completely empty. From a cubicle at the back that could have served as an office a long time ago emerged two figures, their footsteps making hollow echoes on the concrete floor.

"Crawford, you piece of shit!" Morrison snarled at the short, bald individual. "I thought I recognized your asthmatic wheeze."

"I am equally delighted to see you, Dr. Morrison."

"Where is my wife?"

"Not so fast. I believe you have something for me?"

Morrison reached into his pocket, extracted the jewel case and held it out, wondering when the FBI would show up. Crawford licked his lips, took the case and opened it. The intimidating figure beside him kept his eyes fixed on Morrison. Unmoved by the proceedings, the van driver dug out a pack of cigarettes and lit up.

Crawford extracted the crystal and held it up to the grubby skylight. He took a nail from his pocket and slowly scratched the surface. When he looked up, his face contorted with fury.

"I thought you'd be smarter than this, Doc," he said and nodded to his sidekick.

"Hold on! Ferguson subjected the crystal to x-rays in one of his tests to determine its atomic structure. It damaged the self-healing property," Morrison temporized in desperation.

"Damaged?"

"It will repair itself in about half an hour."

"Well, it seems we have half an hour to kill," Crawford said coldly, then shrugged. "Excuse me, unfortunate choice of words."

"My wife—"

"You have given me a lot of grief, Doc, and cost me my job and career. However, if you're right about the crystal, the Department might overlook my bad manners and we'll be pals again if I deliver the device...for suitable compensation. Now that I'm semi-retired—the job they gave me is a dead end—I have to secure my future. They're hoping I'll resign, saving themselves a termination payout, but I won't give them the satisfaction."

"Life can be a drag," Morrison grated.

"And I've been dragged through it."

"I want to see my wife."

"She is back there," Crawford hooked a finger over his shoulder. "Don't worry. You'll have time to enjoy her company—in half an hour."

The side door banged open and black-clad men brandishing weapons charged in.

"FBI! Eat the floor! Now!"

Crawford swore and reached into his jacket. His grim sidekick already had his gun out and crouched to take a shot. Morrison flung himself toward the floor as four sharp cracks made his ears tingle and he saw the gunman go down. The van driver had his hands up, the cigarette hanging from his open mouth.

His face twisted in a snarl, Crawford raised his arm and Morrison heard more shots. Something thumped into his left shoulder, making him cry out. Crawford doubled over, dropped his gun and folded to the floor.

It seemed to take a long time for Morrison to fall and the concrete wasn't all that hard. His shoulder felt numb with little pain,

Stefan Vučak

but the buzzing in his ears grew louder. He heard rushing footsteps and someone knelt beside him.

"You're having a hell of a day, Doc," Fisher told him harshly.

"Better than him," Morrison croaked, managing to point a
finger at Crawford's supine form.

"He'll live to enjoy retirement at a maximum security facility."

"My wife…"

"We got her. The back office had its own entrance."

Morrison sighed with satisfaction and closed his eyes.

* * *

"Fascinating," Sharron Ibrahim murmured, entranced as he
gazed at the orange crystal resting on a bed of white velvet.

The beveled edges and groove cut into its long sides belied
the sophistication underpinning the simple elegance of its design.
He reached out to touch it, then withdrew his hand. He looked
up and smiled sheepishly at Abdon Sayar.

"I feel like I was about to touch the Arc of the Covenant."

The foreign minister sat relaxed in a visitor chair and nodded
with understanding.

"And just as dangerous. Both are unearthly and perhaps
something not meant for man to disturb."

Ibrahim's eyes grew large in surprise. "A few days ago you
were extolling its virtues as Israel's economic savior and pushed
me into undertaking a covert operation to get it."

"I pushed you?"

"Forget it. What changed your mind?"

"I haven't changed my mind, but seeing the real thing gives
me a different perspective." Sayar leaned forward. "President
Walters will want it back, you know that."

"Or what?" Ibrahim said with derision. "No, my friend. We
took this course knowing what might happen, and now we have
to face retribution. What can he do anyway? Announce another

UN resolution?"

They looked at each other and both burst out laughing.

A knock on the door made them turn their heads. The PM's private secretary peered in.

"Excuse me, Prime Minister. President Walters is on line three."

Ibrahim nodded and raised an inquiring eyebrow at Sayar. "The shape of our retribution? Right on time." He snapped the jewel case shut and reached across the desk. "This will be on speaker, so zip it." He pressed a blinking white button on the phone pad, then activated the speaker.

"Good morning, Mr. President. I trust you're having a good start to your day?"

"That remains to be seen, Mr. Prime Minister. And how is your day so far?"

"A bag of mixed fortunes, and the evening shadows grow long."

"I've had days like that myself," Walters said, his voice strong, measured and…presidential, Ibrahim concluded.

The American president had reason to be confident, enjoying unprecedented domestic and international popularity, and with it…influence. Although relatively young, Walters had proven himself an astute statesman not afraid to exert his authority in support of American interests. Ibrahim had underestimated this man once—badly—and did not want to repeat the mistake.

"The China Free Trade Agreement? If we can help in any way…"

"It's not the Chinese, Mr. President—"

"The Gulf Cooperation Council is threatening to block their oil supplies?"

"On Saudi Arabia's urging."

"Public posturing, Prime Minister, which Iran has ignored, more than happy to have a high-volume customer like China. You know, of course, Iran is prepared to supply *you* with oil."

Ibrahim gave Sayar a startled glance and the foreign minister raised a finger in warning.

"There have been…overtures," Ibrahim said cautiously, which was true. "However, our Tamar and Leviathan gas fields have ameliorated our energy dependence somewhat."

Reelected with an overwhelming popular margin, something the Council of Guardians were forced to swallow, not liking the erosion of their power, President Hamadee Al Zerkhani had opened Iran to Western trade and ideas. With several nuclear warheads provided by North Korea, Iran had magnanimously suspended its nuclear program, dismantled most of its gas centrifuge enrichment facilities and converted the Bushehr reactor into a verified civilian power generating plant.

Contrary to popular rhetoric by past Israeli administrations, which formed the cornerstone that underpinned much of its reactionary foreign policy, Ibrahim understood that Iran did not seek Israel's destruction. They were more concerned about a nuclear Pakistan dominated by a Taliban regime. When Sayar informed him of Iran's offer, made through a French intermediary, both were initially surprised. After some thoughtful consideration, Ibrahim acknowledged that trade with Iran would be politically an astute move and would go a long way toward further easing of Middle East tensions. Especially since the Palestinian state seemed to be working, although still a shaky and corrupt institution, which nevertheless had to a large extent neutralized Hamas and Hezbollah's *raison d'être*.

Walters gave a fruity laugh. "It would be in Israel's interest to entertain the proposal and demonstrate to the world at large your country's maturing international standing."

Easy for the President to say, Ibrahim mused.

Walters had risked a serious domestic backlash in his first term when he initiated bilateral negotiations with Iran to thaw relations between the two countries. Zerkhani, acutely aware of the advantages having a more open policy toward the Great Satan, the move had strengthened both men's hold on power. Similarly, no longer hamstrung by ultra-orthodox and extreme right-wing micro-parties, Ibrahim's coalition government was in a position to prosecute genuine dialogue to benefit his country.

"It is something we have under consideration, Mr. President."

Ibrahim heard Walters give a soft sigh and tensed.

"Something that is not in Israel's interest, Prime Minister, is the recent activity by your intelligence service. I could hardly believe what Manfred told me. What happened at the Charles de Gaulle airport today did not help to sweeten my coffee."

"Where the CIA tortured and shot an accredited Israeli diplomat!"

"Hardly a diplomat. I understand your Metsada operative will pull through."

"Unfortunately, your CIA and the French DGSI man didn't."

"Will you believe me that I didn't know anything about it?"

"Mr. President, I don't want to hash over the unfortunate events at de Gaulle, or the discussion Ambassador Caplan had with your Chief of Staff. This device, regardless of the means Dr. Morrison used to acquire it, belongs to Israel, and we took the only appropriate option available to recover it."

"The only appropriate option, Sharron? You could have picked up the phone and talked to me. Instead, you demonstrated once again Israel's predilection for taking unilateral action to secure an outcome that a diplomatic approach might not guarantee. I thought we had developed a deeper relationship than that, Prime Minister."

Ibrahim clenched his teeth, torn with conflicting emotions. He still believed that the course he took *was* in Israel's best interest, but acknowledged the truth of Walter's words.

"I *was* tempted to call you, Sam—"

"Why didn't you?"

"Because you might have said no."

Ibrahim stewed for a few seconds in uncomfortable silence.

"You know what you're telling me? As far as Israel is concerned, the United States is not a reciprocal ally...or friend. After Valero, do you remember what Colonel Matan Irian said? 'Israel has no allies, only acquaintances of opportunity.' I did not want to believe it, but you have forced me to reconsider my position."

"I remember it well, and my history, Mr. President. In 1948, you helped create Israel, and in 1967, you stood by us when we were threatened with annihilation. However, we're no longer a fledgling country content to exist on scraps you and the international community see fit to throw our way." Ibrahim sensed that he had reached a pivotal point and made the plunge. "By retrieving the device, I was exerting Israel's sovereignty. Dr. Morrison's claim that he acquired the crystal legally is a fiction. Closed auctions have no recognition in law."

"Then you should have done something about them! But you turned a blind eye to the practice and now stand behind a thin veil of legality when it suits you. Both of us know what this is about, Sharron...potential economic advantage on a huge scale. Possibly unrealizable. Return the device and I'll try to persuade Dr. Morrison to enter into a cooperative UN-sponsored research project for the purpose of sharing any developments with the world."

"That's not a solution, Sam, and you know it. The project might share the knowledge with the world, but only countries with highly advanced manufacturing and sophisticated software capability would benefit from that knowledge. Capability available in the U.S."

"Which you also possess, as does China—I'm aware of their attempts to secure the device—but they're not the only players, of course. Don't you realize that you cannot do this alone, or you *will* be alone?"

"We were alone for more than two thousand years and managed to survive in a world that hates us," Ibrahim blurted out, immediately regretting the words. "Forgive me, I did not—"

Walters exhaled heavily. "I see that I must present my argument in a manner that leaves no room for ambiguity, and I regret having to do this more than you know. Our two countries are engaged in extensive intelligence sharing, strategic, political, and military cooperation, which includes direct and indirect aid—"

"Conditionally given with the proviso that most of that aid be spent purchasing American goods and services, which in fact subsidized your armaments interests."

"Nevertheless, you were able to procure those goods and services at rates not available to you elsewhere, which you then on-sold to South Africa, Turkey, Pakistan…and China, ignoring our objections and concerns, but I don't want to discuss economics. Despite your flawed policies toward the Palestinian people and Arabs in general, the U.S. has guaranteed the integrity of your state with unreserved commitment to exercise force on any aggressor. Since the Valero incident where I threatened the suspension of economic and military aid, Israel has made significant strides to reduce its tactical and strategic dependence on the United States for its weapons and logistical supplies, turning to European providers. That was a decision I approved despite intense lobbying by domestic vested interests. Being a 300 billion-plus economy, you don't need subsidized support, and we have other markets for our goods."

Ibrahim's brow creased with concern. "I'm not certain I understand what you're getting at, Mr. President."

"Our foreign policy has been driven in part by the need to secure oil supplies, which meant placating the Arabs. That no longer applies after becoming one of the three largest oil producers in our own right, and securing supply from Iran and Russia. With a more stable Middle East—the conflict in Syria being ideological and not somewhere the United States wants to engage, and ISIL reduced to ragtag regional terrorist groups, although still dangerous—Israel does not face a credible external threat. Your

Arab neighbors are well cognizant of your military superiority and nuclear deterrent. Accordingly, I do not see the need to maintain a direct presence of personnel and materiel reserves in your country."

"Mr. President—"

"I remember something Prime Minister Netanyahu said in 2010. 'I know what America is. America is a thing you can move very easily, move it in the right direction. They won't get in our way.' We won't get in your way, Sharron. You can consider the 2013 United States-Israel Strategic Partnership Act suspended. If you want us to be allies, we need to negotiate from mutual understanding consistent with our individual foreign policy needs. You have taken advantage of our goodwill for too long and the cup is empty.

"I have instructed the State Department to issue deportation notices to your embassy and consular staff identified as Mossad operatives. Israel's blatantly clandestine operations have become too serious and can no longer be tolerated. I have also instructed the Defense Secretary to order the 6th Fleet to interdict boarding of commercial shipping bound for Gaza under the pretext of weapons searches in accordance with UN Security Council resolution 2341, which you persist to ignore."

"We have a right to inspect those ships!" Ibrahim exploded. "The defense treaty between Israel and Palestine gives us that right."

"A treaty you imposed on them in return for easing travel restrictions between Gaza and the West Bank."

"Sam, Hamas is still a credible threat. They have not disavowed their objective to destroy us, still demanding a return to 1967 borders and establishing Jerusalem as their capital. Some of the ships we stopped carried arms not consistent with the needs of a peaceful state."

"With you as the sole arbiter of what a peaceful state needs.

Instead of furthering enmity, work with the Palestinian govern-ment to carry out their own inspections. Until then, the U.S. Navy will act to protect merchant shipping trading with a recog-nized state. I quoted a proverb to you once and I feel that another is warranted. 'You have set at naught all my counsel, and would hear none of my reproof.'"

"Proverbs 25, I believe," Ibrahim murmured, all color having drained from his face. The foreign minister turned to Sayar, look-ing ill. "Sam, you cannot mean what you just told me," Ibrahim said.

"This is not some conference in Geneva where we sign elab-orate agreements that will never be implemented. My Secretary of State will probably not agree with me, I know he won't, and some in Congress will question the wisdom of my decision—the Jewish lobby will definitely bring pressure to bear—but interna-tionally, a more impartial and balanced approach to U.S.–Israeli relations will be well received. For the first time, Prime Minister, your country is about to become truly independent with all the obligations independence implies."

Ibrahim did not know which he felt more: anger, humiliation, or desire to lash out. To be lectured and dictated to was intoler-able.

"This is pure intimidation, Mr. President, and an extreme ex-ample of the type. You must realize the potential for social dislo-cation in Israel, and the Middle East in general, your announce-ment implies. All this over an alien computing device?"

"The device merely served to highlight a platform of self-serv-ing policies Israel has pursued for some time, which successive American administrations were prepared to tacitly approve in ab-sence of positive discourse. My administration is not willing to maintain this delusion in order to placate emotional domestic rhetoric that kept you from developing and implementing mature policies. Return the device, Sharron, and together, we shall forge a relationship based on realistic appreciation and understanding of our respective national needs. Do think about it," Walters said heavily and the line went dead.

Ibrahim switched off the speaker, wiped his greasy face and sat back. Crossing his legs, he gave a wan smile.

"Forge a realistic relationship, he said. Hah!" He slapped the desk with both hands, stood up and started pacing. "He is a self-centered, egotistic, bullying bastard, and I will be *damned* if I'll give him the crystal."

Clearly in shock, Sayar swallowed hard. "You never wanted Mossad involved when we first talked—"

Ibrahim swung around and raised his hand. "I don't blame you for anything, my friend. I made the decision—"

"Because of my bad counsel, Israel faces not only another humiliation, but a serious international complication if the President follows through on his threats."

"They are not threats," Ibrahim said, fists clenched, and strode to the window. After a moment, he turned. "I shouldn't have shot off my mouth, but the magnitude of what he announced caught me completely unprepared."

"A new breed of politician we haven't seen before," Sayar mused. "He lacks guile. A result of his Air Force training, I guess. We're not used to straight talk, although he belittles his considerable diplomatic skills."

"Pity he didn't exercise them now." Frustrated, Ibrahim walked to his desk and sat down. "Remember his goodwill visit in February? Charming and gracious, but behind his clear penetrating eyes lies determination and a resolve to act, which he just demonstrated all too vividly. That decisiveness is one of many reasons why he enjoys such unprecedented popularity. Regrettably, Walters will do exactly what he said he would."

"He has already started by expelling our special attachés. That's going to hurt."

"His other announcements will hurt us even more."

"I could not help noticing your anger, though."

"Of course I'm angry, at him and myself, for allowing the situation to deteriorate. Not that I had any choice."

"The proverb he quoted, rather apt don't you think?"

"Damn his proverb! And damn him!"

Sayar suppressed a snicker. "Sorry. There is nothing amusing about this."

Ibrahim glared. "You're enjoying this, aren't you?"

"Sharron, get a grip on yourself."

"Okay, I'm calm. Tell me what you think."

"You know, however unwelcome, cutting the umbilical with America could be good for us, and the President was right about one thing," Sayar contemplated speculatively, working the angles. "With our military superiority and nuclear deterrent, we don't need their protective umbrella. We can be free to exercise our foreign policy without fear of veto from Washington."

"Valero should have been a salutary lesson for us, and in many respects it was," Ibrahim said, understanding exactly what Sayar was saying. "With our coalition, we were no longer beholden to extremist parties to hold government, but our thinking remained reactionary rather than measured."

Sayar pursed his mouth, holding steepled fingers in front of his chin. "Perhaps, and only partially true, but I still believe we made the right decision to take the crystal. If the United States does walk away, I doubt the voters here will care too much. Polling has consistently shown that although American support is appreciated, more than 48% of the population resents the need for that support."

Ibrahim looked meditatively at the foreign minister, admiring the ease with which he adopted the lecturing pose, his considerable intellect coming through. An unconscious trait Ibrahim found irritating at times. The mannerism however, did not stop him from appreciating the value of his friend's input.

"If only it were that simple, Abdon."

Silence drifted through the room, allowing a moment for re-flection.

Sayar shifted in his chair. "The scope of what Walters said…"

"I know. He used the Mossad incident as a platform to an-nounce a clear shift in relations," Ibrahim said slowly.

"Something the White House must have considered doing for some time, and we gave Walters the perfect moment to make it under the façade that we pushed him into it by our action to get the device."

Ibrahim pulled at his chin. "You're probably right, but forging a new relationship he mentioned is conditional on us handing over the thing."

"Not necessarily. What are you going to do?"

"I never rush into a decision when there is time to consider options."

"This time, we don't appear to have any."

"There are always options."

After a sharp knock, the door opened. "Excuse me, Mr. Prime Minister. Premier Dzhang Qishan requests a moment of your time. Line two," the secretary said.

Sayar grinned broadly. "Troubles come in threes?"

"Or an option, perhaps?"

"Sir, you should also know that Senator Lockhart just held a press conference in front of the Senate announcing a Mossad op-eration to recover some alien crystal."

"Thank you, Moshe," Ibrahim said, and the secretary closed the door. "Ah, shit."

"I take it back," Sayar said, still grinning. "They come in fours."

"You know, I hate you sometimes," Ibrahim grated.

He reached across the desk to switch on the speaker and open the line, then glanced at the wall clock and made a quick calcula-tion. Already past midnight in Beijing, it must be something im-portant for Dzhang to call, and he suspected he knew what it was.

"A pleasure to hear from you again, Mr. Premier," he said smoothly, although not a pleasure at all. "I trust that you and your family are enjoying good health, sir?"

Hidden behind a veil of smiles and silky phrases, never offering offense, preferring to dance around an issue, the Chinese were nevertheless deft negotiators. They were happy to spend months or even years grinding down their target until they achieved the desired objective. Unlike the Europeans and Americans, the Chinese shunned confrontational absolutes, content to settle for a workable compromise, favorable to them, of course.

"Well enough, Mr. Prime Minister, and thank you for your concern. However, my health would improve greatly in mountainous air."

"The brown pall hanging over Jerusalem makes me question sometimes whether the price we paid for our technological advancement and materialism worth the erosion of our cultural heritage."

"Unfortunately, the wheel of time turns only one way, and one of its spokes has carried me with it."

"I know the feeling well, Mr. Premier," Ibrahim said dryly, the conversation with Walters burning fresh in his mind, and heard a guffaw.

"Then you know why I called, and please excuse my rudeness for being so abrupt and for calling this late."

"Perfectly understandable. Both of us have little time to contemplate the unfolding of an apple blossom."

"Well said. I knew you would appreciate my difficulty. Mr. Prime Minister, allow me to come to the point. The unusual computing device in your possession has the potential to advance both our countries' interests beyond mere economics. You're aware of this and I shall not belabor the obvious. You must also be aware that any benefit accruing from the device is probably years in the future and will require considerable intellectual and material resources to realize. China is prepared to enter into a purely commercial partnership with Israel to realize those benefits. Even if the device cannot be replicated or made to work, the insights alone gained from its study could yield enormous returns."

Ibrahim glanced at Sayar, who shrugged. Nothing was lost by considering a possible deal. A more open and friendly China would be very advantageous for Israel, especially in an atmosphere of deteriorating U.S. relations.

"What are you proposing, sir?"

"A package, hinged on access to the device. We're ready to accelerate negotiations for a Free Trade Agreement—"

"In the face of a hostile Gulf Cooperation Council?"

"The risk can be mitigated. Israel has advanced rocketry technology, and you have launched satellites. We would invite applicants from your country to our astronaut training program, including potential inclusion to manned Moon missions and building of our space station."

Ibrahim raised his eyebrows. These were high stakes chips indeed. On its own, manned space missions were outside Israel's reach. Cooperation at that level would have considerable technology multiplier effects.

"I admit it's a very enticing package, Mr. Premier."

"Although not complete. For your immediate defense needs, we're prepared to offer you warships and patrol boats at a considerable discount, with options for a joint build of those vessels. This would include subsidized supply of missiles and conventional munitions. I'm aware that you manufacture many of those things yourselves, obtaining much of your logistics from the United States. However, that pipeline is by no means secure."

"In what way?"

"Need I elaborate, Mr. Prime Minister? The Americans are not pleased that you have channeled some of their advanced military technology to us…and others. Given how you retrieved the alien crystal, they will be even less pleased, and will undoubtedly curtail supply of that technology, leaving you without an alternative source. Your European suppliers lack the necessary sophistication."

Ibrahim nodded, admiring the reach and supremacy of the Chinese intelligence apparatus, something Mossad had encountered on several occasions.

"No, you do not need to elaborate, and President Walters has already expressed his displeasure in a very tangible way."

"I am sure he has. As part of this, ah, package, I'm proposing the setting up of a joint research program—"

"And we hand over the device."

"That follows."

"If this is going to be a partnership, sir, Beijing could send its researchers to us. We have a strong physics community and our software engineers are among the best. It's feasible that your scientists could learn something from us."

"A possibility that has not escaped our attention. There is another item for your contemplation," Dzhang said and waited for several seconds. "Despite having major gas fields, your country's energy demands cannot be guaranteed in the long term, and we're aware of your intention to build another nuclear plant. China is prepared to help you build that plant. Not fueled by uranium or plutonium, but thorium, using proven technology we developed and are rolling out."

This one managed to startle Ibrahim. He doubted that China developed the technology, most likely based on stolen French or Indian designs.

"An attractive offer indeed, Mr. Premier."

"Unfortunately, the offer has a limited timeframe, Mr. Prime Minister."

"And if Israel does not accept it?"

"Everything is off the table, as the Americans would say," Dzhang said lightly, but Ibrahim knew it was meant seriously.

"I appreciate your candor, sir, and I shall give your proposal due consideration."

"Thank you for your time, and I look forward to hearing from you."

When the line went dead, Ibrahim switched off the phone speaker.

"Another bastard," he muttered and gave a long sigh.

"He made some good points," Sayar countered.

"But…"

"We should not hand over the crystal to him or anybody. I agree with you there. Once they have it, Dzhang's package could evaporate, or at best be dribbled out in pieces over years, making it useless. Then again, I might be unreasonably cynical."

"I would suggest realistic," Ibrahim mused. "You realize, of course, by revealing the existence of the device to the world, Senator Lockhart has poured fuel on an already volatile situation."

"He would not have done it without Morrison's urging."

"No, the Doctor knew exactly what he was doing—making life uncomfortable for us. Getting back to Dzhang's deal…"

"If we accept any part of it, the Americans will see this as a fundamental shift in Israel's strategic alliance, and they would be right."

Ibrahim shrugged. "President Walters has made that shift for us. He can hardly complain if we consider other alternatives."

Sayar sat up looking concerned. "Do we want to go down that direction, Sharron? Once we make that first step, going back might not be possible. We're a Western-oriented culture with a shared history and religion. Walters may be upset at us right now, but it's a situation we can repair, and we can rely on them to be a strategic partner, something we cannot say about the Chinese. They have no interest in the Middle East, although they're interested in the Mediterranean, and they don't care about a conflict we might have with our Arab neighbors, except to sell both sides weapons."

Ibrahim laughed. "Now you *are* being cynical."

"Even if the Chinese accept your counteroffer to base their scientists here, they will look for ways to steal the device."

"Of course, but we can set up isolation protocols that anyone wanting to get the crystal would find hard to break. Except for our people, who cannot be compromised in any way, no one should be given direct access to the device. I like what Dzhang is offering, but the crystal remains here, even if that means we must reject his proposal."

"We could make a similar offer to the Americans," Sayar said and Ibrahim nodded.

"I know, and I have thought about it, but Walters has not offered us anything in return."

"Ah, I wouldn't exactly say that."

"Mmm, yes. America is prepared to remain a trusted ally, even though we continued to abuse that trust."

"On their terms?"

"What did you expect?" Ibrahim gave a long sigh. "It might have been better for all of us if that crystal remained buried."

"Perhaps others are already thinking that. What are we going to do about the threat Walters made to stop inspections of Gaza shipping?"

"They will continue and we shall see what happens," Ibrahim declared with resolve. "The Palestinians have their state and we're enjoying a tentative peace, but like I told the President, Hamas has not disbanded. We cannot afford to drop our guard."

"Sharron, the only way to stop the American navy is to fire on them. Personally, I don't want another USS *Liberty* incident. Unlike President Johnson who swallowed our attack on the NSA spy ship for political reasons, Walters would not hesitate to retaliate."

"I know. We will fire warning shots only. I don't want an engagement either, but under international law, we're covered."

"You're forgetting that Security Council resolution," Sayar

pointed out.

"I'm not forgetting anything. Walters doesn't live in the shadow of terrorism, and I will not be dictated to!"

"You'll talk to Seddon?"

"In the morning," Ibrahim said. He had to update the defense minister anyway. "But first, you and I need to find a way to present this development to our respective Parties."

* * *

The large *Arleigh Burke*-class guided missile destroyer left creamy white froth in its wake as it cleaved the deep blue Mediterranean waters. Dawn had broken, leaving the eastern sky still bathed in blood. Smooth and glassy, the sea reflected what would be another clear day devoid of cloud. Captain 'Hardy' Mercer sat in his command chair on the bridge observing his watch officers at work, liking what he saw. Well trained, they carried out their respective duties without the need for extraneous orders.

He could have used some extraneous orders yesterday. After four days tied to posts at the Iskenderun Naval Base on a goodwill visit, his sailors running riot through the small Turkish town, Mercer's comfortable world was shattered when the XO showed him a tasking order from CNE-CNA/C6F to sortie immediately for Israel. He had hoped to see the new Chinese *Qin*-class Type 098 strategic missile sub close up, which supposedly used a magnetic fluid water jet propulsion system without a screw allegedly capable of doing 100 knots, but the Turks would have none of it, tying the sub to a pier out of sight of American prying eyes.

When he read the orders, Mercer handed the flimsy to Watkins without comment.

"I've seen it," the XO said. "Old Jarvis never wastes words, but this…"

Mercer shrugged. What was there to say except execute his mission even if it didn't make sense. They would have to hustle though, to cover the 500-odd nautical miles to reach their assigned station.

After checking Vice Admiral Mason Jarvis' authenticator, he issued orders to round up the crew and get USS *Porter* and its sister ship USS *Ross* ready to sail. Commander, Naval Forces Europe-Africa/Commander, U.S. 6th Fleet, did not have a sense of humor and expected the two elements of DESRON 60 to be on their way by 1700 hours. Based at Naval Station Rota, comfortable in his spacious Spanish office, the admiral expected the impossible every time.

They made it with nine minutes to spare as Turkish onlookers watched with amused tolerance the frantic activity of two American warships readying themselves to sail.

"I won't mind getting out of here," Watkins commented dryly.

"Giving the Turkish girls a breather, XO?" Mercer added wryly, a quizzical smile lighting his face.

"Now, Captain. I'm only sharing my charms, is all. They deserve my attention."

"And the girls back in Norfolk?"

The XO shrugged. "The only thing I got back there is an apartment I haven't seen in four months, a pile of bills, and a car that probably won't start. I have to distract myself somehow."

Mercer rolled his eyes. Watkins was impossible. A superb administrator and tactician, he ran the ship with an easygoing style that underpinned his professionalism. On shore, however, the XO turned into a relentless hunter pursuing female game.

Watkins looked grave when the actual tasking order came through later that night, and he had reason to be concerned.

"They are our allies, Skipper!"

"*Were* our allies, XO," Mercer said, watching the play of emotions on his friend's face. "To them, America was a pliable tool to be used or discarded as they saw fit. Tomorrow morning, we'll find out if we're still allies."

"Captain, we're now at nine miles," the Tactical Action Officer announced calmly, pushing back the headset connecting him to CIC, waking Mercer from his reverie.

"Very well. COMMO, give them a hail on Channel 16," he ordered softly, but clearly enough not to have the order misunderstood.

The communications officer touched the mike attached to his headset.

"Cargo vessel. This is the United States warship USS *Porter*, DDG-78. Please state your port of departure, cargo, and destination."

The speaker crackled. "This is the Turkish registered carrier *Abdullah*, Istanbul to Port of Gaza. Carrying general foodstuffs and agricultural machinery," declared a heavily accented voice. "Is there a problem?"

"No problem, sir. We'll be providing escort. Maintain course and safe landing."

"You mean, I will not be intercepted by those Jewish pirates?"

"Not this time, sir. Out."

"Time to the central maritime zone?" Mercer asked.

"Eighteen minutes."

Before creation of a Palestinian state, Israel established three maritime zones off Gaza, nominally under joint management with the Palestinian Authority, but in reality, they had no say in monitoring shipping entering the Strip. A central zone extended twenty nautical miles from the coast and all foreign shipping was forbidden entry. That restriction was never relaxed when Palestine gained independence, despite international protests and two UN resolutions condemning Israel's blockade of a sovereign country's lawful maritime traffic.

It looked like President Walters had grown weary of this and decided to do something about it. Mercer approved. Israel was not a law unto itself, even though they behaved like they were.

"Captain, we have one Super Dvora Mark III-class patrol boat closing on *Abdullah*. Distance, five nautical miles. Speed, thirty knots. Ten minutes to intercept."

"Probably out of Ashdod," Mercer mused.

Around thirty-five kilometers north of the Gaza Strip border, the Israeli Southern Command must have tracked *Abdullah* and sent out the intercept boat from their premier naval base. Probably more than one. The Dvoras always worked in pairs.

The Dvora Mark III was the latest generation in the venerable Dvora family of Israeli fast attack craft, capable of traveling up to 50 knots. Armed with one Typhoon 30mm stabilized cannon on the bow and stern, 12.7mm machine guns, surface-to-surface AGM-114 Hellfire missiles, and Mk 46 torpedo tubes, the little ships were nasty business.

Against an *Arleigh Burke* destroyer, it wouldn't stand a chance.

Massing 6,900 tons and 505 feet long, painted drab gray, USS *Porter* was a powerful ship. Armed with multiple Mk 41 vertical launch cells that could launch Tomahawk or Standard attack missiles, RIM-162 Evolved Sea Sparrows for stand-off defense, VL-ASROC antisubmarine missiles, five inch/54-caliber main gun, torpedo tubes, and a Phalanx CIWS close-in defense system, the ship could hold its own against almost anything. Two MH-60 Sea Hawk helicopters housed in a stern hangar extended its reach when sub hunting. Pushed by four GE gas turbines powering two shafts, going better than thirty-six knots, the ship was also unusually fast.

"Are we being painted?"

"Nav radar only."

Mercer glanced at Watkins. "Action stations, XO. Designate the Dvora as Target A and hail her."

"Aye aye, sir." The XO picked up the 1MC mike. "All hands, set Condition Able. This is not a drill." The claxon blared and the crew scrambled to their assigned stations. Watkins turned to the communications officer. "Give him the bad news, Monk."

"Israeli warship, this is USS *Porter*. You are advised to break contact and not approach cargo vessel *Abdullah* for the purpose of boarding and carrying out inspection of cargo. Please acknowledge."

"USS *Porter*, this is INS *Paragon*. You are interfering with the legal execution of my orders without citing your authority and I cannot comply."

Mercer picked up the mike. "What button?"

"Channel five."

"INS *Paragon*, this is Captain Mercer commanding. Your government was notified of our intention to interdict Israeli naval forces under UN Security Council resolution 2341, denying you the ability to arbitrarily intercept the peaceful flow of commercial traffic into the Port of Gaza."

"Captain Mercer, this is Lieutenant Harmon. In absence of official notification from Tel Aviv, I'm obliged to execute my orders."

"I would suggest, Lieutenant, that you contact the IDF Chief of Staff and query your mission orders with some alacrity." Mercer turned to Watkins. "Light him up with the AN/SPY-1D radar in case he thinks we're kidding."

Grinning, the XO nodded. "Aye, sir."

Painting the Israeli patrol boat with the powerful search radar would alert Harmon that the destroyer's Aegis warfare system was fully active and ready to respond to any development. Mercer hoped this would be enough to deter the Israeli commander from doing something foolish. Jarvis left no room for doubt in the updated Rules of Engagement. The two DDGs would deny the Israelis access to merchant shipping bound for the Port of Gaza, and Mercer was authorized to employ any and all means in compliance of his orders short of using deadly force unless fired upon.

Mercer didn't like it and figured USS *Ross* liked it even less. If things went wrong, which was entirely possible given the current situation, the brass would sacrifice him to patch up a possible international embarrassment.

Well, master under God, you wanted command. Now is your chance to show the Navy that it hadn't made a mistake when they gave you Porter.

"Where is *Ross*?"

The TAO looked up from his CIC repeater screens.

"Twenty-six miles off our port beam, Captain."

"Any other merchant traffic heading our way?"

"Negative. We have the place to ourselves."

Mercer suppressed a grin at the cocky answer. "Order *Ross* to close and maintain a separation of ten miles."

"Order *Ross* to close, aye, sir."

Watkins ambled over. "You have that feeling, Captain?"

"Yeah, I have that feeling, Paul," Mercer mused and stroked his chin. "Go down to CIC…and take *him* with you," he said, hooking a thumb at his fire-eating TAO.

In a major tactical situation, Mercer would command the ship from CIC, but existing threat factors were low and the XO played the Aegis system like a virtuoso. He also wanted to stress the young TAO and build up his confidence. Training simulations weren't the same thing. Anyway, if things deteriorated, the Combat Information Center only a deck down, and he had adequate situational awareness to anticipate any development.

"Sir, *Paragon* knows it cannot take us…"

"Exactly, but it's still maintaining course for *Abdullah*, and that means only one thing."

"Harmon is calling for support. Fast movers?"

"If they mean business, I expect to see F-15SEs out of Tel Nof at any time. Ready the Sea Sparrows and the Phalanx, just in case."

The XO gave Mercer a hard look. "Our presence is meant to be a demonstration of intent, Captain, not an invitation to shoot us up."

"I don't know what's going on, Paul, but intent means carrying out our orders, and that includes warding off a possible attack."

"The Israelis wouldn't—"

"Just go down and look after things."

"Aye aye, sir."

"How is the crew taking this? Some are Jewish."

"They are Americans, not Israelis, Captain." Scowling, Watkins motioned to the TAO and the two walked off the bridge.

Mercer pursed his mouth. He did not worry about the crew, not really, but anything to do with Israel tended to be evocative on many levels and generated powerful emotions. Out of habit, he glanced at the Electronic Chart Display Information System screen and checked the radar plot. *Paragon* had increased speed to thirty-four knots in an attempt to flank *Porter*.

"Helm, make revolutions for thirty-eight knots and turn to zero-three-zero."

"Increasing revolutions to thirty-eight knots and turning to zero-three-zero, aye," the helm petty officer responded as he spun the small maneuvering wheel installed to replace the original joystick. Some things simply could not be modernized.

"CIC, Captain. Light up the Dvora with the AN/SPY-62."

"Target illuminated," the TAO answered.

The squirt from the fire control radar did nothing to deter the Dvora, and Mercer did not expect that it would. Harmon was either pushing his orders to the limit, knowing he would be stopped, or he had received new orders, which Mercer suspected was the case. What he could not figure out was why the Israelis were developing the tactical scenario—unless the diplomatic option had already been expended?

The possibility of Israeli forces engaging him did not sit well, but then, nobody asked how he felt about it. He had enough on his mind without worrying about the strategic dimension.

Silhouetted against a thin line of land that hugged the horizon, *Abdullah's* fat hull looked dark, trailing a thread of black smoke, well within Israel's shore missile batteries. As *Porter* approached the twenty-mile central maritime exclusion zone, it too could now theoretically be classified as a target. However, Mercer doubted that Israel would want to prosecute him regardless of any perceived provocation. They liked their action close and personal. However, the last thing he expected was getting into a shooting match with them.

"Bridge, XO. Showing a second Dvora approaching *Abdullah* from the north. Range, six nautical miles. Also showing two F-15SEs coming in from north-east, probably Tel Nof. Four hundred and fifteen knots indicated air speed. We're being painted by their APG-82 attack radar and they have missile locks with AGM-65 Mavericks."

The air-to-ground tactical missile, armed with either a contact or delayed-action fuse, its powerful 300-pound charge could do considerable damage if it struck. Fired from close range, its 620 knot speed did not give the intended target a lot of time to react. Mercer had no intention of allowing the F-15s to get close. Ironic that he could be attacked by ordnance made in the United States.

"Label them Target B and C," he ordered immediately. "Light them up." These were serious threats and he had to honor them.

Well, the Israelis weren't bashful at asserting their authority, even against a supposed ally.

"Illuminated. Target A is now 2000 yards from *Abdullah*."

Mercer glanced at the ECDIS and saw that he would not close with the merchant ship before *Paragon* reached it. Just then, the air shook as the F-15s roared over *Porter*, wingtip to wingtip going port to starboard. Very businesslike, he thought.

Dvora's Hellfire missiles only had a 600 yards range, and its Typhoon 30mm, 1000 yards. As long as *Porter* stayed outside that envelope, it was invulnerable. That could not be said for the F-15s.

Mercer scowled and picked up the mike. "INS *Paragon*, this is USS *Porter* actual. Alter course or you will be fired upon." He hoped to get a response, but knew he wouldn't, he nodded. "CIC, Captain. You have weapons free. Train the main gun on Target A and shoot one round 100 yards off its bow."

"One round, aye, sir."

The bow turret swung to port slightly. The crack and recoil that ejected a puff of white smoke made some of the watchstanders look at each other, realizing that this was not an exercise and they might see missiles heading their way. With a fifteen-mile range, the Dvora was well within *Porter's* main gun tube envelope.

A tall column of white water appeared in front of the attack craft and began to fall as the Dvora ran through it. It had to have shaken them up, because it veered sharply to port.

"Bridge, CIC! Vampire! Vampire! We have two incoming Mavericks from starboard! CIWS is in autonomous mode. Impact in six seconds."

Too close for Sea Sparrows to engage or fire chaff, the close-in weapons system would have to handle the threats. Mercer saw the forward mounted Phalanx barrels swing to starboard, followed immediately by a sound of ripping cloth as the Vulcan Gatling gun spewed streams of armor-piercing tungsten penetrator rounds at the incoming missiles. At seventy-five rounds per second, the Mavericks would find it tough to get through, but not impossible.

Mercer did not see the missiles, but the brown smudges of their detonation were clearly visible, as were the dull claps of explosion.

"Bridge, CIC. Both incoming destroyed."

Mercer immediately turned to the communications officer.

"Go to Guard and warn the F-15s to break off. If they fire again, they will be shot down."

"Aye, sir."

By broadcasting on the aircraft emergency channel, the Eagles would get the message, as would the Israeli IDF command. Mercer wanted no misunderstandings when the chair warmers started picking through the action.

"Bridge, CIC. Target A is underway again, Captain."

"Fire another round."

Radar-controlled, the shell fell within a three-yard circle of probability, drenching the Dvora. Knowing that the next one might land on him if he continued with his pursuit, Harmon wisely slowed and powered down.

"Bridge, CIC! Vampire! We have two more Mavericks incoming!"

"Give Target B a salvo of RIM-162s!" Mercer said calmly, staring at the ECDIS. Diplomatic fallout or not, he was not about to allow anybody to shoot holes in his ship.

Two Evolved Sea Sparrow missiles leaped from the stern cell and accelerated after the retreating F-15 as it roared over *Porter* port to starboard. His tail threat receiver screaming at him, the pilot jinked hard to port and clawed for altitude. Hugging the deck, being in a low energy position, he could not hope to evade the Mach 4.6 missiles closing on him. Triggered by their proximity fuses, both detonated within thirty yards of the Eagle and it broke up, shedding airframe parts and burning fuel. The pilot did not manage to eject. The second F-15 did a barrel roll and headed for land.

Mercer clearly saw both Mavericks streaking toward *Porter's* port side, trailing a thread of white smoke. One disappeared in an orange flash, but the other kept boring in. He thought it would hit, then it vanished, the shockwave making the ship tremble. Sharp pings on the bulkhead indicated shrapnel hits. With extensive topside armor placed around vital combat systems and machinery spaces, there would be some dents and need for dabs of paint, but his ship was safe. All bulkheads were steel from the waterline to the pilot house, designed with double-spaced plates to prevent fragment penetration.

"Bridge, XO. Both incoming destroyed. We sustained hits and Damage Control is on it. Targets A and C are withdrawing. The second Dvora is closing with Target A."

"Thank you, XO. Keep me advised," Mercer said.

"Captain, *Ross* is showing hull down port side at ten miles," the OOD announced.

Not much for them to do now, Mercer thought, but having another DDG in close support would be a powerful deterrent to any adventurous fighters. The question, of course, would the Israelis now back off or come in force?

"CIC, Captain. Stand down from Condition Able, but maintain a full readiness watch."

"Aye aye, sir."

Mercer leaned back and allowed himself to relax, feeling tension ooze out of his body. Modern electronic warfare made for an exciting time. *Abdullah's* captain had a ringside seat of the action and would undoubtedly talk, giving the media a field day. There would be more than shrapnel damage to consider when the political dust settled.

He did not look forward to writing his after-action report to Admiral Jarvis.

Chapter Nine

Night had settled over the sprawling Zhangnanhai grounds, but the stars were invisible, hidden by the pervasive glow of city lights and the olive drapes that shielded the tall windows. August had nearly ended, and with it, the oppressive heat and humidity. Despite spending decades in Beijing, Dzhang had never gotten used to its fickle climate.

Feet stretched out, sitting comfortably in a beige couch that faced a relatively plain executive desk, he glanced around the spacious, but simple office. Beside him, steam rose from a white porcelain pot sitting on a low coffee table inlaid with a traditional mountain setting against a black background. It probably took the craftsman months to get the mother-of-pearl, gold, and silver flakes set perfectly into the beautiful piece.

Zhou Yedong looked up from his computer and laid down the translucent blue jade cup with a click. On the wall behind him, Mao's round face stared myopically into the room. Impeccably dressed in a dark blue gabardine suit, white silk shirt and striped red and gold tie, tall, muscled, a bulbous nose protruding beneath a high forehead, hair still black and combed straight back, the Communist Party president projected power well. Sixty-three, extraordinarily young for his post, which only served to demonstrate his political skill and ruthlessness. Preferring settlement to confrontation, the president did not shy away from acting decisively when an issue could not be settled amicably, and tonight could be one of those pivotal moments.

Dzhang pointed the remote at the LED TV mounted into the wall bookshelf that also served as a liquor cabinet, stacked with traditional Chinese and Western beverages.

331

Stefan Vučak

"I taped this earlier. I thought you might be interested to see it before you talk to President Walters."

"You could have given me a summary," Zhou grumbled, apparently annoyed that his long day was about to get even longer. The twelve-hour time difference with Washington made calls awkward for everybody.

Dzhang didn't show much sympathy. His day was not going to end anytime soon either. The best he could hope for was getting to bed before midnight, not looking forward to another owl session like the one last night with Sharron Ibrahim.

"A summary would not have given you the body language visuals you need to see," he said and sat back.

The screen cleared just as Granger, the lanky White House press secretary, entered the room and stood behind the lectern. A survivor from the first term, Granger still ruled the press corps with an iron hand, deftly shielding the administration from gratuitous criticism, but able to acknowledge bloopers that came up from time to time, with a dry sense of humor. He did not obfuscate or prevaricate, willing to hang out the government's dirty laundry for everybody to see, a policy of openness President Walters demanded from every department, and one that had apparently cost more than one secretary his or her job. This was behavior alien to Dzhang, where the government and its ruling organs had to be presented without flaws, which, of course, generated much unstated ridicule from the people at large.

Granger looked grim as he swept his eyes over the press gaggle.

"I have two announcements, and I will not be taking any questions at this time. Each of you will be given a briefing paper that will elaborate on my statements."

A murmur swept through the room as vastly experienced senior journalists looked at each other, digesting this departure from the norm.

"However, I am sure that our meeting tomorrow morning will be more

lively," Granger added dryly, which generated the predictable round of polite laughter.

"Following discussions with Prime Minister Sharron Ibrahim, the President is announcing a policy shift in the Administration's relationship with Israel. Past Administrations have found the Middle East a quagmire of conflicting interests and priorities, which colored, and sometimes damaged, our foreign policy. With the establishment of a Palestinian state three years ago, many previously intractable issues were resolved, which had opened a window of opportunity to review the strategic ties the United States has maintained with the state of Israel since its independence in 1948."

The silence lay thick in the press room as reporters scribbled or held up recorders.

"Enjoying relative peace with no credible external threats, especially with the gradual normalization of relations with Iran, Israel had matured as an independent country and prospered economically. Accordingly, military and economic aid that helped it grow is no longer warranted, and this aid is being withdrawn."

Granger waited patiently for the inevitable buzz of startled comments to die down.

"With a more stable region, the Administration is also scaling down its strategic commitments in the area and will be cutting down its 5th Fleet presence. With a powerful military capability, Israel is able to manage its national security needs without the overwhelming presence of U.S. personnel and logistical bases on its soil. The Administration is keen to emphasize that this does not diminish its intention to maintain regional stability, but that stability can be encouraged and maintained through diplomatic discourse. However, when discourse is seen to fail and force is the only option left to resolve an issue, the United States will not hesitate to employ the military option, which leads me to my second announcement.

"With independence, Palestine should enjoy all the rights, privileges and obligations attached to statehood, including taking necessary steps to ensure its security, a fundamental responsibility of any state to its citizens. This privilege implies unfettered sea commerce. Despite two UN Security Council resolutions, particularly resolution 2341, Israel has persisted in its insistence

to carry out inspections of civilian shipping attempting to enter the Port of Gaza, citing the need to prevent the flow of weapons to terrorist groups such as Hamas who still seek to undermine Israel's security.

"At 7:40 a.m. local time, USS Porter, an Arleigh Burke-class guided missile destroyer, while escorting a Turkish registered freighter toward Gaza, and trying to ward off an Israeli patrol boat, came under missile attack from two F-15SE strike Eagles belonging to the Israeli Air Force. In the ensuing action, the patrol boat was prevented from closing with the freighter and one F-15 was shot down. The destroyer sustained minor damage."

Predictably, this generated another burst of excited comments.

"The Administration acknowledges that although IDF Navy and Air Force commands acted with an unwarranted level of aggression, they were perhaps unaware of the shift in U.S. policy, but it condemns Israel's use of preemptive force against an ally without taking an opportunity to clarify the situation using available diplomatic channels."

One of the reporters jumped up. *"Granger, does this have anything to do with the crystal Senator Lockhart announced in his press conference?"*

Dzhang lifted the remote and switched off the TV.

"You have seen enough."

Zhou looked thoughtful and nodded slowly. "I *have* seen enough. You were right to show me this."

"President Walters wants the computing device, Yedong, and he demonstrated that to Israel in a most vivid way."

"Which gives Israel options not previously available, you mean?"

"We can now deal with them without the American shadow hanging over them," Dzhang pointed out.

Zhou shook his head. "America is demonstrably an interested party, my friend, but you're essentially correct." He glanced at the wall clock. It showed two minutes to eight. "Perhaps we shall find out how far their shadow extends."

A knock on the door and Zhou's personal assistant peered in.

"Sir, your call to President Walters has been made. He is on line one," he said and withdrew.

Smiling faintly, Zhou activated the phone speaker. "Good morning, Mr. President."

"And a good evening to you, sir. You know, we must do something about these time zones."

Zhou laughed softly. "It's an intractable problem, Sam."

"Still, it's damn awkward. I don't want to add to your day, and I want mine to begin on a positive note. Tanner is not pleased that I'm talking to you. He doesn't trust my diplomatic skills and fears I will somehow irretrievably damage any prospect of an amicable solution by being too blunt, which regretfully I am, and for which I apologize unreservedly."

He preferred to spend some time on inconsequential dialogue to soften the atmosphere, but Dzhang understood the Western penchant for direct language. It grated on his sensibilities, and he knew that Zhou did not like it, but both had learned to tolerate the Westerner's lack of cultural breeding.

"I don't mind, Sam, and I do want to go to bed early," Zhou told the lie smoothly.

"In that case, allow me to continue being blunt. You're aware of my shift in policy vis-à-vis Israel—"

"Triggered by Mossad's activity to retrieve an ancient computing device."

"Then I do not need to elaborate. I do want to give you a warning, Yedong. The activities of your Second Bureau to procure the crystal are not appreciated."

Dzhang saw Zhou wince, acknowledging the subtle rebuke.

"An internal rogue operation, Sam. I only became aware of it yesterday."

"Initiated by a fellow gem collector perhaps? That's how Dr. Morrison became aware of this device. However, he did not resort to murder of two Israeli citizens and a Hong Kong dealer to get it."

Zhou gave Dzhang a startled and angry look. Dzhang blanched, staggered that Walters would know this. He spread his hands in a gesture that said 'later'.

"The person responsible was disciplined," Zhou said stiffly. "However, my reason for calling you was to hopefully reach an understanding on how everybody could benefit from this strange crystal."

"We want the thing as much as you do, and I'm aware of the overture you made to Prime Minister Ibrahim. The difference in our objectives, Mr. President, is that I don't seek the device on behalf of the United States government, but to have it returned to Dr. Morrison."

"Isn't that the same thing?"

"I want to make sure that you understand me perfectly, Yedong, as this defines a major cultural divide between us. You seek the crystal to advance China's national standing, as does Israel, which I appreciate. The difference is that I want Dr. Morrison to exploit its potential within our capitalist system which you so decry, and the freedom our rule of law guarantees. I don't deny that the Administration has an interest, as it does in the strategic application of his QD pigment, but we will not knowingly force him to give it up or steal from him the results of his enterprise under a blanket of national security."

"You would enter into a partnership?" Zhou asked in wonder.

"Isn't that what you wanted to talk about?"

Dzhang hid a smile. Walters had no need to belittle his diplomatic skills, having neatly undermined Zhou's position.

"A partnership, yes, but with Israel and the United States government, not a corporate entity."

"The cultural difference I mentioned?"

"Sam, I understand the Western mindset, although it's foreign to most of us. I will not deny that we made Prime Minister Ibrahim a proposal for cooperative research and development of the crystal's potential. Despite your policy shift, I know that America

336

will maintain strategic ties with Israel...if they return the device. I propose that we offer them a solution where they don't have to make an impossible choice."

"Get them to work with both of us," Walters said.

"And defuse what might be an intractable problem that could lead to unnecessary complications between us," Zhou added. "This is too big for Israel to handle alone."

"Something I mentioned to Sharron, but this is also too big for the two of us, Yedong. Extend the scope of your cooperation and place it under UN auspices, where any benefits gained would be shared by the world. You have witnessed the creep of mega-corporations taking control of our economic mechanisms, eroding government institutions themselves. You have largely been immune to this, but by giving Chinese entrepreneurs access to limited free market instruments, you have inadvertently opened a door to freedom. I believe neither of us wants to see the computing device this crystal represents exploited by the mega-corps. It would only strengthen them."

Dzhang lifted his head and locked eyes with Zhou. The American president had made a very insightful point.

"What you're suggesting, Sam, is laudable, and perhaps even noble, but you must be aware that your vision faces individual national interests that cannot be bridged. With Senator Lockhart's announcement, you have probably received calls from world leaders demanding an explanation, all of them undoubtedly asking how they will benefit from this crystal. Giving it to the UN will placate nobody, because nobody trusts the UN's integrity or impartiality, and they would be right."

"All legitimate problems, I agree," Walters said. "Nevertheless, with goodwill and leadership on our part, these are problems that can be overcome. You may not agree with me, preferring to reach an independent settlement with Israel, which is your right, and I will not interfere, and neither will my intelligence services. You must recognize the reason for this."

Zhou looked thoughtful for a moment. "The device is simply beyond the scope of any one country to develop, regardless of the sophistication of its technology or industry."

"Precisely. As for your proposal to enter into a joint venture with Israel, it has merit—once Dr. Morrison gets the crystal back."

"Which you will help him get," Zhou said and laughed.

"If you manage to obtain it, Yedong, I hope you remember that you are now part of a community of nations, and not an independent agent."

"Something to think about, Sam. Please extend my regards to your lovely wife, and I would welcome you to Beijing again. This time, with an opportunity to see some of our country and its national treasures."

"Thank you, Mr. President. Let me know when you can come to Washington. Good night, sir."

When the line went dead, Zhou stood up, walked to the coffee table and poured himself a fresh cup of tea. He pulled the spare chair closer and sat down. Taking a sip, he looked up.

"An interesting conversation."

"With a lot left unsaid," Dzahng added.

"He is a fool to think that I would be swayed by sentiment," Zhou retorted. "Not for something this important. There is a global dimension to this, I agree, but not how he thinks. The seat on the IMF Executive Board will be ours soon, and with it, the Go Global Strategy back on track. With control of the West's financial institutions and the international bond market, we will dictate the world's monetary policy. The corporations he is so fearful of will bow to us if they want to survive. We will share the crystal, but on our terms, and certainly not under some UN regime. Walters is a hopeless idealist and doesn't understand us."

"Oh, I think he understands us all too well, Yedong," Dzhang said slowly. "Did you note the wistful tone in his voice when he spoke about us being part of a community of nations? He hoped you would understand that you cannot do this alone either. You spent time in America and you know them. He relied on that."

"Meaning that he is prepared to confront us for the possession of the crystal?"

"He confronted us last year over La Palma, and he confronted Israel just now in no uncertain terms. He would not hesitate to confront us again."

"Mmm, perhaps. We need to increase pressure on Israel. With the shift in American foreign policy, Israel's bunker mentality will be reinforced and they might be amenable to embracing a new ally."

Dzhang frowned. "Do we seriously want to get mired in the Middle East? Look what it cost the United States. This alien crystal device was a gift from heaven for Walters, giving him an excuse to extricate himself from a hopelessly tangled ideological region. We have enough problems with our Muslim population and the Uyghurs to take on new headaches. We already annoyed the Arabs with the prospect of a Free Trade Agreement—"

"Which you managed to ameliorate," Zhou pointed out.

"But not eliminate. Imagine their reaction if we formed a strategic alliance with the Jews!"

"I would worry if they were a unified block, but Muslim countries are not all Arabs and they're not unified. Their internal Sunni and Shi'ia differences makes them hate each other more than they hate the West. Some would grumble and posture, certainly, and threaten to deny us oil supply, but as you pointed out, we have alternatives. Besides, Israel might be more receptive to entering into an alliance if we demonstrated a tangible example of our support," Zhou mused.

"How?"

"The inspection blockade of shipping into Gaza the Americans seem determined to breach, I doubt the Israelis will take this lightly. America bloodied their nose and their God-given right to do anything they want has been challenged."

Stefan Vučak

"You're saying that they will seek another confrontation?"

"I'm counting on it. We have one of our *Qin*-class Type 098 missile boats on a goodwill visit to Turkey, I understand," Zhou said.

"Stationed at the Iskenderun Naval Base and due to return via the Suez Canal at any time, I believe. It might have sailed already. Secretary of State Tanner not very happy with Turkey when they allowed the *Qin* to sail in."

"I know. Turkey is a valued NATO ally, but one whose patience is being severely strained by EU's continued blocking of full membership. The Europeans are naturally wary of Moslem hordes flooding in. Look what happened with the uncontrolled influx of refugees during the Syrian war. With America scaling down its NATO presence, Turkey could also be amenable to a shift in strategic partners."

"So?"

"We order the *Qin* to sail for Gaza and make its presence felt if the Americans have another confrontation."

"Once it's in position, what then?" Dzhang demanded. "Order it to fire on the Americans? Without a formal treaty with Israel, we have no business interfering."

"We will not interfere, but show intent, something the Israelis will notice," Zhou countered. "We will observe, nothing more. Walters was right when he said that we're now part of a community of nations. I want to show him that we're becoming a dominant part of that community, and Pax Americana no longer rules. Get that device for us, Qishan."

* * *

Morrison blinked and opened his eyes fully. Sunlight slanted into the room and white gauze curtains stirred in the light breeze. He felt relaxed, content and at peace, not burdened by anything. He turned and winced as a stab of pain that shot through his left

340

shoulder, shattering his comfortable dream state. Looking down, his upper left arm and body were swathed in a bandage. Memory returned and he tried to sit up, but only managed a weak gasp.

"You shouldn't strain that arm, my dear." The familiar musical voice made his heart flutter and he turned his head toward the sound.

Propped against the cushions in a bed next to him, Juliana flashed him a beaming smile and his insides melted. Her raven hair neatly combed, small mouth lightly colored with lipstick, large brown eyes laughing at him, he couldn't take his eyes off her.

"What—"

"We invalids must stick together," she told him firmly. "That nice FBI man…Fisher…he arranged it."

"I'm in a hospital?" he asked brightly, which demonstrated his mental sharpness.

"New York–Presbyterian again. Don't worry; the government is footing the bill for this."

"Generous of them. What happened? I remember getting shot…"

"You were lucky. The bullet went clean through. It tore some muscle, but your shoulder blade and collarbone are intact. No violent exercises for a couple of weeks, then we can resume where we left off," she said and gave him a suggestive grin. "My side will be up to it then," she added, which made him break into a broad smile.

"I can't wait. Did they say how long I'll be laid up?"

"Four or five days. I could leave tomorrow, but I decided to keep you company."

"Going to nag me, eh?"

She giggled, then winced. "Stitches," she said. "It will give us a chance to talk."

He glanced out the window and frowned. "It's morning!"

"You noticed. They operated on you yesterday afternoon and

341

you were all doped up when they wheeled you in. You woke up once, and when you saw me, you smiled and went back to sleep. You snored during the night."

"I don't snore!"

"You did last night. You don't remember any of it?"

"Nothing."

She gave a long sigh. "And after all the trouble I took to look presentable." She noticed him watching a bunch of flowers beside her bed.

"Stan and Sandra will be in later. They came yesterday, but you were out. You gave them a fright, you know. You bled like a pig."

"That's a nice thing to say to an invalid," he grumbled.

Juliana reached across the space between them and patted his good arm.

"Never mind, my dear. I reconciled myself years ago to the fact that men think only of themselves. We wives come a distant second, and only as an afterthought." Her eyes softened and she regarded him with adoration. "I won't forget what you did for me, Kevin, even if only an afterthought."

Feeling all puffed up with virtue, although misplaced, he managed a shrug without inducing a painful reaction.

"Shucks, lady, I would have done it for anybody."

"But you did it for me, Mister. All your troubles resolved?"

He exhaled loudly, happy with the world, happy to have Juliana with him.

"All resolved," he said and meant it, then frowned. "Well, not really…"

Her laugh a merry tingle. "Living with you, my dear, has never been dull, and I doubt that it ever will. First, it was the nanograss panels, then the QD pigment, and then the crystal. I wonder what you'll come up with next."

"We could have similar problems with the pigment," he warned her.

"I know, but you'll work something out. You always have." Glancing at the large LED TV bolted to the far wall, she raised a slim finger. "You won't believe what happened. One of our destroyers shot down an Israeli fighter off Gaza, and the President has announced a radical cooling off with Israel. Everyone is buzzing trying to work out what's going on. The current guess is the whole thing was triggered by Lockhart's press conference. Your doing?"

"I asked him to announce the existence of the crystal and reveal who was after it, but I doubt that triggered the incident," Morrison said cautiously. "It's possible, though." He reached out and she placed her hand in his.

"You know, I don't actually care. I had time to think things over and I reached a conclusion I was too dumb to see before. Nothing is more important to me than you. The pigment, the crystal, my business, nothing. Thinking otherwise has landed both of us in bandages. It's not worth it, and when we get out of here, we'll have that trip I spoke about."

She looked dreamy. "That would be lovely."

A knock on the door made him look up. When it opened, his face lit up.

"Allison! This is a surprise."

With a bunch of assorted flowers in hand, his usually stern assistant gave a shy smile and walked in. Dressed in a pale-gray business jacket and knee-length skirt, her ash-blond hair trimmed severely short, her small frame a picture of perfection.

"I was on my way to the office," she breathed, "and I thought I better see how you two were doing," she finished awkwardly, a departure from her usual crisp, decisive self. She cleared her throat as she approached Juliana's bed and held out the bouquet.

"Everyone at the office wishes you a speedy recovery, Mrs. Morrison."

Juliana took the flowers, reached for the diminutive woman, and hugged her.

"Thank you, my dear. And it's Juliana, remember?"

"Yes, ma'am."

"I don't get a hug?" Morrison demanded archly.

Allison flushed and hesitated before leaning over him, washing him with her light citrus scent. He kissed her cheek and hugged her hard with his good arm.

"If I haven't told you lately, Allison, I would be lost without you."

Clearly moved, she gave a small sniff, then fixed on her office face.

"I don't know what you mean, sir."

"Never mind. Just don't leave Solaris, okay?"

"I am quite content, Doctor."

"Has Moore taken over yet?"

Her eyes flashed as she smiled. "He wanted to move into your office yesterday, but I chased him out. He only laughed at me. I hope I did the right thing."

"Exactly right. He has no business rummaging around my office. It was a kind thing coming to see us."

"Mr. Trotman called, wishing you well, and apologized for not being able to see you, but he'll be back from Boston tomorrow. Dr. Ferguson also sends his regards."

Morrison turned to Juliana. "Remind me to call him."

She arched her head in disdain. "I'm not your slave, you know."

Morrison looked helplessly at Allison. "See what I have to put up with?"

Not wishing to get tangled in a family altercation, she shifted her feet.

"I will call if anything urgent comes up, sir, but Mr. Moore seems to be on top of things." She patted down her skirt and headed for the door. "Get well soon, both of you."

"Thank you, my dear," Juliana said with a flutter of fingers.

"Nice girl," she added when the door closed, giving him a speculative look. "Did you two ever..."

"Juli!" Morrison was genuinely shocked. "She is a valued member of my staff, that's all."

"Just pulling your chain, darling man."

"I definitely have to get you out somewhere," he said and ran a hand through his hair. "Do they serve breakfast around here?"

It had been a while since he and Juliana spent whole days together, and he realized this forced reunion would require some adjusting. Both held demanding jobs and it was difficult aligning free time. A break from the normal daily grind was exactly what they needed to rekindle the fires.

* * *

Prime Minister Sharron Ibrahim replaced the phone in its cradle, digesting the substance of Premier Dzhang's conversion, not sure he liked the taste. He now stood on the crossroad of destiny, as did his government and country to which he had devoted his entire life, sacrificing everything to bolster its security, which meant doing some things that were not entirely honorable. Did expediency justify what he had done? Did seventy years of war? And what did he and Israel have to show for the blood spilt?

He punched a button on the phone.

"Yes, sir?"

"Moshe, call the Foreign Minister and ask him to see me," Ibrahim said and cut contact.

This was too big for him to decide alone, and as leader of the principal coalition party, Abdon Sayar had a right to provide input. Ibrahim slowly nodded, appreciating the irony. After decades of ideological enmity, no one would have predicted the merger of the right-wing Likud Party and what was then the center-left Labor Party. Yet, that was exactly what happened three years ago, the shotgun marriage forced on him and Sayar by President

Walters following the disastrous Valero refinery incident. To everyone's surprise, and the chagrin of extremist religious and far-right micro-parties, the union had worked, bringing much needed stability and certainty of direction for the country. Would it last once he and Sayar faded into political oblivion? He hoped so. The alternative would be a return to radicalization of policies where successive governments were held hostage by the zealots. It would be a return to darkness.

Ibrahim heaved himself up and strode to the window overlooking the Knesset and the Dome of the Rock glinting in midday sunlight. He could not hear or see the streams of traffic making their way through the city, but knew they were there. That activity represented peace and prosperity, and confidence in a future not threatened by suicide bombers and rioting Palestinians. Peace *can* work, given a modicum of goodwill shown by everybody. Would Premier Dzhang's offer guarantee Israel's peace?

He needed to discuss that with Sayar.

In the old days when his country was young, still searching for an identity, identifying the enemy was easy. They were Arabs and gentiles. No orthodox Jew would admit that he shared a common history and ancestry with tribes that occupied Judah and old Israel. A long time ago, there might have been pockets of people calling themselves the Israelites, but centuries of cultural mingling with Canaan tribes had blurred those bloodlines. It took the emergence of Islam in the seventh century to gradually fan the flames of sectarian hatred, even though in the formative centuries, all three religions had managed to coexist peacefully. Ibrahim wondered where everybody took the wrong turn.

No, he did not have to wonder. He knew. Once they gained political power, radical extremists on all sides poisoned what could have been a harmonious, cohesive culture, gaining much from each other. Israel's radicals had maintained a 70-year war, and would have continued to wage it, were it not for the Valero incident, regardless how misguided its objective. Perhaps God does look after fools and the blind. Ibrahim was adamant his people should not see those days again.

Given two cups, two directions, which one should he pick up?

He returned to his desk and worked steadily through documents his staff determined needed his attention, compartmentalizing his conversation with Dzhang. He could not afford to be fixated on a single issue, regardless of its importance.

He greeted the foreign minister with relief when Moshe ushered him into the office.

"No interruptions," Ibrahim told his secretary and swept a hand at a chair. "Thanks for coming, Abdon. We have a few things to discuss."

Sayar made himself comfortable and crossed his legs.

"I gather it's important or you would have handled it."

"Dzhang called."

"Ah, that explains it. I thought you wanted to hash over this morning's incident."

Ibrahim lifted his hands in exasperation. "It was partly my fault. I should have updated Seddon last night."

"Perhaps, but Kemmet overreacted. He is a hawk and looked for an excuse to exert his authority. You know that he has his eye on Seddon's job."

"He won't get it, not after this," Ibrahim said firmly. "As the IDF Chief of Staff, policy decisions are not part of his terms of reference. His rash action cost us a valuable pilot and an aircraft...and reinforced to President Walters our image of a reactionary Israel, which is the last thing we need right now."

"What are you going to do?"

"Promote Kemmet to Vice Admiral. It's a ceremonial position without authority."

Sayar laughed. "He will send a flight of Eagles here, but that's sidestepping the issue," he said, turning serious. "My party caucus is asking questions, Sharron: the alien crystal, our talks with Walters and the Chinese, and now a confrontation with the American

Navy."

"I'm not surprised. Some of my Likud front benchers were bending my ear all morning. I asked the Whip to call a meeting for this afternoon of all coalition members where you and I will announce our revised foreign policy."

"Which is?"

"That's what I want to talk to you about."

"Fine, but we need to affirm our policy to maintain inspections of all shipping bound for Gaza, or come up with a new model, and you better tell Seddon before something else happens. The next cargo tramp heading our way won't wait for us to make up our minds, and neither will the American Navy."

"I already talked to Seddon. We continue our inspections—"

"You'll be placing our patrol ships in an impossible position. Unless you want to confront the Americans with a Sa'ar missile corvette."

"We send out one of those, it will guarantee a confrontation. Still, it might not be such a bad idea at that, but under no circumstances will the Sa'ar or the Dvoras initiate or return fire regardless of any provocation, and definitely no buzzing by our fighters. Intelligence reports a container ship from Piraeus is due to make landfall this evening, which gives us time to prepare."

"Prepare for what?"

"We will put a news crew on the Sa'ar with a live feed to the networks. If the Americans react, I want the world to see who started it all."

"They won't see anything if they sink the Sa'ar."

"I doubt that will happen, but the Americans will have to board the ship to stop it reaching the freighter, and that would be a technical act of war."

"They'll do it."

Ibrahim raised an eyebrow. "With the press filming everything?"

"The Americans have the world's sympathy behind them, and

we cannot cite violation of our territorial integrity, not with that UN resolution hanging over us. Unless the Americans engage the Dvora and someone gets shot, we'll be proving to the world that UN resolutions don't mean a thing."

"They don't, but they placate the masses, making them believe the Security Council is actually an effective instrument. What would you want me to do?"

"The Dvoras work in pairs. The American destroyer might be able to stop one, but not both."

"They have two destroyers on station, you know."

"Not sailing side by side, they don't. If we're an independent nation, we have the right to exercise the instruments of our security."

"Not by inviting a confrontation!" Ibrahim snapped.

"We roll over and allow the Americans to dictate to us?"

"That damned UN resolution gives them that right!"

"And we have a right to protect ourselves!" Sayar came back hotly. "Look, I'm not suggesting that we engage the Americans, but focus on the objective of our inspections."

"The freighter?"

"Exactly. We allow the Dvoras to do what they have always done. They warn an incoming ship that they're about to be boarded. This time though, with the Americans listening in, if the freighter refuses to stop, the Sa'ar will fire on it. Unless the American warships are sailing alongside the freighter, there is not much that they can do."

"They can stop the Dvoras getting into range," Ibrahim said and pulled at his chin. "Perhaps a media team can have another purpose."

"What do you mean?"

"A deterrent. There will be other ships tomorrow, and if we maintain our presence, there is bound to be an incident. One dead pilot is enough. Contact the Palestinian Foreign Minister and begin dialogue how to address our mutual security needs, with a demand that he stop the flow of weapons to the radical Hamas elements."

"We tried that before—"

"And it didn't work, I know. I might be a bit slow sometimes, Abdon, and need a prod to get me moving in the right direction, but the prod the American Navy gave us this morning cannot be ignored."

"You're not asking that we stop all inspections?"

"We might be forced to if the Americans maintain their naval blockade. We don't want to see the Gaza Strip become a weapons pipeline into the region, and I'm sure they don't want that either. That would only aid and abet extremist elements on both sides, but giving the Palestinians more autonomy in border control and a guarantee of free shipping should be well received. Until then, we continue inspections. The Americans will see that we're making a genuine effort to engage with the Palestinian government, they might pull back their ships."

"This will require a large lump of trust on our part, Sharron. Not everybody in the coalition will like it."

"If the Palestinians are able to demonstrate that they can control the flow of weapons traffic, our policy shift will be vindicated. If they cannot, we showed the world the ineffectiveness of a measured response, which will justify resumption of unilateral inspections."

"And take the wind out of the Americans." Sayar smiled faintly. "It will be a lively session this afternoon, that's all I've got to say."

Ibrahim stared hard at his deputy. "Do I have your support?"

"Of course, and I'm surprised that you had to ask. It's a reasonable approach. We can squabble over details to appease the diehards, but the core policy should be accepted. Now, what did Dzhang want?"

Ibrahim sat back and grinned. "You know how they are, dancing around an issue before they say anything of substance. Even then, what they say is subject to interpretation and analysis. It's no wonder that it takes them years to agree on something important. For a change though, Dzhang came to the point with a minimum of preliminaries. What China is offering, my friend, is a security alliance with Israel."

Sayar slowly nodded. "Not totally unexpected, and the logical next step—if we hand over the computing device."

"If we hand over the device."

"What did you tell him?"

"I told him it was not a decision I could make alone. What did you think? That I would commit Israel to a major strategic shift without consulting you?"

Sayar waved his hand. "You see what their end game is, don't you? It's all part of their Go Global Strategy. They're not interested in us *per se*, but gaining a foothold in the Mediterranean."

"You mentioned that before."

"They already approached Turkey, enticing them into a closer economic and political bilateral relationship, and they offered to underwrite Greece's debt, opening the door for Greece to leave the European Union. The EU hasn't done those two countries any favors, paying them off to stop the influx of refugees into Europe, leaving them with the problem of unwanted bodies on their soil and a national debt they cannot repay. With the UK out, a fractured Europe would play directly into Chinese hands. Getting us into their sphere of influence would consolidate their positon in the region."

"And we would consolidate that position for a perceived economic gain that might never be realized," Ibrahim added thoughtfully. "Marx was right when he said the West would give the communists tools to defeat it."

"Even if we were to consider an alliance, examine the practicality. How would the Chinese help us in a conflict? Short of establishing a naval presence, what could they do? Lob an ICBM at somebody? The Knesset would have us impeached if we suggested a Chinese naval base on our soil. An alliance would not be a gain for us, but a public relations coup for them, and further erosion of American global influence. China's objective is to become the world's dominant economic and political force, and they will do whatever is necessary to achieve that objective. Offering us an alliance is a demonstration of that intent, given under the guise to help us develop the quantum device."

"I am cognizant of the ramifications, Abdon, but somewhat taken aback by your position. I thought you would be happy if we severed the umbilical with the Americans, as you put it. What brought on the change?"

"I haven't changed my position. We took our relationship with the United States for granted, assuming that they would support us always. Regardless of the triggering reason for their shift, President Walters reminded us that grown up, we must choose how to face the world, free to succeed or fail without the safety net we presumed would always be there. Part of being grown up also means exercising responsibility, which we haven't always done."

Ibrahim ran a hand over his chin and sighed. "I feel like a kid who was kicked out of his home and told by his father to fend for himself."

"It's a sobering realization," Sayar agreed.

"I keep asking myself one question, and I give myself the same answer. The Americans stood by us when nobody else did, and I believe they're still prepared to stand by us, even if it's on different terms. But like you said, we're grown up and our relationship should be forged with that in mind. I don't doubt Dzhang's sincerity, but it is driven by opportunism."

"At least he doesn't pretend that it isn't. If it were not for the computing device…"

"Yes, the device. I keep returning to the telling point President Walters made. He doesn't want the crystal on behalf of the

United States government. He wants it back in Dr. Morrison's hands. I did not make the distinction then, but I do now."

Sayar snorted. "Of course he wants it in their hands, but he is being an honest broker. At least I think he is. He believes he can make a deal with Morrison to exploit the crystal." The foreign minister looked thoughtful. "You wanted to do that from the start, and I talked you out of it."

"I'm not holding that against you. Walters was right about one thing. We cannot do this alone. We have the scientific and technological expertise, but not the resources. Although not impossible, it would be difficult to curtail or stop some existing research to provide manpower for a project that is bound to last years without hurting our existing development programs."

"I think you're exaggerating the scope of the problem, but I understand what you're saying. Where does that leave us?"

"Looking to answer the same question. Whom can we trust?"

"There is something else to consider," Sayar said moodily. "Now that the world is aware of this device, we can expect overtures from others, and I don't mean with offers of cooperation."

"I know. We'll have to increase our security blanket or defuse the problem, Abdon, before everyone loses objectivity. Now that we have the thing, I simply don't like the thought of giving it up again," Ibrahim added angrily.

"Not giving up, Sharron, but sharing. We may have been far too clever and manipulative for our own good. Perhaps it's time to exercise genuine statesmanship and trust you mentioned."

Ibrahim chortled, but without humor. "In a world where no one trusts anyone, that might be hard to come by."

"We trust the one nation whom we trusted all along," Sayar said simply. "They can be manipulative, selfish, indecisive, wanting to make you tear your hair out, but we haven't been playing it straight every time either."

"You know, it was easier when the two of us stood toe to toe in the Knesset, venting vitriol at each other, kowtowing to our sectarian coalition partners," Ibrahim said, regarding Sayar with amusement.

"And we exchanged insults like it mattered," Sayar agreed with a wistful look on his face. "I derived a lot of pleasure watching you struggle to contain your resentment of my Harvard education, which you thought gave me an air of superiority. Perhaps it does. What you didn't know, you old fool, is the admiration I held for your calm, measured arguments—when we were not shouting at each other."

Ibrahim couldn't believe it. "You knew, and all this time you never said a word?"

Sayar shrugged. "It made you work harder to demonstrate your superiority, and telling you would have deprived me of the pleasure of watching you squirm."

"Avoda bastard."

"Yes, we had fun then. We knew our enemies, and knew our friends. At least we thought we did. It *seemed* simple."

"I was reflecting on that before you came, wondering if it has become too complicated for me. I still think in familiar squares, when all the time, everything has changed. My party might be better off with someone younger and more vigorous at the helm. Someone with a more modern perspective on the world, unfettered by the chains of history we helped create. It would be good for us if we had term limits. You and I have held power for too long."

"So, feeling sorry for yourself?" Sayar demanded quizzically. "Making decisions is getting tough, is it? You want to switch it off and let somebody else carry the load?"

"You?" Ibrahim asked and chuckled. "I'm not ready for pasture yet, and your turn will come. Meanwhile, I shall curb my childish resentment, and it's childish." He shook his head in wonder. "All those years and you never said a thing."

"Which has now left me with a problem where to find a new source of amusement. Having bared our souls, my conspiratorial partner, it's time we got back to work."

* * *

A stiff easterly pushed short, steep waves before it, making USS *Porter* pitch, sending creaming water crashing over its sharp bow. Streams of threadlike cirrus cloud marred an otherwise clear afternoon sky. It would have been pleasant on the open weather decks if it were not for the hot wind coming off the Arabian Peninsula.

Captain Mercer sipped hot coffee from an enameled mug blazoned with the ship's crest, and allowed his mind to drift. This morning's engagement had stirred a hornet's nest, and predictably the media picked apart the action in minute detail, pontificating learnedly on U.S.–Israeli relations, impact on regional trade, effect on world stock markets, and shifts in power blocks with China an interested party. They had a lot to say about a strange computing device dug up in Jerusalem, and what it might mean for the country able to harness it. Mercer thought the whole scenario was overcooked, but papers had to fill their pages with something, and commentators relished a new unfolding drama, always making the situation seem to teeter on the brink of total disaster.

There wasn't any drama as far as Mercer was concerned. He did wonder about the larger picture like everybody else, but his immediate focus was on the mission at hand. He had his orders and he intended to execute them, content to let others sift through the bones. As a senior captain, he knew very well what it meant to down an Israeli F-15, and that a cloud of *Stunner* missiles could come boiling over the horizon, targeting *Ross* and his ship.

The 6th Fleet had visited Israel's naval ports at Haifa and Ashdod, and he found the people there to be generally warm and friendly who did not mind having a flood of American sailors descend on them. That could not be said for some IDF officers who seem to be carrying rather large chips on their shoulders. Resentment that much of their hardware and logistics came from the United States and they had to defer to their big brother across the Pond?

Tracking the Liberian-registered Greek container ship *Seven Seas*, three days out of Piraeus, Mercer figured he would see if the IDF command still bore a chip. He glanced to starboard across the bridge, just able to make out *Ross* ten miles off, hull down, her superstructure barely visible in the sea haze. He bit his lip and turned to the communications officer.

"COMMO, order *Ross* to close with *Seven Seas* and hold at five miles."

"*Ross* to close with *Seven Seas*, aye, sir."

"Officadeck, you have the watch," Mercer told the OOD. "I'll be in CIC."

"Captain is off the bridge!" the marine guard shouted as Mercer stepped over the hatch coaming.

Down a deck, he blinked as he entered the ship's darkened fighting center. Watkins immediately vacated the central observation seat. Mercer lowered himself onto the still-warm leather padding and quickly scanned the two main screens of the Aegis Combat System showing the tactical disposition, weapons system status, countermeasures, search radar and navigation plot. He glanced at the sonar and anti-submarine warfare desk, the screens were clear. The four watchstanders, the young Tactical Action Officer and the taciturn ECM officer pretended that they didn't notice the Old Man come in.

"Any sign of the Chinese Type 098?" Mercer demanded.

"Nothing," the XO said with a rueful smile. "At around 28,000 tons, the thing is enormous. Despite its size, I'm told it's quieter than cat's slippers. A nasty boat if they want to tangle. Do you want to stream the towed sonar array?"

Mercer pulled at his chin. "If our Chinese friends are around and want to watch the U.S. Navy at work, we'll show them how the job is done."

"Copy that. More good news for you, Skipper. Our bright intelligence officer received word that a Russian *Severodvinsk*-class attack submarine might also be in the area."

"Great. We should have sold tickets if this is going to be a show."

Based on the *Akula* and *Alfa*-class boats, the new attack subs were replacing the aging *Akula* and *Oscar*-class submarines. At around 15,500 tons submerged, the *Severodvinsk* was a massive sub. Intelligence said that when submerged, it could do better than forty-eight knots, which was faster than an *Arleigh Burke* DDG.

Major power navies liked to watch each other play and evaluate the opposition's capability and doctrine. All good fun, but Mercer did not feel comfortable having a concentration of assets around him at this time. There had to be a good reason why Russia and China had subs here, and he suspected he knew what it was, but until CNE-CNA/C6F told him otherwise, he would ignore the visitors—if they were around. The last intel report he had showed the Type 098 heading for Alexandria, presumably to transit through the Suez. Perhaps that might not be the case, which made for interesting speculation.

"Captain, *Seven Seas* is now six miles from the third zone boundary," the TAO announced, "and we have three surface contacts. Two are identified as Dvora IIIs, and the other is a Sa'ar missile corvette. Range, eighteen nautical miles on our port quarter. We're being painted with nav radar."

"Very well."

Mercer exchanged glances with Watkins.

With a displacement of 1,400 tons fully loaded, the 280-foot ship not large, but it carried frigate-class armament, the most relevant here being the Barak surface-to-air and Harpoon anti-ship missiles. The Baraks put paid to any ideas Mercer had to field his

MH-60 Sea Hawk helicopters against the Dvoras. He *could* deploy the Hawks, but in an exchange, they would be swatted out of the air. Was the Sa'ar there to show teeth? It definitely added another dimension to the scenario, and not a pleasant one.

"XO, position *Porter* four miles off *Seven Seas'* port side and tell *Ross* to do the same. Send a flash message to Rota. Admiral Jarvis will want to know what's going on. Action stations, if you please."

"Aye aye, sir."

There wasn't much change in CIC to that order, but Mercer knew his ship was readying itself to meet any challenge, including offering battle. With *Porter* due to rotate back to Norfolk in two weeks, and Marion sure to be waiting for him at the pier, he did not want too much excitement right now. At the same time, the warrior in him made his eyes shine and all his faculties ratcheted up to full awareness.

His presence was an extension of the Command Authority, and everything he did reflected on the Navy and the president. He might be an instrument of policy, but he was also a thinking instrument, which highlighted the problem of hierarchical command everywhere. Regardless of how well articulated, orders were merely a reflection of intent, and were subject to misinterpretation. This in turn led to the cover-your-ass syndrome and bureaucratic obfuscation, something Mercer never liked, but which some of his brother officers practiced to advance their careers.

Better to be blamed for doing something than for having his thumb up his ass—with restraint, of course. In the wrong hands, USS *Porter* could unleash unimaginable violence, but the Navy did not give powerful destroyers to megalomaniacs, not in peacetime anyway.

He appreciated how Jarvis must feel reading his flash, wanting to be on the spot directing things, but forced to trust his commanders. That's how one grew gray hairs. It brought a wry smile of sardonic amusement to his craggy features.

Watkins caught him at it and raised an eyebrow. "Something amusing, Skipper?"

"Visualizing Jarvis gnawing his knuckles when he reads our message."

The XO chuckled. "Comes with the three stars."

Suddenly, the overhead speaker hissed. "*Seven Seas*, this is Israeli warship INS *Lahav*. Heave to and prepare to be boarded." Coming over the general Channel 16, the voice crisp and businesslike.

Watkins jerked his head at the ceiling and sighed. "Those guys are determined to keep pushing."

"And we'll handle them in the same way," Mercer said. He reached for the mike and pressed button five. "INS *Lahav*, this is USS *Porter*, Captain Mercer commanding. Be advised that *Seven Seas* is under escort to the Port of Gaza. Please withdraw."

"Captain Mercer, this is Commander Rabin. *Seven Seas* is about to enter a restricted maritime zone. It will not be permitted to violate Israeli territorial waters until it has cleared Customs inspection."

"Commander, in accordance to an agreement between the Palestinian government and the Israeli Ministry of Foreign Affairs, Customs clearance will be carried out on docking prior to unloading cargo," Mercer said and clicked off.

Someone in Jerusalem must have burned more than one barrel of midnight oil to get this arranged, which should have defused the immediate impasse. It should have, but the presence of naval vessels was clear proof that the message had not gotten through to the IDF chain of command—or was ignored. Mercer was keenly aware that the IDF regarded itself as guardians of Israel's security and did not always defer to civil authority, which had caused more than one regrettable incident. He hoped the approaching ships were not about to create another incident.

He was not privy to details of the hastily contrived arrangement, and there were undoubtedly many issues remaining to be resolved, but as an interim measure, according to the communique from Jarvis, Israel appeared to accept the provisional steps in absence of a formal treaty between the two governments.

Mercer did not know what went on behind the scenes, but his original orders remained in force: Prevent inspection by Israeli forces of commercial vessels entering Gaza. Not much wiggle room there.

The speaker hissed. "Captain Mercer, I am ordered by IDF naval command to escort *Seven Seas* into the Port of Gaza. I am further ordered to place personnel on board to act as observers until *Seven Seas* docks to ensure the crew does not jettison any contraband."

Watkins shrugged. "It's a development, but one that doesn't let us off the hook."

"Mmm." Mercer switched on the mike. "Commander, your vessels will be permitted to escort the *Seven Seas*, maintaining a distance of 2000 yards. You may not attempt to board."

Mercer signed off and glanced at the XO. "Send a signal to Rota stating the facts of the situation and request an advisory."

"Aye, sir. I hope that Sa'ar driver keeps his head," Watkins said and strode toward the communications console.

Mercer shared that sentiment.

"TAO, order *Ross* to close with the *Seven Seas* and hold at 500 yards, denying access to Israeli vessels. Move us to the same distance."

"Aye aye, sir."

Mercer glanced at the nav plot. The Gaza Strip coastline clearly visible, as were the blips of all ships slowly converging on it. Nobody had lit off their tactical radars yet, but that could soon change. He hoped that sanity would prevail, and he was prepared to enforce it if necessary.

"Captain, sonar. I have machinery and reactor pump noises

consistent with a *Severodvinsk* attack boat signature 2300 yards off our port stern. She is blowing tanks. I think she is coming up."

"Very well, sonar."

Terrific, Mercer mused. Just what he needed, an audience.

"He must have been drifting or we would have heard him," the sonar operator added.

The young Tactical Action Officer looked up. "Shall I launch a Sea Hawk, sir?"

"Negative, Lieutenant. Don't be so keen to shoot them up. They just want to see what everybody is up to."

The comment raised grins from the watchstanders.

"Captain, sonar. I have another contact 2100 yards off our starboard stern. No screw cavitation. She is blowing tanks. It could be the Chinese *Qin*."

"Everybody anxious to get a looksee," Watkins muttered sourly.

"As long as they maintain their distance, they can set up picnic tables for all I care," Mercer said, studying the Aegis tactical screen.

Since they were all in international waters, although the two submarines were probably scraping bottom being this close to shore, he could not do anything, and nobody had done anything to make him upset—yet.

Lahav and the two Dvoras were maintaining their closure rate with the *Seven Seas*, giving no indication of their immediate intentions, but if they didn't do something soon, those intentions would become very clear. Commander Rabin must have observed the two American destroyers moving into an interdiction position.

Watkins nodded to the communications petty officer, glanced at the message flimsy and handed it to Mercer.

FLASH FLASH FLASH FLASH FLASH
FM: CNE-CNA/C6F ROTA
TO: USS *PORTER* DDG-78
SUBJ: PURSUANT TO ORDERS
OPERATION INTERCEPT
PERSONAL FOR COMMANDER DESRON 60
DETACHMENT
//BT//
1.   MEDIA CREW ON INS *LAHAV* PROVIDING LIVE
FEED
2.   DENY INSPECTION OF *SEVEN SEAS*
3.   CURRENT ROE IN FORCE
VADMIRAL M. JARVIS SENDS
//BT//

Mercer slowly lifted his head. "We're on TV, XO."

"Looks like it, Skipper. A different kind of reality show, I'd say."

"I would say the same thing. At least old Jarvis didn't keep us wondering. Light up the Dvoras when they reach 2000 yards. I don't want us in range of their Typhoon cannons."

"That won't do anything for *Lahav's* Baraks and Harpoons. We're already well within range."

"I know, but with a media crew on board, I doubt that Rabin will initiate anything. If I were him, I would let the faster and more maneuverable Dvoras close on *Seven Seas* and attempt to board, broadcasting to the world how the aggressive and undisciplined American Navy sunk them in the execution of their lawful duty."

"Getting cynical?" Watkins said and raised an eyebrow. "You would really sink them?"

"Our orders are to deny them inspecting the *Seven Seas*, XO. If that means sinking them, then that's what I'll do."

"And if the Chinese or Russian boat starts something?"

"Then things will get exciting."

Watkins gave a sour laugh. "I didn't join the Navy to go down with the ship, you know. My ambition is to get my two stars and have hot and cold petty officers at my beck and call in a cushy Pentagon office."

Mercer grinned and patted the XO on the arm. "You know what they say. If you can't take a joke, you shouldn't have joined."

"Captain, both Dvoras are now at 2500 yards, maintaining course and speed," the TAO announced.

"Very well. Light them up with the SPY-62 and bring the main gun to action state. Order *Ross* to fire warning shots if the Dvoras cross 2000 yards. Fire for effect at 1200 yards. He has weapons free."

"Aye aye, sir."

Mercer picked up the overhead mike. "INS *Lahav*. You are advised that both Dvoras are now targeted and will be fired upon if they cross 1200 yards separation."

The radio hissed. "USS *Porter*, I'm obliged to place a monitoring team on the *Seven Seas*. The Dvoras will not engage your vessels or offer any resistance if fired upon. I must carry out my orders, sir."

"Commander Rabin, I acknowledge your orders. Query. State purpose of media crew on board *Lahav*."

Mercer did not need an explanation, wanting the Israeli skipper to know that the whole thing was a farce. Farce or not, he faced a serious tactical situation that had no apparent solution. If he damaged or sank an Israeli vessel, it would create an international storm the White House would not relish being in the center of, and neither would CNE-CNA/C6F.

Well, there might be a solution…

"Commander Rabin, I propose a possible resolution that will enable both of us to comply with our orders."

After almost a minute of expectant tension, the speaker hissed.

Stefan Vučak

"USS *Porter*, please state your proposal."

"I will permit you to place personnel on board *Seven Seas*...with an equal number of U.S. Navy personnel."

If the Israelis were anxious to stop dumping of any contraband by the container crew, Mercer was happy to let them. He was specifically ordered not to allow inspection of cargo—until *Seven Seas* reached Gaza. It would then become someone else's problem.

"This is INS *Lahav* actual. Your proposal is accepted, sir. With your permission, I will have one Dvora approach your ship to take on board a contingent of five personnel who will board *Seven Seas* to act as neutral observers."

"TAO, order *Ross* to stand down all weapons," Mercer said immediately and clicked the mike. "Thank you, Commander Rabin. You have permission to detach one Dvora only and affect personnel transfer. Your cooperation is appreciated."

"And so is your solution, Captain Mercer."

"I was not anxious to start something you would regret, Commander."

"Acknowledged, USS *Porter*. Neither was I. Out."

"Cocky bastard," Watkins said with a snort.

"You have to have balls to drive a missile ship."

"Does that include you, Skipper?"

"Never doubt it. Stand down, XO, but maintain an alert watch, and keep an eye on those subs."

"Aye aye, sir. Your solution, I would never have thought of it."

"You will have to start thinking laterally if you want to get those two stars," Mercer said and laughed, vastly relieved that sanity had prevailed. "We might have stretched our orders somewhat, but given the alternative, I don't think old Jarvis will mind."

Watkins pulled at his chin. "I wonder if Rabin would have been as accommodating if he didn't have the media on board?"

"We'll never know, will we? I am simply glad that we didn't

have to find out the hard way." Mercer nodded with satisfaction and stood up. "I'll be on the bridge. I want to see what our Chinese and Russian friends look like."

Two weeks and he would be heading for Norfolk, with Marion waiting.

* * *

The Secret Service car passed through the gate and slowed as it pulled under the portico of the White House West Wing Lobby entrance. Morrison gave Juliana a reassuring nod and squeezed her hand. It all seemed so surreal. Yesterday, he was in the hospital enjoying being fussed over, his gunshot wound healing nicely according to the surgeon, and today, he was in DC meeting the White House chief of staff.

Cottard would not say much, only that the administration wanted to discuss a proposal to resolve domestic and international issues surrounding the quantum computer device. They could discuss it over the phone, but he had reasons why he would prefer Dr. and Mrs. Morrison to come to the White House. Since he no longer had the crystal, Morrison was puzzled why the White House wanted him involved, unless Cottard really sought to hash over his QD pigment.

The papers and the general media had not stopped pontificating and dissecting encounters between U.S. and Israeli warships off Gaza, and the significance of Russian and Chinese submarines in the area. What frustrated everyone, nobody was talking at the official level. The spokesman for the Israeli prime minister issued a terse statement, saying the matter was under deliberation with all parties involved. Under pressure to provide some clarification, all the White House press secretary would venture to say was that the international ramifications of the incident were being reviewed, and a statement would be released in due course. This, of course, did not satisfy anybody. In absence of hard facts, commentators and editors entertained some preposterous scenarios.

The preposterous for Morrison was having an Air Force Gulfstream V fly him and Juliana to Andrews, where grim Secret Service types dressed in severe black suits politely bundled them into a waiting car. He did not mind the VIP treatment, not having to suffer through the hassle of a commercial flight, especially since neither of them were fit to travel, the doctors at New York–Presbyterian preferring to keep them there a while longer. Then again, doctors tended to be overprotective. Besides, being out of that antiseptic-smelling environment had perked him up.

The back door opened and Morrison got out, his arm held in a black sling, careful not to touch anything with his left shoulder. He waited for Juliana to join him and looked around the immaculately kept North Lawn, keenly aware of the charged atmosphere surrounding the venerable building, which some said was the seat of Western power.

A Latino marine guard, resplendent in his dress uniform and gleaming rifle, opened the entrance door and came to attention. A relatively short individual wearing a well-cut dark blue suit, sporting black-rimmed glasses, strode through, nodded to the Secret Service agents and fixed on a broad smile.

"Dr. Morrison…Mrs. Morrison, I am Adam Howard, White House Deputy Chief of Staff. Welcome to Washington. I'll take you through security and escort you to Mr. Cottard," he gushed, wearing a bemused grin.

"Thank you, Mr. Howard," Morrison said guardedly as they shook hands.

"How is your arm, Doctor?"

"I won't be punching anybody for a while, but the support gear should come off in a few days, followed by what will probably be uncomfortable rehabilitation."

"It's always like that. I trust you're feeling well, ma'am?"

Somewhat flustered, Juliana cleared her throat. "No running

for a couple of weeks."

"I prefer cooler weather myself for that," Howard said and extended a hand at the open doorway. "Please…"

Inside the brightly lit reception area, Howard steered them past hurrying staffers making their way between the two wings. At the security desk, he gave them each a visitor badge and invited them to go through the detector portal. It gave a sharp beep when Juliana walked through, and she handed her small purse to the guard on the other side. After rummaging through it—Morrison could never figure out why women had to lug a drugstore with them—the guard nodded and handed back the purse.

The walk through the West Wing deflated his excitement somewhat. The place was crowded with glass office cubicles and open work spaces. It could have been any business environment, but looked slightly dated. The building only had so much space to accommodate an expanding administration. He understood though, the White House did not hold all the administrative personnel, which spilled over into adjoining buildings. Animated conversation filled every space, people talked on phones or dashed to wherever they were going, not noticing the two visitors.

Howard stopped at an open alcove occupied by a stern elderly lady picking at her computer keyboard, and leaned conspiratorially toward Morrison.

"That's Chapelle Davies, Cottard's guardian; absolutely formidable. She has no compunction saying no even to a senior Cabinet secretary. Underneath her armor, she is really quite sweet."

"I heard that, Adam," Davies said sternly and looked up. "Saying no to cheeky deputies, too. You can go in."

"Thanks, Chapelle. You're a doll."

"Go on, you."

Howard knocked once on the highly polished wooden door and opened it.

"Manfred, our guests," Howard said brightly and waited for

his visitors to walk through.

"Thanks, Adam."

Howard nodded and closed the door.

The chief of staff beamed warmly, stood up in his five-foot eleven frame, dark gray blazer unbuttoned, receding hair, face hard but pleasant, and walked away from a desk cluttered with files, binders, keyboard and a computer screen.

"I'm glad you could come, Dr. Morrison...Mrs. Morrison," he said and offered his hand.

For someone who held the second most influential post in America, Cottard's office looked cramped, crowded by a modest wooden desk tucked into a corner, a dark brown sofa pushed against a wall, four visitor chairs, and a bookshelf filled with odd memorabilia, periodicals and stacked paperbacks.

As if reading his mind, Cottard hooked a finger over his shoulder. "I used to have a larger office down the corridor—this was the President's working dining room—but I found it a chore walking over when I had to see him. Please, make yourselves comfortable," he offered, waving at the sofa. He pulled a chair closer to him and eased himself down. "I trust you had a pleasant flight?"

"I could use a Gulfstream when I need to visit my plants," Morrison said cautiously, relaxing in the amicable atmosphere. Cottard exuded a calming effect, looking genuinely concerned. "Far more conducive than a commercial flight."

"I dare say. Can I offer you anything? Coffee, wine? I have a nice Canadian rye if you prefer."

"Coffee would be good, thank you."

"I'll have one too," Juliana said.

"Chapelle!" Cottard yelled.

Seconds later the door opened.

"Coffee all around, please."

She nodded and closed the door.

"I would be lost without her," Cottard said amiably. "She

keeps telling me that I'm hard on her, but she's been saying that even when I was still a Hill lobbyist."

"I have an assistant who is like that," Morrison said. Without Allison's quiet efficiency, he would find his days more disorganized.

"They are indispensable." Cottard paused, apparently arranging his thoughts. "Dr. Morrison, you are no doubt wondering why I wanted to see both of you personally."

"Your summons is somewhat unusual, but you must have a good reason."

"Believe me, I do. First of all, I want to assure you that the White House was not aware of activities by some of our agencies to procure your QD pigment, or the quantum computing device. I trust the apologies you received have tempered your opinion of this administration." He gave a wry smile. "In some respects, I am indebted to Senator Lockhart for bringing the developments to my attention, considering what has happened over the last few days."

Morrison crossed his legs. "I accept what you're saying, Mr. Cottard, but we both know that this is not the end of it. There will always be some busybody in one of your departments, a Congressman pressured by my competitors or a defense industry lobbyist, who will want to wrest my intellectual property to gain a political or economic advantage. I'm prepared to work with the industry in the distribution and application of my pigment, but on my terms. As a businessman, I want to recoup my investment. If DARPA or any other agency seeks to develop a pigment variant citing national security, they and this Administration will find itself answering to the Supreme Court."

Cottard lifted his arms. "Peace, Doctor. You have my assurance that the U.S. government will not seek to compromise your IP. However, I cannot say what any future administration might do, but elections are three years off, which is more than enough time for you to establish Solaris Technology's market dominance.

I am also aware that it would be cheaper for the government to deal with you than attempt to circumvent your patents by spending millions of taxpayer money developing an alternative product. Although it hasn't stopped us in the past," he added wryly.

"I take it that you looked at the possibility?" Morrison said with a scowl.

Cottard shrugged and spread his hands in defeat.

"It took me a while to dig through the bureaucracy walls, but I managed. Being chief of staff has its advantages. I can say that DARPA has reviewed the theoretical basis of your patents, Doctor, but you have staked a large claim, which left them scratching their heads for another approach."

A knock made them all look up as Davies walked in bearing a tray, which she placed on the small coffee table.

"Thanks, Chapelle," Cottard said as he lifted a silver carafe and busied himself pouring them a rich-smelling brew.

Morrison added a sugar cube and a dash of cream to his. He took a sip and lifted an eyebrow in appreciation.

"Excellent. If it isn't a state secret, I would like to know the blend."

Cottard laughed. "I wouldn't have a clue, but I'll get Chapelle to email you the details," he said and leaned forward. "Getting back to this dreary business, you must realize the impact your QD pigment will have on existing photovoltaic producers, Doctor, and the energy industry in general."

"That is why they want to destroy me. I'm also aware that uncontrolled release of the pigment will have serious implications for existing power generating utilities. Despite that, I will make cheap energy available to all. My competitors have had a good run with old technology, and I haven't done badly either with my nanograss lines. They can hardly complain when a new and better product comes on the market. Just because they haven't come up with it is certainly not a valid reason to suppress innovation. They would not have hesitated to roll out their own version of the pigment if they had it. Free market forces at work, Mr. Cottard."

"Which sometimes produces casualties," Cottard agreed soberly. "Tell me, Doctor. How do you plan to make the pigment available to all, which I assume means supplying developing countries?"

"I would like to explore that with the Administration. In return, I will guarantee that Solaris will not license manufacture of the pigment to third parties, which should satisfy whatever national security concerns you may have."

"Mmm. You would subsidize distribution to those countries?"

"Something like that."

Cottard rubbed the underside of his bulbous nose. "A lot of details to work out, but doable, and very generous on your part. We both know that lack of power is one of the main reasons those economies aren't getting anywhere. Call me when you have a marketable product and I will put you in touch with the relevant departments."

"I appreciate that," Morrison said and took another sip of coffee.

Cottard shook his head. "You're going to face some interesting challenges, Doctor."

"I don't doubt it."

"While we're discussing challenges, you weathered a major one this week, which unfortunately has left both of you physically and mentally scarred. I'm referring to the quantum device, of course."

"It has been a rather unusual experience," Morrison agreed dryly, and Cottard guffawed.

"You can say that."

"Since I no longer have it, I'm starting to believe that I am better off without it, and the device is now someone else's problem."

"Well, perhaps. You're aware of the media coverage surrounding the Gaza incidents. So much potential in such a small thing…but it might also be a gate to chaos."

Morrison brought the cup to his lips and paused. Ferguson had used very similar words.

"That is something mankind has faced with every leap in technology."

"Yes, certainly, except in this case, we didn't make that leap. At least I don't think we did."

"The crystal's origin is definitely fuel for debate and speculation," Morrison agreed, and his face hardened. "I understand why everybody wants it, but I deplore the methods used by the Chinese and the Israelis to take it from me. That, Mr. Cottard, includes your Department of Energy."

"Those issues have been addressed."

"I appreciate what you have done on my behalf, but I am disappointed that the U.S. government felt free to trample on a citizen's rights using the all-encompassing umbrella of national security. The experience has made me more cynical, which might not be a bad thing when it comes time to distribute my QD pigment."

"I sincerely regret what you went through, Doctor, and you, Mrs. Morrison. You have justification for your cynicism, and perhaps a case for redress, but what if I told you that you can have your crystal back?"

Morrison was genuinely startled. "You have it?"

"Ah, not exactly. The Israelis have it, which I suspect you know."

"Then what is the—"

"They want to negotiate."

"I don't understand."

"When men of honor decide to be honorable, many things are possible."

"I thought the White House had turned a cold shoulder toward Israel."

"Let me just say that Prime Minster Ibrahim has had a reality check."

"And that reality check made them return the device?"

"In a manner of speaking. There are conditions, of course."

"What conditions?"

Cottard smiled; a secret, predatory grin that made Morrison immediately suspicious. The chief of staff stood up.

"Why don't I allow Ambassador Caplan to explain everything." He pointed at a side door. "Shall we?"

Not sure what was going on, Morrison shot Juliana a glance. She shrugged and got up.

Cottard walked into the other room and waited for the two of them to come through. Juliana gave a startled gasp, and it took Morrison a moment to get over his shock at being in the Oval Office.

"Mr. President, Doctor Morrison and Mrs. Morrison," Cottard announced with a large dose of malicious glee.

President Walters heaved himself up from one of the two beige sofas that flanked a low coffee table set up in front of his working desk, and held out a hand.

"Doctor, a genuine pleasure," he said in his unmistakable radio announcer New England accent. Dressed in a perfectly cut dark blue suit and red tie, the president seemed wrapped in power, his fighter pilot eyes taking everything in.

Morrison cleared his throat as they shook hands, appreciating Walters' strong grip.

"Thank you, sir. You have managed to catch me completely flatfooted."

Walters laughed with genuine warmth. "Believe me, I understand the feeling." He turned to Juliana. "Welcome to the White House, Mrs. Morrison."

"Thank you, Mr. President," she husked and blushed. "It is

an honor to meet you."

"Given what you two have gone through, it's the least I could do," Walters said, giving them an appraising look. "I'm told that your wounds are not too serious, but I regret the circumstances under which you got them."

"A result of conflicting interests, Mr. President," Morrison said dryly.

Walters chuckled and nodded to the individual sitting on the sofa. "Allow me to present Ambassador Caplan."

Not tall, wearing a small bulge around the middle, the diplomat appeared friendly as he stood up.

"Mr. Ambassador," Morrison said politely, shaking hands, unable to suppress a tinge of resentment at what Israel had done. He saw Caplan sense this, but the diplomat appeared to ignore it as he turned to Juliana.

"Mrs. Morrison…"

"A pleasure to meet you, sir."

Walters clapped his hands and waved at the sofas. "Now that we're done with the overtures, let's get on with it." As everybody sat down, he glanced at Cottard. "You told him?"

Cottard nodded and Walters gesticulated at Caplan. "Alon?"

The ambassador locked his fingers and leaned forward.

"Doctor Morrison, I want to extend a formal apology on behalf of Prime Minister Ibrahim for the circumstances under which your quantum device was taken. Although Israel is not directly responsible for the injuries you and your wife have sustained in this very regrettable affair, the Prime Minster acknowledges that our involvement was a contributing factor."

"I appreciate that, Mr. Ambassador."

"Although we have a clear claim on the device, we cannot deny that you acquired it under what were quasi-legal circumstances. What I have been asked, sir, is to propose a three-way partnership to explore the device's potential and develop possible applications. I shall not take up your valuable time explaining the background to this offer. Suffice to say that President Walters has presented a number of, ah, strategic reasons that convinced the Prime Minister of the value of this partnership."

Morrison nodded, perfectly aware of those strategic reasons. The media had gone to great lengths enumerating the scenarios. He cleared his throat.

"Given the circumstances, this is an unexpected proposal, sir. If I were to entertain it, you must realize the problems such a partnership would represent."

"Involvement by other countries, you mean."

"China for one, having failed in its attempt to obtain the crystal, will not rest until it's in their hands. We would face similar attempts by others, leading to probable diplomatic conflict, expressed in several unpleasant ways...aimed at me and my family."

"Succinctly put, Doctor, and it's something that my government and the U.S. Administration understand. However, there are steps we can take to ameliorate those difficulties by involving the United Nations, but first..."

Caplan reached into his pocket and held out a red jewel case.

Morrison recognized it immediately and felt color drain from his face.

"I believe this belongs to you, Doctor," Caplan said gently, sympathetic to Morrison's feelings.

Morrison took the case and opened it. It lay there in its bed of white velvet, oblivious to the storm its existence had created. As he stared at it, he could almost feel the resonance of its glow seep through him.

He offered the case to Juliana. Licking her lips, she gazed at the enigmatic device.

"It is...enchanted," she whispered.

"The very word, I am sure," Walters murmured. "I had the same reaction when I saw it. It's something...unearthly."

Morrison picked up the device and fondled it. He slowly turned to face Cottard.

"This unfathomable crystal…something you said stuck in my mind, sir. So much potential in such a small thing…but it might also be a gate to chaos. Perhaps those who buried it were wise to conceal it from us. In some future time perhaps, we may have the maturity and wisdom to know how to deal with such a gift. I don't believe that moment is now, which events over the past few days have demonstrated all too vividly."

Emotions churning, he raised his hand and smashed the crystal against the coffee table. Cottard gasped and leaped to his feet. Caplan's face turned a mottled red with fury. Only Walters appeared unmoved, and slowly nodded when Morrison looked at him.

In four pieces, the crystal had lost its magical attraction. It was simply a broken thing. Morrison picked them off the carpet, feeling a moment of mild regret, swept away by an overwhelming sense of release.

He held out a piece to Caplan.

"A memento for your government, Mr. Ambassador—and your researchers."

He offered two pieces to Walters.

"If I may, Mr. President. Give one to China and the other to Russia. Your Department of Energy already has a sample."

"What is this?" Caplan demanded, staring hard at Walters.

"Later," the president growled irritably.

"I will keep the remaining piece," Morrison said. "It will make an interesting addition to my mineral collection."

Walters chuckled as he took the shards. "I cannot say which I feel most, Doctor. Outrage or admiration for your courage, but I understand why you did this." He glanced at Caplan. "I suggest that this might be the best solution possible for everybody. Don't you agree, Alon?"

Caplan fondled the piece between his fingers and gave a rueful shake of his head. "Perhaps it's better this way, although I would not have dared do it."

Walters rubbed his hands and stood up. "Now that we have had our little drama, I want to invite all of you to the residence for lunch, where we can turn our thoughts to more pleasant matters."

As Morrison rose, Juliana gave him a radiant smile, reached for his hand and squeezed.

It was all the reward he wanted.

About the Author

Stefan Vučak has written twenty-one novels, which include eight SF books in the Shadow Gods Saga. His *Cry of Eagles* won the coveted Readers' Favorite silver medal award, and his *All the Evils* was the prestigious Eric Hoffer contest finalist and Readers' Favorite silver medal winner. *Strike for Honor* won the gold medal.

Stefan leveraged a successful career in the Information Technology industry, which took him to the Middle East working on cellphone systems. Writing has been a road of discovery, helping him broaden his horizons. He also spends time as an editor and book reviewer. Stefan lives in Melbourne, Australia.

To learn more about Stefan, visit his:
Website: www.stefanvucak.com
Facebook: www.facebook.com/StefanVucakAuthor
Twitter: @stefanvucak

More Books by Stefan Vučak

https://www.stefanvucak.com/Books/

www.ingramcontent.com/pod-product-compliance
Lightning Source LLC
Chambersburg PA
CBHW030651120726
47905CB00001B/159